BEVERLY NAULT

Fresh Start SUMMER

The Seasons of Cherryvale
Book One

a novel

FRESH START SUMMER

BY BEVERLY NAULT

ISBN 10: 1-60039-182-6
ISBN 13: 978-1-60039-182-8

www.lamppostpubs.com

Fresh Start Summer

The Seasons of Cherryvale
Book One

BY BEVERLY NAULT

To anyone who's ever needed a fresh start.

Which pretty much includes the entire human race.

2 Corinthians 5:15–17

My inspiration and prayer warrior, my sister, Brenda Keller. Thank you for listening, brainstorming, and believing in me. And thanks for your legal eye so Cherryvale's within the law.

A special thanks to Pam Harris Bishop. Your own fresh start inspired many of the events in Cherryvale. My bff since sixth grade, who knew how our "stories" would weave together? Your laughter, passion for all things family, God and all His critters, as well as your friendship, mean the world to me.

My mom, Barbara Schrader, thanks for inspiring me through your own talents and the do-overs you've faced. Oh, and thanks for being a terrific cheerleader at all my horse shows. And all my ventures since then, for that matter.

Thanks to my writer's support system: Kathy Tyers, my gentle but firm CWG mentor and teacher. My critique partners, especially Rebecca Farnbach, Dona Watson, Joanne Bischof, Dan Harmer, Dave Henkel, Jackie Harts, Lynn Donovan and Fred Tingler, your suggestions made my make-believe world possible beyond my own imagination. Kevin, thanks for allowing me to write while on the job. Carol and Cindy, thanks for taking on more hours so I could spend more time in Cherryvale.

Mary McDonough, my dear friend, I'm in awe of your own fresh starts. While we worked on your memoir, *Lessons from the Mountain*, you gave me helpful information about the life of a celebrity. But more than that, your energy, your passion for life, and your confidence taught me to be a better person.

Ashley Ludwig, thanks for "getting" my story and making it better. (You visited Cherryvale more often than any one person should have to.) You challenged me to grow, dig for a better turn of phrase, and develop my characters and their world with love and wisdom.

Lindsay, you're not only gorgeous, smart, and a wonderful daughter, you encourage and inspire me. Your enthusiasm for tackling life inspired me through long hours at the keyboard. Evan, your incredible wit, love for the Lord and gentle spirit bring me endless joy. Thanks to both of you for making me one incredibly proud mom.

My husband, Gary. You rubbed my sore-from-hours-at-the-keyboard neck, kept said computer humming so I never had to worry, and never doubted I could accomplish any of my wild ideas, including becoming a novelist. Thanks for laughing at my jokes, having my back, and being the best husband, friend, and father for whom a wife could ever wish.

To my Lord and Savior Jesus Christ. Thanks for your ultimate sacrifice that gave the world the opportunity for a fresh start. I write for You alone.

Map of CHERRYVALE

To Franklin City
The Path
Main Street

1. Bypass Buffet
2. Hospital
3. Lawnmower Parts Factory
4. Maggie's Place
5. Baby's Shed
6. Stables
7. The Pit
8. Grace's House
9. Bed & Breakfast
10. Market Basket
11. Atty. Lew Farrell
12. The Daily Grind
13. Community Theater
14. Lunch Bucket
15. Cherryvale Real Estate
16. Read & Reel
17. Dr. McCoy Vet Clinic
18. Mayor / City Offices
19. Loaves and Dishes Deli
20. Sam's Hardware
21. Your, Mine & Hours

CHAPTER ONE

Grace Harkins ignored the rush of whispers as her oldest friend stormed from the church. She imagined dozens of angry glares boring into the back of her head while Maggie's footsteps echoed around the church walls. The door opened to a flood of summer daylight, and shut with a resounding slam.

Pastor cleared his throat. "As I was saying, the film crew will arrive and set up in the Park tonight. Filming begins tomorrow..."

Grace twisted her purse straps while he finished explaining about the movie shoot. It took him forever to finish the weekly announcements and say the closing prayer. She leapt from her seat on the "amen" to hurry outside in Maggie's wake.

"What was that all about?" Grace's sandals slap-slapped her acute embarrassment as she headed down the concrete steps to the park benches. "Don't you think having a movie filmed in Cherryvale will help keep our businesses open and—what?"

"What in the name of granny's good sense is Pastor thinking?" Maggie stood with a glare and stomped away from the bench where she'd been waiting, taking long strides ahead toward the parking lot. "This town will not be the same when they leave, you watch!"

Pastor Crenshaw descended the steps and stopped to speak with

Sam and Abby Madison—owners of the hardware store and Sam, the town's resident actor.

"Hush, Maggie, they'll hear you." Grace managed a tight smile and nodded at them, keeping her own voice hushed. "Our Vacation Bible School can use their donation if we send enough volunteers. He read the script and approved it."

"Using the Lord's people for evil gain, that's what those movie folk are doing. It's what they always do!" Maggie insisted with a stomp. "Expose our young people to wicked Hollywood influences. And disrupt peaceful communities. You should recall better than anyone."

Grace gaped. *How on earth could Maggie still carry around that ancient grievance?* "That was so long ago. Besides, why can't we be a good influence for them? Cherryvale is the flip side of fast living, after all."

The first Sunday of her retirement, Grace resisted letting Maggie's sour mood ruin this glorious, golden summer day. The cherry blossoms had dropped and their sage green canopies swayed and danced in the morning sunshine like young girls showing off new summer frocks. Grace's winter coat rested in its cedar chest, and even her cotton skirt and light sweater felt too heavy. She pulled sunglasses out of a straw handbag and slid them on.

Twins Cassie and Carson galloped up to them. Like colts escaped from the barn, the kids' energy levels soared with summer-vacation excitement, a rainbow of laughter over the cloud of Maggie's gloom.

"Hey, Miz Grace, come play chase with us." Cassie giggled and chased Carson across the green lawn.

"Not now, honey." She pointed to her sandals. "Don't have my running shoes on, maybe later."

"It's got that old guy, Jeff Field!" Connie McCoy bounced past, cellphone glued to her ear, voice squealing in teenage glee. "And Tiffany Lane, too! I loved her in that street-racing movie last year—"

"These kids can't go ten minutes without those things stuck to their heads." Maggie switched sermon-ettes without skipping a page in her impromptu lecture series. "They're all growing eardrum cancer. I saw a piece on 20/20."

Grace was glad for the change of subject, even if it was another rant. "Maggie, ever since you moved back to the Vale you've been watching too much news and picking out only the bad. My kids got me a cell phone for my birthday and I think they're handy. See? No butt-dialing here." Grace slid hers out of a special pocket in her purse and flipped it open to demonstrate. She looked up, but Maggie had launched her own search expedition into Purse Everest—Grace's nickname for her ever present, enormous bag.

Maggie's mass of red curls bobbed as she plunged through the deep cavern trolling for the prize.

"All I have to do now is remember to plug it in," Grace muttered. The low battery indicator flashed at her as she slid it back into its pocket. "Mark wants to know I can call someone if I need to, since he's at the hospital till all hours." Her tummy growled, reminding her that it, too, needed recharging. "Where shall we eat this week, the Bypass Buffet or the Lunch Bucket?"

"They're all pagans." Maggie's voice muffled up from the depths of her bag, unwavering from her anti-Hollywood soapbox. "They'll trample all over town with their Scientology and piercings. And who knows what kind of cigarettes."

"Hey, Miz Grace." Connie skipped up to join them and peered over Maggie's shoulder. "Miz Maggie, that's the biggest purse I've ever seen. Hiding bodies in there?"

Grace stifled a giggle as Maggie shot Connie a uni-eyebrowed glare.

Connie continued, undeterred. "I know I'm supposed to start working at your place tomorrow, but can I maybe start later in the week?"

"Let me guess." Maggie re-surfaced from her purse dive, eyebrows at half-mast. "You want to be in that movie."

"I can work today, but could you do without me tomorrow?" Connie's straight auburn hair framed hopeful brown eyes.

"I certainly don't want you working if you don't want to be there."

Maggie plunged back in. "I expect you on Tuesday morning. Eight AM sharp."

"Yes, ma'am, thank you!" Connie bounced away, thumbs flying over her cell phone. "See ya, Miz Grace."

"See? It's started already." Maggie mumbled from the chasm. "Disruptions. No peace. Who knows what kind of people."

Grace bit down on her lower lip and shoved her sunglasses up her nose. She'd worked hard all her grown-up life and meant to enjoy herself this summer—Maggie's troubles weren't going to ruin her plans. Instead, she ran her eyes over the sleek, fully restored classic Mustang. "It's a treat to ride in Baby. You haven't taken her out of that old outbuilding all winter."

Good one, she can't resist talking about Baby. Grace waited for Maggie to say something but she continued digging through heaven knows what.

"Found 'em!" Maggie jabbed the keys skyward in victory, then punched them into the driver's-side door. She leaned over and flipped up the lock so Grace could get into the Wimbledon white-with-red-leather-interior 1966 Mustang convertible.

"Joe did such a beautiful job on her." Grace pulled the seatbelt across her lap and clicked it in place, enjoying the aroma of leather and lemon wafting through the sun-warmed interior.

Maggie kerplunked the carpetbag onto the backseat and reached for her own belt. "We both had our dreams, and restoring Baby was Joe's. At least he finished before..." A wash of emotion flooded her face before she caught herself. She gripped the wood grain steering wheel at ten and two. "He researched everything to the last detail. I shouldn't make her stay cooped up in that stuffy shed."

Grace gave her a moment, admiring the authentic chrome knobs and simulated-wood dashboard. She glanced over at Maggie. A white bandage peeked out underneath the sleeve of her cotton shirt. "What did you do to yourself?"

"It's just a scratch. That donkey can be quite a mule, but he means well."

"You're trying to be a one-woman animal rescue mission." Grace clicked her tongue. "You need someone around the place to help you. All those animals, especially the larger livestock. What if one of them takes out past abuses on you?" She gestured at the bandage. "Worse than a scratch."

"Can't afford anyone else right now." Maggie shook her curls. "I can barely pay Connie as it is." She tugged her sleeve down in a futile attempt to cover the wound.

"Then only take small animals, tame household pets turned over because their owners can't afford them anymore."

"I'm not about to turn away an animal because of its size, or past. The big, cranky ones need me just as much as the small, polite ones do."

The air in the car suddenly felt thick, strained. "I know it's the way you and Joe planned, but—"

"Life goes on, Grace." Maggie lifted her chin, and turned the ignition. The engine rumbled to a finely tuned hum. "Now where shall we eat?"

Grace knew too well the woman's preference to keep her emotions private. "Baby sounds terrific. Joe would be happy to know you're enjoying her, Maggs. Let's see what the line's like at the Bucket. If it's crazy, we can drive over to the Bypass."

Cooler air flowed through the vents as Maggie steered the classic onto Main. They cruised past 1800s-era reproduction storefronts nestled along brick-edged sidewalks, and rode in silence for a few blocks. The rubber tires rolled over simulated pavers with a rhythmic thock-thock.

Grace remembered not so long ago when the now postcard-pretty Cherryvale had been more suited for a horror film backdrop than a family film.

Along with the rest of the country's recession, the town's income thinned into financial drought. Businesses closed and families moved away until Mayor Purcell called an emergency meeting and invited Cherryvalers, or "Valers" as townies called themselves, to brainstorm.

"We can make opportunities out of adversity," was his rallying cry.

Grace, selected chair of the committee for her organizational skills and keen eye for detail, led the charge in the town's spectacular renovation.

"The window boxes we put in last fall are starting to bloom nicely." Grace allowed herself a moment of pride. "Aren't they going to be lovely?"

"More work for the storeowners." Maggie kept her eyes on the road as she delivered her next prophecy. "They'd better deadhead those begonias or they'll be a mess when it rains."

"Sam's not just a hardware store guy, you know. His set design skills on the facades really make them special. We spent hours researching old photos in his store room from the town archives to get rid of those ugly 1960's straight lines and concrete."

"Looks too much like a theme park if you ask me."

Grace plowed ahead, determined to sweeten Maggie's sour mood. "I think they're European–looking. But you'd know better than me.

"Some things are better left alone."

Grace drew in a breath and tried to ignore Maggie's dig. "I know the town's not anything like it was when you left, but the tourists are back and the economy's improving. I'm sure it'll trickle over to your farm soon." Grace searched Maggie's face for a sign of softening, but her jaw set firm as the roots of the hundred-year-old cherry trees that circled the town square.

Maggie slowed and Baby idled at the curb in front of the Lunch Bucket. A line snaked from the acrylic pie case, out the screen door, and down the sidewalk. "Bucket's full. We'll never get our table." She craned her neck to find a break in the traffic and pulled back into the flow. "Ever since that travel article, we've had no peace. Look at all these cars."

"It's not like when we were girls and we could walk down the middle of the street." Grace checked the line at the Loaves and Fishes deli across the street, but a crowd jammed up against their counter as well. "All these people bring money, better for the town anyway."

"I guess I can get used to day visitors." Maggie sniffed. "But this movie, that's just too much." She turned the 'Stang toward the highway bypass. "And you mark my words. This town will not be the same after those wackos from the Land of Fruits and Nuts invade."

"Isn't that what you want for your farm?"

"Wackos?"

"You know what I mean." Grace watched her beloved hometown sliding by. She barely remembered what it had looked like before the makeover. And none of the changes had begun the last time Maggie came back for a short visit to bury her mother after breast cancer took her. Maggie had flown into town, landed long enough to help her dad with the arrangements, and left again, promising Grace she'd be better about keeping in touch.

When she found out Maggie and Joe were moving back, Grace wondered how the world traveler would adjust to Cherryvale.

As if she could read her thoughts, Maggie opened up. "I enjoyed our years traveling and living abroad, but I looked forward to moving back to small-town life. Living in big cities with Joe was exciting, but lonely, Grace. You don't know what it's like to rub elbows with heads of state and leaders of countries. They can keep their gowns and red carpets. We don't need throngs of unruly paparazzi and autograph hounds."

Grace snorted. "No one is going to want our autographs."

Maggie smirked. Inside, Grace cringed. Not now, not ever had Maggie failed to remind Grace of the glamorous life she'd led before moving back to Cherryvale.

While Grace chauffeured Wendy to ballet class, Ian to soccer, and graded papers for her high school classes, Maggie shopped in Paris and Nice, took photographs on safari in Africa, and relaxed on cruises down the Nile. She'd lived, traveled, and socialized wherever Joe's job as an energy consultant took them.

Maggie tailgated a crawling SUV. "They called me, you know.

"Who?"

"Location scouts. Wanted to use my place to film." She slid the car into neutral and revved the muscle car's engine to send the poky driver a message.

Grace turned in her seat to look at Maggie. "You should let them—they pay for location shooting. Besides, the publicity for your rescue work—"

Maggie sucked air between her teeth. "Of course I told them no. I don't care if they offer me a million dollars. I don't want any part of what they're doing."

"No one else remembers what happened except a handful of Valers." Grace fell back against the leather seat. "That was all so long ago, why can't you—"

"Let it go? I know. Turning up dirt only digs up old bones." She leaned on the horn, the blast changing the subject. "Would you look at this chucklehead? Get over if you're lost!"

The car finally pulled over and Grace managed an embarrassed smile at the other driver as Maggie powered the 'Stang into fourth.

Grace sighed and watched the fence posts of Cherryvale Stables flicking past, wishing she were home digging into that pile of classic novels waiting for her. But friends—even difficult ones—came first. *Didn't they?*

The large dining room buzzed with a mix of the after-church crowd, families out for a Sunday meal, and truckers on long hauls across the busy interstate. Maggie scowled at the crowd, but Grace secretly welcomed the business to the once economically-threatened cafeteria.

Dawnelle set two glasses of iced tea on the table and flipped open her tablet. "Anything new over in your little corner of heaven?"

"A movie company's using Cherryvale for filming." Grace slapped a sweetener packet. "They need Valers to be extras."

Maggie shifted in her chair and studied the menu.

Grace continued, "The film's about a girl raised in foster care trying to find her dad, and all she has to go on are pictures from an old scrapbook. Tiffany Lane's the star. And Jeff Field plays her dad."

"Sounds exciting." Dawnelle's pencil hovered. "You two ladies going to be in it?"

Maggie flicked her wrist. "We have more important things to do than hang around like a bunch of teenagers gawking at movie stars."

"Jeff Field!" Dawnelle sighed, hip to the table. "Those dimples melt my butter every time." She gazed out the plate glass windows for a moment before returning to the present. "You ladies want the buffet?"

"I'll have the meat loaf with fruit." Maggie handed Dawnelle her menu. "And put the gravy on the side this time."

Grace looked directly at Maggie. "Buffet's fine for me."

"I'll get your drinks." Dawnelle scribbled the order, her mouth tight, then scooted off to the kitchen.

Grace leaned toward Maggie. "Why don't you get the buffet like everyone else on Sunday?"

"Because I don't want food that's been sitting out for hours. The French think American buffets are like pigs eating at a trough—"

"It's more work for Alice." Grace hissed in a whisper. "She has to make your lunch herself when you don't eat the buffet. Her back's been killing her, and—what?"

Maggie's spoon paused mid-stir. She poked it at the picture window behind Grace, flicking iced tea around the table. "Would you look at that?"

Grace wiped the tip of her nose and twisted around to see where Maggie indicated with the culprit utensil.

Truck after truck, van after van, passed outside. One by one, they slowed on the freeway and angled onto the Cherryvale exit.

"West Coast Sound and Motion Picture Unit Support Services," Grace read the lettering on their sides. "ECM Lighting. Western Costumes and Wigs."

Clinking and chattering hushed to a blanket of silence. Everyone turned to watch.

"I'm warning you! Our quiet town will never be the same because of these—these invaders!" Maggie stage whispered, not missing a beat as another truck rumbled past. "I hope you're not thinking of getting involved with them."

Heads swiveled from the buffet line in their direction.

"Maybe I am. Maybe I'm not." Grace's cheeks heated. "It's my first summer of retirement and I can plan what I want to do, when I want to do it." After a long beat, the room returned to its normal buzz.

Grace looked up at the approaching Sam Madison and his wife, Abby, lunch check in hand.

"You two ready for your close-up?" Sam formed a half square with his thumbs and framed them through his "camera lens."

Grace flashed him a cheesy smile.

"How about you, Maggie?" He swung over to focus on Maggie, but threw up his hands in mock terror at her disapproving frown. "Yikes, negative mojo."

"Sam's only kidding, Maggie." Abby tugged at his sleeve. "Come on, goofy, let's leave the ladies to their lunch."

"Why is everyone so giddy about letting these people intrude on the peace and quiet of our town with their ridiculous lifestyle and"—Maggie looked directly at Sam—"and uneducated slang?"

"It's just a movie, Maggie." Sam scowled back.

"Sheriff doesn't need hordes of rowdy strangers all over town. The department's barely recovered from the cutbacks as it is." Maggie shook her head. "And with all these types—"

"What types?" Sam's six-foot-three frame towered over them. "Not everyone in entertainment is evil."

"Of course you're not." Grace tried to play ambassador. "Maggie's just wary of the lifestyle we hear so much about."

Maggie stirred un-dissolved sugar in the bottom of her glass. Grace focused on the mini tornado in the bottom of the amber solution.

Abby slipped her elbow through Sam's arm. "C'mon, let's go over to the sign-ups. 'Bye, Grace. Maggie."

"In a minute, honey." Abby spun away to pay their bill, but Sam turned back to face Maggie. He pointed his check at Maggie's frizzled head and spoke in his booming voice trained to reach the back of the room. "Might I remind you that Cecil B. DeMille's whole intention was to bring the Bible to life on the screen?"

"I don't think *The Scrapbook* is the next *Ten Commandments*, there, handyman."

"Maybe not. But, I've never been as excited about the industry. New filmmakers like Dallas Jenkins are making real headway getting worthy stories back on the silver screen. God can use whomever and whatever he desires to reach people. Even in the movies." He lifted his baseball cap, smoothed all twelve strands of hair over his bald spot, replaced the hat with a sharp tug, and strode away to join his wife at the cash register.

Silence deafened.

Grace imagined the entire room staring at the back of her neck as Dawnelle plopped the plate of meatloaf in front of Maggie and sauntered back through the swinging kitchen doors.

Oblivious, Maggie speared her lunch with abandon.

Grace reached for her glass and tipped it back to gulp the last few drops of the cool liquid. A clump of ice clattered loose, splattered onto her blouse and into her lap.

"Really, Grace? Could you be clumsier?" Maggie fussed. "You're drinking like a thirsty camel after a sandstorm. Everyone's staring at you."

Tell her off, Gracie! She's the one causing scenes. Grace worked up the nerve to deliver a clever comeback, but her lips were numb from the ice floe and her heart caught in her throat with the depth and breadth of what she wanted to say.

Maggie dumped gravy on her meat loaf. "What? Are you having a stroke? Speak up. If you're trying to be silly, it's quite inappropriate, now eat your food before it gets cold." She stabbed the glob with her fork.

"I'm not the same timid girl you pushed aside in high school." Grace looked directly into the woman's gaze. Maggie's eyebrow shot up into red curls. Clearing her throat, she continued. "The days are long gone when you can…well…intimidate me."

"Hmph."

Or so I thought.

Grace and Maggie rode back to Cherryvale attempting polite conversation until awkward silence grew into a third companion. Grace couldn't remember the last time she was so relieved to see her own house when Maggie finally stopped at the curb.

"Want to come in for a cold drink?" Grace got out and watched Maggie fiddle with the gearshift. "I have that box of old linens the hospital sent over for your place."

"Maybe another time. I have a lot to do to get ready for the opening."

"Anything I can do to help?"

"I'll manage." Maggie shifted into drive. "Give my regards to Mark."

"Wait!" Grace hated letting their afternoon end with such tension. "Pull into the driveway, I'll help you get it in Baby's trunk. It's pretty heavy. They really loaded it down with rags for your animals."

Maggie sighed but slid Baby's gearshift into reverse and backed up the long driveway next to the sprawling ranch-style home.

Grace unlocked the front door and Maggie stepped into the foyer behind her. Grace passed the creamy tan sectional sofa and gently worn leather easy chair nestled around a stone fireplace that rose to meet the beamed ceiling. Grace grabbed a newspaper and coffee cup. "My goodness, look at this mess." Guilt tinged her pride, thinking of Maggie's cramped farmhouse. Folding the paper and placing it in a magazine basket on the hearth, she glanced at Maggie who still hadn't spoken since they'd gotten out of the car.

Maybe if I hum, she'll replay the one about the merits of ancient hymns versus 7-11 music. Grace bristled against the awkward silence and wiped her hands on a dishrag, aware of Maggie's silent witness on her every move. She looked at the sink, changed her mind, and slid the dirty cup onto the top shelf of the dishwasher.

So much for not being intimidated. "Would you like a drink?" She looked squarely at Maggie. "Lemonade or iced tea?"

Maggie shook her head, lips a tight line.

Grace couldn't remember the last time Maggie-the-Mouth had gone so long without speaking. *I'm not about to apologize for growing a spine.* Grace cleared her throat. "I'll be right back."

She strode to the opposite end of the living room, down the hallway, opened a closet door, and grabbed an old pillowcase bulging with cast-off towels and linens. *Too bad old feelings and our unfortunate past can't be bagged and used to line critter boxes like these old discards.* Back in the kitchen Maggie studied a piece of paper.

Maggie held up the paper. "What's all this?"

Finally the silent treatment was over. "Here's my contribution. The big box is on the service porch." Grace set the bag down.

Maggie waved the sheet under her nose as she read aloud: "Take a tap-dancing class. Plant a vegetable garden. Clean the attic. Overcome fear of flying."

"It's just some things I've wanted to do for several years, and well, you know me. If it's written down, I'll get to it. Except maybe that flying thing." She shivered. "That's Mark's idea."

Maggie picked up a magnet and replaced what Mark called her Great Retirement Manifesto onto the door of the stainless steel fridge.

Maggie shrugged. "Looks more like a chore list. You should try and enjoy yourself. Your drive to organize everything and everyone will make you crazy. You can't do it all."

"That is how I enjoy myself." Grace considered the items she'd anticipated tackling for years. "I hate it when things aren't wrapped up and neat and tidy. You know that. Mark says..."

Maggie had grown silent again, studying the pottery rack, dishes aligned like soldiers standing shoulder to shoulder. "Only you would be able to keep wedding dishes intact all this time." She lowered herself to one end of the banquette.

The backhanded compliment slapped hard. *Really, Maggie? And only you could find a negative in keeping an orderly household.* She cleared her throat, taking the high road. "It's sturdy stuff. I've replaced some pieces over the years. Ian and Wendy were pretty rough on them when they were learning to set the table." Grace paused a beat, grabbed two glasses. "I think I will pour us that lemonade." *A glass of lemonade and sayonara, sourpuss.* Her thoughts sounded sibilant and sharp even to herself. She forced a softer tone. "Made it yesterday. Mark enjoys it fresh squeezed." From the opposite end of the kitchen table, she slurped lemonade until her tongue sizzled.

Maggie's glass sat untouched. "Didn't this kitchen have linoleum when you bought it?"

"You remember that? You were only here once before you moved away."

"You did a nice job. I still have pictures of a Tuscany kitchen we rented in Italy...a few summers ago." Maggie's gaze danced around the custom cabinets, polished chrome appliances, and granite countertops. "There's no way I could afford to fix up Dad's old place..." Maggie's eyes fixed on the microwave clock and she hauled herself up. "I'd better get back and help Connie feed, I'm sure her mind's occupied with that movie. Thanks for the drink." Maggie lifted the pillowcase. "And your contribution."

Together they maneuvered a heavy cardboard box into Baby out of a small utility room off the garage.

Maggie slammed the trunk. "Tell Mark thanks for the hospital's castoffs."

Grace shut the back door and listened to Baby rumble down the driveway. *I feel bad for you Maggie, but this is supposed to be my time and you're not going to ruin my first summer of retirement.* She crossed the kitchen and moved her Manifesto two inches to the left

In the bedroom, Grace changed into seersucker capris and a T-shirt, pulled her hair into a ponytail then wandered into the family room. She removed the Lifestyle section from the Sunday paper and turned to the crossword puzzle.

Without papers to grade for school anymore, she could indulge herself in the satisfying challenge of filling in the tiny boxes with her tidy lettering, or spend hours reading her favorite classics. She straightened her pile of to-be-reads. *Gone with the Wind* at the very top.

Soon, I'll be back at Tara, my dear, Scarlett.

Grace sucker-punched a couch pillow to plump it then realized the action felt really good. A few more one-two hooks and she realized the blows were really meant for Maggie.

Who cares what she thinks? What if I want to volunteer for a movie, it's my life.

A seam popped and feathers poofed. A white cloud wafted to the floor and she giggled, sucked a floater, and gagged.

Nothing like a little humility check, she thought, extracting the white down from her tongue.

What are you trying to tell me, Lord? Feathers? Chickens. I get it. Her thoughts dipped to farm fresh eggs, and her prayer partner, Shelby. A sigh, she gathered up the mess she'd made. *Seek wise counsel. I can work off that lunch and buy my week's worth of eggs while I'm at it.*

Grace picked the last dainty quill out of her hair, plopped her straw hat on her head, and went outside. She stowed her wallet in a gingham-lined wicker basket strapped to her hot pink, cushion-seated Comfort Cruiser's handlebars and guided it along pavers through the backyard and onto the path that passed behind their home. She turned the pedals in a rhythm quick enough to get her blood moving, but not so fast that she couldn't enjoy the afternoon ride.

The footpath around Cherryvale, called Cherry Path or simply "The Path" by Valers, served as an alleyway around town and enjoyed a special role in the community. At Christmas, families decorated their portion of the rail fence with colorful lights and festive decorations. In the summertime, gardeners placed bowls, buckets, or barrels from their recovery gardens' harvest to share with passersby.

She glided to a stop, unlatched a gate, and rolled into a small yard behind a two-story white clapboard building that housed the Lunch Bucket. After leaning her bike against a tree, she climbed two concrete steps and tapped on the screen door's frame. From somewhere inside, she heard Arlene holler, "Back door customer!"

Footsteps approached on the linoleum. Shelby, Grace's prayer—and accountability—partner, opened the door.

As the Bucket's owner and chief waitress, Shelby could always use a break, especially for Grace. She shouted over her shoulder into the kitchen, "I'll be back in ten!" Shelby stepped into the yard, shoved her pencil behind her ear, and slid an order pad in her apron pocket. "Hey, girlfriend. Here for your eggs?"

Grace nodded. "And a shoulder."

"Sit." Shelby pointed to a wooden bench that circled the broad trunk of a sprawling oak, sat down beside her, leaned back, and closed her eyes. "Quite a crowd here today. You and Maggie eat somewhere's else?"

"We went to the Bypass. It was awful."

"I been tellin' you their cook is too daggone happy with the lemon pepper over there. It's 'lemon pepper this' and 'lemon pepper that.' Sheesh!"

"No, not from the food—though, yours is better. It's Maggie, Shelby. She's taking all the fun out of this for me."

"Fun out of what?"

"I've been looking forward to my first summer after retirement for so long. I loved teaching, but I have my own plans. I feel bad for her, but do I have to, well, to . . ."

"To widow-sit?" Shelby's voice could be gentle when she wanted. "Maggie's still hurting. When they moved back here and Joe checked out, you could almost watch her change from sort of tolerable to downright bitter overnight."

The wind rose and lifted the oak leaves, their dappled shadows dancing on the bench and the grass around their feet.

Grace swung her shoe, playing with a thistle that poked through the grass.

"You two were tighter'n a rusty hinge way back when," Shelby pointed out.

"I know. But I've got things I really need to do."

Eyes closed and her head resting against the trunk, Shelby spoke words that pierced directly into Grace's heart. "Did God put you in this place right here, right now so's you could have clean closets? Really?"

Grace winced. "You know me too well." She listened to the hens scratching and fussing behind them. "And way to make it about Maggie instead of me."

"I know Maggie can be as hard as Cherryvale Pond in winter. But if anyone can crack her, you can." Shelby stood up and rolled her shoulders. She looked directly into Grace's eyes. "You ever iron out what happened between you two before she left town?"

Grace squirmed and twisted her gold band, third finger left hand. "That's ancient history and everyone's over it. It wouldn't serve any purpose to dredge up all that old stuff again."

"I'm just suggestin' it might help to get it out. I think it's mighty coincidental that Maggie's upset about a movie." She climbed the concrete steps. "Sometimes God puts people in our lives for His reasons. Not ours." The hinges squeaked at her tug. "You gonna come through for Him or think of yourself first? Help yourself to the eggs. I heard Lady Gaga's layin' cackle earlier."

The screen door plopped closed, and Grace remained on the bench pondering Shelby's challenge. After a few minutes, she removed the basket from her bike's handlebars, unlatched a gate into the chicken coop, and stepped into a small enclosure. The musty smell of straw, hen feathers, and earth rushed up to greet her. The eggs were so fresh they were still warm in her gentle grip. She plopped several coins in the honor basket, realizing she'd received more than a couple eggs from her wise friend. She'd had a word from above.

Pedaling home, Grace's knees lifted in slow rhythm as she considered her motivations and wrestled with her priorities. She negotiated bumps to keep the gems from breaking. The cautious pace forced her to enjoy the evening air, sultry in spots from the early summer sun, now cooling in pockets shaded by overhanging branches.

Neighbors sipping lemonade on their Path side porches waved, others tended sizzling grills or worked their vegetable gardens. The smell of seared burgers woke her tummy and reminded her she only picked at her lunch with Maggie. Shrieks from the next yard punctuated splashing into what she imagined must be a chilly pool.

One small house a few doors from her own stirred a familiar pang. Overgrown with bushes, almost completely hidden from view, Grace remembered the owners who'd given up and left town before the makeover spurred the economy back to health. In total disrepair and neglect, the house earned an unfortunate nickname.

A pathetic remnant of the recession, The Pit always looked lonely, no signs of life or sounds of a family's love coming from inside. A stone walkway to The Path crumbled in pieces, and the fence, overgrown with weeds, begged for a new coat of paint. *Lord, bring someone who can cherish this little house, and may it be a happy home again.*

The lonely cottage made her even more anxious to get home with her basketful of treasures. She pedaled on until she heard excited voices coming from the real estate office's parking lot.

Her curiosity tickled, she steered between buildings to the street side. Late afternoon shadows crawled over tables set up under green awnings. People waited in a line that snaked toward the street.

Carolyn Sims beckoned her over, a yellow sundress beautiful against her deep-chocolate-toned skin. "Are you signing up to be an extra in the movie?"

"It does sound like fun." Grace wondered if there was room on her to-do list, then glanced down at Carolyn's six-year-old twins, Carson and Cassie. They beamed at her, with identical gap-toothed grins, casting a warm blanket over her heart. She ducked down to their level and ruffled Cassie's rainbow-clipped and braided head. "Are you two going to be in the movie?"

"Yeth!" Cassie squealed, her recent tooth fairy trade accentuating her lisp.

Carson let go of his mom's hand and grabbed Grace's handlebar. "And we're going to meet Tiffany Lane!"

"*Maybe* you'll get to meet her," Carolyn reminded him, affectionately rubbing his thick close-cropped black hair.

Sam and Abby Madison approached. Grace caught Carson's eye and indicated them with a nod. "Here's a man who knows all the etiquette. We're wondering if the commoners can meet the stars this week."

"Don't tell me you think Tiffany Lane is cute." Sam grinned at Carson.

"Nah, but Cassie does." Carson kicked at the ground with his sneaker toe. His sister thumped him on the arm.

"Oh, okay." Sam caught Grace's eye with a knowing wink. "You're supposed to ask first before speaking to one of the stars." He pointed at the film crew working the table. "See the girl doing the sign-ups, the one with the ponytail? Her name is Holly. She can ask the actors to give you an autograph, or maybe even have your picture taken with them. It's all in this letter they'll give your mom. Here, you can have mine." Sam gave Carolyn his handout. "I'm familiar with the rules."

"There's a small part open, and he's going to read for it." Abby patted her husband's broad chest.

"It's just a couple lines. They added it in rewrites." Sam lifted his baseball cap and smoothed a few strands across the top of his head.

"After all these years, you can finally put a little of your talent to good use." His wife grinned up at him. "He was in some movies before we met, you know."

"I remember that," Grace said. "I haven't seen you perform since the city makeover fundraiser."

Sam shrugged. “Keeping the hardware store going’s been all we could manage lately. I’m looking forward to this town having some fun for a change.”

“Now that Cherryvale’s in recovery, we should do another show at your theatre,” Grace suggested. “Kind of a celebration.”

His face lit up. “Maybe for the Harvest Festival. That would give us plenty of time to plan. Speaking of planning…you should be in it, Grace. You were so busy with the arrangements last time that we didn’t see you on stage. I’ll bet you’re hiding talent we’ve never seen.”

Grace remembered with a shudder her last time onstage. She shook her head, looking for anything to change the subject. “I’m much better at organizing. Say, what does that flyer say?” She pointed to the handout.

Carolyn read from the piece of paper. “Background Artist’s Do’s and Dont’s.”

“Background, mommy?”

“Another word for extras.” Sam assumed his stage voice to answer Cassie’s question.

Connie McCoy paused next to them, thumbs hovering over her cell phone. “You know. The people you see in the background. Right, Mr. Madison?”

Sam nodded. “Good girl, you were listening in my Acting for the Camera class last summer.”

“They’re also called atmosphere because they make the scene look realistic,” Connie added. “You told us they’re more like re-actors than actors, like when there’s an explosion and people running.” She thrust her hands in the air and screamed in mock terror. “AH! Run!”

“Mommy!” Cassie’s dark brown eyes grew rounder as she clutched her mother’s legs. “Are there going to be ’splosions?”

“If there are, we won’t be close to them, will we, Sam?”

“I don’t think we’ll be exposed to anything like that,” Sam assured the little girl.

“Will we wear costumes, Mommy? I can wear my Princess Tiana one!” Cassie offered.

"They should tell you..." Sam pointed at a section of the upside down paper. "Right there."

"Let's see." Carolyn read from the list. "'Street clothes appropriate for summer, no logos or red or white.' Sorry, hon. No princess attire."

"They'll keep track of everything you wear and probably even take pictures of you," Sam added. "That way if they have to reshoot a scene on another day, it doesn't look funny if your clothes switch from one color to the next all of a sudden!" Sam twirled his hat around, crossed his eyes and stuck his tongue out.

While Cassie and Carson giggled that happy kid laughter that always made Grace's heart sing, Carolyn lowered the paper. "Are you sure you want to do this? It says we have to be there at 8:30 in the morning. You wouldn't be able to sleep in on your first day of summer vacation."

"Yes!" Carson and Cassie jumped up and down.

"Okay, okay. But everyone's going to bed early tonight."

Groans.

"Not so glamorous now, is it?" Grace teased.

"We'd better get going if you're going to learn those lines, dear." Abby turned to Grace. "They're auditioning him tonight."

"Break a leg." Grace lifted a foot to shove into motion.

"Are you going to volunteer?" Sam wanted to know.

"I guess not." Grace braked and looked up and down the line. "Looks like there'll be enough people from church to make the numbers."

"What about doing something just for fun now that you're retired?" Carolyn urged. "You and your lists, Grace!"

"Please, Miz Grace." Cassie grabbed Grace's fingers from the hand-grip and tugged. "You can sleep in the next day."

She felt more than a hand tug from the little girl. She and Cassie bonded long ago when Grace took shifts during the night when the twins had colic. Carl needed his sleep to run the newly opened Inn. While Carolyn cuddled Carson, Grace would swaddle Cassie and walk up and down The Path to soothe the tiny girl.

Had that really been six years ago? She leaned over and kissed the soft brown forehead she'd loved to cradle in the crook of her neck. "I'll think about it, honey, but I have a lot of things to do." She pushed off and tried to ignore a knot of regret in her stomach.

Gliding along The Path toward home, she argued with herself. *Decades of junk wait for me in those closets and drawers.* Somewhere in the closet of her soul, Grace's own memories lurked.

Indeed. I have no time for frivolous days hanging out on a movie set.

Still, it might be fun. What's another day? Those closets can't read a calendar.

Grace set the wicker basket on the kitchen counter, slid open the little door on her appliance garage and pulled out her mixer.

This'll take my mind off Maggie.

One of her traditional and most loved Sunday afternoon chores, Grace always found comfort in puttering in her kitchen, especially preparing her trademark muffins, a family heritage and a Cherryvale favorite.

She'd been making them for years, and still remembered the day she stumbled upon the recipe. When Ian and Wendy were in elementary school, like other working moms, she'd searched for healthy, creative snack ideas that were easy to prepare and keep on hand. One day, while she thumbed through her grandma's 1896 Boston Cooking School Cookbook, the heirloom practically opened itself to a flour-smudged page percolating with the aroma of vanilla and cinnamon. The one-egg muffin recipe and notes scribbled in its margin stirred her imagination. "Cherry in the spring, raisin in winter," her grandma's neat lettering advised.

By following the penciled-in suggestions and adding her own ideas for seasonal stir-ins, she perfected the recipe for tummy-filling, healthy kids' snacks. Her family, and eventually everyone else in Cherryvale, playfully argued about which were the best: cherry in the spring, carrot or zucchini in the summer, either pumpkin or squash in the autumn, cranberry and apple pie spice in the winter.

She whipped up batches on Sunday afternoons for after-school snacks and, because the recipe made thirty, she took a dozen or so outside as her own contribution to The Path's bounty. The fresh-from-the-oven aroma greeted passersby walking their dogs or jogging past, and before the fresh-baked delicacies cooled, there would be nothing left but crumbs.

They were partially the reason she'd given up driving a car in town and started riding a bicycle. Riding gave her mobility and fresh air, and helped prevent her from developing her own muffin tops. Shelby teased her about the great muffin mileage she got.

Today Grace decided to indulge in her favorite pick-me-up: double chocolate chip. She set the mixer to low and poured herself a glass of iced tea as the phone rang.

"You coming to the clinic soon?" Mark knew the first batch would be hot out of the oven at any minute. She could almost hear him salivating.

"Sorry, I'm a little behind schedule." She hurried to fill the basket while she told him the day's highlights. "And guess what? Pastor announced that a movie's being filmed in the Vale. They want us to help out as extras and they'll make a donation to our VBS funds."

"Are you going?"

"I don't know."

"Why not? You love our VBS. And movies."

"I've got plans. There's the hall closet, the pantry needs re-painting. And . . ."

"And what?"

"Maggie says we shouldn't. The evil Hollywood influence and all that. Do you think she's right?"

"Well, I guess it depends on—" A crackling, urgent voice interrupted him. "That's me, I gotta run. Trauma coming into the ER. I'm sure you'll do what's best, honey. Page me when you get here. Love you." Click.

Just speaking with Mark tightened the tug at Grace's knotted conflict. On one hand she wanted to spend time organizing and attending to their home. Even though Mark never complained, she knew she'd neglected keeping it in proper order. Besides teaching school, she'd spent most of her free time the past couple of years on the Cherryvale makeover committee.

"When I retire, I promise to clean all those closets and the attic too," she'd promised.

"Twenty years of clutter bugs you more than it bothers me," Mark repeatedly assured her.

Well, that made her feel even worse. Now she felt torn between supporting the newly widowed Maggie and enjoying her own retirement.

Sipping her tea, Grace admired the gracious kitchen, a testimony of Mark's love for her. On the eve of her fiftieth birthday, Mark arrived home from a long shift at the hospital and while she ladled out a bowl of soup for his dinner, told her to pack her bags.

"Why? What did I do?"

"I'm kidnapping you."

"Don't have to." Grace blew at her bangs. "You're already stuck with me."

"And don't I know it. Get your overnight bag ready. We leave first thing in the morning." Mark's blue eyes danced at her over his bowl of soup. "That's all I'm telling you."

"I don't know what to pack."

"Hmm." He studied her. "Comfortable slacks and a blouse. And a fancy dinner dress."

"No pajamas?"

"If you insist," he teased.

"You rascal!"

The next morning after breakfast, they drove the hour to Franklin City. Without even checking into the hotel first, Mark turned their sedan into the parking lot of a two-story redbrick colonial and escorted Grace into its elegant foyer. Inside, they were greeted by a young woman in a gray silk pantsuit, with a firm handshake.

Mark made introductions. "Grace, this is Madeline. Madeline, my wife, Grace. Top-to-bottom makeover, just like we talked about."

Oh, here it comes. One of those don't-wear-those clothes ambushes.

Grace's mouth dried up and she searched Madeline's clipboard to see if it said anything Stepford on it. "I'm getting a makeover?"

"Not you." Mark grinned. "Our kitchen."

Our...kitchen? "Oh, honey, you're kidding!" Grace wrapped her arms around Mark's neck and kissed him full on the mouth. "I take back everything I ever said about you. You are a nice guy."

Mark threw back his head and guffawed, then kissed her right back.

When Grace finally released him, Mark handed Madeline a canvas bag. "Here's the wish book. I managed to hide it from her in the backseat. Now if you ladies will excuse me, I'm going to embarrass myself on at least twelve of eighteen holes." With that, he left her to realize a dream she thought she'd kept a secret for decades.

Six months later, the warped avocado green countertops, chipped harvest gold appliances, peeling laminate flooring, and thrift store dining set were history.

Jerusalem stone floors, hickory cabinets, and a gleaming white farmhouse sink still made her heart leap each morning when she walked in for her first cup of coffee. She especially adored her cook's heaven on earth: the baker's station with all her flours and spices arranged alphabetically and the measuring cups stacked by height.

Grace opened one of the Aga oven's four doors, and slid in batter-filled trays. She eyed the proper placement for maximum cooking efficiency, but her thoughts went back to the day's events. *Maggie needs to make other friends, she can't rely on me all the time. Maybe we were best friends a hundred years ago but that's changed. I deserve to enjoy my retirement. Not my fault Joe up and died.*

Grace closed the oven door with a smack, kick combo. Wiping down the counter, she picked up the untouched glass and dumped the lemonade into the sink. *Besides, Maggie's made of tough stuff. She'll be just fine.*

Henry Weston's head felt dizzy watching his brother, Stan, pacing a trail in the dining room Persian rug. He swallowed and resumed shoveling mashed potatoes into a pile then poured gravy into the middle.

Just outside Cherryvale, the boys lived in the mansion all alone, had kept to themselves, both attending private schools. Alone, apart, the two were all the other had in the world. For better or worse.

"I'll watch over him," Stan promised his parents when they were young. "Don't worry. He's too stupid to get in trouble." Then when they tragically died within a year of each other, Stan realized he now had access to Henry's inheritance as well as his own.

Stan slapped the phone down on the oak table. Large enough for twelve, it had once held their extended family at holidays and family gatherings. Those days were long past.

Henry focused on dabbing a biscuit into the gravy pond.

Stan took a bite of chicken leg then wagged the poultry at his brother. "Make sure you get that delivery to Franklin City. Tonight." His cell phone interrupted. "And don't dilly-dally. You were hours late last time. Hello?"

Stan's tirade befuddled Henry. He fumbled and lost control of his knife. A dollop of strawberry preserves he'd been balancing midair to a hot biscuit somersaulted in a gooey glob, missed the napkin hanging from his overalls and settled near his belly button.

Stan closed the phone, threw back a gulp of beer, and wiped his chin on a sleeve.

"Why do I have to go tonight?" Henry whined, scraping at the jelly. "It's Sunday, there's nobody there."

"Just do it and don't argue. They need those files first thing in the morning. Put everything in the lockbox by the front door."

Stan's phone vibrated and chirped again. "We've got a meeting with the county on Friday, but they already told me there's not enough easement. We're up a creek without a paddle. Hello?" Stan listened to the caller, pacing the length of the room.

Henry poured another glass of milk from the carton on the table.

"We have to do something!" Stan shouted into his cell, startling Henry into spilling milk on his pants. "If we want to get this contract, we've got to increase production, and that takes—Okay, let me know." Stan flipped his phone closed and drained the bottle of beer.

Henry scooted back, sopping up milk with a soggy napkin.

Stan sighed, grabbed another napkin, and pulled Henry up, spinning him by the shoulders to face him. He swiped at the jelly blob and re-hooked Henry's makeshift bib. "I thought that special boarding school would have taught you some manners. You're such a dunderhead; you can't even eat without—"

"Stan?" Henry's voice wobbled as his brother finished cleaning him up.

"What?"

"Are we in trouble?" Henry swallowed. "Bad trouble?"

"What do you mean?"

"On the phone just now." He pointed to Stan's cell phone. "You said we can't finish the contract. Don't we need that?"

"Peterson's threatening to give the contract to the Michigan division because the lease on our facility's almost—Oh, who am I kidding, you don't understand. Just get that paperwork delivered. That's all you need to know."

"If the lease is up, why can't we just go somewheres else? Or build a new factory?"

"I told you this the other day, nitwit." Stan rolled his eyes. "The county's right-of-way is to the north and that petting zoo woman's place is in our way. It's not working out like I thought it would when her old man died."

"So, what does that mean?"

"Just get this folder of invoices to the accountant if your tiny little brain can manage that much." Stan grabbed his cell and headed for the door. "And don't get into any trouble."

"You're not gonna send me back are you? I wanna live here with you. That group home—"

"I ain't," Stan caught his breath and started over. "I am not sending you back. Unless you prove to be useless. He fumbled with his cell.

"Stan?"

"What now?"

"Can I have some money?"

"What for?"

"It's a long drive." Henry licked his lips. "Might wanna stop and get a Slurpee or somethin'."

"Here." Stan dug out a bundle of bills from his wallet, separated out some ones, and threw them on the table. "Just do like I said." Stan spun on his Italian loafers and bolted out the door.

As the BMW revved and squealed down the driveway, Henry mumbled, "It's my company, too." He drained the last swig of his milk and patted his pockets, pulled out a set of car keys, grabbed the dollar bills and muttered, "I'll show him," as he walked out past a metal box on the dining room sideboard.

CHAPTER THREE

"They probably don't even have cell phones out there in Bananaville," Tiffany Lane groused to her tiny, teacup Yorkie, Leonardo. His long lashes fluttered up at her while she tugged down a black-billed cap and tucked in her bangs.

She slid large-framed "Jackie" shades up her perfect nose, and pouted at her equally perfect reflection…if she did say so herself.

Her driver negotiated the Los Angeles traffic and pulled the Town Car over to the curb at LAX. She waited behind dark-tinted windows and her driver handed porters matching Gucci bags.

She flicked off the television, tossed the remote on the seat, and lifted Leo from his pillow to snuggle him into a teal, faux-crocodile bag that matched his Swarovski-jeweled collar.

With a click, Gus opened the door to her cocoon. She stuck out one then the other long leg to teeter on a pair of red patent Jimmy Choo stilettos.

"Have a nice flight, Ms. Lane."

"I wish."

Two pre-teen girls ran over. Gus held out an arm to body block them from swooping in on their star attraction.

"Oh, terrific," she muttered to Leo, scratching his fur with her acrylic nails. "Vultures."

"Please, Tiffany, can you give us an autograph?" One of the girls leaned around the bodyguard's bulk to call out to her.

Remember, your fans are your meal ticket. Blah. Blah. She could hear her manager now.

"Let them through." Tiffany clacked to a stop, shoved Leo's carrier at Gus, and took their papers and a pen. She scribbled her name, grabbed Leo and stepped around the fans as if they were viral.

"Is that the near-dead dog you rescued?" One of the girls turned to her friend. "She found him in a dumpster and spent a ton of money to save his life. Hey, can we have a picture of—"

Tiffany spun on her stiletto heel and clickety-clacked away, their request fading in the shushing automatic door at her back.

Cast in a nationwide commercial at nine months of age then on a sitcom that lasted nine years, Tiffany performed for studio cameras all day and fled paparazzi the rest of the time. Her approach to the world: trust no one. Her view: from behind dark glasses.

She and Leo were flying east to join the crew filming her final scenes in *The Scrapbook.* At least in such a primitive town, maybe she wouldn't have to worry about the stupid paparazzi chasing her.

In a high-rise office building several freeway interchanges from LAX, Jeff Field prepared to join the film crew as well. His friends jabbed fun at him, but costarring with Tiffany Lane required copious amounts of prayer and patience. Known for her explosive attitude, many directors refused to hire her, and her costars found it equally annoying when she interrupted filming with unprofessional behavior.

"I'll be on location for about two to three weeks finishing the rest of this movie. I'd appreciate prayer, if you guys can remember me." Jeff slid his upholstered chair underneath the mahogany table where they'd been having a Bible study. "I just want to get to this little town and back as quickly as possible."

A new Christian, Jeff attended the group whenever his shooting schedule allowed, but he still had a lot to learn about this new life that began almost a year ago.

"Thousands of people pray for you, Jeff." Rick Westly, a chaplain in a ministry dedicated to reaching folks in entertainment, had been inviting Jeff to have lunch or coffee for years. After a series of failed relationships, and many years of searching for significance in the world, Jeff agreed to meet. He almost canceled, but he was curious. Something he couldn't explain compelled him to keep the engagement.

They met for lunch in the studio cafeteria reserved for "named" stars and studio executives. Decorated in modern teak, sleek chrome lights, and plush carpeting, it offered more privacy than the cafeteria downstairs, but Jeff worried that someone might see him meeting with the Christian minister.

"If we know your specific needs, we can pray for you in a more personal way," Rick told him over salad. "We know how hard it is, how your every public move is photographed and scrutinized."

"How much is it going to cost? When I met with the Scientologists—"

"No. No money, Jeff." Rick's smile appeared warm and genuine. "There may be costs to you, but not in the monetary sense."

"What do you mean by that?"

"Let me ask you this. Are either you or your daughter completely happy? I read you haven't lived with her since she was little."

Jeff didn't feel challenged or surprised that the guy knew all about his personal life. Most people did.

"Because you deserve to know you are loved by God. Jeff Field the person, the dad. Not Jeff Field the actor, assumed to be a cog in the wheel of a big machine."

Nail on the head. He did feel like a dispensable cog. "I guess I'm not completely happy, no." Any day, a younger, better-looking actor could take over and he'd be a nobody overnight. Bumped off the throne of Hollywood's royalty. He glanced around and made eye contact with a casting director considering him for a blockbuster green-lighted for next year. "I don't believe in God . . . scientifically." He stuck his fork into a piece of chicken.

"Evolution?"

"Been proven by scientists."

Jeff followed Rick's gaze out the commissary window. Technicians pushed dollies with sound and lighting equipment, and a costumer dragged a rack of vintage dresses into a panel truck. A golf cart filled with people in business suits reading from clipboards and talking on cell phones rolled past.

"Suppose we were from a couple hundred years ago, and we built a time machine and landed on the red carpet at a movie premiere."

Jeff snorted. Now he's pitching a script treatment. Beautiful.

"Okay, bear with me," Rick chuckled. "For the sake of illustration. We get hustled into Grauman's, sit and watch this flick, and when it finishes, they ask us what we think of it. We don't know a good performance from bad, much less how they made these pictures of people moving on the wall. To us, it was all magic."

"You want me to admit there had to be some kind of intelligence behind the scenes who designed the world?"

"How else do you explain the hours of scriptwriting, auditions, location scouting, set building, score preparation, Foley and score recording, filming, post-production—"

"I get it." Jeff waved a hand in surrender. "You're not a fan of evolution. But how do you know your particular brand of religion is right for me?"

"I'm not talking religions made up by people who either want to be God or become Him." Rick wiped crouton crumbs off his mouth with his cloth napkin. "I'm talking about a relationship."

Rick folded his napkin and laid it next to his plate. "You cast this one. Either you play God, or you need God. And what about your daughter?" Rick looked at his watch. "I've gotta get over to Studio City by 1:30. I hope you'll let us know how we can pray for you. And your daughter. Julie, right?" He reached into a leather bag. "Would you take this as a gift from One-to-One? From the Master Script-Writer Himself." Rick moved a handsome leather book across the linen cloth. "Go on, it's a gift."

"Uh, thanks." Jeff slid the Bible under his napkin and glanced at the next table, but the people were engrossed in their own conversation.

"Start with the book of John." Rick stood and held out a hand to shake Jeff's. "It tells the story of another gift. If you have any questions, you have my cell."

All afternoon during table reads and costume fittings, Jeff thought about the book in his dressing room.

Later that night, Jeff poked at a nuked dinner in the blue glow from his plasma TV, alone in the living room of his Hollywood Hills mansion. Not pushy, Rick had left Jeff with many questions. And a warning. "Be forewarned, when you sign up for this gig, you won't know what's in the script ahead of time." What would all this mean? And how will Julie react? She'll have more reasons to avoid me if I tell her I've become a religious nut.

Pushing back the tasteless meal, he lifted the book out of the gym bag he'd shoved it in after lunch. It took a few minutes of fumbling, but he finally found the book of John. By midnight, he accepted a role in the kingdom of heaven.

"Okay, Lord. Sir." Jeff stumbled on his unfamiliar lines of the prayer, not sure how to go on, but suddenly filled with hope. "Bring it on."

Maggie bumped the screen door open. Only a few people filled The Lunch Bucket, one couple at the soda fountain huddled over an ice cream sundae, and Shelby stood behind the register cashing out a family.

"Is the mayor in here?"

"Good afternoon, Maggie." Shelby moved around her and picked up a tray. "No, he ate lunch but left hours ago, why?" She lifted salt and pepper dispensers off a table and clacked another set next to them, moving from table to table.

Maggie dogged her. "I need to speak to him about letting these movie people run amok all over town."

Shelby glanced at the couple at the counter. "No one's fixin' to run amok," she whispered. "But if you're against something, it's a free country and your opinion's gonna be considered. I think you'll have to wait 'til tomorrow when the city office opens. File a complaint if you must."

"Paperwork never gets anything done."

"Maggie, they're just here to do a job. It's not like they're coming here to stomp on our morals and run off with our scruples."

"Like you said. It's a free country, and everyone's entitled to her opinion." Maggie crossed the room and paused before opening the door. "But just wait." She gestured, Purse Everest swinging from her forearm. "This town will not be the same if they are allowed in."

The door smacked and rattled against the frame, and Shelby let go a deep sigh. "That woman's tougher'n an opera tune at a sing-a-long."

Tiffany's taxi wound through a compound of catering trucks, transportation and utility vans, trailers, and tents set up in Cherryvale Park. Crews were unloading cables, carts, tables, chairs, and black and silver boxes, building an instant mini-city.

Tiffany opened her wallet to pull out two crisp ten-dollar bills. "The third honey wagon on the left."

"Honey-what?" The driver pulled to a stop as the meter clicked to nineteen dollars, and she flicked the paper money onto the seat next to him.

Leo stirred in her lap, sniffing the air, and she lifted him, slung the straps from his carrier and her Coach bag over her shoulder, and stepped out of the cab.

Tiffany unlocked the trailer door and stepped in. "Just put my bags inside the door." She let the door slam behind her.

The driver pushed it open and slid the five suitcases into the trailer. He watched her scanning and tossing envelopes onto the table in the kitchenette. "I hope you enjoy your stay, Miss Lane."

Tiffany turned her back on him, flipped open her cell, and walked down the hallway to the bedroom. She lifted the phone to her ear and spoke into it. "I'm here, you can unpack me."

Behind her, the trailer door thumped shut. She slapped the phone closed, tossed it onto her satin comforter, and settled Leo onto his pillow covered in matching fabric. In the marble-lined bathroom, she kicked off her shoes and turned on the shower, anxious to wash away the aroma of airports, cabs and common people.

A few minutes later, Holly Benson called, "I'm here, Tiffany," as she let herself into the trailer. Steam billowed from the bathroom and she sighed. The director, Radford Harper, was notorious for flinging additional work at his skeleton crew. She still burned from his hefting her the additional job as Tiffany's watchdog to her P.A. responsibilities. Already over budget and behind schedule, the producers insisted on cutbacks. Even the bodyguards had been let go, the producers willing to risk the stars' safety over shelling out more money.

Tiffany caused most of the problems: arriving late for her call times, flubbing lines, and indulging in diva moments. So Holly and others in the remaining skeleton crew had taken extra jobs to get the movie in the can.

"Have a nice trip?" Holly raised her voice over the shower noise.

Getting no response, she dragged a suitcase in from the living room, flopped it onto the teal satin comforter, and unzipped it. While she arranged the couture clothes in the closet and designer underwear in dresser drawers, the shower stopped. Tiffany's cell phone bleeped and vibrated.

"Phone's ringing, want me to get it?"

"Who is it?" Tiffany yelled through the door.

Holly leaned over and read the caller ID as it chirruped again. "Says 'unknown.'"

"Get rid of them."

Her first day as Tiffany's personal assistant, and already the attitude she knew so well. Holly punched the talk button. "Hello?"

"Tiffany?" A woman's voice.

"I'm sorry, she's not available. Can I help you?"

"Where is she?" Something about the caller's tone prevented Holly from hanging up. "She's busy, but I can give her a message."

"Tell her I called."

"I'm sorry. Who are you?"

"Her mother."

That's it! Her voice sounded like Tiffany's. "Wait. Hang on a minute." She moved toward the bathroom door and shouted over hair dryer noise. "Tiffany, it's your mother!"

No response.

She knocked and repeated, louder this time. "It's your m-"

The door yanked open, slammed against the bathroom wall, and Tiffany grabbed the phone from Holly. "I heard you!" She jutted her chin in range of its mic and spat, "Leave me alone!"

Leo sat up on his pillow and cocked his tiny head as Tiffany snapped the phone closed, hurled it onto the bed, and thundered back into the bathroom. "Finish unpacking already, I'm sick of the mess. And get the maintenance department over here to fix that stupid shower door, it's almost off the hinges." She slammed the door and Leo quivered.

Holly stroked the top of his smooth head. "I'll bet you could tell some stories, couldn't you, buddy?"

Leo sighed, circled, and lay down, lowering his muzzle onto tiny paws.

Holly finished stacking twelve pairs of shoes, no doubt fresh off Rodeo Drive, in acrylic shelves, zipped the last bag closed, and let herself out the front door. *The next couple weeks are going to be a real treat.*

Henry twiddled with the radio dial to coax Rascal Flatts through the static and joined in a flat monotone. Then something flashed across the road and he stomped on the brake.

The rusty van shuddered and squeaked, kicking up bits of rubble as Henry fought to keep it from grinding off the tarmac into the ditch. Finally it stopped, a cloud of dust settled, and the radio announcer promised clear, hotter weather. The motor hiccupped, sputtered, and died.

Henry coughed and lifted up on the door handle. He shoved his shoulder against the door and it gave way so he could step out. Crunching over deep gravel around to the front, he looked up and down the shoulder. "Must'a been a deer or something runnin' across."

He paced up and down the shallow ditch but didn't see anything except a man walking toward him on the other side of the road. He stopped, waited for traffic, and crossed over to Henry.

"Car trouble?" The stranger checked Henry up and down then eyed the beater van. He shifted a dusty vinyl bag from one hand to the other.

"Thought I hit somethin." Henry stooped to check between the tires.

The guy didn't move. "I don't see nothin."

Henry spied the traveler's hard-soled shoes and sunburned forehead, his greasy hair dripped sweat. "You need a ride somewheres?"

The stranger rubbed his chin. "Where ya goin'?"

"Franklin City then back home. But I can't stop and do nothing else or Stan'll get mad." Henry wiped his palm on his pant leg and stuck his hand out. "My name's Henry. What's yours?"

Ignoring Henry's outstretched hand, he patted a shirt pocket. "I just got out…er, just left there. Not goin' back." He moved closer so he could see into the VW. "Why're you headed up that'a'way?"

"Papers for the accountant."

"Any cash?"

"I got a couple bucks. Gonna get me a Slurpee." Henry grinned. "Hey, what's your name?"

"Max." Max shuffled toward the centerline then stopped when a car horn blared and swerved to miss him. "Got any smokes?"

"Nah, Stan says it's no good to smoke. He chews." He nodded up the road. "There's a Nifty Mart 'bout a mile back. Ya can't miss it if'n you wanna buy a carton. I better git." He pulled open the driver's side door, but looked at Max. "Was 'at you, whining?"

"Do I look like a whiner?" Max sneered.

"Thought I heard...what if I hit a critter?" Henry, stricken to the gut, knelt at the edge of the ditch and strained his eyes. Something was out there. He glanced up, sharp. "Looks like a dog!" He hunkered again, whistled and listened. "I won't hurt ya!"

A black and grey dog, covered in mud and burrs peeked out from behind a stand of scrubby oaks among tall weeds.

"Looky, it's a puppy. C'mere, boy." Henry held out his hand and the dog's ears pricked up. As he took a couple of tentative steps away from the trees, an even larger dog stepped out and studied them.

"Dang, that 'uns huge!" Max yanked open the passenger door that creaked in protest, jumped in and slammed it shut. Max heaved on the handle to roll the window up, but it stopped at the halfway point. "Git in, that's a killer dog there."

Henry didn't move, and the smaller one stepped toward the ditch, the tip of its tail switching slowly.

"They're friendly. I think they're just hungry." The "killer" dog stayed near the tree, and Henry jumped over the small ditch. He crouched low and spoke in a soft voice. "I won't hurt you, come on." The scent of strawberry jelly still lingering on Henry's overalls must have floated on the breeze to twitching nostrils because, in unison, all four ears popped forward and they leapt as one to the source of the enticing aroma. Their weight combined into a misguided missile and together they catapulted Henry backward into a thick patch of ferns and brambles. The jumble of filthy fur, flying tongues and breakfast-smeared dungarees rolled together, wagging tails spinning in the excitement.

Max watched from the car, his hand frozen on the window handle, the glass wedged halfway up. Henry finally managed to scramble to his feet. "Off me, you two, I ain't got no dog biscuits in my pockets." The dogs fell away, ears down at the false advertising.

"Thought they were gonna eat you alive for sure," Max called from his safety seat.

"Reckon I smell better than I taste." Henry leaned against one of the trees and wiped his forehead with his sleeve.

The mongrels gave up and lay down, panting in the shade.

"Look how skinny they are. You can count their ribs. Bet they're thirsty too." Henry jumped back over the gulley and the pair scrambled to their feet and followed him. "Let's take 'em, they're lost."

"I ain't ridin' with them mutts." Max pulled on the handle, but stopped when the largest one stuck his muzzle up to the window. "Back off, Cujo!"

"We can get 'em some food at the Nifty." Henry slid the door open, and "Cujo" and his buddy jumped in, their noses sniffing noisily for crumbs on the dirty carpet.

"He likes you." Henry grinned, turning the key. "Them's doggy kisses."

The van's engine started with a belch and snort, and then spewed gravel as Henry did a u-turn across the highway.

"Gimme some money." Max eyed Cujo as he slurped the back of his grimy neck.

"What for?"

"You want me to buy them somethin' to eat, don't you?"

Henry held the steering wheel with one hand and pulled out the wad of one dollar bills that Stan had given him. He fumbled, trying to peel off a couple, but Max grabbed the whole thing.

Henry cast a worried glance. "Get me a cherry Slurpee, too." He pulled into the parking lot of a strip mall and stopped in front of the Nifty Mart. Max opened his door and bounded out before Henry could shut off the engine.

The dogs lay down on the floor and panted, their tongues lolling out the sides of their mouths. Henry fiddled with the radio knobs.

A few minutes later, Max got back in. "Smells like dead carcasses in here. Shove in that lighter." He opened a carton and pulled out a box of cigarettes.

"Where's my Slurpee?"

"Didn't have enough money for dog food, smokes, and a Slurpee."

Max unwrapped a couple of Twinkies and tossed them in the back. The two scrambled to their feet and in an instant devoured every crumb of the moist cakes, down to the last morsel of their creamy filling. They licked their jowls and sniffed around for more.

"That wadn't enough to feed two growed dogs," Henry scolded. Max lit a cigarette and took a long drag. "Stan's gonna be mad. He give me that money for a drink when I finish..." Realization crawled across his face. "Dang it. 'At's not all he's gonna be mad about. Shoot-fire." He cranked the engine and shoved the VW in reverse.

"Where ya goin' in such a hurry?" Max dragged the seatbelt across his lap and the dogs tumbled as the van twirled around and sped back up the highway. "Hey, I thought you needed to go to Franklin City. It's the other way."

"I gotta go back home. I forgot something." They bounced along for several minutes, the dogs lay down and snoozed, Max puffed his smoke. Soon, Henry slowed and turned the van onto a private driveway, pausing in between two brick pillars.

He entered the code into a digital pad, and twin iron gates swung open. They drove up a long drive and parked underneath a porte cochere leading to a handsome brick Colonial with leaded glass windows. The complicated roofline suggested a generous home of immense square footage—Max gave his jaw a thoughtful rub, and slid a glance back to the driver.

"Wait here, I'll be right back." Henry got out of the van.

Max opened his door. "This where your apartment is?"

"Nah." Henry straightened with pride. "It's my house. Mine and my brother's. Don't live in no apartment."

The dogs jumped out behind Max and sniffed and relieved themselves on a wide grassy lawn. Max followed Henry up to a set of double doors and into the marble foyer where an oak banister curved around a massive crystal chandelier. The dogs ran in behind them and, from the sound of it, found the downstairs powder room and helped themselves to a drink. Max examined gold leaf wallpaper and sconces, fingered an oil painting hanging near the double doors while Henry disappeared into the dining room.

"Got it." He came back into the hall carrying a metal file box.

"Say, buddy." Max adopted a cool tone. "You live here with your parents?"

"No. They died a couple years ago. Just me and Stan, now."

Max curled his lips, showing Henry his tobacco stained teeth. "Maybe I will ride along to Franklin City with you. Keep my new bud company." He reached up to put his arm across Henry's shoulder. "We've got lots to talk about."

On the outskirts of Cherryvale, where The Path meanders past the town park, the houses are spaced further apart than in town. On a parcel of acreage across from the veterinary clinic and Maggie's petting farm, lay the Cherryvale Riding Stables. This evening, Dr. McCoy supervised a very special event with owner, Rose Perkins.

"One more push and this baby should be out!" Greg McCoy, Cherryvale's vet, crouched in deep straw at the business end of a foaling mare. He tugged two slimy legs protruding from the groaning mama. Greg swiped the sac away from the muzzle so the chestnut foal could take its first shallow breaths, its long lashes blinking open.

"I never tire of watching this miracle," Greg whispered to Rose, who stood behind him watching the delivery. She flicked her long, blonde braid down her back. He wiped his damp forehead with his elbow, and focused back on the miracle at hand.

Rose handed him a clean moist towel. He wiped his hands and face then shoved it absently in his back pocket. Together they watched the mare, waiting for her to stand and allow the baby to nurse.

After resting a few moments from the exertion, the new mom raised her head, stretched her front legs forward, pulled her body weight onto them and then onto her back legs to a standing position. She shook herself from head to tail. Stepping gingerly toward the infant, still slick with new birth, she swished her long tail and whickered a soft greeting of welcome.

For several minutes, she sniffed and snuffled, checking him muzzle to tail. The foal dozed; his warm damp coat steamed a mist into the evening air.

"He looks like he's in a cloud." Rose kept her voice low. "Like the angels just lowered him from heaven to earth."

Greg and Rose crouched toward the stall's half door and stepped into the aisle.

After a beat, the baby stirred and tested his own front legs. They watched as the foal attempted to take control of his newly upright situation. He looked around, four tiny hooves planted squarely in the straw as Mom nickered encouragement.

Wobbly at first, then with gathering confidence, he lifted each foot a bit too high, lowered, and tried them with his body weight. After a few test circles, he leaned his long head against his mom's broad chest for a reassuring nuzzle. He bumped her stomach, exploring and searching, at last rewarded by a long drink of his first meal.

"That's what I wanted to see." Greg swiped his brow with the cloth again and stuck it back in his pocket. "I'll clean up the afterbirth if you'll rinse my instruments."

While Rose washed, Greg finished his task. Together, they replaced equipment in the containers on the back of his pickup parked at the entrance of the stable. As he closed the lid on the customized storage bins, a siren sounded, racing past the stables. The blare stopped almost as soon as it passed.

"That sounds close!" Rose looked up, sharp.

"Looks like they stopped at Maggie's." Greg raced toward the petting farm, Rose matching his strides. At the section of the Cherrypath that connected the properties, a beam of light approached.

Grace, her bike's headlight illuminating The Path, pedaled up alongside them. "I was on my way home from the hospital and heard a siren. Did you see where they went?"

"We think they're headed for Maggie's." Rose trotted next to her. Greg disappeared into the blackness down the lane.

"Let's go!" Grace leaned forward in her seat spinning as fast as her legs could manage.

The Cherryvale Volunteer Fire Department trained their hoses onto a small out-building that sputtered and smoked.

Greg cleared the fence in one leap. "You okay, Maggie?"

She turned to him, her red curls sticking to her sooty face, slick with sweat, eyes wild in the firelight. "I couldn't get them out!"

"Who?"

"A new litter." She pointed to the flaming structure. "I got them in yesterday."

"Where are they?"

"They're in a cage next to the washtub." Maggie's face screwed up. "But you can't—"

Already at the door, Greg dragged the wet towel from his back pocket and held it up to his nose and mouth. He lunged under streams of water, and kneeling, gulped a mouthful of clean air. Grabbing the knob with a shirttail, he pushed the door open.

He crawled toward the tub, his target for the victims. Faint mewling beckoned to him in the darkness. Barely audible over the whoosh of water on flame and the shouting voices outside, they gave him a target through the dark wall of smoke. He coughed, crawling low through the lung-stinging cloud toward the cage of babies. Greg groped at the latch, but jerked his seared hand away, gasping; the pungent air burned his nostrils. He forced himself to take shallow breaths through the cotton, wrapped his shirttail around his fingers, and tried the latch again.

He fumbled and got it open despite the layers of cloth, then groped on the bottom of the cage. A pile of fuzzy bodies huddled together in the far corner. Greg lifted them out one by one, cradling them against his chest. He scooted backward out the door, but one of the little babies squirmed loose, flopped over, and rolled into the darkness.

Grace and Rose ran up with Maggie, and they took the kittens from him. A burning timber fell down the side of the building, and as Greg set a kitten bundle in Rose's arms, they moved as a unit into the safety of the yard. Grace caught one before it slipped to the ground. His arms free, Greg leaned over, resting his hands on his knees, gulping deep breaths of the cool evening air.

"Start CPR...and give them...short shallow...breaths into their muzzles. Like this." He leaned over, demonstrating on Rose's charge, first coughing to clear his own lungs. Then he placed his mouth over the tiny nose and mouth of a grey tabby. He gave a couple of short puffs and the tiny body squeaked and squirmed. He handed the baby to Grace, spun around and went back in.

Grace cradled the small body and looked up at Maggie. "What happened, how did this start?"

"I told you there would be trouble as soon as those movie people hit town." Maggie said with a snarl. "Satisfied?"

CHAPTER FOUR

Bring those babies over here," Maggie commanded, trotting with her armload toward the Administration building.

Grace followed her across the yard, cradling her own armfull of fluff, her eyes stinging with the acrid smoke. Maggie disappeared inside a door marked "Office" and Grace sat down on a step and tried to take a deep breath, but the heavy, acrid air gave little relief. She peeked down at several tiny faces bathed in soft light from a wall lantern over her shoulder. Cradling the tiny bodies, she watched the men's progress against the flames hissing into the night air.

Maggie reappeared carrying a cardboard box and set it on the porch. Grace lowered her kittens onto the terry cloth alongside the other babies Maggie placed in the makeshift home.

Rose hurried toward them, massaging the chest of another small victim. "Greg found this one and went back in to check for more. He wants to know how many kittens were in there."

Maggie counted heads in the box. "There's still one missing."

"You go back. I'll take that one." Grace took the baby from Rose, who spun on her heel and ran back to the inferno. She inspected the tabby's fur coat. Satisfied with his condition, she placed him in the box with the others.

Greg's large frame appeared out of the smoky darkness, and Rose came up behind him into the glow of the porch light.

"Found him under the toe kick of the sink." He gave the latest victim to Grace and leaned over, breathing in fresh air and coughing out smoky crud.

Troy, one of the volunteer firefighters, hurried up carrying a portable oxygen tank. He thrust a facemask toward the vet. "Put this on. Your lungs are filled. Ladies, make sure he wears it. I'm going back to the line." Troy trotted off, and they turned their attention to the limp kitten-body.

Grace breathed into his little muzzle.

Greg spoke through his mask, his voice echoing inside the plastic chamber. "Anything?"

Grace shook her head and bent over the kitten's face and puffed.

"Short breaths, that's right." Greg hacked inside the mask, his voice raspy and deep. "Rub its chest too. Easy."

Grace followed his instructions, but the body remained limp.

"Let me try." Greg pushed the mask up on his forehead, turned the baby over and lightly thumped its back, then breathed puffs of air into its snout. Turning, he coughed to clear his own lungs, then placed the mask over the ball of soot covered fur.

Please, Lord, help this tiny baby. Grace realized she held her own breath when a hoarse mewing erupted from Greg's palm. "He's alive!" she exhaled.

The kitten gurgled while Greg held the oxygen mask over the entire little body and it began to squirm and wiggle. Greg gave up and lowered the survivor into the box of mewling littermates.

"You're welcome. No need to carry on like that, little guy," Greg croaked. They all laughed as meows and purrs sang out, welcoming their brother into the fur pile.

"We'll have to call him Smoky," Grace suggested.

"This is for you, not the animals." Rose slid the plastic mask back over Greg's nose and mouth.

He cleared his throat, visibly uncomfortable from Rose's attentions. Greg leaned over, peering in the box to check the other kittens.

"It seemed to work." His voice sounded echo-y. "I'm going to help the guys with the fire." He snatched off the mask and started to walk away, but teetered.

"No!" They cried in unison.

Grace scrambled to her feet and placed her hand on his back before he could fall over. He steadied, and she lifted her hand from his shirt, smudged and moist in the yellow porch light. "You have some cinder burns."

"Grace, take the box o'critters and Super-Vet into the kitchen. I'll see what I can do to help with the fire," Maggie ordered.

"Yes Ma'am." Grace picked up the box. "But shouldn't Greg go to the hospital? I'll call Mark on my cell." She dug in her pocket for her phone.

"I'm fine. I just need to rest a minute," Greg protested.

Grace carried the box, and Rose helped Greg carry the oxygen tank. They paraded through the smoky haze toward the bungalow's back door, past barns and sheds of pot-bellied pigs, sheep, goats and Maggie's milking cows.

In the small kitchen, Grace placed the box on a window seat next to Greg, and Rose sat in a high-backed wooden chair at the oak table. Grace poured glasses of cold water at the kitchen sink and took a refreshing drink.

"I'll see if I can find a first aid kit." Grace opened a cabinet and caught a package of unopened saltines as it tumbled out. She tried cramming it back, but gave up. Instead, she plopped it with the pile of old mail on the countertop. "We can start cleaning you up with this until Maggie comes in." She grabbed a kitchen towel and moistened it under the kitchen faucet.

They heard Maggie clomping across the service porch, and she burst in. "Oh my, oh my." She stomped over and peered in at the kittens, then began opening cabinet doors and closing them, crossing in front of Grace and back again. "I think it's out, but the building's ruined." She slammed the fridge door without taking anything out.

"Sit down..." Grace handed the wet towel to Rose and pulled out a chair and pointed to it. "Maggie. Sit. I'll make coffee. You're flitting around like a blindfolded bee."

"It's late. You people can go." Maggie picked up the box. "I'll take my carton of cats and you people can get home." She stood in the middle of the kitchen.

"Maggie, put down those kittens. We need to clean Greg up. He won't go to the hospital." Grace motioned to the vet. "If you'll get some bandages and ointment, I'll make some decaf. You have some, don't you?"

"I might have tea somewhere." Maggie sat down, holding the box on her lap.

"I'll get the bandages if you'll tell me where to look." Rose popped up. "Come on, Greg."

"Try the medicine cabinet in my bathroom. Look behind...never mind, I'll show you." Maggie peered into the box and paused, then set it down again, and shuffled down the hallway, Rose and Greg following.

Grace poked in drawers and cabinets for tea bags. Footsteps and tapping interrupted her tea-less expedition. She reached over and opened the door. Troy's glistening, smudged face leaned in.

"Come in, Troy." Grace held out a glass. "Drink of water?"

"I'm filthy, no thanks. I wanted to tell Maggie that we've cleaned up the hoses and we're leaving. We soaked the rest of the structure pretty good. There won't be any flare-ups."

Maggie appeared in the doorway. "Did you see anything that looked suspicious?"

"What do you mean? Like an accelerant?" Troy thought a minute. "You think someone set the fire?"

"What else would have caused it?" Maggie challenged.

"Old building, old wiring—"

"I demand someone investigate and the culprits punished." Maggie jabbed a fist into the air.

Troy blinked at Maggie, then Grace. "The county will send someone over to do a complete analysis, but I don't—"

"Good night. And thanks anyway." Maggie lifted her chin. "I'll speak to Sheriff directly."

"Maggie's had a rough evening, Troy." Grace tried to smooth things over. "What about that water?"

"No. I've got to sleep a few hours before my shift at the factory. How's Greg? Any dizziness?"

"He's got some burns, but he quit using the oxygen after we got inside if you want to take it." Grace lifted the heavy metal cylinder and handed it over. She closed the door behind him and the kitchen fell silent.

"If it wasn't for bad luck lately, I wouldn't have any luck at all." Maggie lifted Smoky and cradled him in her palm.

"At least no one was hurt." Grace hesitated then continued. "You were kind of short with him, he's not in charge of investigations."

"I told you as soon as those movie people hit town there would be trouble, didn't I?" Maggie laid the kitten with the others. "They're out for revenge."

"Why would they—" Another knock interrupted, and Grace opened the door again.

"Excuse me, ladies. Maggie, Troy said you wanted to speak to me?" Sheriff Don Melton stepped into the kitchen, wiping his black service boots on a rag rug inside the door. He twisted the brim of his Stetson in his hands and nodded at Grace.

"I want you to rope off my burned building with police tape," Maggie instructed.

"Why? It's not near the public—"

"Here, take my prints now so we can move forward tomorrow." Maggie held out her hands, palms up.

"Maggie, I don't think—"

"I'm a taxpayer, and I demand you launch a full investigation for arson."

"Who would want to burn up that little building, Maggie? This place is old…run down…"

"You mean my father didn't take care of the place?" Her eyebrows shot up into the red curls that stuck against her forehead.

"How much trouble would it be to investigate?" Grace wondered. "I mean, to rule out foul play so Maggie can sleep at night?"

"If you'll hire an electrician, I guess it wouldn't hurt to make some calls. It's really a county matter since firefighting's just done by volunteers here." Sheriff thought a second, twisting his hat brim. "We have a meeting with the boys from the highway department in the morning to organize extra security for the movie unit. I'll make the call after that."

"And while you're distracted with stars in your eyes, my place is vulnerable. I expect you to send extra patrols by every hour." Maggie's voice sounded stern, but wavered a bit. "It's obvious I'm a target."

"I don't believe you're a target for anything."

Maggie's left eyebrow shot up.

"I'll have someone drive by whenever we can spare a unit."

"I should say so."

"I've gotta run." Sheriff fitted his hat down on his head and grabbed the doorknob. "See you, Grace."

"I won't be intimidated, even under these circumstances." Maggie raised her voice as the door clicked shut behind the retreating sheriff.

"What do you mean under the circumstances?" Grace asked.

"I think I would like some tea. Did you find the tea bags or did you just muddle up my cabinets?" Maggie disappeared in the direction of the living room china cabinet.

Greg shuffled back into the kitchen buttoning his shirt and collapsed into a chair at the table. Rose joined them, sliding her cell phone into her jeans pocket.

Still wondering what Maggie meant, Grace addressed them. "Find any ointment for those burns?"

"How does she find anything in that mess?" Rose held up a tube. "I think this ointment has an expiration date circa *The Brady Bunch*."

"My daughter can help me put something less expired on them tomorrow." Greg eyeballed the medicine Rose struggled to open.

"Speaking of whom, I'll take a rain check on the tea also. I've gotta get home. Connie'll be wondering where I am."

"I called and told her you were here with us," Rose assured him.

Greg inspected his burns, his frown lines deepening.

Maggie came in carrying three dusty china cups. "I'll get the first aid kit. Grace, the tea bags are in the cookie tin."

"We found it." Rose indicated the antique tube. "He wants to self medicate though."

Grace took the cups from Maggie and ran water over them in the sink. "You have a sick animal at your place this evening, Rose?"

"My mare foaled tonight." Rose cut an admiring glance at Greg. "Doc says it was a textbook delivery."

"Isn't that lovely." Grace ripped the last paper towel off a roll and wiped it around the rim of a cup. "I just love their spindly legs and watching them romp in the pasture..."

Maggie came in. "You three don't fool me, trying to change the subject. I heard. I know this place is a wreck. I'm doing the best I can. Geez Louise, with everything else, all I need is my friends criticizing me in my own kitchen." She grabbed the ointment from Rose and tossed it toward an overflowing can in the corner of the kitchen. It landed on the heaping pile then slid off onto the floor.

Grace glanced at Rose and back to Maggie. "We weren't criticizing. We're worried. Fire is dangerous."

"Ya think? Wait there." Maggie stomped past Greg onto the service porch. Her voice muffled through the wall. "Don't you think I want to know what started it..." She emerged from the porch and tossed a cotton shirt to Greg. "Here's one of Joe's shirts. That one's ruined."

"No, it's okay, Maggie, really," he protested.

"What am I going to do with men's clothes? You keep it."

He unbuttoned the singed shirt and peeled it off. Grace cringed as he tugged fabric from burned skin.

Maggie grabbed the ruined shirt and shoved it into the garbage.

"Maybe a smoldering butt started the fire. A careless visitor to the petting farm might have thrown it," Grace suggested.

Maggie's wrenched frown tightened a turn. "It's more likely that people take revenge when other people make their opinions known."

"About what?" Rose looked from Maggie to Grace.

"Maybe someone didn't like my comments yesterday at The Bypass. Or, they might have heard me say something at the Bucket. And I might have said something down at the mayor's office."

"Oh, Maggie." Grace turned to Rose and Greg with a sigh, and then faced down her friend's growing wrath. "You don't think someone from the movie..."

Rose stared at Grace. "From the movie what?"

"Maggie thinks someone from the movie..."

"Set the fires?" Greg wiped the soiled cloth over his wounds. "Did you see any of them poking around?"

"I guess almost anything's possible, even if we don't want to blame anyone prematurely." Grace rinsed her paper towel and tried to help Greg, but Rose took over.

Maggie looked out the window into the darkness. "Our last visitor left about 4:30 but I wasn't home yet. Connie helped me feed, then she left. I took a bath and then I came in here to rinse out my soup bowl and saw smoke."

"A butt could have smoldered that long and then caught fire. I'll help you make more 'No Smoking' signs," Grace offered. "That could happen. We haven't had any rain lately."

Maggie tapped her fingers on the counter. "Next to the building where I quarantine new animals? There's nothing to see back there. No reason for anyone except Connie to be over there."

"My daughter better not be smoking." Greg's tone kicked into high.

"No. She wouldn't." Grace laid a hand on his shoulder. "She's well brought up and level-headed."

"All kids experiment." Greg slid a cell phone from the clip on his belt. "I'm calling her."

"Probably asleep. She said she was going to bed early." Rose watched him dial. "She's so excited."

"Excited about what?" Greg rolled a sleeve of the plaid shirt to his elbow.

Rose watched him button the shirt over his broad chest and the twinkle in her eyes gave Grace a revelation. Could Rose be interested in Greg? She knew they spent a lot of time together because of Rose's horses. She tried to remember seeing them around town together and failed. *Wouldn't it be interesting if more than one fire kindled here tonight?*

"About the movie shoot." Rose filled Greg in on the developments. "The film crew that's in town needs extras."

Maggie sniffed.

Rose continued. "After she found out you were okay, all she cared about was getting your signature on the parental release form. I told her to put it where you can find it when you get home."

Greg gave up buttoning and let the shirt hang open, and turned to Maggie. "Wasn't she supposed to work here tomorrow?"

Her lips clenched together in a straight line. "Another reason this Hollywood thing's a bad idea. I told Connie she could go over there, but I'm not happy about it." She turned to fill a teakettle at the tap. "If you ask me, the whole lot of 'em should be run out of town before we regret letting them into the Vale."

Grace opened her mouth and instantly shut it again. Maggie'd been through enough tonight, no need fanning the flames. "We'd better let you get some sleep." She pushed back from the table. "Rain check on the tea for me also."

Greg and Rose followed Grace outside and they exchanged goodbyes. She breathed in, just the slightest hint of burn spicing the air along The Path in rhythm with the birds chattering evening farewells, dreaming of a bath and the cool sheets of slumber. Her thoughts wandered back to Greg and Rose and the possibility of their relationship blossoming. That gave her a happy feeling. Greg had been raising Connie alone all these years, and she would soon be out of high school. All she knew about Rose was that she'd moved here and bought the old stable to fix up and teach riding, and board a few horses. She'd been quite attentive to Greg's burns. More than just being neighborly?

The fire returned her mind back to Maggie's comments about the possibility of the film crew's involvement. *Could it be? Surely not.*

Rose watched Grace's handlebar light disappear, then followed Greg up The Path back to her stables. The still night air next to Maggie's remained heavy with smoke. At the fence line into her pasture, Greg waited for her to climb over the stiles. He lifted his boot to follow, but lightheadedness swept over him, and he missed, toppling them both to the ground. They rolled side by side onto the thick pasture grass.

"Greg! Are you all right?" She leaned up on an elbow, worried he might be feeling faint from the smoke in his lungs. "What about your burns? We should take you to the ER."

"I'm okay. The grass is soft. Did I hurt you?"

"No." She held his glittering gaze in the darkness, her pulse racing a notch higher.

"Thought I'd enjoy the view from down here." Greg slid an elbow under his head and looked up at the stars. "Feels like I've been inhaling toasted marshmallows. You mind if I snooze in your pasture for a few?"

"I don't mind." She watched his eyes close, an unruly lock of brown hair flopped over onto his forehead. *Why had she never seen him this way before?*

"Rose?" He turned to face her in the moonlight.

"Yes, Greg?" She leaned his direction, head tilted toward him—ready should he move to kiss her.

"I think I'm lying in poop."

The next morning, Grace slipper-shuffled into the kitchen and groped in the cabinet for her favorite mug, stifling a yawn.

Already at the table, Mark thumbed through the paper. Grace loved that he could take the rare luxury of a quick breakfast with her.

"Hey, Clara Barton, there's an article on the fire." Mark peered at her over his bifocals.

Grace tugged at her chenille robe and perched on a chair next to his, sipping and blinking. He showed her the article, but she squinted at the blurry words. "Read it to me."

"The place is ancient. Her dad really let it go." Mark drained his coffee cup. "What?"

"The last thing I want to do my first summer of retirement is get mixed up in Maggie's messes and listen to her lectures. I've got boxes of curriculum to unpack, closets I want to organize, and—"

"I didn't say anything about—"

"You don't have to, I know what you're thinking." Grace poured cream into her mug and reached for a spoon. She bumped into Mark's chest. "You think I should drop everything and devote myself to Maggie full time but I have closets—"

He tipped her chin and pressed his mouth against hers before she could finish. "Those boxes and closets aren't going anywhere. It's your call, but maybe it's time you talked about what happened a hundred years ago between you two."

His warm brown eyes stirred her heart but his words churned her stomach. "Since you're older than me, you're making yourself almost two hundred when you do that, Dr. Harkins."

"I'm glad every century with you is better than the last or this would be a real drag." He whistled his way into the service porch. "Gotta get to the hospital."

His footsteps and jangling keys passed into the garage and she heard the door slam. The house grew still and Grace felt her conscience doing the salsa again.

All right, all right.

She picked up his dishes and carried them over to the granite countertop, lifted the phone and dialed.

"Maggie? You sleep all right? After you feed the critters, wanna meet for a bite?"

I just heard about the fire at Maggie's last night. It's a blessing only one of her buildings was damaged." Sam Madison slid into the red vinyl seat across from Pastor Bob for their customary Monday morning breakfast.

Shelby circulated around the diner, pouring coffee and greeting The Lunch Bucket regulars. She stopped at the men's table to top off the pastor's mug.

"She's been working hand-to-mouth opening that place. She can't hardly afford to lose any ground." Shelby lifted the carafe spout just before the cup overflowed Sam's mug. "It's took some prayer and stick-to-it hard work to get that place going again, and I recognize hard work when I see it."

Shelby and her cookin' cousin, Arlene, worked hard keeping the diner open through the economic downturn. They kept their faith and extended the diner's hours, and now it thrived. Regulars filled red vinyl booths and chrome chairs from early breakfast to late afternoon. The side facing the street received its own updated look, or "backdated" as Shelby described it, to the original charm with white scalloped trim, green siding and a wide bay window draped with red gingham and baskets of dripping fern.

Regulars to the Bucket kept a coffee mug near the door and, like old workhorses on automatic, grabbed their mugs and preferred the same chair, stool, or banquette bench on each visit.

While Shelby poured steaming coffee and took orders, she listened to the conversations flipping between the movie shoot to the fire at Maggie's. Arlene spun the chrome clipper as fast as Shelby could refill it, flipping pancakes, slapping bacon and hash browns. Every few minutes she'd announce in a sing-song, "Or-der's up!"

As Shelby set plates of scrambled eggs and wheat toast onto the yellow-swirled vinyl table in front of Sam and the pastor, the cowbell on the doorknob tinkled. The roomful of curious heads turned as a cluster of strangers stepped in and waited next to the specials easel by the pie case.

Dressed in cargo shorts, T-shirts and hard-soled shoes, a couple of them wore backpacks slung over one shoulder, others carried walkie-talkies clipped to their belts. The Valers' chatter fell off, and each world stared across at the other over the wooden bench and newspaper rack. Bacon crackling on the grill and tick-ticking of a Coca-Cola wall clock arose in the sudden silence.

Shelby waved the coffeepot in the air like a Nascar flag. "Take a seat anywhere. I'll get to ya in a minute. Specials are on the chalkboard."

Muted conversations ensued. The newcomers slid into vinyl booths and clattered chairs over black-and-white tiles to sit at round chrome and Formica tables. They slid leather bound menus from wooden holders on their tables and the chatter picked back up to its normal hum.

The bell jingled and the screen door opened again as Maggie and Grace entered, chatting and reaching for their mugs.

"Where were you? I've been waiting outside for hours," Maggie snipped as they walked in.

"It couldn't have been hours—" Grace stopped just short of plowing into Maggie's denim-shirted back. She peeked around the taller woman. *Uh oh. Way to start a Monday.* Strangers naively sat in their favorite place in the bay window.

She stepped from behind Maggie and spied an empty table near the kitchen end of the soda fountain. She headed for it and slid onto the bench, her back to the kitchen, forcing Maggie to take the seat with her back to the rest of the room. Maggie lingered where she stood, glaring. Her giant purse clutched under her left arm, her coffee mug dangled from the fingers of her right hand.

Oh, good Lord. "C'mere, Maggs, here's a table." Grace tried to make her voice bright and sweet as if training a reluctant puppy. She waved her coffee cup to lure Maggie. "Shelby, we're on empty over here—"

"You know very well I don't sit next to the kitchen." Maggie turned, casting one last scathe toward the intruders. Despite her proclamation, she slid into the seat across from Grace.

"Shh. It's the only place left." Grace felt her face warming, a familiar sensation lately.

"Who are they, anyway? They're dressed like baggage handlers on a second rate cruise ship," Maggie spat.

"I think they're some of the movie crew." Grace took a paper napkin from its chrome holder and laid it across her lap with exaggerated care.

"I thought they brought their own food. Catering or whatever it's called. Why do they have to sit at our—"

"Look." Grace attempted to interrupt, holding up a half-pint canning jar, motioning with a "Vanna" wave in front of the hand-calligraphied label. "Shelby's got some of that strawberry-rhubarb jelly you like so much."

"—table for breakfast? I knew they'd be trouble."

"Only billiards, never a pool table," Grace muttered under her breath. "We've indeed got trouble in River City."

"What?" Maggie's brows slammed together, a macramé of cynicism.

Think, Grace, think. Quick! While she pauses for breath. "Let's get the special today. It smells yummy. I didn't eat yet this morning and I'm starved."

The swinging door flipped back and Shelby came out, stopping at their table to fill their cups. "Morning, girls. Gittin' the usual?"

"If I have to sit where I can smell the dish ammonia and listen to kitchen noises, I'm not about to eat one of your dubious concoctions," Maggie snapped. "Of course I'm getting my usual."

Shelby set the decanter down with a smack. "Here, I'll leave the whole thing." She leaned over to Grace. "But if you ask me, somebody needs their tank stripped and polished." Shelby turned on her rubber heel.

Grace tipped sugar from a glass decanter into her "Apple for the Teacher" mug, stirring the granules slowly into solution. Maggie sipped hers black, the ape on the side of Maggie's "San Diego Zoo" mug gawked at Grace, as if daring her to try and smooth this one over.

She took a deep breath and ran for broke. "Maggie, I don't like disruptions to my comfortable routine any more than you do, but let's make the best of this. Now, what had you in town first thing this morning?"

Maggie's brow-knot looped again and her eyes cut sideways at the movie crew who were sipping coffee and chatting quietly. "Pour me another cup. I need all the energy I can muster, what with Connie wanting to be gone all day for that dern movie shoot. And being up till all hours of the night with the animals. Where'd Shelby go?" Maggie studied the menu like she'd never seen it before.

"You can't blame Connie. It's exciting to have a movie filmed here, and Cherryvale can use the money."

"I haven't seen anything good come from Hollywood since John Wayne died. It's all smut, they all use drugs, and they're useless. Tiffany Lane is the worst sort. I've seen her in the news, living the wild life..."

"You said yourself you can't believe everything you read. Maybe she's not as bad as the papers. You know how they sensationalize—"

"Even so, it's not the kind of publicity we need. Back in the day we could eat breakfast in peace, drive on our streets without bumper-to-bumper traffic. Now I've got suspicious fires breaking out. And I don't believe it's any coincidence." Maggie turned her gaze to Grace and cleared her throat. "So this morning I lodged a formal complaint at City Hall."

"City hall..."

"That's right! I lodged a formal complaint against the production company." Maggie's voice soared over the clatter of plates and hum of conversations, her barbs reaching her intended victims. "They're all pyromaniacs. You can't watch a movie these days without something or other blowing up. I'll bet you one of them sent me a pyro-warning to keep me quiet."

The dining clatter and friendly chatter fell silent under the weight of Maggie's accusations.

Across the room, a pony-tailed young woman set her menu down. "Maybe we should go someplace else." She pushed back her chair and the other crewmembers did so as well.

Shelby hurried over to their table to run interference, her pad and pencil at the ready. "Honey, there's not anywhere's else to go this early, unless you want to go all the way back up the highway." Then she raised her voice and added, "Most of us are glad you're here, so don't you go takin' no offense at what some people say. We're right proud you're usin' Cherryvale for your picture show. Now, who wants to try my stuffed French toast with homemade strawberry preserves?"

Maggie raised an eyebrow at Grace. "Then you and I will go eat at the Bypass." Snatching her purse from the bench, she leaned forward, but didn't crank down her volume at all. "I don't appreciate the atmosphere in here any longer!"

With Maggie glaring at her, Grace imagined all ears in the room trained on her response, and prayed the red vinyl would melt and swallow her. From somewhere deep inside, her resolve bubbled to the surface. *I'm not letting you run my life any more.* Grace twisted around to check the time. *How do I say that without getting clobbered?*

"Actually, I've decided..." Grace stumbled. "I am going to be an extra in that movie." The last part rushed out like air from a popped balloon, high and squeaky.

Maggie stared at her for a moment, then pushed herself out of the banquette and shot back, "Suit yourself." She blundered across the room, her giant bag beating against her rear end. The screen door slammed on her exit.

Heart hammering, Grace leaned back in the booth. She inhaled a long breath of the bacon and coffee scented air, expanded her lungs, and sang out, "Bring me today's special, Shelby. And a double OJ. On the rocks!"

Just across from the town square, on the other side of Main Street from the Bucket, the City Park sprawled for about thirty rolling acres, partly wooded, partly open fields perfect for flying a kite or spreading out a picnic. A pond fed by a slowly meandering creek—stocked with small mouth bass and catfish—sprawled next to the road, its sloping sides gradual enough for skipping rocks from the shore or wading in for a cool summer dip.

Grace pedaled into the parking lot where a small city appeared overnight. Clusters of trailers, trucks and tents rimmed the field next to the lake. Grips carried loops of cables, technicians unloaded black boxes trimmed in shiny chrome, and a costumer sorted through racks of outfits.

Carolyn Sims pulled her minivan into the parking space near the bike rack, and Grace waved. Carson and Cassie jumped from their booster seats almost before their mom could open the sliding door.

Carolyn stepped aside to let them jump down and pulled out a canvas bag. She slid the door closed and slung the bag's handle onto her shoulder as Grace kicked down her bike's stand. "Ooh! Grace! You brought muffins. Any carrot-raisin?"

"Help yourself." Grace lifted a corner of the checked cloth and Carolyn peeked in and chose one. Cassie and Carson clambered over, their noses barely clearing the basket, and took one each.

"I heard about Maggie's fire. Is everyone okay?" Carolyn peeled the paper off one side of her pastry and took a bite.

"One small building was hurt pretty bad, but no people were injured." Grace kicked the bike's stand up, lifted the basket from the handlebars, and they moved together toward the footbridge. "A litter of orphaned kittens was caught in the smoke, but Greg says they'll be fine."

Cardboard directional signs guided them across the bridge over Blossom Creek to a vacant, freshly mown grassy field. A large white tent rose up near the lake. Carson skipped ahead, and Cassie held her mother's hand as they clomped up the planks of the bridge.

"Will Maggie be here today, Miz Grace?" Cassie pumped her mom's arm up and down. "I want to see how her baby lambth are."

"No, honey. You can go see the lambs another time, though," Grace reassured her. "But they weren't harmed by the fire last night if that's what you're worried about."

Cassie nodded, and her thick black hair, divided into a rainbow of colorful clips, bobbed as she skipped ahead to join her brother.

"I hear Maggie's not a fan of the movie industry, anyway." Carolyn hitched the bag higher on her shoulder.

"I'll say. She's nicknamed them the 'Vaders,' and she's convinced they'll ruin Cherryvale forever." Grace switched the heavy basket to the crook of her other arm. "But I think it's exciting! I've never seen them making a real movie."

They joined a line of volunteers at a sign-in table.

"There's the girl you need to see. The Production Assistant. Her name's Holly." Carolyn indicated the blond sitting behind the folding table. "You might have seen her yesterday."

"Recognize her from the Bucket this morning at breakfast." She stepped up to the table and Holly handed her a clipboard with a liability release attached.

Grace scanned the brief agreement, signed her name, and handed it back.

"You're all set." Holly handed her an instruction sheet. "And by the way, thanks for standing up for us this morning. We're over budget and everyone's tense. Being attacked was a rough way to start our week in a new town."

"Don't you let Maggie ruin Cherryvale for you. The rest of us are glad to have you. We'll do whatever we can to help. Muffin?"

"No, thanks—" she glanced at the name on the clipboard. "—Grace. Nice to meet you." She stuck her hand out. "I'm Holly. I think your friend will like the movie if she'll give it a chance." Holly pointed behind her with a pencil. "Now you need to go over to wardrobe so she can approve and record what you're wearing. And, have fun."

Grace and the three Sims waited for the costumer's approval. An assistant took their pictures and wrote their names on a log sheet, then sent them inside the tent to wait. A sign over the door read "Atmosphere Holding."

Carolyn and Grace poured themselves coffee from a large urn and sat down at a long folding table. Carolyn pulled out coloring books and crayons. Carson flipped open a page to a brontosaurus and chose a dark green shade and began coloring.

"Where's Cassie?" Carolyn looked around as Grace pulled out the chair next to hers.

Grace looked over the heads of the other volunteers. Cassie held court with two scruffy men in hobo-looking costumes. "She's over by the opening in the tent. I'll go get her."

"We're called 'atmothphere.'" Cassie beamed through the space between her front teeth and pointed to herself as Grace joined them.

"How do you know all this movie stuff?" The taller man drawled, one dirty thumb hooked in the strap of grimy dungarees, the other digging at a gap in his teeth.

"I went to Mr. Madithon's theater camp last summer. I can cold read a thide and everything."

His tooth digging paused. "A what?"

"Sides." Grace moved protectively closer to Cassie.

"You mean like macaroni and cheese, or pork and beans?" He gave his belly an absent rub. "That kind of side?"

"No, thilly." Cassie's happy giggle tickled Grace. "Thides are what you thay in a movie."

The men leered at each other. A creepy feeling slithered up Grace's spine. "Cassie, your mom's looking for you." She placed her hands on Cassie's shoulders and gently nudged her toward her mom.

Cassie skipped away and Grace held up her basket, as much an offering as a shield. "Speaking of food, would you like a muffin?"

"Got any applesauce? My grandma used to make 'em with applesauce." The tall man and his shorter, but just as filthy, companion bumped heads in their eagerness to see into her basket.

Judging from their greasy hair and dirty fingernails, Grace decided it made hygienic sense to choose for them and she pulled the basket away. She grabbed two that rested at the top of the pile and handed them over.

"How about blueberry? Everyone likes—" Before she could finish, the last crumbs disappeared and they licked their fingers, crumbs catching in day-old stubble. Across short guy's right knuckles, Grace read the word "HATE" in greasy looking tattooed letters. The anxious tingle bristled up her spine again. The tall one's odor reminded her of wet dog. The shorter one just plain smelled.

She stepped back. "If there are any left after I offer some to the others, I'll let you know."

The breeze rattled the canvas tent, and the men's stench filtered through the morning air toward her. Her lips clamped against the barnyard reek. "You two actors in the movie or on the crew?" She tried to think of some way to pinch her nostrils closed without appearing rude.

"Uh. Yeah." Tattooed-guy shifted from one foot to the other. "We act purty good. Double-double toil and trouble..."

If nauseating your audience is the desired effect, you are quite good.

A squawk and amplified squeal interrupted the pathetic impromptu Shakespeare moment and saved Grace's breakfast from reappearing.

"May I have everyone's attention, please?" A young man spoke to them into a bullhorn from the tent's opposite end.

"Excuse me, gentlemen, it looks like we're being organized. Good day." Grace stepped back and took leave of the aromatic strangers.

"Good morning. My name is Ryan, I'm the Director's Assistant." The young man's earpiece connected to a walkie-talkie clipped on his belt and his clipboard's pages flipped up in the breeze. "This is Holly, the Production Assistant.

"First, thanks for coming out to help us. We couldn't do these exterior shots without volunteers to make the sequences look realistic.

There might be a lot of waiting between takes. I'm glad to see some of you brought books and things to keep busy..."

Ryan continued explaining the day, what to expect, things to do and not to do. "If you can see the camera, it can see you, so please, don't look directly at it. If you do, we have to re-shoot, and it wastes valuable time. Or worse, we'll edit that part, and you'll end up on the proverbial cutting room floor."

They chuckled as he paused, pushing on an earpiece to listen for a moment before he spoke again. "I'm needed on the set; Holly will answer any questions."

Holly held up her clipboard. "If you haven't already signed in, please come by my table." She looked at the two grimy men. "And, parents, please keep your children with you at all times. We can't baby-sit for you."

Grace and Carolyn kept the children busy with their coloring and visited with other Valers until Holly came in and selected several of them for a scene. Through the morning, Carolyn and Grace carried prop shopping bags up and down Main Street with Cassie and Carson skipping along with them, in and out of shops at the director's instruction. Most of the time, though, they waited for cameras to be readjusted, lighting and sound to be set up, and through numerous re-takes. After lunch, Holly took Carson and Cassie to be in a scene, playing in the park and Carolyn went along to watch. Grace spent the afternoon reading. At five o'clock, the director approved the final take of the day with, "That's a wrap!"

After she returned her props and some borrowed wardrobe items to their departments, Grace waited for the Sims at the tent for a few minutes. When they didn't appear, she headed for the parking lot and the short bike ride to a long soak in a steaming hot bath.

She pedaled across the Blossom Creek Bridge as sirens blared in urgency. The volunteer fire department truck blasted past.

After a moment's hesitation, she kept on toward home. *God bless the emergency crew,* she prayed. *And the poor souls who need their help.*

CHAPTER SIX

Flames licked skyward from the roof of the combination Administration and large animal building in a pyro-dance worthy of macabre theater against the late afternoon sky.

Two firefighters ran in and out a smoky side door, evacuating animals housed in the barn section at the rear. They opened stall doors and coaxed the cow and several potbellied pigs to pass through smoke that rolled out like a sick belch from a medieval dragon. When they ran out, Maggie shooed them into a nearby pen. She squinted through the smoke when she realized her ponies hadn't followed.

"You'll have to drag them out! They'd stay and burn if we let them!" She shouted over the whoosh of water from the fire hose.

The firefighters ran back, and in a few moments, they came back out practically carrying the reluctant ponies who squirmed and whinnied in fear. They balked at the noise and smoke and planted their hooves firmly. Maggie grasped each one by the halter and leaned her hip into their shoulders in a crazy to and fro that would have been funny under different circumstances. She shoved and tugged on them all the way across the yard and shut them in the closet of a smaller barn. Maggie heard their hooves skittering and clacking as they trotted around inside, confused and crying out, adding to the chaotic shouts, bleats, and cackles.

She ran back and caught the eldest ewe as it scampered out of the barn. The others' instinct would be to follow, so Maggie dragged her the entire length of the barnyard protesting in raspy baahhs toward a seldom-used corral at the back of the property.

The other sheep bumped and rushed past, missing the gate opening. After a few frustrating minutes of guiding the frantic animals, she managed to scoot their furry butts through the narrow opening. Finally, they were all in one bunch and they scampered into a far corner and huddled, knit together in a moving mass of singed wool and wide-eyed confusion. Maggie swung the gate closed, jimmied the rusty lock until it loosened, slid it into place, and slumped against the fencepost to catch her breath.

"I saw the smoke." Rose panted up to Maggie's side. "And ran over."

Maggie indicated her cottage with a nod. "Look in the shed next to my house and bring out as many of the travel crates or cardboard boxes you can find. It looks like the fire's getting close to my rabbit hutches."

Rose darted off that direction. Maggie went over to a row of chicken coops that lined a walkway next to the ticket booth. Holding her breath against the acrid smell, she opened a chicken wire door and groped through the straw. Shaking her head, she backed up and trotted away from the lineup to take in fresh air, and then went back. It took three more tries before she pulled out a lop-eared rabbit that squirmed in her grasp. She carried the survivor to a crate Rose set on the lawn.

Together, they moved several more rabbits and some chickens and ducks into travel crates and cardboard boxes. They lined them up under the eaves of Maggie's bungalow where they'd be safe from flying cinders.

When they were finished moving the critters from harm and they were sure they wouldn't escape, Rose and Maggie went back to the barnyard to survey the damage. The remains of Maggie's office lay heaped in piles of slush, soggy and unidentifiable from the preventive dousing.

"Are all the animals out of danger?" Rose watched Maggie picking up empty fire extinguishers that lay strewn about the lawn.

"Lost a couple of lop-ears..." Maggie tossed the empty canisters into a metal barrel with a loud bang. She shrugged and clomped toward some volunteer firefighters who were winding hoses and stowing equipment into the containers on the fire truck.

Sheriff Melton sat in his cruiser speaking on his radio and got out to join Rose and Maggie. "This building held your farm's office, right?"

"We kept every file since my grandpa's day in there. A hundred years of farm reports, and..." Maggie's voice shifted into an awkward cough as she poked at a soggy pile of papers with her boot. "Joe started making backups of our records for tax purposes. Anything from before that's all gone."

"Those old records were useless anyway." Rose glanced at the Sheriff. "Right?"

They stepped around to the rear of the building. Charred two-by-fours were merely a suggestion of the walls that housed cows for milking and pigs for slaughter in the farming days of Maggie's childhood. Her lip quivered, remembering the days she spent helping her dad, feeding the livestock and playing in the haylofts.

"We're cleaned up, Sheriff. I think we've covered all the hot spots." One of the volunteers climbed into the hose truck and shut the door. "Take care, Maggie."

Maggie waved with a half salute as he drove past. The other volunteers following in their cars called out similar good wishes. She turned and gazed at the rubble without really focusing on it. "My grandpa helped his dad build this barn. It's stood through tornadoes and blizzards until now. Something, or someone, has it in for me."

"C'mon, Maggie, let's go up to your house and rest." Sheriff laid his arm on Maggie's shoulders.

"When the building burned the other day, my insurance company said they're sending someone out to investigate the cause before they'll cover anything else. My policy's on hold. Someone's out to ruin me."

"Ruin you?" The Sheriff's back straightened. "That doesn't make sense."

"What doesn't make sense is why, all of a sudden after decades of standing here steady as truth, would these buildings spontaneously combust? I'll tell you. Evil people and evil doings, Don."

"It's getting late. Let me help you feed and water," Rose offered. "I want to get back to my place before dark, especially if there's an arsonist."

"If there's arsonists, the insurance examiner will know. I'll see if I can get them to expedite the inquiry." The dispatcher's voice sounded over the Sheriff's walkie. "I'm needed in town, but first I'm taping off this area. Keep your visitors from wandering around and fooling with any evidence." Sheriff strode over to his car and opened the trunk. "On second thought, maybe you'd better postpone the opening until we have more information."

"It's not like I have a choice." Maggie sounded as if she'd lost all hope. "I don't have the money to rebuild this."

Rose helped Maggie with her evening feeding and watering, and then they moved the boxes of displaced animals onto the bungalow's service porch.

Together, they bustled out the crate of mother duck and ducklings as Greg's truck crunched up the driveway. He jumped out and grabbed the end Maggie carried and together, he and Rose settled the box of birds inside.

"Colicky colt out at the Baxter's." His soiled shirt and jeans testified to the long day he'd spent battling what can be a life threatening tummy-ache to a horse. "Heard about another fire. You all right, Maggie?"

She lifted then dropped her shoulders. "I'm not hurt, but the hutches near the office were too close. Lost a few from the smoke."

Greg straightened from peering into a box at a couple of tortoises who stretched their necks up at him. He searched Maggie's sooty but expressionless face.

Rose caught his eye and indicated a tarp covering something near the fencerow.

Greg nodded and pointed at the row of refugees. "These guys look okay. But, excuse me, I want to catch up with Don before he leaves."

"I need to get back to my place, but I hate to leave you." Rose paused with her hand on the knob. "Are you going to be okay?"

Maggie reached for a glass and filled it at the kitchen sink. "Go on, I understand."

"I could use a drink of water, though." Rose waited for Maggie to offer one, but when the woman didn't move, she found her own tumbler and filled it.

"I admire what you're doing here, Maggie, with the petting farm and animal rescue."

"I guess not everyone agrees." Maggie pulled out a kitchen chair and slumped in it, then remembered her manners. "How's business at your stables? You got any borders yet?"

"It's been slow, but a few new kids signed up for my beginner's class on Saturday morning, and now that school's out, I hope to get more."

"You should do a summer camp or something like that. Parents are always looking for ways to keep their kids busy."

"I've also gotten a few cancellations. I think they want to be in the movie."

"Take deposits?"

"No."

"There's your second mistake."

Rose thought a minute. "And my first one?"

"Thinking you could start up a new business here in Cherryvale. If you don't mind, I'm tired. You can see yourself out, can't you?" Maggie pushed back her chair, moved down the hall and closed her bedroom door. Rose rinsed the water glasses and left them to dry on the drain board, closed the back door to Maggie's cottage, and tiptoed past the crates. Weary to her soul.

Her riding clothes smelled of every kind of animal, plus smoke from the fire, and she still needed to feed her own horses. She trudged along Cherrypath toward home, looking forward to a quiet evening and a hot bath in the loft apartment over her stable.

"All kinds of evil..." Maggie's voice replayed in her thoughts. What did the woman mean? Could someone really be setting the fires?

She quickened her stride, now more eager to check on her own place. But on this stretch of The Path, only moonlight filtered through thick branches here and there. She slowed and caught herself as her foot dropped into a soft spot. How long has it been since someone took care of this stupid path, she wondered.

Rounding a bend halfway between Maggie's and the Stables, Rose could barely see the rough boards of the fence beside the footpath that led to her own property. Ever since she moved here, the people acted friendly enough, but Maggie's warning scared her. She wanted to work with her horses and become part of a community, not live in fear of an arsonist.

Passing a grove of trees that stood tight and thick in the dark woods to her left, she heard a rhythmic thumping that made her heart do the same. She peered into the night, but didn't see what could be making the noise. Nor did she see a tangle of weeds. The toe of her boot caught, she teetered and reached out to grab the fence rail to keep from falling.

Righted, she hooked her elbows over the fence rail and listened, holding her breath. Over the whooshing of her heartbeat in her ears, the steady thump-thumping came from behind the trees. She considered what kind of machinery or animal it might be. She mentally measured the distance to either run back to Maggie's or home before the ax-wielding arsonist found her standing there.

The longer she listened, the higher the chills lifted the hairs on her neck up to her scalp. And the more her curiosity taunted her to discover the source of the noise.

Thump. Thump. Thump. Pause. Another thump.

Rose stepped up on the bottom rail and squinted. Clouds skimmed across the sky, and moonlight winked over the tops of the branches, revealing the source of the mystery noise.

Between two oak trees, knee deep in a fresh trench, Greg lifted a spade over his head and dropped it, breaking up the hard ground. Thump-thump, Rose watched for a moment..

Without speaking, she climbed the fence and picked up a shovel leaning against one of the trees. After a half hour working, Greg poured the final shovelful on the mound and they stood side by side considering the sad result of their evening's work.

After a few moments, Greg spoke in a low voice. "Lord, we commit these beautiful creatures to your fields in heaven. We thank you for each and every one, large and small, furry or feathered…" The vet's broad chest rose and fell. "And, Lord, help us figure out how to help Maggie. And please prevent more fires, whatever their causes. Amen."

"Amen." Rose spoke in a soft voice. "Greg, what is Maggie going to do? The petting farm was the bread-and-butter of her place. Do you think there is an arsonist? Are we all at risk?"

Greg looked at Rose in the moonlight. "If one Valer is in danger, all Valers are in danger."

Cherryvale had hosted hardship before. When the newly constructed highway bypass diverted traffic from town, it relieved congestion but also hurt the businesses that relied on thirsty, hungry travelers.

The Main Street Merchants Committee, organized by Grace Harkins, spearheaded the town's extreme makeover. Valers were relentless in solving problems and meeting challenges to keep businesses operating and families eating. Besides renovating storefronts and shaping up their main street, they devised an unusual solution. Diverse businesses reduced their overhead and combined into unique alliances.

The bakery and sandwich shop merged with the pottery artist. "Loaves and Dishes," as it was whimsically named, sold deli meats and picnic supplies on one side and customers could watch the potter hand-throwing custom creations in clay on his wheel on the other. The consignment store merged with the watchmaker to become "Yours, Mine, and Hours." The bookstore moved into the lobby of the movie theater, and the re-named "Read and Reel" offered a book club and special screenings of the movie based on the latest literary selection.

Overheads reduced and shared expenses affected neighbors, and even the local lawnmower parts factory—next door to Maggie's place—seemed to prosper by hiring workers and expanding product lines.

So Cherryvalers heard the news of Maggie's second fire with the same determination and sense of community.

Greg, Pastor Bob, Sam Madison, and Mayor Jack Purcell sat in a corner booth at the Bucket discussing the best approach to help Maggie.

Shelby set down plates of eggs-over-easy, stacks of pancakes, and piles of bacon on the yellow-swirled Formica table, then she slid into the booth next to Sam. "Any a'you got a bright idea? Her animals need to eat ever day."

"They're sayin' arson." Greg sliced into a tall stack of blueberry pancakes. "It'll take even longer for her settlement to come through, if it does at all."

"The church don't have that kind of reserves, do it Brother Bob?" Shelby asked.

Pastor set down his "Gone Fishin'" mug and shook his head. "We could give her some canned beans. That's about all we have right now."

Shelby watched the mayor sopping up egg with his wheat toast. "Jack, what about that community chest we started years back?"

"That fund hasn't had over twelve dollars in as many years." Mayor Purcell shook his head. "I think what we need is a city-wide campaign."

"This is bigger than the few of us." Greg sipped his orange juice. "In the meantime, I'll send over a couple bags of oats. I'm sure Rose will lend her some hay."

"You know..." Mayor continued under his breath. "We don't know what that woman's really been up to all these years."

"What do you mean?" He had Sam's attention now.

"What if she's been involved in some kind of foreign espionage and they're catching up to her?" Mayor's eyes darted underneath bushy brows.

"Really, now," Pastor protested. "I don't think—"

"He has a point." Sam waved a butter knife. "We don't know that maybe her husband's energy consultant job might have been a cover-up for something." He slathered butter on toast and bit off a corner. "Very *Mr. and Mrs. Smith*."

The cowbell rang announcing a customer. Rose, dressed in a cotton shirt, jeans and barn boots, paused, then crossed over to their table. "Good morning, Greg. Hey, Pastor. Mayor. Your clerk said you have the keys to the storeroom, Sam. I need to pick up a special order."

"Sure." Sam dug in his pocket for his keys.

Shelby looked up and down Rose's slender frame. "Set yourself down and have a stack. You'll fly right off if a strong wind blows."

"Join us." Greg pulled a chair over from a nearby table. "We're brainstorming how we can help Maggie."

Rose eyed the plates of hotcakes and scrambled eggs. "I guess I wouldn't say no to some of your stuffed French toast, Shelby."

"You got it, honey." Shelby lowered her voice to inject one last comment. "Nobody's mentioned Maggie's other problem."

Rose smoothed a paper napkin across her jeans. Greg swabbed a fork full of hotcake through a syrup puddle and shoved the mess into his mouth. Mayor clinked a spoon around his coffee cup. Pastor Bob studied a speck on the Formica.

"I'll say it." Shelby removed a pencil from the bun at the base of her neck, loosening another tendril. "She ain't a favorite around town." She caught Greg's eye before he glanced away. "Especially since she's been so vocal against the movie shootin' here. And for the amount of money they're likely to bring in, folks may not care to help her out any."

"Indeed, Shelby, we're supposed to love our en—" Pastor wiped his napkin across his lips and started over. "What I mean to say is, those creatures need our help right away. Rose can't be expected to carry both her operation and Maggie's."

Greg nodded at Rose. "I offered to send over some sacks of grain and thought you might have some hay to loan her."

"Of course." Rose met Greg's eyes, but he picked up the syrup pitcher for another splash.

"Good start." Shelby tapped the table with her pencil eraser emphasizing her point. She spun on her white sneakers and hung Rose's order on a chrome clip for Arlene.

"Speaking of the movie, we have a celebrity among us." Mayor poked his fork at Sam. "Rumor says you're auditioning."

"I do. I read for a small part, and I shoot tomorrow."

A round of teasing and "your head will be too big for you" jokes followed.

Shelby set a coffee cup in front of Rose and filled it. "We have quite a few hams in this town, don't we, Sam?"

"I get a fair number when I hold auditions. You ever done any acting, Rose?"

"Me?" Rose's cheeks flushed and she ducked her head. "I was in a talent show in school. I did a hula hoop number in a poodle skirt of my mom's."

"A talent show." Sam sat up straight. "We could do that. That could be our fundraiser."

"The Cherrypickers are available." Mayor didn't skip a beat. "We're not booked until the Fourth of July picnic. Of course we should audition more local acts."

"I can re-mount scenes from last season's musical productions." Sam lifted his ball cap and smoothed blond whispies. "Everyone will want to perform for a good cause—and a chance to be on stage."

Shelby chimed in from the cash register. "I play a mean washboard."

Greg grinned and lifted his voice. "We're not paying them to listen; it's the other way around." They laughed as Shelby stuck her tongue out at him.

"Excuse me. May I offer a suggestion?" Two strangers sat in a nearby booth. They were dressed in Doc Marten work boots and black t-shirts and khaki shorts. The man who spoke stuck his hand across the aisle. "I'm Emmett, Emmett Johns, and this is Hank." Mayor shook hands with Emmett and they all waved at Hank, who lifted his mug in salute.

"We couldn't help overhearing." Emmett's broad grin matched his flowing white hair. "Perhaps we can help enlarge the scope of your show. Attract an audience larger than just Cherryvale."

Shelby moved from behind the cash register to be nearer the discussion.

"I'm *The Scrapbook's* electrician, and Hank's the best cameraman you'll ever want to work with. We can give you some pointers on doing a live broadcast."

"You mean put it on television?" Sam sat up straight.

"We can get the neighboring counties, or even the whole state, involved." Shelby waved her arm with a wide flourish.

Mayor studied Emmett's face. "Are you sure you want to help with this? You know she—Maggie—she's the one that lodged the complaint. Tried to stop your filming."

"Yeah, we know about her. We run into her kind a lot. But the animals don't have anything to say about it. Maybe we can convince her that we're not all of the devil."

"Some of the other crew'll pitch in with their technical help," Hank went on. "We'll have to clear it with the studio. Publicity department might even help us. If they think it'll help promote the movie."

"A telethon means we'll need a phone bank. I'll have my secretary set that up." Mayor pulled a notepad and gold pen from his pocket and scribbled. "I'll draw the permits myself."

"I'll produce the show, and my wife, Abby, can handle the ticket sales!" Sam slid out to shake hands with Hank and Emmett. "I'm going to make phone calls and line up some acts. You folks settle on a date, and I'll make sure the theater's available. This must be our highest priority!" Sam made a theatrical flourish in the air with his baseball cap. "But first I have a shipment of fertilizer coming in this morning."

"Let's meet in the church basement tonight. Is that all right, Pastor?"

"Absolutely, Mayor."

Over the next several hours, news of the talent show spread along The Path and throughout the community. But over at the movie shoot location, day two of filming had serious problems.

"Please, Tiffany, please come out, the director's losing it!" Jeff stood outside Tiffany's trailer door.

"Harper's a butt. I can't work like this!" Tiffany hollered through the door.

"Can I come in?" Jeff waited several seconds and, detecting no movement inside, tried the unlocked doorknob. He pushed in and stepped into the dark interior of Tiffany's customized trailer. Slivers of light from mini-blinds striped the plush carpet like prison bars. When his eyes adjusted, Tiffany's form appeared in the shadows. She'd curled up on the sectional sofa, her feet tucked under her.

Leonardo jumped out of her arms, sniffing and yipping at him from the edge of the sofa. Tiff didn't look at or acknowledge his presence.

Jeff held out his hand for Leo to sniff, and satisfied, the tiny dog circled and lay down with his head on his paws. Jeff sat on the end of the couch and waited.

After a few minutes, Tiffany spoke. "Aren't you going to lecture me about time being valuable and how I'm wasting money?"

"No."

More silence.

"Why not?"

Jeff spoke in a low tone. "Because I know you're aware of that. You've been in this business longer than most of these people. Tiffany, you are more important than any money it's costing the studio."

"That's crap and you know it."

"What? That you're more important than money? Movies come and go. Gigs come and go. But you're one-of-a-kind. Irreplaceable."

Tiffany scooped up Leo one-handed and buried her face in his neck, looking at Jeff between the fringe of his triangular ears. Smeared makeup gave her a skeletal look.

"I know more about what you're going through than you might realize. Talk to me. I'm a good listener. Talk to someone before you explode."

"You trying to make a move on me?" Tiffany's eyes narrowed. "Perv."

"The dialog in this movie's hitting a raw nerve with you, admit it. Too close to your own—"

Insistent banging on the trailer door interrupted.

"Tiffany, you have to come back to the set! Now!" Holly's anxiety practically melted through the particle door. "Harper threatened to call your manager!"

"Good luck finding him," Tiffany sniffed. "Never even answers my phone calls."

"C'mon, girl. I'll go with you." Jeff offered a hand to help her off the couch, but she didn't stir.

"You're not in this scene."

"That's okay, I'll keep you company. We'll talk more later."

Clutching Leo to her chest, Tiffany sighed, and unfolded her long legs. She shoved past Jeff and clattered down the metal stairs to follow Holly back to the set.

A few minutes later, Tiffany slumped in her canvas chair and pouted while her makeup technician repaired the damage to her makeup. Out of range of her hearing, Jeff implored the director. "I know she's difficult to direct, Radford. Go easy on her, though. There's something affecting Tiffany emotionally. Remember she's only seventeen."

"If you want to play psychotherapist to that diva, it's fine by me." Radford popped and crunched an antacid. "But if she pulls another stunt like this, I'm black-balling her, and she's history in this business. We took a chance on casting her in the first place."

Jeff watched the director rub his tender midsection. Obviously, keeping the production on time and on budget had Harper's ulcer spreading like a bad review. "What set her off this time?"

"I asked her to change a line delivery, then she told me I wasn't clear and I should be specific about what I wanted, the little—" Radford muttered under his breath and winced as Tiffany stood up. "Let's go everybody!"

Jeff watched them shoot for a while. Once Tiffany put her game face on, he made a "let's talk" signal and escaped to the peace inside his own trailer.

CHAPTER EIGHT

"And...action!"

Grace looked up to see Sam Madison—dressed in a yellow rain slicker—clomp toward a small shed carrying a bucket and fishing rod. He stopped next to a prop bait stand. Made from a large board painted by the scenery department to look like a small shack, the scenery attached to the pier with clamps, it leaned against temporary scaffolding. Sam waited a beat, dumped a bucket of baitfish into a barrel. He turned and spoke, gazing past the camera, too far away for her to hear his lines.

Another actor spoke a few lines before Radford looked up from his director's monitor and yelled, "Cut! Thank you. Set up for Tiffany's close-up." The director jumped down from his perch and began gesturing at light reflectors. Hank moved around with Radford while he explained angles and distance.

"All this walking's not hard work, but my feet are getting tired." Grace lowered herself onto a clean patch of grass next to Carolyn. "I don't know if I'm cut out to be a professional background artist."

Carolyn eased down next to her. "Too bad Abby couldn't get away from work long enough to watch her hubby's big scene."

"I hope it makes it into the film. Our own movie actor." Grace watched Carson at the water's edge. "The flat ones work best, buddy." Grace worked her throbbing left foot out of its sneaker prison. "Could this little town stand to have a full time star in its midst?"

Carson picked up a handful of rocks and stood on the dirt that sloped gently toward the water. He turned a shoulder and flung a rock that plopped and sank.

"Don't get your clothes dirty, honey. They might want us to be in another scene."

"Mom." Carson flicked a sturdy pebble and managed a double skipper. "I'm tired. I wanna go home."

Cassie wandered over to watch her brother skipping rocks.

"Good one!" Grace called to Carson. "This is a tough way to make a living; I had no idea." She wriggled her toes in the grass, catching sight of Holly angling their way.

Cassie and Carson ran over and collapsed in the grass.

"How much longer do you think we'll be here?" Carolyn looked up at the PA. "My kids are beat."

Holly flicked over a paper on her clipboard. "It's three pages of script, a long, then a two-shot. One establishing." She smiled at their blank looks. "It shouldn't take too long. Unless something crazy happens. You're wrapped, Grace. You can go."

"How about uth?" Cassie mumbled from the cradle of her mother's arms.

"That's what I came to talk to you about, Mrs. Sims. Mr. Harper wants Cassie in this shot with Tiffany. Even though you're all volunteers, he's offering her a bump—a little pay. It won't be much, but we can even give her a credit too. If you can stay, he'd appreciate it."

"What do you say?" Carolyn tipped her head to look into Cassie's deep chocolate eyes. "Do you want to work some more or go home?"

Cassie sat up. "Do I get to pet her puppy?"

"She'd do it for the chance to pet the dog." Carolyn grinned at Holly. "She loves animals."

"I'll see what I can do. She'll probably let you pet Leo. And she'll still get paid." Holly held a hand out to Cassie. "You wanna come with me now? Hair and makeup want to check you over."

"Get ready for your close-up." Grace gave her a thumbs-up. "Break a leg."

"Huh?" Cassie's eyes grew large and she searched her mom's face.

"Showbiz talk. I'll explain it to you while we walk," Holly assured her. "The rest of you can watch from over here." She glanced toward the sun on its descent. "Just don't walk around; your shadows might crawl across the shot. Ready, Cassie?"

Cassie let Holly lead her by the hand next to the fake bait shop where she sat in a canvas chair. A makeup artist tamed her hair in the colorful clips and powdered her face. Then Holly showed Cassie where to sit on a bench under a "Fresh Bait" sign.

"I'm glad she gets to sit. I think she's practically asleep as it is," Carolyn observed.

The heat of the day slipped slowly toward dusk, and the lake water tap-slapped against the grassy slope near their feet. A light dew settled as the sun's rays grew longer.

Skitch-sk-ploop!

Carson resumed skimming rocks. "I don't have to stay clean, do I, Mom?"

"No, have fun, but when they give us a warning, you'll have to sit down." Carolyn sighed, watching her son. "I'm glad they picked Cassie. Maybe Tiffany will speak to her."

Grace watched Tiffany, carrying a little dog in the crook of her arm, sauntering over to the set. "Wouldn't that make her day?"

"Cut!" The sun kissed the horizon as Radford glared at the cast and crew waiting for his next command. "Back to one. Again. What take is this, anyway?"

"Twelve, Mr. Harper." Holly stroked Leo beside her in Tiffany's chair.

The director stood up from his perch, stepped away from the cluster of cameras and monitors and motioned to Tiffany. "Walk with me."

She glanced up from her acrylic nails, rolled her eyes, and trudged over to stand next to him behind a light reflector.

"What exactly is the problem, dear? I need some emotion from you. I could get more out of that tree than you're giving me." He glowered, and then changed his tactic. "I've seen you switch between full-on sobbing and cool composure quicker than Hollywood changes A-lists. Why can't you bring it today?"

"It's all these distractions. That brat keeps yawning during my lines." Tiffany flicked a white-tipped thumb in Cassie's direction.

They watched as her little head nodded forward, her eyes hooded halfway shut, mouth opening in a tiny snore.

"She's a sweet little girl who's had a very long day." Radford glared at Tiffany. "You, my dear, are the brat."

"If your drones could control their extras, I could do my job." Tiffany grabbed a dozing Leo from her chair and tucked him under her arm.

"Finish your monologue with some sort of emotion. Shoot, I'd settle for a whimper from your dog at this point so we can wrap for dinner. It's not rocket science."

"Leave my dog out of this." Tiffany shoved Leo toward Holly, swung her blonde hair in Harper's direction, and stomped back to her mark.

The director dragged a hand through salt and pepper chin stubble. "Holly, wake up the little girl." He breathed in then finished in a measured monotone, "Please."

Holly knelt next to Cassie. "Honey, can you stay awake for a few minutes?" She stroked a brown cheek until Cassie's eyelids fluttered open. "Hi. Want a sip of water?"

Cassie sipped and one of the makeup girls powdered her cheeks again and stepped away. Cassie's long dark lashes fluttered up at Holly. "Ith Tiffany mad at me?"

"She's okay." Holly re-clipped a wild tendril of Cassie's brown hair and lifted the little girl's chin toward her. "She's been working for a long time on this movie and I think she just needs to get home."

"Maybe she misseth her mommy."

"We're almost finished," Holly reassured her. "You need to keep your eyes open a little longer. Can you do that?"

"I'll try." Cassie lifted her chin and scooted her bottom to sit up straighter.

Radford paced back and forth. When Holly stood up, he called his orders. "All right, people we're losing the light, not to mention my patience. Back to one."

"Okay, Cassie, this is it," Holly whispered.

Like a precision machine, each crew called out their equipment's readiness in rapid succession.

"Picture's up," came first.

The clapper held up his board. Digital numbers ticked, recording the sound marker into Hank's camera. The board pulled away, allowing the camera lens to focus on Tiffany with Cassie in the frame behind her. Except for the assistant director calling cues, no one moved or dared make a sound. A late afternoon breeze stirred the tops of the oak trees, and the surface of the lake fluttered into a tiny chop.

Radford made a final visual sweep of the scene and took a deep breath. "Background—action!"

On his call, the extras resumed their assigned motions, re-enacting, for the umpteenth time, the same movements: picking up a bucket of bait, casting a fishing line, strolling along the dock. Hank stood ready with the steady cam, focused and waiting.

Radford laid one arm across his chest, chewed on a thumbnail, and studied a monitor as if it held the secret to eternal youth. "Miss Lane—action. Please."

Standing on her mark, Tiffany opened a prop envelope and read the letter's contents in silence.

"My darling daughter." Holly read the voice-over narration from her script sides. "One of the hardest things I ever did was leave you. When you were born, my cancer had spread..." Holly stopped and looked up, waiting for Tiffany to continue the letter aloud in her own voice.

Radford glanced at the light meter while Tiffany picked up the dialogue, her tone stumbling with emotion over the last words. "...and so, my precious daughter..."

The sun dropped behind the trees and the world dimmed as if God slipped a shade over a giant light bulb.

Cassie's eyelids fluttered closed.

Harper's back arched and he twisted toward Tiffany.

Still in character, she continued reading the prop letter. "...never give up hope. Someday you will find your father. His name is..."

Tiffany lifted her gaze, focusing on a distant point beyond the camera. Actor's tears spilled down her made-up cheeks.

Radford gnawed his thumbnail.

The sun continued its inevitable journey.

Just over Tiffany's right shoulder, Cassie's heavy head tilted back, her eyelashes dropped to her cheeks and her mouth yawned wide until a full on, up-too-early-missed-my-nap gurgly kiddie-snore erupted.

The long arm of the boom mike shot up as the sound echoed into the sound engineer's headphones. He jerked his head up. Motioning to Radford, he caught the director's attention and pointed at the snoring lass.

"Cut!"

Tiffany twirled around, and seeing the dozing little girl in her shot, blasted, "You idiot child! Get out of my sight. You're ruining my scene. You're ruining my life!" The enraged actress raised her arm to the girl.

Holly leapt to body-block her from making contact. Cassie, wide-eyed and fighting tears, plastered up against the rough wooden boards of the fake bait stand.

Startled from his catnap by the screaming, the little Yorkie jumped from the canvas chair to follow his mistress's voice. Yipping at the air, he bounded past Tiffany and landed on the bench next to Cassie, grazing her knee with his pointy little teeth. Holly shoved the yipping dog off the bench.

Tiffany reached down to catch him before he fell to the ground, cuddling the ball of fluff to her chest.

"Miss Lane!" Radford bellowed and practically stood on tiptoe to glare up at the diva he'd argued against in every pre-production meeting. "Shut up that overgrown rat and get it out of here before I cut him into pieces and serve him to the crew for dinner!"

Tiffany postured, towering over Radford "Now wait one minute, my contract allows Leo—"

"I don't care if your contract allows you to ride a kangaroo on set, you will keep that dog under control! And don't you ever speak to another actor—or me—in this manner. Ever!"

"She's not an actor." Tiffany looked down squarely into Radford's face. "She's a set piece!" Backing away, she announced, "I can't work like this! I'll be in my trailer!"

Bullying her way past the circle of cameras, mic booms and folding chairs, she wadded up and hurled the prop letter.

A grip scooted to avoid the missile and knocked into a light pole that slammed to the ground popping a two-hundred dollar bulb in a mini sound-and-light show.

Carolyn and Grace raced over, and Carolyn hugged her sobbing little girl.

Holly frowned at Cassie's wound. "I radioed the set medic, he'll be over pronto."

Carolyn hugged her whimpering daughter. Carson ran up and held Grace's hand, watching his sister with concern.

Grace glanced down at the twins and squatted next to Carolyn. "Hey, Cassie, Carson."

"What Miz Grace?" Carson sat next to her.

"Do you know what a baby ear of corn calls its father?"

Cassie stopped crying and asked, "No, what?"

"Pop corn!" Grace told her.

Cassie giggled through her tears, and Carson's eyes lit up. "I have one. How do you know the ocean is friendly?"

The medic run up and knelt next to Cassie. Thankfully, the little girl's attention remained on their joke-telling. "How?"

"It waves a lot." Carson fell back on the grass giggling at his own joke.

"Do you want to tell one, Cassie?" Grace hoped the diversion would continue to distract her, but Cassie watched the attendant unhook the hinges, lift the lid and slide on gloves. Cassie's lower lip trembled as he wiped her wound, then applied ointment.

The scratch bandaged, Carolyn signed incident paperwork, handed the pen and paper back to the medic and looked up at Holly. "Can we go now?"

Holly looked over at Radford, who leaned against a monitor, head in his hands. "We are NOT wrapped ladies and gentlemen."

Grips stopped their work, frozen in place, cables half wound into neat circles. Sound techs held mics at half-mast over open and waiting cases.

Radford gazed out from the command post, and Holly caught his eye. His shoulders dropped. With a shrug, he revoked his previous direction. "Never mind. It is a wrap." He stepped through the cables and murmured, "Holly, see me in my trailer—ASAP."

Holly rubbed a circle on Cassie's back. The little girl's sobs were now quieted to an occasional blubber-gasp. "Honey, I'm so sorry she scared you."

"Tiffany wa-wath mean t-to me." Cassie peered through eyelashes damp with tears. "And her dog b-bit me."

Carolyn gave a wan smile over her daughter's head nestled against her shoulder. "At least she won't have wild dreams of running away to Hollywood when she grows up."

"Not after the trauma we've put her through." Holly blew a sigh. "I'd be surprised if she wants anything to do with any of us ever again."

Jeff puttered in his trailer after grabbing a bite at the catering tent. He tried to review his lines but threw down the script and flicked on his computer to check his inbox. He hoped to hear from Julie, but only spam and an e-mail from his agent waited. Dusk changed to dark. He stretched and flicked on the television in his trailer, but the peaceful evening lured him outside. He clanked down metal steps and breathed in the cool twilight air carrying a faint, sweet perfume. Jasmine or honeysuckle? He always got the two mixed up.

Tight muscles in his back relaxed as he strolled the perimeter of the makeshift city, past the caterers washing up. He stepped over inch-thick cables that ran from power generators and solar panels to the sleeping trailers and honey wagons used for changing and restrooms. Moonlight shone on the water across the park, and he could see the crew had already removed the bait shop scenery and filming equipment.

If everything went well, he'd be summoned to Radford's trailer to look at the overnights, and the final scenes would be in the can. For the first time while on location, Jeff felt a sense of loss. Leaving this small town and returning home to Los Angeles would be difficult. In their few days in Cherryvale, he felt at home.

He wandered around the compound toward Tiffany's trailer. Though he didn't relish the thought, he intended to keep his promise to check in on her. Hand to the trailer door, he jumped as it slammed back against the metal wall.

"Thank God! Jeff!" Holly grabbed him by the shoulders, eyes wild with fright. "I think she's done it! She's killed herself!"

Grace stretched her legs out through the squishy warm bubbles, cell phone to her ear. "We waited around a lot, but when we actually worked, it was kinda fun."

"How many scenes are you in? Am I going to have to hire you a bodyguard?" Mark teased.

"Only if someone has really good vision or likes tiny little women. They put me so far from the cameras, I'll be surprised if I'm even recognizable." Grace heard Mark's desk intercom announce an incoming ambulance.

"Hold on. They're bringing someone in."

Grace overheard the transmission through Mark's muffling fingers. "Victim's Tiffany Lane! Possible su—"

"Gotta run, hon." The line went dead.

Grace stared at the phone, punched "END" with a soapy finger, and opened the bathtub drain.

Jeff wrapped his arm around Holly's shoulders as the ambulance pulled away, sirens screaming into the night air. Radford stormed back into his trailer barking at his assistant as he went.

"He's not going. But we can. My rental car's over here." Jeff pointed.

Holly sniffled and followed him to the parking area. "Did you hear about the blow-up?"

"Kind of hard to miss." Jeff trotted up to a Suburban and clicked the doors open. It brr-uppd and the lights flashed.

"I let myself in her trailer to check on her after her meltdown." Holly pulled open her door, climbed in and ran her hand over her bleeding left ankle. "She was part of the problem on set."

Jeff glanced at her wound. "We'll get you looked at too."

"Anyway, I knocked a couple times. She had music on freaky loud. She didn't open up, so I went in a-and th-then…" Holly choked a sob.

"You can tell me about it later if you want." Jeff mashed on the brake, checked for traffic, and steered the car over the curb onto the tarmac.

"Her bathroom door, it was locked, so I busted it open." Holly swiped at her nose, composed herself, leaning back in the passenger seat. "That's when Leo bit me." She rubbed her ankle.

"Ungrateful little..."

"He was just trying to protect her." Holly slid her gaze to meet Jeff's. "She was—she was on the floor holding the shower door handle—her wrist was bleeding…th-there was s-so much blood." Holly snuffled and faced forward. "Do you know where you're going?"

"The EMT driver gave me directions. I remember seeing the hospital when I drove in from the airport. Town's small, it can't be too far—there it is." Jeff turned left then right into the parking lot of a two-story brick building. He put the car in park and shut off the engine. He hesitated, hands still on the wheel. "Holly, can I ask you a personal question?"

"What?"

"I want to pray for Tiffany before I go in. Would you join me?"

"No." Holly opened her door but didn't get out of the car. "Okay, yes."

Relieved, Jeff prayed for Tiffany, for the doctors, and for an answer to what troubled the young actress. New to praying in front of others, his gut urged he should learn how, and soon.

The two sat for a minute without speaking, the only sounds were from a car passing and the low voices of smokers on a nearby bench. Jeff opened his door first and helped Holly hobble to the sliding glass doors.

"She's stable." The nurse at the ER desk shrugged. "That's all I can tell you now, if you'll have a seat." They stepped back to find a chair in the waiting room.

"Can someone look at this as well?" Jeff pointed to Holly's reddened ankle.

"Fill this out. Did you know the dog? Or was it a stray?" The nurse handed Holly a clipboard.

"No. I know him."

"Good. Well, not good. But a stray dog poses all kinds of other problems." The nurse nodded to Jeff, a blush at her cheekbones. "By the way, Mr. Field, I enjoy your work."

"Thanks." Jeff managed a tight smile, an automatic reaction.

"That looks like something you can take care of at home unless you want to wait several hours." She watched Holly dab at the wound with a tissue."

Holly sniffed, her emotions over finding Tiffany causing a catch in her throat, and Jeff put an arm across her shoulder as she sat down in a vinyl chair.

The nurse caught Jeff's eye. "Let me see what I can find out." She mouthed and slipped through a swinging door.

Holly set the clipboard down and Jeff wandered over to a coffee vending machine but didn't gamble any money in it. Instead, he pulled out his phone. "I should call the set and let Radford know we're here."

Before he could dial, the outside doors swooshed open and Grace rushed in. "I heard they brought Tiffany in. What happened, have you heard anything?"

Holly stood up. "Uh, we just got here. The nurse told us to wait—"

"I'll see what I can find out." Grace passed the triage desk.

"Who's she?" Jeff tilted his head, watching her disappear through a door marked 'Employees Only.' "She a nurse or something?"

"Something." Holly picked up a tattered magazine and lowered herself back to the chair. "She's an extra."

Before she could flip past the letters to the editor, Grace reappeared.

"They finished stitching her up and they're moving her to a room upstairs."

Jeff regarded Grace with wide eyes. "You work here?"

"My husband's chief of staff; they have to put up with me." She held out a hand. "Boss's wife, you know. My name's Grace."

Jeff shook her hand.

"I know I break rules. Can't get past the days when we were a small country clinic and didn't have all these restrictions." Grace tapped the side of her head. "I can read a chart from ten yards though and I overheard who they were bringing in, so if you want to report me..."

"Not at all." Jeff chuckled. "We're just glad to know she's in good hands. No one's going to turn you in." He pulled a handful of change from his pocket and studied the machine's selections.

"Oh, don't drink from that; it tastes like last week's lab samples. I'll get you some coffee from the nurses' break room. Follow me."

"I have to admit if you found out Tiff had been brought in..." Jeff looked through the glass doors into the parking lot. "I'm worried the paparazzi—"

"I was telling my husband about the movie shoot." Grace held up her cell phone, switching it to off before sliding it back into her purse. "I overheard the EMT's over the nursing intercom. Don't worry. The staff here will keep her privacy. Speaking of which, though, your presence might give it away. Come in here."

They followed her past the reception desk and into the interior offices. Grace picked up a carafe from a machine on a long Formica counter and poured coffee into three Styrofoam cups.

"Keeping our privacy's not as easy as you'd think." Jeff accepted the strong, steaming beverage. "There's always a snitch. She should have a code name."

"Been done. They're calling her Windy Angel—see the nursing board?" Grace pointed to a white board gridded into large squares. Each patient's name listed their doctor, their room number and any procedures ordered for them.

Jeff's eyebrows lifted as he tried out the name with Tiffany in mind. "Where'd they come up with that?"

Holly chortled and attempted to cover it with a cough, "Boy are they way off."

"Maybe Angel's for Los Angeles." Grace shrugged. "C'mon, let's see if we can visit her."

She led them to the elevator, and when they got out, Grace leaned over to whisper to a nurse working at a computer. She cupped a hand around Grace's ear, and a grin flashed across her face. Grace thumbed toward her own bottom. "She has a kite tattoo."

Holly and Jeff looked first at the nurse, then back at Grace, then back at the nurse as if they were watching a tennis match.

"Tiffany." Grace nodded. "That's where they got the name Windy—the kite's for blowin' in the wind, right?"

"Miss-Tough-as-Nails has a kite tatt?" A smirk spread across Jeff's face and he turned away.

"Who knew?" Holly shook her head, her ponytail swinging. "Angel's still a stretch, though."

They walked across the hall to Tiffany's room, as directed. Grace knuckle-wrapped on the door and pushed it open, stepped aside to let Jeff and Holly in, then she stepped in behind them.

Tiffany lay motionless, eyes closed, long blond hair spread across the starched pillow, her pale face washed clean of makeup. She looked fragile, innocent.

Another nurse watched monitors around the bed and nodded at Grace when they walked in. She flashed Jeff a smile as she scooted out.

Holly moved to the side of the bed and rested her hand on the rail. "Are—are you okay?" She stroked the back of Tiffany's hand below her wrist-to-elbow bandage.

Tiffany moved her arm but didn't open her eyes. "Where's Leonardo?"

"We left him in your trailer. He'll be okay by himself a little while. I'll take care of him while you're—" Holly glanced at Jeff.

He moved to stand near her pillow. "Tiffany, whatever's going on, we hope you let someone help."

"Jeff and I prayed for you," Holly blurted, fiddling with a lampshade. "I don't know if you believe in that stuff."

"Hmmph." Tiffany shifted her legs under the stiff sheet.

"What's the matter, honey?" Holly pushed Tiffany's bangs off her forehead. "Are you in pain?"

"It pains me that people talk about me when I can't defend myself."

"We weren't talking about you." Holly bit her lip. "We were praying for you."

"Save me your sermons. The world's too messed up for any self-respecting God to be in charge." Tiffany shifted as much as the IV would allow her to face away. She caught sight of Grace.

"Actually, God cares a great deal about you, Miss Lane." Grace stepped closer.

"Who are you?" Tiffany challenged.

Grace moved closer so she could see the girl's face over the bed-sheets. "I'm Grace. Grace Harkins. I was at the shoot today. When I heard you were, well, hurt, I wanted to come see if there's anything I can do to help. My husb—"

"I don't know you and I don't need anything from you." She peered at Grace. "Wow. You're old."

Grace smoothed her hair, kinked at the ends from rushing out of the bath and pedaling through the breeze. She took a step back in her mind, but firmly stood her ground against the rude teen.

Tiffany buried her face in her pillow. "All of you go away." With her good arm, she clutched the white sheet and pulled it up to her ears.

Grace moved to stand next to Tiffany's pillow and leaned in. "When someone feels the worst is when they need friends the most. I'll go away, but please let Holly or Jeff—"

"Get out, old woman, don't you get it? I don't need anyone." Tiffany grit her teeth as she tugged with her bandaged arm. "Ow."

"Call if you change your mind." Jeff's tone attempted to soothe.

"Yeah, we'll come back." Holly pulled open the heavy door.

"Hol?" Tiffany's muffled voice sounded small.

"What?"

"Make sure Leo gets his dinner."

"I will."

Grace reached out to smooth the young girl's hair from her face, but Tiffany's glare warned her away. She tiptoed to the doorway, but stopped and looked back at the small mass under the shroud. "I can come back and check on you later."

"Don't bother."

Outside her room, Grace made a suggestion. "Let's see if my husband has a minute." She spoke to the charge nurse, who nodded and picked up a phone. They took the elevator to the admin floor and Grace showed them into Mark's private office.

"That shower door handle was loose the other day when I unpacked her bags." Holly searched Jeff's face. "I hope that's all it was."

"Was it a real attempt, or a cry for help?" Grace wondered aloud, gesturing at the visitor chairs for them to sit. "It's possible they'll hold her for a psych eval."

"Maybe it's exhaustion. We've been working pretty hard getting this film finished." Jeff slumped onto a leather settee.

Grace lifted a coffee carafe and swirled the swill at the bottom. "Sheer exhaustion combined with dehydration could have caused her to be lightheaded." Pouring the goop into a sink in Mark's private bathroom, she swished clean water and refilled it. "Is there any reason to think she's got other problems, mental or physical, they need to know about?"

Jeff and Holly exchanged glances.

"She's been known to bring issues to the set with her," Jeff spoke slowly. "I hate to say it, but it's getting worse. This could be her last film unless she can pull herself together."

Holly nodded. "The word's out she's unprofessional. There are too many people easy to work with waiting for the opportunity. It's not a field you can slack off; I don't care who you are."

"Hey, honey, I got your page." Mark stepped into the room and Grace made the introductions. "Of course I can't tell you anything, except the obvious you saw for yourself. She was brought in with a wound on her wr-uh-arm." Mark met Jeff's eyes. "You might have to stop production for a few days if she's in any scenes. I'm not letting her go just yet."

"Oh, terrific." Jeff dropped his head. "Radford's already furious. He wouldn't even come here. She's the reason we're behind schedule as it is."

"I know she's emancipated, but what about family or friends?" Mark sat down at his desk. "Anyone on the crew or production staff close to her? Someone who might be able to shed light on her mental state?"

Holly held up her cell. "I just got a missed call from Hank." She looked at Grace. "He's our cameraman. I'll text and tell him she's okay if that's all right with the hospital rules."

Mark nodded.

"Tiff doesn't have friends." Jeff shook his head. "Unless you count the party leaches that hang around her back in LA."

Holly looked up from texting. “Her mother calls once in a while, but they aren’t close. I can get her number off Tiff’s phone.”

“You can tell the poor thing’s hurting.” Grace caught Mark’s gaze. “I want to know more about her and if there’s anything we can do to help.”

“I met her mom once when I guest starred on Tiffany’s television series.” Jeff leaned back. “But she mostly had guardians. Her mom lives in Europe, goes by Ruby Santorini now.”

“We should try to contact her, anyway,” Grace observed. “If she’s any kind of mother at all, she’ll want to be here.” She laid a hand on Holly’s. “I’ve helped call family about these kinds of situations. I’d be happy to help.”

Holly exhaled in relief. “The director told me to handle family. I guess this is it.”

“Any questions you want me to ask her?” Grace grabbed a pad and pen, at the ready.

“Kind’a curious about that kite tattoo.” Holly’s lips quirked a quick smile, then returned to serious. “But no. It’s all you, Miss Grace. And, thanks.”

Grace dialed the long list of numbers to make the international connection and heard a series of clicks and tones. She checked her watch again and counted the hours on her fingertips. The time difference to Italy would make it about suppertime there.

She listened to several quick rings, then a woman's voice answered, "Pronto."

"Hello. I'm looking for Ruby Santorini." Grace waited. "Um—do you speak English? Are you Signora Santorini?"

"Momento."

Chatter and noises, then, "Who is this?"

"Ruby Santorini?"

"What is it? I'm having a dinner party."

"You don't know me, ma'am. I'm Grace Harkins. I live in Cherryvale. In America. Your daughter, Tiffany, is here. Filming a movie."

"Get to your point, Mrs. Arkin. I shouldn't leave my guests alone. We have the opera later. If you want an autograph or something you'll have to go through—"

"No, it's not that. She's been injured. I thought you might like to know."

"How did you get my number? Why didn't the studio call me?"

"She's in the hospital. I got your number from the production assistant, Hol—"

"I don't know who you are, but I'd appreciate if you'd mind your own business, *capisce*? Tiffany's always pulling something to get attention. I'm not playing her games any more. *Cu'oco's* fussing at me to let him serve. I have to go."

"I'm sorry to bother you." Grace felt her face warm over—this woman on the other end of the line was the koo-koo one! But, she persisted. "Can I ask you one more thing?"

"You have a lot of ner—I'll be right there, Guiseppe."

"Do you know anything about her tattoo?"

"Mrs. Barkins I am not discussing—what tattoo?

"It's Harkins." Grace gathered her patience. "She has a small kite tattoo."

Ruby's voice became husky. "A kite?" And just as suddenly, her next remark masked any glimmer of maternal concern. "Ask her yourself, and good luck getting anything out of her."

"What about Tiffany's father? Is there some way we can reach him?" Grace hurried before the woman hung up. "He should be notified."

"I suggest you go back to your soap operas or PTA meetings or whatever small things keep you happy." Ruby's ire raced across the ocean to chill Grace in her cozy kitchen. "And leave me alone." The line went dead.

Grace stared out the window, unable to focus. How could a woman be so self-centered, so uncaring about her own daughter?

Jeff counted the ceiling tiles in his bedroom.

Again.

Voices from the nearby costume trailer—no doubt their gossip discussing Tiffany's drama—drifted through an open window on the evening breeze. The crew worked late, cataloging and sorting costumes and props, wrapping the shoot. Most would leave for Los Angeles the next day.

Jeff lifted his arm, turned his wrist and looked at his watch. He picked up his cell phone, pushed a speed dial number, and waited for the connection.

"Thank you for calling Westbury Academy. If you know your party's extension..."

Jeff punched another button.

"Westbury Academy. Rebecca speaking."

"This is Mr. Field. Is Julie around?"

"Hi, Mr. Field. Lemme check."

Voices and fumbling, then, "Hi Dad. What's up?"

"I miss you. How's your summer going?"

"It's okay. I'm working on a project so I can't talk long."

"I won't keep you. When's your last final? Do you want to plan some time with your old man?"

"Didn't you get my email? Victoria's parents are taking her to Disney World and they invited me."

"Yeah, I got it." Jeff lifted his tone, trying to sound bright. "Don't you wanna see your old man?"

"Dad. It's Disney World."

"I get it. But Thanksgiving together for sure."

"Can you put some more money in my account for shopping in Florida?"

"Of course. I love you, Jules."

"Um. You too. I've gotta go, they're waiting for me." Click.

"Bye." Jeff rolled over and set his phone on the bedside table struggling with conflicted emotions. On one hand, his own daughter seemed more like a second cousin he only saw at weddings and funerals. When his wife died eight years ago, he'd sent her to boarding school and visited her occasionally during parent's weekends. What did he know about raising a daughter? On the other hand, he missed that little girl he'd been so proud of when she was born. While he pictured the little tyke with pigtails running to meet him so long ago, the phone rang.

He answered without checking caller ID, hoping Julie had a change of heart.

"Hi, Jeff, it's Grace Harkins. Got a minute? I tracked down one of her parents."

"Tiffany's?"

"I called her mother."

Jeff rolled his eyes. "The warm and charming Ruby invite you over for espresso next time you're touring Europe?"

"Not exactly."

"Don't take it personally. Ruby lives strictly by A-list rules. How many names did she drop?"

"Beg pardon? "

"If your name's not a household word or your fortune's not in the top 100, you're nobody to her."

"And even more reason to track down her father. Maybe if he knew how much she needed him, he'd be more a part of her life."

"Tiffany's getting old enough. She doesn't need her dad."

Grace caught her breath. "Jeff. Every child needs a father. Even if they don't want to admit they do."

Jeff grew silent for a beat. "Of course you're right."

"What was your father like?"

Jeff wondered at this bold woman on the other end of the line. "Absent."

"How did that affect you? Do you remember him at all?"

"I felt when he left, he rejected me…" Jeff's voice caught. "I don't talk about him like this to anyone, well, ever."

"I've seen lots of kids who blamed themselves for their parent's divorces."

"It never leaves you."

"And worse, it sets you up for a lifetime of pain. Hard to accept love from your heavenly Father when your relationship with your earthly father is dysfunctional."

Jeff thought about Tiffany lying in the hospital bed. Was it possible her accident had been a lesson for him? "Grace, I'll do what I can for Tiffany, but right now I have something else to take care of."

As he dialed the phone, he remembered Rick's warning. "Look out, once you turn your life over to the Lord, you may be in for a wild ride."

Strap yourself in, he told himself. I think Rick's prediction is about to come true.

The church basement hummed with chatter and activity as Valers gathered to organize the fundraising telethon.

"Quiet, everybody! Hello!" Pastor Bob waited for conversations to end and for everyone to take a seat on the folding chairs. "We have a lot to cover, so let's get started. We already have committee chairmen, so please sign up to help. But first, let's ask the Lord for His blessing."

After the amen, Valers wandered around the church basement to volunteer for everything from handling publicity, to answering telethon phones, to the dreaded clean up committee.

"I almost forgot." Pastor interrupted the vigorous chatter. "I want to introduce you to Emmett John and Hank Wilson. They're on the movie crew, and Emmett has contacted channel 56 from Franklin City, who are donating several hours of broadcast time beginning Sunday night. Let's give them both a hand."

Maggie leaned over to Grace and whispered above the applause. "It's no big deal. Just extra publicity for their movie don't ya know."

"Oh, I don't—"

"I'll bet their PR people love this kind of thing," Maggie interrupted and clenched the straps of Purse Everest, her lips a thin line.

Grace thought of a hundred ways to respond to Maggie's attitude, most of them unkind, but she took the high road. She made a point of clapping loud and long before sliding her gaze back to her friend. "Why are you so skeptical? They've been no trouble and now they want to help. I met some of them at the shoot and most of them are perfectly lovely."

Maggie sat back, mouth an *o* of surprise. "You went?"

"I did." Grace, chin up, mustered newfound boldness. "I wish you'd stop being so negative and mistrusting. I'm truly sorry about the fires and all. But honestly, your attitude has gotten, well, tiresome."

"Suit yourself, then." Maggie stood, upsetting her chair backwards in a clatter. "Guess I know who my friends are." She pushed her way toward the door, weaving in and out between clumps of people.

Grace stared, arguing with herself over whether to run after Maggie or sit her ground. But if she ran after her, Maggie would most likely play the 'I know more about the world than Grace does' card.

Globe traveler Maggie never missed an opportunity to remind her she'd taken pictures of rare rhinos on African safaris and slept on riverboat excursions down the Amazon. Grace stared at her folded fingers and willed the strength to pray. One would think Maggie would be grateful to have a hometown eager to help a near stranger. *Lord, please send someone with the patience to help Maggie. I'm the wrong person for the job.*

Grace considered the challenges. Maybe all that moving around robbed Maggie of a sense of belonging, of community. Or maybe Maggie was just stubborn and self absorbed, and no one could break through that tough exterior. *That's it. I quit. She's in your hands, now, Lord.*

Grace set her jaw and stood up to volunteer for a committee.

Carolyn Sims flicked the light off and pulled the door closed on her small office in Sweet Dreams. The summer bookings were starting to pick up, but she'd hoped by now there would be more future reservations for the Bed and Breakfast. If the summer didn't bring more customers, she and Carl would have to think about returning to the day jobs they'd quit to buy the place. She pulled a pound of ground beef from the freezer and set it in the microwave to thaw, opened the refrigerator door to count eggs and check the level of milk. She wondered if she had enough for tomorrow's breakfast when the swinging door between the kitchen and den opened. Cassie wandered in.

"When's dinner, Mommy?"

"It'll be late tonight. Do you want to take your bath first?"

"I'll go thee what Daddy's doing." She paused by the fruit bowl. "Can I have a apple?"

"Of course."

Carolyn divided the granny smith into sections and crunched on a piece as Cassie pushed open the screen door and shuffled across the wide porch. Carolyn watched her baby girl cross the yard toward Carl's workshop then turned back to check on dinner. Cassie calmed down and quit crying on the ride home, but wouldn't talk about Tiffany's tantrum anymore. Maybe her dad could get her to open up.

Cassie jumped off the swing and wandered to the edge of the yard. A pretty butterfly, just like the one in her alphabet book under B, skimmed and lighted on the blossoms in her mommy's cutting garden. The butterfly swooped and turned, clearing the fence railing next to The Path. Cassie knelt under the fence's bottom rail and followed her sweet new friend.

"Wait. Wanna see my booboo?" She lifted a corner to expose her scratch made by Leo's tooth, but the butterfly lifted off and landed in the middle of some pink flowers, opening and closing its wings. She smooshed the bandage back, then reached out to touch the soft wings, but he flew away again. "Nobody wants me around them today." Miss Shelby would be too busy with her restaurant people to let her gather eggs in her chicken coop. Carson just wanted to watch dumb old cartoons. Cassie realized in just a few more hops, maybe a skip and a jump, she could be to Miz Maggie's. She could hurry over there and be back before mommy had dinner ready. The animals were always glad to see her.

Carolyn removed a crock of thawed meat from the oven and dumped it into a bowl, added an egg, some breadcrumbs and spices, stirred them together and formed a loaf. She returned the bowl to the microwave and punched buttons to start the meatloaf cooking.

She poked her head into the den where Carson watched a cartoon on television. "I'm going out back to see if there's anything ripe. Dinner's in about twenty."

"Okay, Mommy."

Carolyn strolled out the back door and closed her eyes, taking a moment to enjoy the early evening breeze. A flight of starlings, startled by the banging of the screen door, lifted off the hedgerow that ran across the back lawn. She watched them pass overhead and noted the days were already growing noticeably longer.

She stepped over a low fence of rabbit wire into the vegetable garden and snapped off a couple of daisies for a centerpiece, then found one tomato ripe enough for their salad. Nothing else appeared ready to pick, so she went to the back of the property and rounded the corner of Carl's shop. What started as a hobby carving wooden planes had become a steady business. Overnight guests admired the work he displayed in the Inn, and one special order led to another. Thanks to internet sales, the business took off.

He hand-carved custom scale models of all kinds of aircraft, from fighter jets to general aviation private planes. Meticulously accurate, he followed photographs and engineering specs, copied tail numbers and matched each aircraft's exact color scheme to the last pinstripe and whorl.

Carolyn walked up to Carl, bent over a yellow Breitling, and waited for him to lift his brush from a red flame along its nose. "That's gorgeous. Shipping it soon?"

"Birthday party's coming up at an air show in Branson." Carl held the model under a lamp to check his work. "His wife's going to mount it so it appears to fly over a cake decorated with tiny trees and houses doing a snap roll." Carl flicked his wrist and dropped the plane toward the floor.

"How's she going to do that?"

"Says she's going to use cotton candy contrails."

"Neat." Carolyn leaned against a sawhorse. "Did Cassie tell you what happened today?"

"Haven't seen her since you got back."

Carolyn scanned the yard. "She didn't come out here a little bit ago?" The swings were empty, no tiny child dug in the sand box.

"No." Carl followed her gaze.

Carolyn's voice shook. "I'll see if she went back inside."

"I'll check the front yard and The Path."

"Cherryvale Real Estate, can I help you?"

"I'd like to have a look around. See what you've got on the market."

"Yes, Mr. Field!" The receptionist's nervous giggle meant she'd recognized him. "Are you looking to rent?"

"Um." Jeff hoped she would manage a professional reaction to his next remark. "Or, maybe purchase."

"Oh, how exciting! Are you going to live here in Cherryvale?" She practically sang the word "live".

"Maybe. But, could you keep this to yourself? I'm exploring my options, nothing's for certain."

"Of course, Mr. Field." Her voice resumed a normal pitch. "I think there's still someone here. Let me check."

Jeff listened to Billy Joel sing "Uptown Girl" while he waited, followed by "Cat's in the Cradle." Irony. His stomach curdled as he thought of Julie's reaction to his idea.

Cat Stevens faded and the line clicked back on. "I have Jacqui Solenz on the line. Goodbye, Mr. Field."

Another click, and the real estate agent introduced herself in Kathleen Turner-esque husky tones. "Cindy tells me you're interested in looking at some properties."

"I'm thinking of making some changes. And I think Cherryvale might be the place to start."

Jacqui asked Jeff a couple of questions about his tastes then suggested they meet the next day. “I’m late for a meeting, but why don’t you take a looky-loo drive around town before dark. Be sure and walk The Path,” she told Jeff. “It’s a unique feature. I’m not sure if there are any particular properties on it worthy of your, well, expectations, but it will give you a good feel for our community.”

Jeff drove up and down the quiet lanes, enjoying the relative—compared to Los Angeles—lack of traffic and smooth, pothole-free streets. When he’d circled the town, he parked close enough to access the unusual artery Jacqui told him about.

He took out his iPod, stuck the phones in his ears and turned up the volume. He passed several houses, his broad strides covering several yards at a time. After a few minutes of this hurried march, his gait slowed to a mellow saunter and he pulled out the plugs.

Over tinny racket from the ear buds draped on his shoulder, a goldfinch called *per-chick-er-ee*. He shut off the device the better to hear the surround sound bird symphony. The anxieties over his career and doubts about his ability to parent dissolved. A feeling of serenity hidden for decades surged through his veins. All at once, the meaning of the word “evensong” became clear. Shoving the player into his pocket, he allowed the gathering peace to take a firm hold of his heart and soul. Lightning bugs flickered and danced above the hedgerow along the fence, beckoning him forward along The Path.

“Cassie! Cassie, where are you? Come in for dinner!” A mom’s voice called into the night as he passed a regal Victorian. The woman waved, and he lifted a hand in reply.

A sign hung over The Path: Sweet Dreams and Flying Machines – Ask about Our Stay and Fly package.

“Cassie!” The screen door slammed and the woman disappeared into the house.

He glanced up and down the lane but didn’t see a child, so he strolled on. How would he handle the day-to-day routine of child care alone? *Does an almost sixteen-year-old need anything besides a debit card and a car to drive?* He shook his head. *I am crazy to even consider this.*

He ambled on, admiring pristine houses of varied styles, their lots stitched together by the pathway into a quilt of generations old and young.

Brick colonials, lattice-adorned Victorians and regal French provincials graced well-maintained lots generous enough for swimming pools and tennis courts. Further along, he passed modest ranches, Craftsmen and colonials with swing sets, tree houses and barbecue pits in fertilized and manicured lawns.

Other walkers greeted Jeff with waves or smiles. Worried he'd be recognized and detained, he ducked his head, glancing up when he thought The Path clear. After three or four groups passed without making any movement to ask for an autograph or gush over his latest blockbuster, he relaxed, lifted his chin and allowed himself to enjoy the beauty of the enchanting alleyway through this unusual community.

Dogs barked at him, more in friendly hellos than warnings. A housecat followed for a while, slinking under the orange and yellow crepe blossoms of a chrysanthemum bed at the fence line. The gray tabby kept pace with him for a few houses, then turned homeward, pouncing at moths and shadows.

Among the houses with manicured lawns and weeded vegetable gardens, one property obtruded like an ugly word in a beautiful poem. A miserable grove of trees and sprangly shrubs blocked Jeff's view. In the dusky light through the wooded fortress, he almost missed the faded sign advertising the mystery structure. Something about the forlorn blight on the otherwise enchanting lane required further exploration.

He tried a gate latch, but rust froze the mechanism. He glanced up and down the Path, tested his weight on the top rail, kicked off, and cleared the fence into weedy overgrowth. Brushing his hands on his jeans, he ducked and shoved through twisted forsythias that scraped his back and neck like yellow claws.

Overturned and broken flagstones through knee-high weeds and wind-blown trash suggested a forgotten walkway to a cavernous porch. He moved closer and ducked under an overhanging branch. He emerged into an opening, finger-combed a lock of hair from his line of sight and straightened. A gently sloping roof, its exposed rafters supported by massive square columns, extended over a porch that disappeared down each side of the house. A flock of crows took off from the rafters, squawking and fussing. The remains of an early century Craftsman bungalow lurked beneath wild branches and tangled morning glory vines.

Despite the rubble and neglect, Jeff sensed noble grace beneath the smothering vines, trash, and broken shingles. He tested the bottom step, but an unwelcoming creak warned him the buckling boards would surely swallow him into a pit of dry rot and rodent nests. He backed down and worked his way through shoulder high grasses to the street side and gazed up, admiring the classic architecture.

The style stirred memories of another leaded-glass front door in a neighborhood far away and long ago. The "For Sale" sign squeaked on a nail near the curb and returned him to the present.

Fading light encouraged him along, so he fought through the brambles and jumped the rails. He cast a lingering gaze at the blemish, a stain on an otherwise beautiful fabric of the neighborhood that wedged into his soul with every turn of its idyllic Path. Shadows crawled toward him and a firefly's beacon flashed—a miniscule lighthouse to the lost ship of his soul.

He moved with urgency now, ideas forming as he strode. Lost in the possibilities and wondering if he should pray for guidance, he rounded a bend and looked up at a soaring steeple. Brilliant white against the orange sky, lingering sunrays illuminated it like heavenly klieg lights. The irony of stumbling on the building straight out of a location shoot book at the same moment he had a profound desire to pray hit him. He approached, wondering if the doors would be open on a weeknight and lights from basement windows answered his question.

The door into the parking lot opened and several clusters of people emerged, talking and laughing. Jeff decided to move on before anyone recognized him.

Too late. Emmett John looked up from the knot of people. "Hey, Jeff! Come on over, let me introduce you to some of these folks."

Jeff found the gate and went in.

After Emmett introduced him to the others, he explained their meeting. "Did you hear about the fire at the animal rescue farm?"

"Yeah, I did. Was anyone hurt?"

"Some of the animals died, but no humans were harmed."

"Kind of an emergency, then? How can I help?"

"We're organizing a talent show," Sam continued. "Maggie's gotta feed dozens of animals until her insurance kicks in." Sam's face animated into a broad smile. "Would you consider being our emcee? We could attract more viewers with a celebrity."

Jeff thought a moment. "Wouldn't mind an excuse to hang around a few more days. If it works into my schedule. When are you planning to have it?"

From the street side, a voice over a loudspeaker interrupted. "May I have your attention?" An officer spoke from a patrol unit. "A small child is missing. Her name is Cassie Sims. Please be on the lookout for a six-year-old, African American girl dressed in shorts and a blue t-shirt. Search parties are organizing at the Sweet Dreams Bed and Breakfast. Everyone's help is needed."

CHAPTER TEN

Henry wrestled the VW van onto the rutted dirt road from the tarmac and shuddered to a stop on a patch of mashed grass. The junker spluttered, coughed, and died. The two patchy-coated dogs, ribs bumpy under mangy coats, clambered to their feet and squeaked feeble warnings. Pathetic yips skidded into choking yelps as they reached the ends of rusty chains. Their ears sagged as Henry maneuvered the heap beyond their reach.

"What happened? You call her?" Max teetered in a dilapidated beach chair, dressed in stained coveralls unzipped to the waist, and a wife beater t-shirt. The two-man tent at his elbow flapped tattered shreds in the late afternoon breeze. He drained a long-necked beer and clinked the empty bottle onto a growing pile. "Did you scare her any?"

He squeaked open a cooler lid, swirled his hand through melted ice and held up two dripping bottles. "Brew?"

"Yeah, she's scared all right." Henry squatted on the cooler lid and unscrewed his top in one motion. "We're not gonna have any trouble with her, nosirree."

"Did you pick up some chow?"

"No. Uh..."

"You went all the way into town and didn't git us... Gimme the keys."

Max pushed up out of the rickety aluminum, swayed, and fell backward into the chair's plastic webbing that popped through, his butt sagging to the dirt. He leered over his knees and shoved the bottle through three days' growth, took a long drag and belched.

"Wish I had me some of them muffins we had at the park 'at nice lady give us." Henry smacked his lips.

"If wishers were horses."

"What's 'at mean? Wishers were horses?"

"Don't you never shut up? You still got some of them smokes we swiped?"

One of the dogs yawned and whined.

"Shush!" Max snarled. "It look like we have any food?"

Henry took a box of cigarettes out of his suit jacket and tossed it to Max. "Why'd you tie them mutts up, anyway? If we let 'em go, they could eat rabbits. Or something." He watched them circle, scratch dirt and lie down, their chains tangling and knotting with each revolution.

"They'll come in handy, I done told you. How do you put your pants on, anyway? Your mama didn't git you no brains, I swear."

"Leave my mama outta this." Henry jutted his chin. "I ain't stupid. I kin hold my own."

"This is how it goes down." Max flicked a rusty lighter until it flamed up. He took a drag, and the smoke mingled with his evil plan. "We scare the old bag so she moves off and you and your brother git her property. Ain't that what you want?"

"Yeah. But what if she won't scare easy?"

"Plan B, idiot."

"What's 'at?" Henry squirmed, his voice up a notch. "I ain't gonna hurt nobody."

"I'm workin' on the details, gimme a break." Max's annoyed energy propelled him to launch from the chair and he stood up, the metal arms clinging to his bottom. "Besides you want to show your brother you can handle the business, don't you?"

He wrestled the chair loose to fling it away. The aluminum arm tangled in his sleeve, the chair banging a shin. With a curse, stamp, and kick, it flung free. His coveralls puddled around his ankles.

"Uh..." Henry eyed the stocky man's boxers.

"Don't just stand there!" Max spat and tugged at the holey shorts. "Gimme a pair a jeans or something."

Henry crawled into the tent and tossed out a wad of greasy denim while Max sat in the dirt and fought the coveralls past his pair of Brogan's. With a grunt and tug, the heavy shoes gave up their stinky grip on dingy tube socks. Dragging the pants up, he groped for a zipper on the inside out pants and shuffled toward the van. "I'm gonna git us some chow. You comin'?"

"Lemme change outta this preacher suit."

"Where'd you get that anyway?"

"It were my dad's. Do I look perfessional?" Henry turned back to the thin, hopeful-eyed hounds. "We gonna get them dogs somethin' to eat?"

"You can get 'em anythin' you find, but I ain't givin' you no cash. I hear the dumpster-dive blue-hic-plate special's all the rage. Hurry up, I might eat one of 'em if you don't quit lazing about."

"Max, why don't we sleep in that garage over there instead of this ole tent? It leaks."

He flashed yellowed teeth and spit a little down his chin stubble. "You want, we could go live in that mansion you got."

Henry studied Max's soiled t-shirt, the armpits stained to the waist, and the week old growth on his chin. "Nah, Stan's not too friendly these days. But he'll like it when you help me git that woman to move so we can have her land. Then you can meet him. I'll tell him you helped me."

Max dug at a tooth with a thumbnail. "Guess I can wait. You wanna break inna that shack, do it. I'm sleepin' outdoors. Suits me. I can git away in a hurry if I need to." He swiped the keys off the cooler lid and teetered toward the van, hiking up his backward pants that hung gangster style over his boxers. "Let's go."

Henry lunged for the keys and hopped one-legged, quick changing into his own dungarees. "I'll drive. It's my car. 'Sides, you cain't even put your pants on frontwards." He stuck the keys between his teeth, pulled up the zip, threw his shoes in and climbed into the driver's seat while Max fumbled to correct his wardrobe malfunction.

The dogs watched, heads cocked and whining.

Henry jumped down, unhitched the chains and opened the van's slider. "Git in, you!" He shoved the door but it stuck open a crack, stuck on the slider. "Dang door. Stay in there!" He cautioned the mutts, climbed in, re-started the heap, and they corkscrewed over deep ruts to the street. A flock of sheep grazing near the fence startled and scattered, their lambs bleating and leaping like furry gazelles across the pasture.

"Them dogs could take down one of them lambs for dinner on the way back." Max thumbed back at them. He took a long last drag, then tossed his butt out the window, leaned back and closed his eyes. "Wake me up when you find us a good mark. But go to Franklin City. We don't wanna bust our cover in Berryville yet."

At the place on The Path where big weeds grew tall, Cassie knew she should turn around and go home. A quick peek into the workshop and she'd known that her dad would be distracted with his latest model all night if Mommy didn't call him in. She stepped out onto The Path. She wanted to show her animal friends the ow-y she got. Then she could run back home before Mommy even knew she was gone.

In a few more skips, the fence around the horse stables ended, and she spotted one of the buildings near Miz Maggie's barn. She leaned against a fence and rubbed her sore leg.

She looked into the pen. Nothing. Where'd they go? *Wait a minute.* A glance up showed the sheep crunching hay behind a different gate than when Mommy brought her the other day.

"What are you doing here? Why aren't you in the big barn?" She tried to touch a baby lamb's moist black nose, but chicken wire kept her hand away. Pulling up onto the bottom rail she leaned down. *Still can't reach.*

Curious muzzles sniffed and nuzzled. Cassie swung a leg over and plopped down into the soft dirt. Her leg made her wait a minute. Drat, Leo's sharp tooth! The excited sheep rushed forward and she fell over backward. Noses snuffled over her, but when they realized she didn't have anything, they wandered away.

Her bandage flapped open, and Cassie sat down, leaning against a little building to mash on the flappy end to make it stick.

She gave up and reached for a wisp of hay and held it out to a lamb. "C'mere, come get it." The lamb startled, reared and twirled, bumped its mother. Curious, he turned back and sniffed at Cassie's offering. He nibbled at it then lay down next to the warmth of Cassie's legs.

"Be still little lamby and go to thleep." Cassie stroked the downy head and hummed. Soon, her lullaby made her own eyelids flutter closed and her head nodded onto her chest.

Grace pulled a spoon through preserves bubbling in a large stovetop Dutch oven and lifted it to her lips. She inhaled the explosion of cloves, tart berries, and peppery-sweet aromas that mingled together and blew across the steam. She tipped the contents into her mouth and added a dash of cinnamon.

Leaving the pot to simmer, she removed a bag of fresh lettuce from a refrigerator drawer and snapped several crisp leaves into ceramic bowls. Juice trickled down Grace's elbow as she sliced them into wedges deep red on green, like the poppies blooming in the town park's lush green grass. A dash of vinaigrette, and the salad joined bowls on a tray Grace already prepared with utensils and spinach muffins, one for Mark, one for herself.

She carried the tray into the den where Mark had kicked off his shoes and melted into his leather recliner. Through the sparkling panes of a wide bay window, the sun sank behind the trees beyond The Path.

Grace settled into her favorite corner of the sectional. Mark clicked the remote. Vanna turned a batch of lit letters on the muted television screen while he asked the blessing.

"Have you worked out the hospital schedule for Founder's Day?" Grace asked after the amens.

"I'm splitting the day with Phil. He's willing to work so he can have Labor Day off to move his son to college." Mark bit into a butter slathered muffin. "Yum, honey. You making plans?"

Grace caught him up to her latest volunteer activities. The Founders Committee recently announced this year's special project would be the long overdue "Path Restoration and Repair Day." Founder's Day in Cherryvale almost equaled the Fourth of July in activities and festivities. After working together all day, the Valers threw backyard barbecues and then gathered at the Park for a concert and fireworks.

"Since we're on The Path, we'll be in the thick of things this year, so I thought we should offer our yard for a resting area and fire up the grill." Grace watched Mark's reaction.

"That's big."

"And I'd like to invite Rose, I've gotten to know her better since I've started riding lessons." Then added, "and possibly Jeff" that hinted the melody of a question.

"Jeff." Mark paused mid-chew. "The fellow who washes our windows?"

"No, his name's Ted. Jeff Field. The actor from *The Scrapbook*."

"Ah." Mark sipped his merlot. "Rose and Jeff. You're not match-making by any chance?"

"Me?" Grace feigned interest in Wheel. "A new lease on life!" She guess-pointed her fork at the puzzle then slumped against the couch when the contestant from Dayton spun on "bankrupt." "Too bad. I'll clean up." She uncurled her legs and jumped up.

Mark waited for her to set his bowl on the tray, and when she reached across for his napkin, pulled her onto his lap.

"Why don't you let Rose pick her own men?" He pulled her close and snuffled into her neck.

"I just think it would be a nice gesture. Their filming's extended because of Tiffany, and it would be sad if he sat all alone while we have a party." Grace giggled as Mark munched on her earlobe. "And, what's wrong with seeing if maybe he and Rose might hit it off. She hasn't lived here that long and might enjoy making a new friend."

"I thought Rose was seeing Greg McCoy, didn't they go to that Sunday school social a few months back?"

"I think they ate pie together at the same table, but I don't think there are sparks."

"You're going to get some sparks going, all right." Mark found a ticklish spot under her ribs.

Grace giggled, squirmed, and stood up with the tray, padding in her house slippers toward the kitchen. "I think it's the friendly thing to do, and if they hit it off, then they hit it off."

"What about Maggie?" Mark called as she disappeared around the doorframe and she stuck her head back in.

"We can invite her, but she's taking a trailer-full of animals to the park. She'll be too busy. So you're okay with a party?"

"All right." Mark picked up the remote. "I'll flip burgers so you can throw darts, er, arrows, my little cupid."

After dinner, Mark begged off for bed, his morning shift having caught up to him.

Grace flicked off the television, put on her reading glasses and picked up the mystery she'd been reading. Just as the cat's meows were about to inspire a solution to the murder, the phone rang.

Grace flipped the book a double-tumble onto the floor and reached to pick it up before the bedroom extension woke Mark. "Hello?"

"Cassie's missing," Carolyn skipped pleasantries, her voice shrill. "Sheriff's organizing search parties. Can you help?"

Grace slipped her shoes back on, jotted a note on the kitchen chalkboard in case Mark woke up looking for her, grabbed a flashlight, and dashed out to her bike.

Grace pedaled up to Sweet Dreams and leaned her bike against the porch railing. She climbed the stairs, the screen door burst open and

Jeff, Emmett, and Hank emerged, checking flashlights, headed for the street.

"Hey, Grace, we were going to join a search party." Jeff pulled keys out of his pocket. "We don't know the town, but we can follow directions."

"Wait." Grace started up the steps. "I'll run in and tell Carolyn I'm going with you."

"We'll be in my rental car." He pointed. "The SUV at the curb."

Inside, Grace hugged and assured a worried Carolyn, then trotted down the sidewalk and climbed in Jeff's passenger seat. He introduced her to Hank and Emmett, and they filled her in on the search details.

"Her parents said their safety password is 'Boogie Woogie.'" Jeff pulled into the road.

"Clever." Grace slid her seat belt across her lap. "How long has she been missing?"

"Now that I think about it." Jeff checked traffic. "I went for a walk about two hours ago and I heard Carolyn calling her for dinner. That was around six. Where's the elementary school? They assigned us the playground to search."

"Tiffany, please try and eat." Holly lifted a warming cover off a plate of dark grey and light brown lumps and shuddered before setting it back down. "I'll get you something from the cafeteria. I need coffee, anyway."

"Go back to your trailer," Tiffany mumbled. "Just make sure Leo's okay before you go to bed."

Holly hesitated leaving Tiffany alone. "We were wondering if your mom has called to check on you."

"Why does she care? I'm not her money train any more so I'm of no use to her."

"Oh." Holly tried a new tack. "So, what's with the tattoo?"

"Did you see it?" Tiffany checked, pulled the bed sheets closer.

"No, the nurse told me and Grace—"

"So much for privacy. I do have an image to uphold, you know."

"She didn't mean anything. Grace knows everyone around here, but she won't tell your secret and neither will I."

Tiffany lay silent for a beat. "It's nothing." She rolled over and shoved the sheet just below her waist to reveal a tiny red and green diamond shape with a tail that hooked like a cat's at the end.

"Does the kite mean anything or was it a drunk-pick?" Holly knew plenty of people with mystery tatts from wild nights.

"I wasn't drunk." Tiffany growled, then her tone gentled, the first indication there was a real girl behind the magazine cover facade. "When I was little, I saw my dad once at a park." She drew in a long breath. "They were...he was...with another little girl. Flying kites." She shoved a fist up her cheek and turned aside. "My mom started crying and made me throw away our picnic. We left." Tiffany stared through the window into the parking lot dotted with streetlights. "Later I heard her tell my grandma she'd seen him."

"Did she know you found out?"

"If she did, she never had the decency to tell me. Better that I grow up a bastard child than risk her embarrassment outing me, I guess."

Holly didn't speak at first, unsure whether she made it worse or if she helped Tiffany uncover memories she needed to share. She decided to take the plunge since the worst was out. "So you got the kite to remind you of him."

"Yeah, on my butt cheek so I can keep it all behind me. Get it?" Tiffany's voice resumed her edge of sarcasm. She pulled the sheet to her chin and closed her eyes.

"You rest for awhile." Holly moved toward the door. "I'll go check on Leo."

On the patio where cell phones were permitted, Holly dialed Jeff's number to fill him in, but he answered with his own news.

"Hi, Hol. Did you hear? The little girl that Tiffany yelled at on set today is missing. We're not far from the hospital now. We'll come pick you up if you want to help with the search."

A painful scrape across Cassie's thigh woke her in time to see the ewe jumping over. A tiny, sharp hoof gouged her leg. She tried to stand, but the lamb, panicking to keep up with its mother, bumped her against the rough boards.

Cassie looked around, hiccupping and puffing to catch her breath through the pain. Tears welled in her eyes, and as she put weight on her good leg, the searing pain lightning-shot up her thigh and she crumpled, her blood-soaked little hand trying to cover the gaping flesh. The crimson flow oozed between her fingers and trickled down to her ankle.

She pulled herself up and squished toward the gate as her sneaker filled with blood. A car rumbled past. "Help! Mommy!" Cassie watched an ugly van pop and jump over ruts like a porpoise she'd seen at the ocean one time. Her heart sank as the car made a loud noise and swerved onto the road, a tail-light flashing red at her before it disappeared. Her heart hurt along with her leg. She missed her mommy's reassuring hug.

She looked up for the sun, but it had gone to bed while she slept. Boy, was she going to get in trouble. Cassie scrambled to her feet and limped over to find the gate's latch. Her fingers fumbled with the lock, different from the one at their house. She jiggled, pushing and rattling it, but it stuck. The lambs and sheep bleated, shoving against her, urging their new flock-mate to open the gate and let them out. She tried to climb over the fence, but her leg hurt too bad.

One hand on her boo-boo, the other on the latch, she pushed and jiggled. "Thtupid gate, open!"

Cassie felt a tingle in her nose, like when she tried her daddy's hot taco sauce. This was different, more like when you blow out birthday candles and the stink goes up your nose. Sure enough, smoke seeped between the rafters of the shed behind her.

"Let me out!" She kicked the stubborn wooden door.

Sobbing, she thought of her daddy's calming words last time she got scared. *Take it easy, Cassie.* Remembering his deep, rich voice soothed her. *You can do it.*

The lambs looked at her with wide, brown eyes.

"Don't worry guys. I'll get you out of here..." Taking a moment to feel for the latch, she twisted it, testing a little piece to see if it would move.

With every jiggle and rattle, the sheep bumped her more. Pain shot fire, hip to toe. One lamb's wool looked red and smeared. Smoke stung her eyes and they watered. Maybe her mommy wouldn't be mad if she saved the lambs from fire. Even if it was after her bedtime. That gave courage enough.

Once more, she tugged at the metal slider, and this time it loosened at her touch. The heavy gate swung open. The herd surged over her, their white mass like angry storm clouds gathering before a storm, ramming her head against the gate. She staggered, pushed forward by their momentum and they trotted off into the night, bleating, and scared.

Steps away from the burning building, Cassie fell in a tiny heap, unconscious, and bleeding.

Sweet Dreams and Flying Machines Bed and Breakfast bustled as a makeshift command post. Valers made sandwiches in the kitchen, others relayed information on cell phones, and the entire VBS committee prayed for the little girl's safe return in a corner of the sun porch.

Carolyn Sims busied herself making coffee and food in the kitchen where Sheriff sat at her table, having stopped by to give her an update on the search teams. Mid-sip in a well-deserved cup of coffee, his shoulder-mounted radio squawked.

"Another fire at Maggie's. I'm sorry, Carolyn." He drained the last drops and settled the Stetson on his head. "I've got to go over there. One more thing happens in this town and I don't know what we'll do. We're stretched thin now."

"Shut off the power at the main! The lines are sparking!" Sheriff Melton twisted a knob and sprinted toward the flames dragging a garden hose, directing the stream toward the engulfed shed.

Spitting and hissing, the flames smoked and curled, dying back. Sheriff watched for flare-ups while Maggie rounded up stray sheep and coaxed them into the enclosure. The roof still smoldered, but the fence stood untouched. Maggie examined the rusty latch for clues how the creatures managed to shove through.

"Maggie." Sheriff interrupted her thoughts as he wound the hose into a neat coil. "This place is obviously a hazard. I want you to shut off the electricity to all your outbuildings until you can get them re-wired." His voice lowered. "And I'm shutting you down for customers until that happens."

"I had the electrician out after the first one burned. He said that it wasn't electrical," Maggie pleaded. But with the smell of smoke still heavy in the air, her argument fell like the ashes that floated to earth around them.

"Is there someone who wants you out of business? Or worse?"

Maggie stared at the scorched shell of a shed. "What business? I haven't even had the official opening."

Something snuffled behind them and she flicked on her flashlight. "Did you hear that?" She flicked the beam over weeds beyond the corral.

"Wait, I have a stronger light." Don switched on the searchlight mounted to his car door and swung it around to sweep the yard, fence and gate.

They followed as the beam skimmed and skipped over and through the grasses around the truck.

"There! What's that?" Maggie dashed over. She knelt beside a red sneaker poking through the weeds and Don focused the light. "It's Cassie Sims!" She leaned over the pale child. "She's breathing."

"Don't move her." He knelt beside her. "Cassie, can you hear me?"

Cassie's eyelids fluttered and she looked up. "W-where's my mommy?" The little girl leaned on an elbow trying to sit up. "Oh, my head!"

Maggie caught her before she fell back into the grass.

"Let's get her to the hospital." Don carefully picked her up and followed Maggie to the cab.

"Buckle up and I'll lay her across your lap."

"Shh, kiddo." Maggie surveyed the leg wound. "This cut's pretty bad."

Don tossed a box of gauze from his emergency kit to Maggie. "Hold this firmly over that leg wound." He circled the truck at a trot, jammed the keys in the ignition, the truck roared to life and he slammed it into reverse.

Maggie pressed the towel down but the gap in Cassie's leg oozed open with the jiggling of the car's motion. She held on to stop the flow as the sheriff swung the patrol unit onto the road.

"Hurry Don, the bleeding's started again."

He reached down to flick a switch on the dashboard. "Hang on! I'm going lights and sirens all the way." The wailing sound of distress once again filled the Vale.

"They found Cassie. Mom!" Carson jumped up and down in the

kitchen. "They're taking Cassie to the hospital. But they found her!" He waved the phone in the air.

"The hospital?" Carolyn's shoulder slammed into the doorframe, her hand over her mouth.

Abby Madison wrapped an arm around her shoulder. "C'mon, I'll drive you."

Carolyn grabbed her purse but stopped to address the group of volunteers. "Thank you all so much! Thank you for praying, searching and..." She hugged her son at the door. "Carson, you stay here. I'll call you just as soon as we know how Cassie is. Please keep praying, everyone."

"They found her at Maggie's, Carl." Carolyn's breaths weighed heavy with a mother's concern over the cell connection. "They're taking her to the emergency room. Apparently she's hit her head or something. The dispatcher didn't tell me much."

"Thank the Lord! Let me tell everyone here at the schoolyard..."

Exclamations of praise went up as Carl relayed the news. "I'll meet you there." He pushed the end button and uttered a quick prayer of thanks.

"They found Cassie!" Grace snapped her cell phone shut. "She'd wandered over to Maggie's and got hurt, so they're taking her to the ER." She relayed the news to her search committee while they hurried back to the car. "And, there was another fire there tonight."

"That must have been the sirens." Jeff steered the rented Suburban toward the bypass. "Anyone want to be dropped off first? Otherwise, I'm headed for the hospital."

Grace, Holly, Emmett, and Hank agreed they were hungry, tired and dirty, but couldn't go home without checking on Cassie's condition.

The glass doors whooshed open, and they stepped into a waiting area packed with volunteers from the other search teams.

Grace wound her way through the crowd and found Sheriff Don. "What's the news?"

"The fire didn't appear to do her any harm, thank the Lord." Don swiped his head with his forearm. "Carolyn and Carl already went back to see her. She had a pretty nasty head wound and a gash down her leg."

"I'll see what I can find out." Grace eyed the Employees Only doorway.

"Hey, Ms. Harkins," a nurse greeted her.

"How's little Cassie?" Grace asked. "Are her parents with her?"

The nurse glanced toward the mob and spoke formally. "Unless you're family, I cannot share that information." Then she leaned forward and pretended to look for something on the counter next to Grace. "They're giving her blood and suturing a wound on her leg."

"Thanks, hon, I'll keep out of your way." Grace stepped back and into the waiting room as Maggie hung up a wall phone next to the vending machines. With a deep inhale, she made her approach.

The smell of smoke hung around Maggie like Pig Pen's dust cloud. "Are you all right? Don told me what happened."

"Know that little utility shed that's at the end of the lane?" Maggie wiped a sleeve across her brow, smearing soot and grime into her frowzled ruby tresses. "All the sheep were in there from the last fire. When we got there, they were loose. I guess Cassie opened the gate somehow. That latch sticks, I've been meaning to replace it. I might have lost them if she hadn't let them out."

"What was she doing there by herself?" Grace patted down her pockets, wishing she carried a hankie to offer Maggie. Nothing but a lone house key and her cell phone in her back pocket. "How'd she get hurt?"

"Hit her head on something, maybe the sheep pushed her over in their panic to get away from the heat. Also got a nasty cut." Maggie gave a curt slash across her own thigh to demonstrate.

"Another fire?" Grace automatically lifted an arm around her, but Maggie moved away, headed for the glass exit doors.

"Got to get those sheep rounded up before they scatter all over the county. Don's taking me home."

"Do you want me to come help?"

"I called Rose. She's meeting me over there with her new dog. He's a herder, I guess."

Grace fought over her mix of emotions. A small part of her felt glad Maggie could call on Rose. The rest hurt that she chose someone else. She watched Maggie join the sheriff as he finished with his report to the triage nurse. They left through the glass doors without a wave goodbye.

"Thanks for your help." Grace saluted Jeff, Emmett and Hank on their way out.

"You need a ride home?" Jeff held up his keys.

Instinct compelled her to stick around. "Think I'll stay a bit longer. Thanks anyway." They exited as well, and Grace turned in time to see Carolyn gesture from the swinging doors.

"I was hoping you were here."

She hurried over to hug the surprisingly calm woman. "How is she?"

"Groggy, but she'll want to see you. Lost some blood and bumped her head, but she's making sense and seems perky even through the medications."

"Has Mark been called? Do you want me to call him?" Grace followed Carolyn through the swinging doors. "He'll make sure everything's being handled right."

"Don't wake him up. I'm happy with everyone's care. Abby'll stay with Carson until we get home." Carolyn led Grace through a gap in curtains surrounding Cassie's bed. "Look who's here, Sissie."

Grace's chest caught at the sight of precious little Cassie in the big bed hooked to tubes and hoses. "Hey, honey, you gave us quite a scare." She laid a hand on a tiny brown wrist.

Cassie's dark brown lashes fluttered up at Grace. "I helped Miz Maggie's theep get out so they wouldn't burn up."

"Yes, you did." Grace caught Carl's eye. "You holding up okay?"

"I am, now we found our little runaway." Carl's tone grew stern.

"I'm starting to side with Maggie. We just need our town to get back to normal. I was scared—"

"Carl." Carolyn shot him a warning glance. "We agreed to talk about that later."

"You scared all of us, honey. I'm so glad you're okay." Grace pecked Cassie's cheek and lingered near her ear, whispering. "I'm going home, now. But in the morning I'm making you a batch of your favorite muffins. Octopus flavored with puppy kibble, right?"

Cassie managed a weak giggle. "No, thilly. Blueberry."

"Of course." She rolled her eyes, her hands palms up. "I am being silly, I'd never forget my girl's fave."

Cassie's expression grew serious. "Miz Grathe."

"What?"

"I thorry I made you a-scared."

"We're just glad you're okay." Grace stroked Cassie's arm. "But don't do it again, all right?"

"If Tiffany yells at me again, I'll tell my daddy."

Grace glanced at Carl and back at Cassie. "Is that why you ran off, because Tiffany lost her temper?"

"Yeth." A single tear crawled down Cassie's cheek and onto the pillow.

"Well, that was wrong of her." Grace shook her head. "And don't think it was your fault in any way."

"I know what we can do."

"What's that, honey?"

"We should pray for her."

"Oh, Cassie, you're so right." Grace wished she could grab up the fragile little body and squeeze, but settled for cradling tiny hands in her own. "Your mommy and daddy must be so proud of you."

Grace hugged Carl and Carolyn goodbye and stepped out of the enclosure. Carl followed her out to the swinging ER doors. "Thanks again. I know you organized the search parties."

"Nonsense. When I got there, everyone was already in motion."

Grace paused. "If you want to cancel our plans for tomorrow, under the circumstances, I totally understand."

"I think it'll be fine if I leave for an hour or so. I'll let you know." Carl's white teeth flashed in a quick smile. "You're not getting out of this again, Mith Grathe." He mimicked his daughter.

She wandered back into the waiting room, now almost deserted, debated going home, but Cassie's words prompted her to take a left turn. The elevator door opened and she stepped on and rode the elevator to the much quieter second floor.

Tiptoeing down the hallway past darkened patient rooms, she stopped at Tiffany's door and nodded at the security guard.

He motioned for her to go on in, but she hesitated. She'd intended to pray silently for the girl and then leave, but a bedside lamp was on and, high on the wall, the television flickered.

She tapped and leaned in. "Mind if I come in?"

The slender lump underneath the covers reminded Grace of her kids playing before bedtime when they were little. They loved to stuff Wendy's bed with pillows, then when Grace went in to kiss them goodnight, she'd pretend not to know where they were until they jumped up, laughing at their joke. "Here we are, Mommy!"

Somehow she doubted this lump would end up a giggling mass of tickles.

"Tiffany?" Grace stepped closer. "You asleep?"

The sheet lowered and eyes the color of a tropical sea peered out. Tiffany muffled from beneath the cover. "You're up late."

"We were looking for Cassie, but we found her, praise the Lord."

"Who?"

"Mind if I sit?" The evening's events caught up to Grace, a freight train delivering a boxcar of exhaustion. She picked up the remote from the wheeled bed tray, muted the late night chatter, and rested on the edge of the bed. "Remember that little girl from the shoot? Had a hard time staying awake?"

Tiffany's eyes narrowed and she stared at the television.

"Somehow she ended up at a farm off The Path—my friend, Maggie's place. Not that far from her house, but she's just a little thing, and she was all by herself. She got hurt when a fire broke out."

"Fire?" Tiffany's gaze slid to a vinyl chair under the window. "So this little girl. What happened to her?"

"They're working on her downstairs in the E.R."

Tiffany rested her bandaged wrist across a pillow on her lap. Grace studied her face for a reaction.

"Tiffany? Can't you say anything?"

"What do you want me to say?"

"I thought you might have felt a little... something for her, since..."

White-tipped nails tugged on the sheet and Tiffany slid down and rolled sideways in her linen cocoon. "I didn't tell her to run away and get herself hurt."

Grace studied the wall of white sheet Tiffany held between them. "When I cause someone's feelings to be hurt, I can't rest until I apologize."

"Well, I'm not you."

Grace dragged the vinyl chair over and sat where she could see Tiffany's face. "How are you feeling?"

"Like you care."

"I do care. I wouldn't have come in to see you if I didn't care."

Tiffany didn't stir for a moment, then she peeked up at Grace through thick, dark lashes, her eyes red-rimmed and puffy.

Grace's heart melted. "Tiffany, I know when a person tries suicide, they send a psychiatrist by. Have you been able to speak to one, yet?"

Tiffany slid her bandage under the pillow. "I didn't try to off myself. I told everybody. It was an accident. The shower door has a sharp edge."

"Okay. You didn't try to 'off yourself.' But you did blow up at the set today. You can't fool me on that one."

"Why should I talk to you? I don't know you."

"I've got lots of experience with teens. I was a high school teacher for over twenty years. And I've got grown kids." Reminded Grace of a job interview. "And I won't go blabbing anything. I know you want to keep your privacy."

Tiffany lay silent for several more minutes. Finally, the white sheet fluttered as Tiffany took a jerky breath. "You know what a stage mother is?"

"It's not a good thing to be, I know that much. Is that what yours was like?"

"If they wrote Stage Mothers for Dummies, she'd be Chapter One."

"So you were a commodity to her."

No response.

"You know. A product."

"I know what a commodity is."

"And to a stage mother, all she cared about was having a famous daughter and your earning potential."

"Yep."

"What about your father?"

"Not part of the picture."

Grace shook her head, took a box of Kleenex and offered it.

"You wanted to know."

"Is there something about this movie role that's upsetting you?" Grace handed her a tissue so she'd stop wiping her runny nose on the bed sheet.

"Nah. A gig's a gig."

"You're tired, so I should go. If you want to talk..." Grace paused, but Tiffany shut her eyes and rolled back toward the wall.

Guess I need to pray for two hurting little girls tonight. She started to tiptoe out, then, a small voice made her pause.

"Grace?"

"Yes?"

"I want to know how that little girl does, you know. When she's better. Can you call me?"

"I sure will, honey. I sure will."

CHAPTER TWELVE

Grace chatted with the guard outside Tiffany's room for a few minutes, catching up on his kids she'd taught several years back. She checked the time and pressed the elevator button, rode up and got out on the admin floor. Almost five A.M. and Mark, even though he was chief of staff, still insisted on taking his share of early morning shifts. He would have arrived while she was with Tiffany. Unless there was a logjam of patients in the ER, he started the day in his office looking over the previous shift reports.

The outer office overhead lights were still off and the computers asleep as she tiptoed past his secretary's empty desk. She stood in his doorway for a moment and watched her handsome husband scribbling in a patient's chart. "I thought everything was digitized and recorded these days."

Mark looked up at her. "Hey! Come on in." He replaced the fountain pen in its holder and closed the file. "Still have to sign my name the old fashioned way." He moved to peck her on the lips. "I wondered if you were still here." He studied her face. "Still worried about Cassie? They're moving her into Peds."

Grace snuggled into his chest and buried her face in his white lab coat. "You can't make this stuff up."

Mark squeezed her in a bear hug and rested his cheek against the top of her head. "Know what you mean. With the paparazzi and autograph seekers camped outside and Cassie's little adventure, we're a-twitter in here too. I had to arrange for more security, so my month's budget is seriously strained. Want coffee? Stale and bitter, like the doctor ordered." Mark picked up a carafe from his sideboard, already pouring.

"Sure." Grace plopped into a leather visitor chair. "Did you examine Cassie yourself?"

"Yes. She's stitched up and tucked in. She should be all right. It's not like her to go wandering away from home."

"No. She was at the wrong end of a Tiffany meltdown." Grace inspected the framed degrees on the wall behind Mark's desk alongside family pictures. The mom inside made a mental note to bring in updated pictures of Wendy and Ian.

"What's got you so thoughtful?" Mark handed her the Styrofoam cup and sat in the chair next to her.

"Maybe Maggie was right. Ever since the production hit town, things are going wrong. Now Carl's siding with her as well."

"Things go wrong and right every day, Gracie."

"Our kids had a great childhood, didn't they?" Her eyes wandered over the smiling faces of Ian, fly-fishing with his dad, Wendy in the soccer team photo the year Mark coached them to state finals. "So unlike Tiffany's."

"The nurses told me she's wearing out her welcome down there."

"I remember those commercials she was in. Cash cow for her mom from an early age. Then her mother marries and move overseas leaving her alone. Such an odd life. I see a glimmer, but not sure I'm really reaching her."

"I'm sure you'll think of something. Speaking of reaching someone…you talked to Maggie yet?"

"This tastes like spit. I better run." She frowned deep into the watery coffee, then tossed the remnants in his sink and dropped the cup into the wastebasket. "Mind if I drive your car home? I rode with my search team here."

Mark slid his hand in a trouser pocket and held the keys to her, just out of reach.

"Why are you pressuring me?"

"You know I'd never pressure you."

"I don't need Maggie." Grace looked through the curtains where the sunlight crept up into the sky. "I still have my retirement list." She swayed, repressing the urge to hurl.

"What's wrong?"

"I just remembered what I'm doing later."

A grin spread across Mark's face. "Your flying lesson."

"I told Carl we could skip it. Under the circumstances with Cassie and all, we can put it off."

"You've done the cockpit lesson. Already put off your flight three times. Say it, Grace."

"I know." She held up a palm. "Once I understand the dynamics and how everything works, I'll feel more comfortable,"

Mark nodded along with her. "Just like—"

"Riding in a car. So you keep telling me."

Mark continued their well-rehearsed mantra. "And Carl—"

"Is a third generation pilot. He'll take good care of me."

Mark held Grace's shoulders. "I already spoke to Carl and told him that if anything changes with Cassie, we'll patch a message through to him, and you can land and be back in no time. But what Cassie needs is plenty of rest and quiet anyway. Didn't you say you were always jealous of Maggie and her world travels? Now we'll have a chance to do that ourselves. If you wait for me, I'd love to give you a ride and watch you take off."

Grace thought about the attractive possibilities of boats and trains.

"What now?" He tipped her chin up.

"You're right. Even Cassie's braver than I am. She saved the sheep from fire—"

"And flies with her daddy. If a six-year-old—"

Mark's intercom buzzed and a tinny voice crackled through.

"Trauma coming in, pedestrian versus auto, ETA two minutes, EMT's report a bleeder."

"Come here, brown eyes." He kissed her, his coffee breath warm on her cheek, then held her face in his hands. "You've got plenty of brave in you."

"I know what's really behind this pep talk. I should work out what's wrong between me and Maggie."

"Something for your to-do list. Wounds can hide infection unless they're flushed clean."

"We better get you downstairs." Grace leaned into him as they made their way to the hallway.

"C'mon, we can neck in the elevator."

"Rascal."

"Clear!" Carl Sims shouted as the Cessna's propeller kicked over and spun faster in rotation.

In the co-pilot seat on his right, Grace squinched her eyes shut. A white-knuckle ride through a thunderstorm replayed in her head, the last time she'd ever climbed into a barnstormer like this one.

Mark humored Grace's refusal to fly for years. Determined to overcome her anxiety so she could accompany him to medical conventions, or maybe, here's a wild thought, they could take a vacation further away than their customary four-wheels-on-the-ground transportation took them. The day arrived and here she sat, strapped in and ready—or not—to go.

In their first lesson, Carl re-introduced her to flight by explaining the science of aerodynamics. He'd been so thorough, she felt like she could design a plane herself. After that, he taught her to fly one of his own radio-controlled model planes over Cherryvale Park one afternoon. Next they spent an hour taxiing in his airplane around the Cherryvale commuter airport between the hangars and flight line until she became familiar with the sounds, smells and motions.

Eventually, Grace convinced herself the reckless venture might not be life threatening. She announced her readiness to go airborne. Still, she'd spent the hour waiting for Mark praying in the hospital chapel. The trauma patients taken care of, he happily drove her out to the airport between Cherryvale and Franklin City for the early morning flight. As her lungs filled with the warm air lifting off the hot tarmac, her doubts rose again, making her woozy. Maybe she should have gone home to rest.

Mark stood near the airport's general aviation center watching them strap in. She turned her heavy and slightly awkward head, weighed down by the headset, to look for another dose of reassurance. In the tight space, she smacked the glass and skewed the headset over her eye.

"It's a shame Mark can't go up with us," Carl tutted. "He loves a good spin."

"He needs to get back. Just wanted to see me off. Bye, honey!" Grace re-settled the equipment over her ears, then stuck her hand up to the side window and managed a brave wave.

Mark gave her two thumbs-up and flashed her a grin. Her heart beat faster as the propeller whirred. She forced a weak smile and reminded herself to breathe.

Carl maneuvered the Cessna forward and she watched the tip of the wing clear the other planes. They picked up speed, rolling along the blacktop.

Carl switched a dial and Grace could hear other pilots chattering. "You can adjust the volume with that little dial on the side." He motioned to her ear.

She fiddled with the tiny knob.

Carl leaned forward, looked left, right, then pulled out, and they glided along the tarmac for several hundred yards until he braked to a stop.

Her stomach lurched with a glimmer of hope. "Something's wrong and we can't go up?" She glanced at Carl.

"Everything's a go, don't worry. This is where we hold, waiting to take our turn in the sky."

Oily mechanical smells wafted into the warm cockpit and a shudder of nausea wiggled through Grace.

"You need a sick-sack? They're in the pocket next to your seat."

Reluctant to take her eyes off the horizon, Grace felt along the door for the paper bag. "I'm all right." Then she repeated the mantra. "Just like riding in a car."

Grace thought back over her journey leading to this day. "I feel like a tetherball at the end of that rope on the playground," she'd told Mark. "I've been going in the same, predictable circles for years. I want to let go of my tether and fly free."

That's when he'd challenged her to overcome her fear of flying, but she'd resisted until one day at lunch with Maggie.

"You don't have a fear of flying," Maggie told her. "You just want to be in control. No surprises. You've always been like that."

That did it. She could handle Mark's patience, but Maggie's taunts were too much.

Blinking back to the present, she looked over at Carl adjusting knobs and levers. She should remember what they were after his patient explanations, but her mind blanked. "Maybe we should wait. You must be worried about Cassie!" She called, too loud in the sensitive headphone, startling Carl. "Sorry."

"Cassie's doing fine, and so will you." He gave her a reassuring knee pat. "Now let's do this."

She opened her mouth to make another excuse, but caught another glimpse of Mark standing next to his car waiting for their take off. So excited and proud of her, he'd even called Wendy and Ian with the news.

Carl maneuvered the plane into position behind a blue and white twin engine at the end of the taxiway. "We're next." He gestured to the plane turning its nose onto the runway and Grace could hear its engines roar louder. Her armpits conspired against her deodorant. Her salivary glands switched off.

"Remember what that plane is called?" Carl pointed ahead.

"A peeper?"

Carl laughed. "Piper."

"I know what you're doing. Trying to keep my mind busy so I won't worry."

Carl tipped his chin and glanced at her. "I have to admit taking you up will keep my mind off Cassie in that hospital."

"So you are worried. We can go back!"

"No. Carolyn's with her, we're already here." He leaned forward to check the skies once again over the approach path.

"I just hope I don't redecorate the inside of your plane before I finish keeping your mind off her."

Carl's eyebrows shot up, then she grinned at him and his expression relaxed.

Not a bad idea. She pulled out the barf bag and laid it in her lap. The Piper rolled forward, passed them going the other direction, and popped off the tarmac.

Carl spoke into the headphones announcing his intentions, and turned, moving them into position facing the length of the runway.

Grace recalled his detailed explanation since this was an "uncontrolled" commuter airport. Too small for a control tower, she learned the pilots broadcasted their movements to each other when taking off and landing. Still sounded like the place was a wild teenager out of earshot of her parents for the first time. *Uncontrolled indeed. Needs a better term. How about 'Pilot controlled airspace?' Much better.*

She returned focus to the blue and yellow wildflowers blooming along the tarmac. They swayed, innocently. Oblivious of the dangers that lay before her. *If I could sit among them for a few minutes, I could quiet my thrumming heart.* She shut her eyes in a quick prayer to remind herself where her confidence lay. She opened her eyes, Carl's deep voice returned her to the interior of the plane.

"This is where we wait for it to be a safe distance for our take off."

The airplane ahead of them grew smaller as it hurtled up and away from sanity and safety. Alarm surged through her veins, all ground school training and preparation erased from memory. Her tongue stuck to her palate, a final plea for amnesty lodged unspoken in her constricted throat and the moment she'd dreaded for years slammed into reality.

"Off we go!" Carl announced, and pushed forward on the yoke.

The Cessna picked up speed, the stripes on the runway zipping underneath faster and faster. The peaceful flower patch abandoned her. She imagined their delicate waves a final farewell as she hurried to her certain death. Buildings zoomed by. She tried to find Mark, longing to see that reassuring smile one last time. Then the bottom of her world fell away. Darkness bloomed at the corners of her vision and she forced oxygen into her lungs. She focused forward, the windscreen an IMAX on the universe as they flew into familiar blue skies smattered with wispy summer-white clouds.

"We'll be over Cherryvale in a minute." Carl's tinny voice came through her earphones. He adjusted dials and punched buttons on a confusing jumble of knobs and switches she couldn't remember the purpose of to save her life.

The mechanical engine and sickly-sweet fuel smells were gone and she forced herself to breathe fresh air that now flowed from the vents. Her cotton blouse felt cool and light.

Working her leathery tongue loose from the roof of her mouth, she managed, "That'll be nice." Curious to see the ground, she hesitated then moved cautiously to prevent smacking the window again so she could see down.

Miniature cars and trucks sun-glinted like rhinestones on silver-gray ribbons of highway below. The roads wound around, trimming green fields ranging in green hues from cobalt to teal to cadmium.

Grace recognized buildings in her Google-earth-comes-to-life experience and pointed. "There's the high school!" She studied the shapes of the familiar redbrick buildings and the running track inside the football stadium.

"I'm trimming the mix. The engine'll change pitch." Carl adjusted a knob. "No worries, it's all normal. Let's fly over your house."

"That would be fun." Grace peered in the direction of home. Excitement welled, along with the realization that she meant it. She marveled at the sudden confidence she had after only three minutes aloft.

Carl turned the yoke and tipped a wing so Grace could see the ground underneath them. Her house formed a U-shape around the brick patio. The half-acre yard, surrounded by trimmed hedges along the sides, across the back, and beside The Path, looked pristine but tiny.

"Looks small from up here, but when I'm cleaning, it sure seems ample." She giggled, giddy at the sight and her reckless abandon at actually enjoying herself.

"I'll buzz the B&B. Maybe Carson's playing outside." Carl straightened the wings and flew over Sweet Dreams, its yard empty of activity.

A parade of cars crawled through Cherryvale's town center, around the rotary and down Main Street. Sheriff's vehicles blocked the entrance to the park, guarding against looky-loos hoping to catch a glimpse of the remaining trailers at the filming compound or the movie stars themselves.

"Don's got his hands full with the paparazzi and tourists, doesn't he?" Carl looked down. "They hired me to fly them over for footage, you know."

Grace turned to look at him. "The photographers?"

"No, the movie people. They call it a second unit or something. I guess they need footage for establishing shots."

"Listen to you, speaking the lingo." Grace peered down again, unable to keep from admiring her beautiful hometown from a new perspective. "Can we fly over the hospital, too?"

Carl nodded and turned the yoke. They glided over the white steeple and broad, gray-tiled roof of Cherryvale Church and continued toward the edge of town, following the slight meander of The Cherrypath.

Grace recognized the riding stables, and next to it, the outline of fences around Maggie's place, the recently charred barn and the small cottage she lived in. As Carl circled to the east, Grace peered at the structures and enclosures where she and Maggie played when they were children.

She scanned the tumbling debris from the recent fires. Each building on the compound held a special memory. She and Maggie acted out their made up stories in the haylofts and sheds. They'd built castles out of hay bales and took turns reigning over their magical hay-barn kingdoms. A paddock became an island hiding treasures, surrounded by pirates dressed like dairy cattle. She longed for those days of innocent friendship, unspoiled by mistakes and misunderstandings.

They swept toward the bypass and over the hospital's L-shaped brick building. Grace's heart sank. "Oh, no. Look at the news vans." Aerial antennas tripled in number in the past hour, and lined the street. "They know."

"Pardon?"

"One of the actors had an accident and the media found out by the looks of it. Mark set up extra security, but his budget's strained as it is."

Carl shook his head. "Those poor souls have no more privacy than a nudist on a city bus."

Grace chuckled, but her smile faded. The young woman inside lay in danger of prying eyes looking for a sensational story.

Carl made adjustments and the plane lifted. "Want to fly her?" White teeth gleamed against cinnamon skin, his calm encouraging her.

Grace's stomach ping-ponged. "What? Me?" She swallowed hard.

"Sure, take the controls. It'll be fine, I promise. I'm just going to take a little nap."

Grace's hands flew away from the controller.

"Just kidding. Seriously, it's a piece of cake. You can't do anything that I can't get us out of. Eventually."

"Don't go all stunt pilot on me, like your granddad!" Grace heard her voice go high-pitched.

Carl's grandfather had been a decorated Tuskegee Airman, his father a Navy pilot. He grinned, looking much like the old picture on display at the B&B. "Scout's honor."

"You keep yourself in stitches, don't you?"

"Go ahead, it's easy." He indicated the yoke in front of her.

She took first a tentative, then a firm grip on the handles and Carl let go. "You have the plane."

She waited for catastrophe, but no death spiral, no alarms announcing impending doom. Silly glee crept up her spine plastered in flop sweat against the leather seat.

"Pull on it a little to feel how she responds."

Grace tugged, the plane's nose lifted and the curvature of the earth fell.

"Push it back in and level her out. Find a spot on the horizon and head for it."

Grace pushed the control forward and she experimented, first in minor adjustments, then bolder, learning the plane's responses.

"Great job, you have a nice touch. Turn left, back toward the runway." Carl made no move to take the controls over.

"You're going to land, aren't you?"

Carl's easy grin flashed. "I'll take her when we get closer."

They flew for several minutes, Carl giving her hints and tips about the subtleties of flight. Before they reached the busy traffic space near the airport, Carl placed his hands back on the yoke, "I've got the plane." Grace let go but immediately missed that feeling of being in control of her fate. *Wow, maybe Maggie was right.*

Carl turned the plane in a sharp left toward the runway, speaking over the radio, but Grace didn't hang on every word this time. She watched the operations buildings and hangars grow larger, and the small craft floated earthward until the wheels glided without skitter or screech onto the blacktop.

They taxied to the parking spot, and before she knew it, Carl shut the plane off. They stowed their headsets and opened the doors to the quiet after the engine noise and pilot chatter. Grace helped him tie down the plane with chains attached to steel hooks in the blacktop and waited while he covered the windshield with a canvas tarp.

He slung a strap of his flight bag over his shoulder. "C'mon inside. I'll buy you a soda to celebrate your first flight. Or would you rather have coffee? It's still early."

"A cold drink sounds refreshing." She followed him inside the fixed base operations facility, or FBO, where pilots could use the restroom or wait for inclement weather conditions to pass. Carl paid for two sodas and handed one to Grace.

"You're not going to drench me?" Grace cast a quick glance.

"That's a ritual for your first solo. This one, you can drink." He tipped his bottle toward hers in a toast salute. "How do you feel?"

"I hate to admit it, but I actually enjoyed it. I know why people get flying fever. Everything looks so neat and orderly from up there."

"Amen, sister."

"So, when can we go up again?"

Carl threw his head back and laughed.

Maggie scraped a plastic scoop across the bottom of a grain bin and poured the last of the feed into several metal buckets waiting in line. She gathered the handles three at a time and stopped at the first pen, hanging each one on a hook. Furry ponies, resembling poorly groomed poodles as they shed their heavy winter coats, jostled and nipped. Their steady rhythmic munching reminded her that last night's fire ruined her last feed reserve. Three fires in as many days. Would the insurance company suspect her of setting them? She'd been late on a few payments, but she always caught up. Would anyone believe her?

For the first time, Maggie tasted the bitter truth. Someone wanted to harm her.

Finished with feeding, she walked back to her small house and its dirty dishes and smelly laundry, tires on gravel made her already prickly skin crawl up and down her spine. You're being silly, she scolded herself. Probably someone who wants to tour the farm. She gathered her wits and prepared to explain the petting farm had closed. Maybe forever.

Rounding the small ticket booth, a man in a dark suit got out of a beater van. She doubted this guy wanted to cuddle a baby lamb. Her spine shivered, but then the thought occurred to her he might be the insurance inspector. What you get for bargain shopping for insurance, by the looks of that heap.

"Can I help you?" She frowned at the approaching figure.

"I'm looking for the owners..." He squeaked the door of his junker van closed, standing next to it, jaw gaping. "Peggy?"

Maggie caught her breath. No one called her that nickname since she was ten. "I-uh-I go by Maggie."

"Course." He straightened so far he almost fell over. "Um, are you the female that runs this-um-amusement?"

"Yes. Did the insurance company send you?" She cast a dubious frown. Everything about his dilapidated vehicle and oddly fitting clothes inspired suspicion.

"No."

"Well, we're closed today, I'm sorry." She took a step back. "I don't know when we'll open. If ever."

The gaunt, unshaven man hesitated, opened his mouth to say something, stopped, and then muttered, "I'll come back." He climbed back into the rust bucket and a gray ponytail tucked into the neck of his rumpled coat dislodged and fell over his collar. Beneath the door, she could see his too-short pants caught on the top of grungy leather boots. After he cranked the engine a couple of times, it started, and Maggie watched him execute a sloppy five-point turn. The van bounced and belched the length of the driveway.

Odd, creepy man. Yet there was something familiar about him.

CHAPTER THIRTEEN

At a roll top desk in the corner of her tiny kitchen, Maggie stared at an epic pile of bills. She picked one up, then another, then shoved the stack aside. She contemplated calling a bankruptcy hotline when the phone rang. A glance at the black box, she considered letting the machine answer, but changed her mind and picked up the receiver, wishing she'd splurged on caller ID.

Skipping the formalities, she challenged the caller. "Now listen, I'm getting tired of this!"

Silence on the other end, then, "You still mad at me?"

"Oh, Grace, it's you." Maggie breathed a sigh of relief. "No, I'm not mad. I thought you were someone else."

"Can I come over?" Grace blurted.

Did she want Grace to see her or her place like this? The line crackled. In the barnyard, sheep caterwauled. "Suit yourself. I could use some company anyway."

Not exactly the most enthusiastic response, but Grace hung up the phone in the small office off her kitchen. She went out back in bare feet and unbuckled the wicker basket from her bike handlebars and set it on the kitchen counter. She lined it with a gingham towel, placed a half dozen assorted muffins in the center, and folded the corners over the top.

She laid a small notebook across the top and slipped a pen behind her ear, her straw hat on her head, and sunglasses on her nose. After checking the contents of her backpack she slung it over one shoulder, and slipped on her sneakers. Guiding her bike across the backyard to The Path, she jumped on. She turned the pedals fast enough to keep the bike moving, but slowly enough to enjoy the warm rays on her bare arms and the bird songs that cheerfully drifted along on the gentle breeze.

A group of plein air painters sat behind easels across the church. She waved and they lifted their brushes in greeting as she glided past.

Every so often, she'd slow and make a note of something in her notebook, then pedal on. It took her a while to go several hundred yards, but the beautiful morning made the delay worthwhile. Getting to Maggie's wasn't something she rushed to do, in any case.

She heard a chirping from inside her backpack, braked, put one foot on the ground, and swung the bag around. Her heart skipped happily when she read the caller ID.

"Hey, Wendy, what's up?"

"Hey, Mom!" Her daughter's voice sounded echo-y, probably in her car. "Can't talk long, just wondered how you were enjoying your first days of retirement. Relaxing like you'd hoped?"

"Anything but that. You'll never believe all that's going on here." Grace heard a ping in her ear and glanced at the screen. "Dang it, I keep forgetting to plug this thing in. I'm losing my battery. Can I call you back tonight?"

"Sure, where are you now?"

"Taking inventory of repairs needed on The Path. It's our Founder's Day project this year."

"I miss The Path, how's it holding up?"

"The section outside town's all grown over and the fence needs new lumber. Could be a bunch of hobos living out there and we'd never know it."

"Mom, they're called The Homeless."

"You're right." Properly chastised by her own child, she cleared her throat. "Any chance you'll be able to come home that weekend? We're having the BBQ in our yard this year."

"Sounds like fun, but I doubt it. I'm the newbie, and I get last dibs at weekends off. I'll see what I can do."

Grace's battery warning sounded again. "I'm about to die. Love you! Call me if you're coming. I'll wash the sheets on the bed in your old room. Oh! I took my first plane ri—" The phone became a dead weight and she snapped it shut. She checked her watch and pushed off, still with a mile or so to go along The Path before reaching Maggie's place. She measured lengths of fallen down fence and estimated how much fill they'd need for the ruts to be smooth enough for hikers and bikers.

Sweaty and tired from the bumpy ride, she pedaled up to Maggie's place, leaned her bike against the porch railing and tapped on the screen door.

"It's open!"

"Brought your favorite." Grace held up the peace offering. "Lemon with poppy seed."

"Thanks." Maggie lifted a corner of the gingham cloth. "You look a sight. Want tea or coffee?"

"Iced tea, please. I rode the long way."

"Why the long way?" Maggie poured two glasses while Grace wet a paper towel at the sink and wiped her moist forehead. "Wouldn't be so bad if you didn't wear jeans on a day like this."

"Have my riding lesson later. I didn't want to go back home and change into my long pants." Grace sank into a kitchen chair and wiped her face and neck. "When I started out, it wasn't so hot."

Maggie handed her a squeeze bottle of lemon juice, Grace counted out three drops, and clinked her spoon through the glass of sweetened tea.

"You and your Great Retirement List." Maggie waggled her eyebrows.

She moved Purse Everest to the living room sofa and sat across from Grace. "Why not just be spontaneous?"

Maggie lifted a pile of envelopes and looked at one, then the other. Grace took a long drink of the cold liquid and watched Maggie going through her mail. She tried to ignore the piles of papers and dirty floors. Living without domestic help was not Maggie's strong suit. And must be a shock to someone used to having dishes washed and laundry taken care of. Mental reminder: appreciate her good qualities, not her challenges to clean up after herself.

"I like having a plan." Grace lifted a corner of the tea towel, revealing her untouched bounty. "Don't you want a muffin? I could use one after all that exercise."

Maggie studied the top paper on the pile she was holding.

Grace shrugged and reached for her hat. "If you're busy, I can push off."

Maggie placed the pile back on the table. "No, I'm sorry, just distracted. Let me get us some plates." She found two small chipped dishes and a couple of mismatched knives from a rack on the drain board and sat back down.

"I remember helping your mama wash dishes at that sink." Grace breathed on a smudge, wiped the knife then placed a muffin on each plate and sliced hers down the middle. "I loved hearing the stories she told us about growing up on this farm."

Maggie lifted the lid off a cracked butter dish and set it between them. She stared through the window toward a tree in the backyard.

Grace sliced off a conservative pat, smearing it across the bottom half of her muffin to nibble along the edge. "Remember how your mama used to fuss at us? 'Peggy! Gracie! Get out of the hayloft!' I miss those days."

Maggie cast Grace a pained look as if she'd been shot. "Why did you bring that up? Peggy..."

"I didn't mean anything. Just your mom's nickname for you." Grace wondered at the emotional response. "I'm sorry."

Maggie turned over a muffin. "I've got lots of chores. I should get busy." She swiped a hunk of butter across without unwrapping it. "Thanks for bringing these." She bit off the top and put the rest back on the saucer, stood and headed for the back door.

"Wait." Grace didn't mean for her voice to be as loud as it sounded. "Maggie, I know you're busy, but let's talk." She patted the seat next to her.

Maggie sank into the chair facing the window.

"We were like sisters as kids, weren't we?" Grace began. "I've tried to make you feel welcome here. Ever since you and Joe moved back to Cherryvale." She wet her tightening windpipes with another long, sweet drink of tea. "And I would never do anything to hurt you…especially now with the fires and all, it's gotta be so scary for you."

Maggie sighed and picked up the knife. She buttered each bite individually, methodically. "You don't know the half of it." She scraped off a long yellow curl and examined it like a convict at a last meal. "But, do go on."

"Well. You have been known to…well, you can…Mags, you're getting…"

Maggie stared at her. "What? What am I getting?"

"Crotchety." Grace stuffed her mouth full, gaze trained on Maggie's heaped kitchen sink.

Maggie popped the final bite into her own mouth, set the knife down deliberately across her plate, and pushed it away. She picked up a kitchen towel, and a fistful of crumbs rained onto the floor.

"Crotchety?" Maggie rolled and twisted the cloth in her hands. "Is that what you think?"

Grace soldiered on. "Your attitude about the movie being shot here is one example. You hated them before they even got here, like some monster was invading." She felt woozy using Maggie's own words against her. "What I mean is—I think maybe you should—you should lighten up."

The kitchen towel tightened in Maggie's fists, she unrolled it, rolled it back up, pushed back her chair. She stood over the sink, her back to

Grace. The dripping faucet punctuated the silence. Somewhere outside, Maggie's rooster made mid-morning announcements.

"Grace, you have a lot of nerve lecturing me. You have your husband, your kids. You haven't been visited by the fire department that I know of, recently. You have no idea what I've been going through."

Grace wished she could crawl out the back door and hide in a pile of hay. "Maggie, I—"

"Let me finish. I put a lot of dreams on hold for Joe's career. We saved and planned to move here when he retired. Don't get me wrong, I loved our life together. We lived places and met people you only read about in the headlines..."

There she goes again, flaunting in my face. Grace waited for Maggie to re-compose herself and then a thought occurred. Something in her tone didn't sound like Maggie was bragging. Could it be that the world-traveler felt jealous of a boring English teacher who lived three miles from where she grew up?

"I loved Joe." Maggie drew in a breath and Grace dabbed the paper towel at her own eyes filling with shared pain. "But our plan—my dream—to settle here and rebuild this place, bring it into this century for animals lost in the economic troubles…that's not happening. And all anyone can talk about is Tiffany Lane this, and the movies that...while the farm goes down in flames." Maggie spun around to face Grace. "I'm losing my dream here, don't you see?"

Grace rushed over and tried to pull the woman in for a bear hug, but she jerked back, so she settled for an arm across her shoulder while Maggie hunched over the sink.

"When Joe died, I lost my companion, my helper, and my husband all at once. He was the brains, the planner. Take a look around and you can tell I'm not the one with organization skills." Maggie swept her arm across the sink full of dishes toward the mountain of papers waterfalling onto the sticky oak. "We lost most of our savings, then his medical bills. And now these fires…"

"Oh, honey, c'mere." Grace tugged Maggie, forcing her into a hug.

They stood together until Maggie pulled away, swiveled the knobs, and leaned over to splash sink water on her face.

"Know what's funny?" Grace unknotted the dishtowel and held it out to Maggie. "I've always been jealous of you and now I think I sense..."

Maggie cut her a sideways glance. "I partied in my day, but look at me now." An eye roll at the stained ceiling tiles. "Now this is pretty glamorous."

Grace followed Maggie's gaze around the farmhouse kitchen's worn 1930s cabinets and peeling linoleum. "I'm serious. You led such an exotic life, moving all over the world. Those postcards you sent from the Taj Mahal and the Holy Land. I couldn't imagine going to, much less living, in those places. I was home knee-deep in potty training and piles of laundry, and you were eating in palaces and staying in ambassadors' guest rooms."

"Anybody can travel." Maggie frowned. "Especially a doctor's wife."

A touch of smug simmered, but Grace remembered it had been Maggie who shamed her into taking the lessons. "Not easily if you can't get on an airplane. Which I am working on, thanks to you." She sobered. "But seriously, between med school loans, the mortgage, then two children in Little League and dance lessons, braces, college tuition..."

"I coveted you, you coveted me." Maggie smiled wanly, dabbed at her cheeks with the towel, and sat, heavy, in the kitchen chair.

Grace lifted her iced tea from the table. "I say we start over. I'll be more sympathetic, you're entitled to some *'tude,* as the kids say. Lord knows the town's barely recognizable since you moved back."

"I can be quite the geezer when my persnickety button's held down too long." Maggie winced. "How old do I sound?"

"No comment." Grace chuckled. "Tell you what. Let's come up with a system. When I get wrapped up in my own issues, trying to control every situation—"

"And when I get preachy or go off on a soapbox tangent—" Maggie lifted her glass to touch Grace's. "—kick me or something."

"Much as I've been tempted, I'm not kicking you. And don't slug me either like that time when we argued over whose science fair project was better." Grace stared at Maggie, recalling their almost sibling rivalry. The project marked the first time they'd seriously argued, but not the last, or the biggest.

Grace cleared her throat and almost panicked, afraid Maggie would bring up the real reason for the monkey on the back of their friendship. "When one of us gets tiresome, we'll let the other know by saying, 'fresh start!' No questions asked." She wondered why she hadn't thought of that idea years ago. "The other person has to jump down from whatever soap box or selfish topic we're dwelling on." *Including pathetic jealousy or silly rivalry.* Then she thought of something her own mother said. "If we let something go unforgiven and unexposed, it's like a mole in the garden gnawing at the roots of a friendship. Like the vegetable plant that's lost its roots, bam, the friendship withers and dies." She placed her thumb and fingers together as if they were rodent teeth working their damage.

Maggie managed a weak grin but her eyes looked strained. "Deal!"

They clinked glasses, but Maggie's face grew even more serious. "*All* things forgiven?"

Grace caught the emphasis on all, but before she could form thoughts into words, the phone rang and Maggie jumped as if a starter pistol fired next to her ear.

"What's wrong, honey? It's only the phone."

Maggie stared at the insistent device.

Grace reached for it. "I'll ans—"

"No!"

Grace snatched her hand back.

"Someone's been calling me and acting crazy. If I answer, they hang up, but if I don't, they leave crazy messages. Listen."

The machine's greeting finished, and at the beep, a barely discernable, rumbling voice spoke. "This message…is—*static*—whoever has—*crackle*—surveys, and deeds—*buzz, pop!*—get rid of you. Soon." Beep.

"Oh, Maggie!" Grace shuddered. "Do you recognize him? Did you tell Sheriff?"

"He told me to make a tape. As if they have time to take care of us law-abiding-citizens right now with all the pestarazzi to worry about." Maggie stalked over and poked through papers in her roll-top. She extracted a page, loosening the cramped jumble. Envelopes and sheets of paper slid to the floor. "Here's a transcript I made of the calls last week."

Grace took the sheet and stared. "Do you think it has something to do with the fires? What's he mean by all that?"

"Darned if I know. This bozo talks about the deed and title of my land, so I've been looking everywhere for copies. What if there is a lien or something we didn't find when my dad died?" She shifted piles of old farming reports, seed catalogs and handfuls of paper clips, scanning, and tossing aside yellowed papers and faded receipts.

"What about getting Jacqui at the real estate office to do a search?" Grace leaned over and gathered papers to straighten the mess. She frowned at faded red and green envelopes. *Christmas cards?*

"Joe set up a filing system in the administration building office for me, but everything out there burned in the fire. Fireproof cabinets are expensive."

Grace watched Maggie digging, creating even more chaos out of mayhem. "Hand me a pile. What would it look like?"

"Lew, he handled Dad's probate, wants me to look for something that references the original titles or deeds to the property. Anything that proves ownership will help. Who knows what the original paperwork looks like? The place has been in the family since my grandfather."

"Did you check at City Hall?"

"The other day while I was there, I filled out a form to retrieve archived papers. Could take months." Maggie placed a pile in front of Grace.

The tower fell over and the top layer slid into her lap. Grace lifted the brittle sheet of lined notepaper and read the title. "'J&M's Top Twenty To-do's.' What's this?"

"Oh, fiddle dee-dee." Maggie reached. "It's nothing. Lemme have it."

"Nu-uh." Grace jerked it out of her reach, focused on the scrawl. "Number one, see the Eiffel Tower. Number two, read *Brothers*

Karamazov." Grace cooed. "That's on my list to re-read too; we could start a book club. There you were teasing me about having a list, and you started one years ago." Grace grinned and skimmed down. "Number eleven, start an animal rescue farm." She looked up, tears welling.

Maggie's eyes glittered with moisture as well. "At least you're getting yours accomplished."

"This has been one of your dreams for a long time." Grace poked at her with the list. "Listen to me. You are not going to give up. We will figure out what is going on. Whatever's happening around here has met its match in Cherryvale."

After tea with Maggie and an admonition to watch out for strangers, Grace plopped her sunhat on her head and pedaled next door to Rose's stables. She leaned her bike against a corral fence where Maggie's sheep, displaced from the latest fire, nibbled grass. She paused a moment enjoying their peace, grazing next to a mare and newborn foal. She went inside, strolling the breezeway that ran the length of the horse stables.

Several pairs of large brown eyes watched her. An appaloosa horse stuck his head over the door into the hallway, curious about the visitor. A tall bay snickered softly and bobbed his head at her.

"Hello, Jake," Grace greeted, reading the nameplate on his gate. She held her hand out for him to sniff, waiting for approval before stroking his long, whiskered nose.

"I didn't bring any carrots. Hey, I make a mean carrot muffin. I'll bring you some next time."

Jake whinnied, tossing his head back.

A blue-eyed shepherd rounded the corner at the opposite end of the barn, and with a low woof, ran over to sniff up and down Grace's blue jeans.

"Hey, Grace." Rose appeared behind him, pushing an empty wheelbarrow. "Just finishing some chores." She lifted a rake and shovel and placed them on hooks.

"You keep such a clean, neat place. It's remarkable. It must be never ending."

"I don't mind." Rose swelled with obvious pleasure as she scanned the tidy barn. "You been here long?"

"A minute or two. Just met your dog." Grace rubbed the golden head leaning against her leg. "His eyes are two different colors; they're beautiful."

"That's Buckwheat. He's an Anatolian Shepherd. He belonged to my very first riding instructor. She passed away recently."

"I'm so sorry." Grace pet the grateful dog while Rose clomped around in the tack room. In a moment, she emerged lugging a saddle across her arm and a bridle draped over her shoulder. "Her family gave him to me. He's a great guard dog and a herder by instinct. I'm training him to bring horses in from the pasture for me."

Grace stroked Buckwheat's head, admiring the cream-colored hair that blended from his forehead into darker hair on his snout. She chuckled as he groaned in appreciation of her attention. "He's a tad skinny."

"Yeah, he's not eating well." Rose considered him. "Grieving I guess."

"I'm so sorry for you too, buddy." Buckwheat licked Grace's hand. "Has Greg checked him over to make sure he's not sick?" She knelt to the dog's level. Buckwheat rolled over for Grace's belly scratching convenience.

"I'll call him if he doesn't start putting weight on soon. Ready to saddle up? You'll be riding Jake. He's my bomb-proof teacher's aide."

"I am if you'll help me stand up again!" She reached up and Rose grabbed her hand to hoist Grace to her feet. "See you, Buckwheat!"

Rose tacked up Jake, explaining the girths and headpieces, bits and horse parts. She showed Grace how to properly place the saddle and pad on Jake's back, tighten the cinch, and double check the equipment for safety. Her straw hat swapped for a safety helmet, Grace stood ready for her lesson.

After a couple of attempts and a boost from the mounting block in the yard, she perched on top of the patient Jake for her first refresher ride in more years than she cared to add up.

From atop the gelding's back she could see parts of Maggie's place. Between listening to Rose's instruction and urging her bottom to remain somewhere in the vicinity of the saddle, she almost forgot about the troubles down The Path.

After the half hour lesson, Grace wobbled on stiff limbs to help Rose un-tack and return Jake to his stall.

"After a couple more lessons, I'll put you in one of my beginner classes. It's good to ride with others. Your seat will improve, and your balance will come back." Rose's gentle encouragement helped ease some of the tightness that crept up her thighs.

"Always up for some seat improvement." Grace patted her rump. "Do you have many classes?"

"It's been slow, but more people are calling, and I almost have enough to set up classes by age now." She looked through the class clipboard. "You might not have to ride with the ten-year-olds if that's what you're worried about."

"I love kids, even if they can ride circles around me." Grace glanced sidelong at Rose. "You must like them, too, if you decided to become a riding instructor."

"I do. But teaching's only one way to pay the bills. I plan to take on young horses and train to re-sell them."

"Horse flipping?"

Rose laughed. "You could say that, but the image that brings to mind is not conducive to marketing."

Grace stroked Jake's nose. "Thanks for the lesson. Next week at the same time?"

"That's right." Rose moved toward the tack room, her arms laden with the saddle and bridle.

"Rose?"

"Yes, Grace."

"How do you find Cherryvale? I mean other than as a place for your business. Have you made friends?"

Rose shifted from one foot to the other. "People are friendly enough."

"I'm sorry; it's none of my business." Grace tucked her chin. "Mark calls me Mother Hen. All the years teaching school…oh, not that you're a kid or anything—"

"It's okay. It's just that most people here are already married, or they're quite a bit younger or old—well, not my age range." Then almost to herself, but Grace heard, "Or seem to have no interest in relationships."

"We're having a get together for Founder's Day. If you'd like to bring someone, we'd love to have you."

"Can I come by myself?"

"Of course. I'll call with the details." Maybe Mark would disapprove, but Rose did seem lonely—almost made her forget the discovery of new muscle groups that protested each rotation of her pedal home.

CHAPTER FOURTEEN

What do you have planned for the day?" Mark chased a bite of scrambled egg with a blueberry muffin. He eyed her shoes. "Walk and Rollers?"

Grace finished tying her Keds and glanced out back. "The girls should be passing soon."

Every Monday, Wednesday, and Saturday alternating with the Farmer's Market, Grace, Shelby, Carolyn Sims, and Abby Madison met for their morning sprint. She loaded the dishwasher with their breakfast plates and kept an eye out the back window for them to make the turn and appear on The Path.

"Why do you still call yourselves the 'Rollers'?" Mark pulled his keys out of his pocket and kissed her cheek. "No more babies in buggies."

"Like Carolyn said, we'll be rolling around our grandbabies some day."

"And then wheelchairs."

Grace wadded and threw her damp dishtowel at Mark's head.

He ducked to avoid the missile. "See ya tonight, granny." It hit the door as he scooted out. She heard him laughing in the garage until the car door slammed.

The ladies appeared, calling her out. Grace jogged to join them on

The Path. The sun promised a gorgeous day and warmed the air of the misty dawn. In cooler spots still in shade, beads of dew clung to spider webs that spread from fence post to railing like grandma's tatting.

Shelby eyeballed Grace. "There's a hitch in your get-along."

"Sore from my riding lesson yesterday." Grace lifted her knees higher. Her thighs stiff like taffy before the pulling. "But thanks for noticing."

"One of your new retirement hobbies?" Carolyn pumped her arms back and forth to the rhythm of their pace.

"Wanted to take up where I left off. Besides, Rose can use the business. Giving tourists buggy rides through town on the weekend won't keep the stables open."

"She seems like a nice girl." Shelby paused to tie a shoelace.

"Shel, you ever see her out with anyone?" Grace circled her arms and trotted in place while Shelby tugged and looped.

"Why? You have some matchmaking in mind?"

"Isn't she about Greg McCoy's age? They have so much in common," Carolyn mused as they stepped off again.

"No." Shelby shook her head, the morning's bun still tight against her scalp. "I never seen them two out together on anything you'd call a date. Now you mention it, I never seen him out with anyone since his wife died in that car crash, leaving him and poor little Connie...How many years ago was that?"

"I still remember that night." Grace's voice sounded hoarse. "Her death is one reason Mark committed to getting the hospital built." Grace did some quick math. "Twelve years ago. They were high school sweethearts, you know."

Abby looked over at Grace. "You have them in your class?"

"I taught her as a freshman, but Greg wasn't in any of my classes."

They walked without speaking for several minutes.

Shelby broke the silence. "How's Cassie?"

"On the mend. She's queen of the remote and driving Carson crazy with Candyland matches." Carolyn breathed in through her mouth, out through her mouth. "I'm so lucky my husband works at home so we can share the joy of child rearing."

"And give you a chance to get away from the B&B." Grace felt her thigh muscles loosen. "You've been full since the movie crew hit town, haven't you?"

"Some of the photographers are still here. Most of them have checked out now. Certainly helped meet this month's mortgage, and next."

They rounded the turn in time to see Jeff Field disappear through The Pit's overgrown hedge. "Excuse me, girls. I see someone I know. You go on, I'll call you with your Founder's Day assignments."

"Since when do you hang with movie stars?" Carolyn snickered, watching Grace jiggle the latch.

"Get on. I'll catch up with you later." She pushed against weeds that twined up into the boards.

Elbowing and giggling, they paused next to the railing. "Remember you're a married lady, Grace," Shelby snorted.

Grace waved them off and they scurried away, tittering like schoolgirls crushing on the quarterback. She ducked through. "Morning!"

He greeted her with his magazine-cover smile. "Hey, there, Grace."

"You lost?" She tilted her head up, scanning the dilapidated structure. "This house has been abandoned for years."

"I keep thinking of the family that must have lived here..." He resumed scanning the architecture camouflaged under broken boards, dangling tree branches and piles of litter. "Saw it when I passed by the other day. Can't get it out of my head."

"A young family lived here but couldn't keep up the payments." Grace wondered why she hadn't thought to organize a cleanup of the place.

Jeff stepped up to inspect a cracked footer under the back door. "You have kids, Grace?"

"A grown daughter, Wendy. Ian's in college, interning this summer. You?"

"I have a daughter." He picked up a tree branch and flung it aside so they could climb the porch step. "We're not close."

Grace stepped over a concrete pedestal from an old birdbath and followed him up. "Where does she...? Sorry, you don't have to tell me, it's none of my business."

"It's okay. She goes to a boarding school in Los Angeles. Very posh. They have a fast track for kids who want to grow up to be snobs."

"Sounds exclusive." Grace started to laugh until his expression grew serious. "If you don't like it, why do you let her stay there?"

He shrugged. "She makes up her own mind. I just pay the bills."

Grace kicked trash aside and knelt to pull on some buckled and warped boards that gave way to a gaping hole through the porch floor. Critters underneath skittered into the darkness.

He swiveled a plank over the gap, tested with the weight of one foot, and when it held, walked across to push open the unlocked door. Someone had made a half-hearted attempt to scrub off graffiti.

"This place should have been bulldozed ages ago." Grace made it across with a dancer's light step to stand next to him.

"Oh, don't say that." Jeff's voice dropped. "It reminds me of myself."

"How could this pit possibly resemble you?" Grace gaped at him then glanced at piles of filth heaped in the corner of the foyer. Pungent odors of rodent droppings and decomposing carcasses ambushed them. Grace pushed the door open wider behind them.

"I grew up in a house with bones like this." Jeff wiggled an oak banister and gazed up the flight of stairs. "I miss that little house. Having a family. Maybe another wife someday." He grew silent then turned toward the door. "It's crazy."

"What?" Grace backed out onto the porch, grateful to be in the fresh air again.

"It's a harebrained idea." Jeff pulled the door shut and focused on a point in the distance. "There's something about this town. It's grown on me. It's quiet...or it must be when there's not a movie crew taking over. I'm just rambling." Jeff held his arm toward an opening in the weeds. "May I see you safely back to The Path?"

"Hold on." Grace lowered her bottom and patted the porch next to her. "Cherryvale has a specialness about it, you're absolutely correct. Our hearts are big and our hugs are long." She looked up at the steeple peeking over the trees behind the cottage. "Did anyone tell you how we came to have that path?"

Jeff shook his head and rested an arm across his knee.

"Its very existence is a testimony to how special this town is."

"Do tell."

"In the winter of 1909, Mark's great grandfather was the town doctor. He just about killed himself, and his poor pony, driving between farms tending the ill in a flu outbreak."

"Hm. Horse drawn wagons and doctors who made house calls." Jeff watched a hawk circle overhead. "Go on."

"To make it worse," Grace continued, "in the middle of the night one of the worst blizzards in decades hit. The snow made it almost impossible for him to get through. So the healthy men and women went out, lanterns burning, bundled to the eyeballs, and started clearing the road. Then someone realized it would be less work if they went behind." She nodded in the direction of The Path. "Because of the town's layout, he could make it in between houses faster by going behind them. So they tore down fences and cleared snow, staying one stop ahead of him as he made his rounds." Grace paused for a moment. "They say they were able to cut his travel time in half."

Jeff lifted his chin and straightened his back. "That's one of the most touching things I've ever heard." His voice sounded thick.

"They worked all night and through into the next day keeping the path cleared for him." Grace cleared the catch of pride from her voice. "They decided after the crisis passed to rebuild the fences a couple of yards back to leave the footpath access open. Partly in memorial to those that died and partly as a testimony to Doc Harkins's selfless attention to his patients." Grace swung her foot. "Not to mention his horse. I hope he got a nice long rest after that."

Jeff considered for a minute. "Quite a testimony to how the people of this town have each other's back."

"You got it." She looked over at his pensive gaze, his mouth a straight line. "Now, who wouldn't want to live in a town like this?"

He snorted. "My daughter for one. Much as I'd like to move her somewhere…anywhere so we could be together. That's why I have to go back to California." He stood up and stretched. "The scare over Tiffany and then Cassie really brought that home to me." Jeff tugged at a loose wire hanging from the rafters.

"Here's a crazy thought." Grace popped up and gasped, her thighs muscles seized again. "Move her here to live with you." She lifted one foot, then the other. "Send her to public school."

Jeff shook his head. "Sorry. You don't know her."

"I know kids. I know they want to be loved, most of all by their parents. What does her mom say?"

"She died when Julie was small."

Grace caught her breath. "I'm so sorry. But that means your daughter needs you more than ever."

"She'd hate me worse if I made her leave her friends." Jeff's blue eyes were serious and penetrating. "That would spoil any chance I have with her."

"She'll make new ones."

He paused. "I guess I can speak to her therapist and see what she says."

Grace turned her head so he wouldn't see her rolling her eyes. "She's your child."

"She needs someone to talk to." Jeff cleared his throat. "I abandoned her for my career. The damage is done." He swiped at a cobweb stuck to his famously dimpled cheek.

Grace considered his comment while he gazed up at the cottage. "Can I ask you a personal question? How old are you?"

"Not that personal. Anyone can Google my age. I'm thirty-six. Why?"

"Just wondering." Grace did some more math. Not too old. "What about your career? I mean when you pack up and move here?"

Jeff caught her eye, a look of disbelief in his face. "She's not even willing to spend her summer vacation with me, much less live together. The kids at the school are her family now. I've ruined my chances with her."

"Humor me." Grace held out a hand and Jeff helped her stand. "Let's just take a look see. Even abandoned things can often be rehabbed."

"All right." Jeff's doubtful tone carried a tinge of hope.

In the oak-paneled great room, he ran a hand down smooth paneling then nudged stones clinging to an old fireplace. He knuckle-rapped a wooden mantle. "Sounds solid. At least the termites haven't found this beauty." They wandered past peeling wallpaper and stained carpet. down the hallway and stopped in the doorway to a pink-tiled bathroom. "Very retro." Jeff observed. He peeked into a bedroom across from the pink bathroom.

"This could be your daughter's room." Grace looked at the cove ceiling and window seat. She imagined a reading nook filled with Judy Blumes and Nancy Drews. Well, maybe not Nancy Drew. "How old is she?"

"Fourteen. No, fifteen. Just a couple years younger than Tiffany." Jeff fiddled with a light switch. "It's funny. I've actually spent more time with Tiffany than I have my own daughter."

Grace thought about the girl in the hospital bed. "Do you think she did try to…you know?"

"It's no secret she's messed up. She's been hijacking this movie ever since we started filming. Like she wants to derail it." Jeff took a deep breath and let it out slowly. "I guess she might have tried something."

"She told me about her absentee mother and no father." Grace glanced up at Jeff and decided to change the direction of their conversation. "You know what your daughter wants to be when she grows up?"

"Huh. She majors in partying." Jeff tried a closet door that fell off a hinge at his touch. "Let's get going. I'm not buying this place."

"Hinges can be repaired, tiles can be replaced." Grace followed Jeff back down the hallway.

"It's not just the hideous tile. I don't know anything about being a father. I'd make it worse than it already is."

Jeff almost made it to The Path but stopped to wait for Grace. "What? What do you see?"

"You're right, we should arrange for a bulldozer. This abandoned, pathetic shambles is beyond hope."

Jeff spun on his heel and ran back to point up to the roof. "You're crazy, look at that classic architecture, you can't replace that..." Jeff glanced over. Grace folded her arms. He nodded then shook his head. "Oh no. I know what you're trying to do."

Grace grinned. "Know what we call this place?"

"What?"

"The Cherry-Pit."

"Ouch."

"I know." Grace laughed. "Isn't that mean? And doesn't it make you love it even more?"

Jeff considered the structure, his eyes sweeping the generous yard and established trees. "It's got great bones," he whispered as if he were speaking directly to the home.

Grace leaned in. "And everyone and everything can use a fresh start from time to time."

Jeff cut a glance over at Grace, a twinkle in his eye. "Grace, you should be in real estate. Or therapy."

Grace rummaged through the cedar chest in her attic, negotiating her way behind boxes of Christmas decorations. The heat of the day penetrated the roof, and her upper lip sported sweaty droplets.

She lifted a garment bag, wrinkled and pressed thin from years beneath the weight of baby clothes, Wendy's prom dress, and a keepsake baseball uniform of Ian's. She felt along the bottom for two bulges. Satisfied, she closed the lid and backed down the ladder into the hallway.

She laid the bag across her bed and stripped to her underwear, then tried on the outfit. Thanks to those hours on her bicycle, it fit almost like twen—er, thirty years ago. Gads. Number seven on the to-do list was shaping up to be quite a challenge.

"All right, people, line up to get your number." Sam Madison stood on the Cherryvale Community Theatre stage addressing performers signing up for the fundraiser.

"If you are going to sing, give your CD to tech." Sam gestured to a volunteer sitting in the sound booth then continued his announcements. Behind him, Hank and Emmett walked the boards, planning where to set up their equipment for the broadcast.

Grace, standing in line behind a dog act from Franklin City, made goo-goo eyes at a slobbering Malti-Poo. Someone tapped her on the shoulder.

"What are you going to do, Grace, stir up some muffins?" Jack Purcell, part time mayor and lead bass player for The Cherrypickers, teased.

"You'll see soon enough!" Her tummy fluttered as the couple in front of her stepped away before she had time to chicken out.

"Hey, Miz Grace, I didn't know you had any talent!" Connie looked up to take her application form.

"Stick around, kid, you'll get an eyeful!"

Doc McCoy's daughter had shown great promise in her English

composition class and now stood to judge her performance. *Better make it good, Gracie.*

Connie scanned the sheet. "How cool is that!"

Grace had a sudden brainstorm. "Say, Connie, when you're finished here, can I have a minute?"

The young girl nodded and in a few minutes, sat down next to her in one of the well-worn theatre seats. "What's up, Miz Harkins?"

"I admire you, Connie; you seem to be very level headed." Connie puffed up a tad at the compliment.

"I have a challenge for you. It's important, but I think you can handle it," Grace went on.

"What do you mean?

"You know that Tiffany Lane is in the hospital, don't you?"

Connie nodded. "Everyone's talking about it. My small group at Youth Night prayed for her."

"Good girl. And something else she could really use is someone her own age who can be her friend. Would you like to come over to the hospital with me and visit with her?"

Connie shoved a lock of long brown hair behind an ear. "I don't know, she's so famous—"

"Even celebrities need friends. You two have a lot in common, if you think about it. She doesn't have a mother in her life, or a father."

"I have my dad."

"Why not see what happens?"

"I guess I can try. I'll drive us over in my Jeep. Let me call Dad and tell him where I'm going."

"Before we get there, I'll make sure the security guard knows we're coming." While Connie went for her purse, Grace dialed Mark's office and got his voicemail. "Honey, I want to visit Tiffany but I need today's password, call me!" She shut off the phone and thought a minute. "I know who'll have it." She stood up when Connie rejoined her. "Let's stop by the Park and ask Holly."

Connie drove Grace over to the park and they walked over the bridge to the film compound. Grace exhaled with relief at a familiar face. "Ryan! Excuse me."

The Director's Assistant stopped. "Oh, hello. You were one of our extras, right? I'm sorry, but we don't need you for any scenes today."

"No, that's not why we're here. I think I'll leave that to the professionals from now on. My name is Grace Harkins." Grace turned to Connie, "And this is my friend Connie McCoy."

They exchanged greetings.

"We won't keep you," Grace continued. "We're looking for Holly."

"Hang on." He spoke into a walkie talkie. "She's in the women's honey wagon."

He grinned at the blank stares. "Sorry. Past that catering tent, it's on the left. Stairs going up to several doors. Marked 'Ladies.' She's in the women's changing room." His radio squawked. "Nice to meet you, I gotta run."

Moments later, they stood among racks of costumes. Holly re-hung garments over the rails. "I'm swamped here and now I'm helping with the fundraiser, so I won't be able to visit Tiffany." Holly told them after they disclosed their mission. "Today's password is 'Swarovski.'"

"Like the bling!" Connie's eyes sparkled with recognition.

"Appropriate, right?" Holly nodded.

"I think someone closer to Tiffany's age will be able to relate to her." Grace told Holly as they walked back to the car.

"I know there's someone inside that wants to connect, but darned if I can figure out what will open her up." Holly shoved her hands deep in the pockets of her cargo shorts as they strolled. "She's older than my niece and younger than my sister, so I'm not doing much good. Besides, she thinks of me as an employee." Then she remembered something. "Say. I did find out something that might help. You know her kite tatt?"

Grace's eyes lit up. "Yes?"

"She has a tattoo?" Connie whispered. "I never read that anywhere, and I know everything about her! Uh, from the magazines."

"Shh. We're keeping that a secret between us," Grace cautioned. "Strictly a need-to-know thing."

"Gotcha." Connie nodded solemnly. "What about the item that shall remain unmentioned?"

Holly told them about her conversation with Tiffany. "I still don't know myself how this might help, but you never know. Maybe you'll do better than my failure."

"You weren't a failure." Grace placed a reassuring hand on Holly's shoulder. "It's obviously important." She gave her a quick hug when they reached the jeep. "We'll let you know what happens."

"Maggie, we need to find your deed and title paperwork." Attorney Lew Farrell switched off a tape player after listening to a copy of Maggie's harassing phone caller. She sat across from him in his visitor chair, twisting the handles on her giant handbag.

"It sounds like mush mouth has some kind of issue with your ownership of the land. Is this the only message you could copy?"

"My power went out during the last fire. I lost the others."

"He could just be a kook. I got a notice to allow entry for your insurance company to send an arson investigator. They might want you to take a lie detector test."

"What about the movie crew? Will they make them take one, too?"

"There's no reason to suspect any of those folks, Maggie. Your back taxes are the red flag."

Maggie clutched her duffel-purse to her chest and towered over Lew's desk. "I would never put my own animals at risk—"

"I know, I know." Lew spread both hands wide toward her. "Relax. I'm on your side." He drummed his fingers, studying a document.

Maggie fell back heavily and resumed curling and coiling her purse strap.

His shoulders sagged at Maggie's expression. "I'd be remiss if I didn't consider all the possibilities." He picked up a pen and made some notes on a legal pad. "But this kook on the phone's our strongest suspect. I'll ask Sheriff to keep an eye out. He's got his hands full with the celebrities and now the fundraiser."

"My troubles are feeding my troubles."

"Ironic, huh?" Lew met her eyes. "Don't give up. And keep a lookout for suspicious activity around your place. Maybe you should get a guard dog."

"All I need is another mouth to feed right now. Wait, I almost forgot."

"What?"

"Speaking of suspicious, a guy stopped one day. I thought he was the insurance adjustor at first." Maggie searched her memory. "He didn't seem to know what he wanted. But he called me by my childhood nickname." She looked up at Lew.

"Oh? What was that?"

"Peggy. Had an aunt named Maggie, so got confusing until she died."

"Hmm. It could be a coincidence. Did he threaten you?"

"No."

"What did he look like?"

"Tall. Average kind of face."

"Not much to go on. Anything odd about him?"

"He drove an old VW van. Wore a suit that looked like a reject from a donation pile. Scroungy."

"Okay. I'll tell Sheriff about him as well, but unless he made threats, I doubt if there's anything he can do."

Maggie's eyebrows lifted and she checked her watch. "I should go over to the theatre. They're having sign-ups today, and after all, they are trying to help me out." At the door, she paused. "One more thing about this guy. He had a long, gray ponytail and hadn't shaved for several days."

"Classy."

Back on street level, Maggie walked past her pickup truck parked in front of the two-story brownstone. Ambling down oak-lined Main Street toward the theatre, the irresistible aroma of fresh brew tempted. Maggie hesitated then pulled open a screen door. She stepped into The Daily Grind, an indulgence she'd denied herself for months. She ordered her fave, a decaf caramel macchiato and waited at the bar for her treat.

Large, iced. The nutty flavor mixed with the liquid candy in a sweet pool on her tongue. Her shoulders instantly relaxed, her back knots working themselves loose and free.

Perched on the tall barstool, sipping and savoring, her eyes wandered over the hundred year-old black and white pictures of Cherryvale's Main Street. She studied the images of horse-drawn ice delivery wagons in front of the feed store. Its image caused a stirring in her soul, a reminder of the small girl growing up in a quiet town.

She would beg to ride into town with her dad and granddad when they needed to buy seed or a replacement part for farm equipment. When the crops had a good harvest, she could order a double fudge sundae from the Lunch Bucket's soda fountain. A rare treat.

Maggie sat up straight. Realization dawned like brain freeze.

She drained the cup, barely savoring the lump of caramel that slid into her mouth from the bottom, wiped her chin, hoisted her bag from the counter, swung her feet onto the wooden floor, and blasted through the screen door.

"Knock knock!" Grace leaned in, peeking at the bed.

Tiffany hung up her phone and rolled over, groaning into the sheet.

"Can we come in?" Grace tiptoed over. "I brought someone with me. This is Connie McCoy." Connie hovered near the door. "Come here, she's not royalty." Grace beckoned at Connie then turned back to the bed-lump.

"Tiffany, we came to visit you for a few." Grace thought about poking the still mass. She took the polite road, instead. "Ahem."

A mumbly under-the-covers mumble emphasized clear resentment, then, "I'm busy."

"Ha ha. Very funny. We can see you're solving world peace." Grace raised an eyebrow at Connie who inched toward the door. "Say something," Grace mouthed.

"Let's go, Miz Grace." Connie tugged at the door handle.

Grace frowned. "No. Tiffany, where I come from, people are polite to visitors."

"Where I come from, people leave other people alone if they don't wanna be bothered." Tiffany's muttering remained monotone.

At least we're getting a response now. Grace gave Connie another elbow to the side.

"W-we wanted to say hi, Tiffany, we don't want to bother you." Connie's unease increased visibly with Tiffany's rudeness. She turned with pleading eyes. "Let's go, Miz Grace."

Grace resorted to classroom tactics. "I guess you deserve to be in such a sorry state if this is the way you treat other people." Sometimes calling a difficult teenager's bluff worked...other times, well, not so much. Grace stared at the sheet and sent up a quick prayer.

Connie gestured at her watch. Grace crossed her arms and lifted her chin.

Gradually, the sheet lowered. Long lashes over those brilliant sea-green eyes rimmed with puffy, red lids glared over the white cotton. "Can't you see I want to be left alone?"

"Holly's busy and can't spend time with you. We..." she shot Connie a glance, "thought you might be getting lonely." She held up a market basket. "Look, I brought muffins. I made several kinds since I don't know your favorite."

Tiffany looked past Grace at Connie. "What do *you* want?"

"Well, Connie here is about your age." Grace hurried to answer before Connie bailed. "She's the daughter of the town vet. You have a lot in common. Connie loves animals. Tell her about your dog, Theo—"

"Leo!" Both Connie and Tiffany corrected her in harmony.

Grace detected a micro-change in Tiffany's manner.

"You know about my dog?" The pop star had a soft side.

"Who doesn't? He's part Yorkie, right?" Connie moved closer. "I remember reading about him in Teenzine. You rescued him. We have five dogs at our house right now. And plenty of cats, mostly from that fire."

"Fire?" Tiffany's features softened even more. She listened about the daily care the little critters needed after their smoky rescue.

Slowly, the fire melted the ice. Tiffany and Connie dished about their pets, common interests, safe ground.

Grace backed away from Tiffany's bedside, out the door for a cup of coffee from the nurse's station while the two chatted.

A half hour later, Grace and Connie rode the elevator down, Connie talking nonstop.

"She's really kind of sweet and not what I expected after you get through the wall she tries to put up against people she doesn't know, oh, Miz Grace I'm so glad we came, I think she liked the cranberry-orange ones best..."

Grace nodded, proud of herself for accomplishing this small step toward connecting with Tiffany. As Connie chattered about the visit, a fun thought came to her.

Could she?

On their drive back to the theatre, when the young girl took a breath, she told Connie about her idea...bold and spontaneous. Okay, not spontaneous, but it was bold, and very un-Grace-like.

A few doors from the coffee shop, Maggie stopped to read a sign taped inside the hardware store window.

CLOSED FOR FUNDRAISER SIGNUPS
WE WILL REOPEN TOMORROW

"Aunt Nelly's noggin, I keep forgetting. Sam's at the theater." She scurried down the sidewalk and hit a wall of people clumped behind temporary dividers. Don's deputies were directing foot traffic, attempting to keep the autograph seekers separate from the row of photographers while allowing for the flow of pedestrians. As she stood there looking for the way into the theater, cameras angled toward her, then dropped when they realized she wasn't a celebrity.

"We're getting lots of publicity for the fundraiser, Maggie," Mayor told her when she managed to wind her way into the lobby. "I've just given my third interview."

"Don't let that fifteen minutes go to your already generously-sized head, Jack. You seen Sam?"

"He's inside working out details with the crew."

She stepped through the swinging door and scanned the room as Sam's baseball cap disappeared behind one of the curtains on stage.

She started down toward the steps to follow him backstage and almost tripped over a tiny ballet dancer stretching across the aisle. "Excuse me, hon, but really..."

"Sorry, Miss Maggie." The little girl scooched her pink-tighted legs out of the way.

"These people really should keep their kids in control," Maggie muttered then remembered they were here to help her. "I'm sorry, what's your name?"

"Chloe."

"Chloe. That's a lovely name. And I like your tutu. It's very pretty. Don't mind me, I have some things on my mind. Thanks for being in the show."

"You're welcome. Good luck with the petting zoo!"

She waved at Chloe and scurried up the aisle, climbed on stage and walked around a leg of the curtain. Sam stood behind the stage manager's desk scribbling on a tablet of thick paper.

"I need to get into your filing cabinets."

"Hey, there you are Maggie. You what?" Sam looked up, a puzzled grin spreading. "Did you see all the talent we have? Should be a great show."

"Sam, something's come up and I need to look in those file cabinets in your upstairs storeroom. From the days your store brokered harvests."

"I can't leave now. I've got to block the entrances and find someone to work the rails."

"Just give me the keys, and I'll let myself in." Maggie held her hand out, palm up.

He dug in his pants pocket and drew out a bundle of keys. "This one's to the front door. The storage room key's among them somewhere." He flicked through several. Someone called Sam's name from the throng backstage.

"I'll manage." Maggie snatched the ring weighted with keys of all sizes and generations and turned on her heel.

I'm coming!" Sam turned back to Maggie. "It's dark up there, be careful." His gaze searched hers. "You coming back over when you find what you're looking for?"

"You won't even miss me." Maggie trotted up the aisle and across the street past a row of reporters smoking and drinking coffee under a pop-up tent in a parking space across from the box office.

She unlocked the glass door under the green canopy. "Shoo!" Pigeons scattered as she stepped in and switched on fluorescent lights to reveal rows of tools, lawn equipment, and display cases. A faint aroma of sweet feed mixed with hay and fertilizer stirred memories of visits to these rooms with her father and grandfather for meetings with the bookkeeper. Her heels echoed across the linoleum and through the empty store, quieter than a church on Monday.

She climbed the wooden stairs, and on the landing illuminated by the light from below, searched through the ring for the key to the storeroom. After a couple of false tries, she finally found the one that unlocked the heavy door. It swung back with an arthritic creak, but refused to give up the heavy key ring even though Maggie jiggled and tugged.

"Stubborn." She left the snarl of metal hanging from the door and felt along the rough paneling for the light switch and caught a splinter in her left thumb. She dropped her bag and peered at her throbbing digit. Too dark to see, much less remove the plank of wood, she stuck her thumb in her mouth and continued to explore the wall for the light switch with her good hand, this time patting instead of swiping.

A memory surfaced, and she reached toward the center of the room. A string dangled from a bulb in the ceiling, and she grabbed the ceramic knob on the end and tugged. A dusty bulb popped, and its yellow glow faintly illuminated the wall and a section of wooden and metal file cabinets.

Faded pictures of dairy cattle, curly, out-of-date calendars and pale county maps hung in dusty frames. A clock with Wonder Bread dots for hours told the correct time twice a day.

She squinted to read the faded labels and, after a quick calculation, decided on a year likely to produce useful results. She pulled open a drawer, its metallic scraping raising tiny hairs on her neck, and also apparently waking up a tiny critter as she heard something thump behind her.

"You better run for cover or I'll feed you to my reptiles." She warned it.

Satisfied, she lifted thick files and piled them on her forearm, holding her wounded digit clear of the grime-covered manila cardstock. Maggie flipped open the first, then set it aside to leaf through the next.

Across a small sheet of browned parchment, she read her great-grandfather's name. The balanced pages teetered and, anxious to keep her thumb from smearing, she let several papers drop. The page skid-sliced her thumb and pain careened up her arm with the paper cut.

She tossed the clipped-together paperwork bearing her grandfather's name on top of the cabinet, and pressed tight to the throbbing injury, kneeling to pick up the scattered papers off the wood floor.

She reached into the dark to pick up a stray page and heard a heavy thunk-thunk.

A thought flitted across her mind. *A giant mouse?* Then, the lights went out. *That turns out the lights?* Then she felt a sharp crack, accompanied by searing pain across the top of her head and she crumpled into a heap.

CHAPTER SEVENTEEN

Connie pulled her Jeep to the curb outside the theatre. A couple of cars were parked in front, and the lobby lights were still on. Grace and Connie jumped out and went inside.

Sam met them at the door, his baseball cap shoved high on his bald spot. "Grace, have you seen Maggie?"

"Not since lunch. Why?"

"She came by earlier and asked for the keys to my store. Said she'd be back in thirty minutes or so, and it's been over three hours. When I checked my pocket for my keys to lock up the theater, I remembered I gave them to her. Do you have her cell number?"

"She doesn't carry one. I'll go look for her. But I still haven't shown you my act."

"You go look for Maggie, I'll put you in the program. I just need to know how long it runs. You mind if I put you in first?" Sam jotted on his clipboard. "I thought we'd use you as an example of community involvement in our voiceover pitch."

Grace took a moment to process that. "Sure I guess that's okay. I can get it out of the way and help answer phones or something." Her mind jumped back to Maggie. "I've gotta look for our guest of honor now."

"Wait, I'll go with you!" Connie followed Grace out the back of the theater.

"How long?" Sam hollered.

"As long as it takes!"

"No, how long is your act?"

"Two minutes!" Grace followed Connie out the door and muttered, "Two minutes too long."

"You're funny, Miz Grace." Connie trotted to keep up with her. "I'll bet you're a terrific dancer."

"Terrific as in talented? No. Terrifically brave maybe. It's more about putting yourself out there, not the talent. You know the whole Bucket List thing us old folks challenge ourselves with."

As they crossed Main Street, Grace could see the front door to Sam's store gaped wide open, the lights blazing through the showroom windows onto the sidewalk out front.

"Shoo!" Inside, a flash mob of pigeons pecked at birdseed spilling on the floor near the register. Connie and Grace whooped and flapped their arms to wrangle them, fluttering and arguing, outdoors onto the stoop. "Now I know where the term foul odor came from." Grace pulled the door shut and caught her breath. They stepped over smeared pigeon droppings and down the aisles, past plumbing, electrical, and home improvement supplies. Nothing stirred.

"Maggie, are you in here?" Grace's call echoed. "Let's see if she's upstairs." Connie stuck to her as she clattered up the wooden stairs to the second floor landing. A dark hallway loomed. "Let's go back downstairs." Grace fought a quiver in her voice and turned to go back down.

"Miz Grace, wait. That door's open and the light's on." Connie peeked around her and pointed.

As one unit, they stepped over to the door. Grace peered around the doorframe. "Maggie?" She cleared her throat. "No one's here. Let's go."

"But all the lights, the birds," Connie reminded her.

"You're right." Grace argued with her flight reflex. "Someone has been here." Even Maggie wouldn't leave lights on, doors open and the feed store vulnerable to feathered freeloaders.

She took a timid step into the room, Connie sticking with her like a bad cold. Among a row of filing cabinets lining the walls, the closest ones appeared untouched. Drawers in a couple of wooden ones toward the back, however, were pulled out and left hanging. Several files poked out above the others, and sheets of paper lay scattered around the dusty floor. As if they'd been dropped in haste.

"Look at the mess," Connie whispered, reached to pick up a pile.

Grace grabbed the girl's shoulder, making her stop. "Don't!"

"What?" Connie startled. "Why?"

"This is a crime scene!"

"Did you touch anything?" Sheriff Melton wrote on a small tablet. He'd driven over as soon as he received the dispatch about Grace's discovery.

"Certainly not. I've watched Jessica Fletcher enough to know better!"

The sheriff shone his flashlight into the dark corners. "Sam, can you tell if there's anything missing?"

Sam paced around the old storage room. "Sheriff, it's been so long since anyone went through those old files that I really couldn't say. They're mostly old sales receipts and records from years ago, before we computerized."

"Grace, since Sam gave Maggie the keys, it's not breaking and entering. There's no sign of any struggle. Look, the key's still in the door." Sheriff jiggled and forced the keys out and handed the ring to Sam. "I don't see anything here except a mess. And that's not breaking any laws, Grace. Although, we all know your standards in that department."

Grace shot Sheriff a scolding look and he dropped his grin. "Maybe Maggie got frightened by a mouse and dropped everything to run."

"Maggie frightened by a mouse?" Grace tutted. "Please. She doesn't scare that easily. She's been on African safaris and a houseboat on the Amazon. You think a mouse would spook her?"

Connie piped up. "And why would her pickup still be parked on Main?"

"Maybe it wouldn't start." Sheriff's radio crackled. "She hoofed it home."

"I've got a bad feeling, Don. Something happened to Maggie." Grace's tummy clenched as she forced herself to say the words.

"You're all being dramatic. Or been watching too many crime shows," Sheriff mumbled under his breath. He headed down the stairs. "Why don't you run over to her place and see if she's there. I'll bet something came up at the farm." More techno-crackle. "I've gotta run. Armchair detectives," they heard him chuckle as he clomped down the stairs.

"I have to go, too, Miz Grace." Connie hugged her. "I know Miss Maggie's okay. Sheriff Melton's probably right. She's around here somewhere." Connie's heels clattered a staccato down the stairs.

"You need a ride home? It's getting late." Sam moved toward the door. "Now that I have my keys back, I need to lock up the theater."

"Did Maggie say why she wanted the keys?" Grace remained in the middle of the room. "What could she have been looking for?"

Sam lifted his ball cap and smoothed the top of his head. "She mentioned something about the days when farmers sold their crops through a broker here." He gazed at a faded picture of Main Street over the row of cabinets. "And something about her granddad. I'm sorry. I wasn't paying much attention, so many details for the telethon." He glanced at the unhelpful clock on the wall. "What about that ride?"

"No thanks, I want to look around a little longer if you don't mind."

"Pull the door closed behind you." Sam shook a finger at her. "And don't clean up that mess downstairs. I'll do that tomorrow. Promise?"

"Scout's honor."

"The door will lock behind you." Sam clomped down the stairs. Grace opened a drawer and thumbed through the files scattered around, looking for a clue. Anything. *Please Lord, what is Maggie trying to tell us?*

Ready to give up and go home, the decades of grime creeped her out and she reached up to pull the string to switch off the bulb and froze. Something didn't seem right. *Why was the dust disturbed on the top of one cabinet and not any of the others? Something was here and now it's gone.*

Letting go of the string, she moved for a closer look. Her toe kicked a soft, heavy object in the shadows. Camouflaged in the dark among a heap of dusty feedbags lay Maggie's enormous bag.

The oxygen seemed to rush from the tiny room. Grace knew Maggie would never leave Purse Everest behind.

She quick dialed the Sheriff's office, but the dispatcher put her through to Don's voicemail. "I found something you should know about." Her voice sounded high pitched and whiny. She slowed and tried to speak calmly. "After you left, I found Maggie's purse. She'd never leave it behind. And there was..." This was going to sound thin. A tingle crept up her spine. "Some dust was disturbed on top of a file cabinet. Call me." Her gut told her he'd insist on more than dirt evidence and a forgotten handbag. Don didn't know Maggie like Grace did.

A few minutes later, with Purse Everest's straps wrapped around her handlebars and the bulk settled in the basket, Grace pedaled down the dark Path to Maggie's place. She leaned over to switch on her handlebar light. It flickered and went out. *Darn batteries.*

Her bicycle tires crunched on the drive up to the unpretentious bungalow. A motion sensitive light flickered on, illuminating the yard up to the front porch. No lights spilled from inside the house or any of the outbuildings.

"Maggie!" Grace stepped up onto the front porch and waited for her eyes to adjust. She groped the door and found the handle. Wishing she'd brought a flashlight or an NFL linebacker with her, she pulled the screen open and tapped on the frame. Hearing no response except her own heart pounding, she tried the knob.

Locked solid. She trotted back down the steps and dug in Maggie's purse. No keys. Searching her memory, she glanced into the shadows and ran back up. She scooted her hand under a clay pot in the corner under a swag of lacy webs. She prayed the spiders lurking would sleep and not scamper up her arm. Her fingers clamped around a rusty key nestled in a pile of icky droppings. Wiping her hand on her pants, she poked at the keyhole, found the slot, and slipped the key in. She opened the door and switched on every light switch she could find. The porch and small parlor lit up.

She called Maggie's name again but knew down to her toes that no one would answer. Several well-loved and long-worn furniture pieces jammed up against the walls and fireplace. In the center of the room, a crate of kittens, a tortoise in a cardboard box, and wonky heaps of scorched supplies were piled after the last fire. The kittens squinted in the bright lights and climbed over each other, mewing at Grace.

She switched on lights in the kitchen, found bowls, and filled them from bags of food in the service porch. She measured out kitten chow, shredded lettuce for the reptile, and dumped pellets into bowls for the bunnies. Grace knew Maggie's animals always came first, and if she didn't show up to feed, something was definitely wrong.

Finished with the houseguests, she removed a large-beam lantern that hung beside the back door and clicked it on and off testing the batteries. Wondering what to feed the larger animals, she pulled her cell phone out of her pocket and found Connie's number. The call went to the girl's voicemail, as did the vet practice's phone, so she exchanged her sneakers for a pair of rubber boots a half size too large and tromped out to the barnyard.

She guessed what the animals should eat, carried bales of hay and studied labels on feedbags.

Grace watched a pot-bellied pig snuffle eagerly into his slop and remembered Sheriff Melton's remarks about "no obvious foul play" and she should "wait before panicking."

"Well, I'm ready to panic now," she told the pig, slapping the gate shut behind her to move on to the next hungry critter. Eventually she was satisfied they'd all been fed something resembling a decent meal, so she tromped back inside the cottage, hoping to find Maggie and hear a simple explanation for the whole drop-file-and-run incident. No such luck.

She flopped onto the couch, massaging her feet, and pulled out her cell to leave Mark a message. "Pray for Maggie, honey, I can't imagine what's happened to her." She hung up and leaned back to shut her eyes, but the light from the kitchen bothered her. Besides, who could rest? She busied herself washing dishes at least a week old piled in the sink. As she pulled the rubber plug to let the water drain, she racked her brain about what else she could do. She considered going through the heaps of mail when the answering machine's blinking light caught her eye.

Grace's now squeaky-clean finger reached over and pushed the play button.

"This is your last warning." A gravely voice raised hairs from the top of her head all the way down into her granny panties. "We'll get it all back…ninety-nine years ago…" Scratching techno-noises garbled the rest. Grace leaned closer. "…before the sun goes down on the..." Then nothing.

Before the sun goes down on what?

She studied the counters piled with appliances and newspapers, farming magazines and sales flyers. Cardboard boxes filled with veterinary supplies teetered on top of dusty canning jars. Before her head could burst into flames from the clutter, Grace grabbed a sack and began stuffing advertising flyers and empty envelopes into the trash. She tutted, remembering the neat and orderly home Maggie's mother and grandmother kept. She and Maggie had spent hours peeling apples for sauce and snapping beans on the back porch for the farmhands. All the while, Maggie complained and fidgeted.

Grace would have stayed indoors all day. She loved sorting and sifting, rinsing the fruit, washing the jars, listening to the women discuss recipes and argue measurements. Yet Maggie always wanted to finish in a hurry, never happy to stay inside. She was happiest outside, building hay-bale kingdoms and climbing up on the tractors, pretending they were pirate ships sailing off to imaginary lands.

"I'm never going to do inside work when I grow up," Maggie said time and again. "I'm going to have someone do all my cooking and cleaning so I can spend all my time outdoors."

All my time outdoors. The life she'd planned with Joe had been about these animals and taking care of them. Maggie didn't care about keeping a clean house.

Grace took a long breath and pulled open stubborn drawers and dug through piles of jumbled papers, looking for anything that might give up a clue. She wiped the counter and lifted the phone handset for a quick spritz. She thought of Lew, Maggie's attorney and, except for Sam, her last known contact, before her disappearance. She hung up, waited a beat, then lifted it again and dialed 411.

Maggie awoke to a throbbing so intense she couldn't tell exactly where it came from. She was sore from the top of her head all the way to her toes. Unable to move or do anything else, she took inventory of her condition.

Pasty tongue.

Thirsty.

She strained to open her eyes, failed. Like her lids were sealed tight. *If I could see something...are they...taped shut...?*

So THIRSTY! A cool drink of water would be heaven.

Can't move my left leg, something heavy is holding it down. My left leg is attached to my right one. They've gone and done it. I'm kidnapped!

What kind of doofus kidnapper tapes your eyes shut? Honestly.

Rough damp boards scraping my back, my legs are tied together and arms are pinned. And my thumb! How it hurts. Am I still in the hardware store? That's a familiar smell. Rubber. Leather. Lemon.

A faint cell phone jingled outside, breaking into Maggie's confusion. A gruff voice mumbled, halted, spoke again.

Scuffling footfalls approached and a door pushed open.

"Don't go in there, idiot!" someone yelled, setting off dogs barking.

"Shut up, stupe!" Another male voice growled, low. His boot thudded onto flesh from the sound of it, and barking changed to a whine. "I'm making sure she's not dead!"

That voice sounded familiar. Maggie heard boot steps moving toward her on the concrete floor. She took a breath and tried to lie still.

A boot poked her side and she broke her silence, groaning an indignant protest through duct-taped lips. Must have satisfied him because he left, slamming the door.

The scents, the familiar layout. Now Maggie knew for certain she'd been locked in the garage Joe used to rebuild Baby. Away from the main compound of barns and sheds and hidden from the road by a stand of pines, no one could see into the clearing. Great. *Prisoner in my own backyard.*

Maggie concentrated on Idiot's footsteps. *Who was he? Who was he with?*

She heard the other man's voice. "What are we going to do with her?"

Maggie couldn't hear the reply.

"We gonna leave her there without food or nothing?"

Maggie strained to hear how Idiot would answer, but heard only a metallic sliding sound, maybe the door on a van? and then quiet except for a dog's whimper. She'd seen a van lately—in her driveway? At the store? Her head pounded, her thoughts muddled. First things first: how to get out of this predicament? The pain in her hand and the ache in her head made it almost impossible to concentrate.

I've got to get out of these ropes and tape. She remembered a Houdini-like act she'd seen in Belgium years ago. Could she dislocate her own shoulder?

"Claire de Lune" played in lyrical tones. Animals with wings sang and flew by. More "Claire de Lune" growing louder, now.

Wait. Not a song.

A ringtone. Her cellphone.

"Hello?" Grace answered in a nasally thick morning voice.

"Hon, are you all right?" Mark sounded anxious.

"Oh, hey, honey. Did you get my message?" She sat up on Maggie's couch, a throw afghan pulled to her chin as it all came back to her. "I'm still at the farm." Fully awake now, she filled him in on the events at the hardware store.

"What did Sheriff say?"

"Said he'd put an alert out, but since it didn't look like foul play, he can't do anything else. He's overwhelmed with all the extra work around town this week."

"Be on the lookout," Mark told her. "What are you going to do now? Are you coming home?"

The living room critters scratched in their boxes. "I should feed the animals. I'm waiting for Lew's office to open. Maggie had an appointment with him yesterday and he might know something."

"I wish I could help, but a pileup on the freeway last night filled our

ER. We're slammed." She could hear him speaking to someone, then, "I hate to add to your day. Never mind, I'll think of something else."

"What?" Grace padded in her socks into the cleaner kitchen.

"We need the beds, and I need to release Tiffany. There's no reason to keep her any longer. But I hate for her to go back to her trailer in a taxi. I'll call Holly."

"That's so thoughtful of you." Grace pulled down a clean glass to pour herself some ice water. "I hate for her to be alone at that trailer at all what with the rest of the cast and crew busy with the fundraiser." She turned the tap, waiting for Mark to finish answering another question on the other end. "What would you think about inviting her to stay with us for a couple of days?"

"Grace..." Mark hesitated. "I don't mind calling the girl a taxi, but you can't continue to get involved in everyone's life and expect to keep your own in order."

"I know. But she's got nowhere else to go, and the paparazzi will find out she's alone out there..." She took his silence as agreement. "It'll just be for a couple days. I'll come over this afternoon and pick her up."

He signed off in a hurry to get back to his patients. She opened the refrigerator door. Her plan had been to practice her routine this morning and bake muffins for the greenroom, but under the circumstances, she'd have to forego the rehearsal. Her tummy protested waiting on the muffins, though, and she began pulling ingredients out. Surely Maggie had ingredients for a couple dozen muffins in her farmhouse kitchen.

About an hour later, Connie pulled up in her jeep. "I got your message when I woke up. Sorry you had to feed by yourself last night. Did you figure out what everyone eats?"

"I guess we're about to find out if anyone's dead or complaining of a stomachache."

They tromped toward the stable. "Mark needs the bed, so I'm going to pick up Tiffany later." Connie measured grain and showed Grace where to dump the buckets of oats. "When you two clicked so well, it gave me another idea of how to connect with her. She really lights up when you mention animals." The donkey flicked its long ears as if to emphasize the point. "I didn't do so badly last night, did I?"

"Especially her dog." Connie scratched the donkey's neck. "Everyone seems fine, good job, Grace. You're a good friend to do so much."

"Thanks. Anyway, I had a thought, and if they're as busy at the hospital as I think they are, we won't get caught."

Connie's face registered a little shock. "You in trouble? What are you planning?"

Grace told Connie her idea, and they giggled and planned their escapade while they finished feeding.

Dressed in skintight couture jeans and designer high heels, Tiffany sat in the visitor chair and looked out the window into the hospital parking lot. She didn't look up when Grace and Connie walked in.

Grace sat on the bed and laid a backpack next to Tiffany. "Good morning, Sunshine!"

Connie leaned against the bed. "You ready to get sprung from this place?"

"I guess." Tiffany worried the bandage on her arm. "Where's Holly?"

Grace fought back a grin. "The hospital administration thought it would be better if we take you home. The media are glued to her, trying to get to you. But we're nobody, so we're taking you home." Grace lifted the backpack and placed it in Tiffany's lap. "We brought escape clothes for you. A disguise. Go on, open it."

Tiffany rolled her eyes and tossed the pack onto the bed. "No thanks, I'll take my chance..." The backpack squirmed and rolled off the bed. Grace dove and scooped it up before it smacked onto the linoleum.

"What the...?" Tiffany drew her stilettoed toes up and hugged her knees. "What the flip is in there?"

Grace unzipped and tipped the opening toward Tiffany. Leo's head popped up.

"Leo-baby! Oh, c'mere!" Tiffany reached in, sweeping him into her arms. "I missed you so much."

Leo trembled from tail to tongue in a licking frenzy and doggy greeting. He snuggled under her chin, his little tail whipping a tiny breeze.

Grace's heart sang at the teenager loving on her pet then interrupted the reunion. "We'd better get you out of here. Even with my connections," she nodded at Leo, "he's not allowed in here. I'll let the charge nurse know you're going with me. Hurry now, change into these clothes." Grace affected a serious tone and addressed Connie. "The eagle flies at midnight." She grinned and pulled open the door, looking left and right before stepping into the hallway.

While Connie kept Leo quiet, Tiffany changed in the restroom. Three quick raps at the door announced Grace's return. She wheeled a chair in and helped Connie re-snuggle Leo into the backpack.

Tiffany emerged, dressed in a pink hoodie of Connie's, a pair of loose fitting sweat pants, and pink Converse sneakers.

Tiffany shook her head. "Are you kidding me? I don't need that. I'll walk."

"Hospital policy." Grace gave her a stern look.

"Like the dog?" Tiffany remarked. Connie giggled.

Grace gave up. "I guess we've already broken enough rules. On with the crime spree." She pushed the chair away from the door and glanced around the room. "Did you get your toothbrush and check the drawers—?"

"Yes, Mother, let's go." Tiffany pushed past and pulled the door open.

"At least cover your head, just in case." Grace reached up and flung the hoodie up so it hid Tiffany's very recognizable long blond mane.

Grace's heart pounded as they sneaked past the nurse's station. Leo whimpered a tiny yelp.

Her heart quickened, but the voices from the nurse's workroom didn't sound the alarm. They trotted to the back stairway and descended to the ground floor. Grace shoved open the door into the staff parking lot and leaned out, checking for stray paparazzi or autograph hounds.

"Coast's clear, let's go."

They crouched, dashing between the parked cars, Connie in the lead and Grace and Tiffany following.

A voice shouted from above. "Look, I see someone!"

Grace couldn't believe someone had gotten on the roof. A camera lens the size of a yule log teetered toward them, and the sound of tires on pavement came from a green sedan that careened around the ambulance bay and straight for them.

"Start your engine!" Grace hollered at Connie. "Tiffany, run!" Grace planted herself in the middle of the aisle, body blocking the sedan's progress toward Tiffany.

Tiffany clutched Leo inside the backpack to her chest and cleared a concrete cherub next to a koi pond. Connie threw the jeep into reverse and weaved down the lane to stop next to her.

Tiffany snapped open the door and fell into the back seat. Connie popped the jeep into first, two-wheeling around the end of the row, and screeched to a halt behind Grace. The passenger door swung wide open and she shouted, "Jump in!"

The green sedan reversed when Grace wouldn't budge, and she turned and sprinted for the escape car. As Connie tore out, they heard the sedan round the corner behind them. Its driver misjudged and clipped the corner of a retaining wall, glanced off, and spun around to crash head-on into a metal dumpster.

Connie stopped, backed up, and idled next to the trash heap.

"The airbag didn't even deploy, and he looks okay." Grace pulled out her phone. "I'll call inside and tell them to come out and check on him. In the meantime, let's get out of here. I'll take the responsibility of leaving the scene." She speed dialed the switchboard. "Tiffany, you lay low until we're clear."

Tiffany huddled on the floorboard with Leo's head poking out of the canvas.

"I'll notify the Sheriff now." Grace hung up. "Under the circumstances, he'll understand why we didn't stick around."

"You telling about Leo?" Connie snickered.

"That will be our little secret." Grace checked behind them. "You just drive, Mario."

They drove out of the hospital parking lot and past a line of trucks whose aerial antennas soared into the afternoon sky like sailboat masts in the harbor. A gaggle of reporters mingled on the sidewalk. No one else moved to follow them or even paid attention as they stopped at the intersection for a red light.

Grace flipped her phone closed and checked for chase vehicles. "Looks clear. I think you can sit up now, honey, but leave the hood on to be safe."

Tiffany climbed onto the back seat and unzipped the backpack. "They're all so jealous of each other, always trying to get the first scoop. The spotter didn't even tell the others we were on the move." She lifted Leo out of his hiding place.

"Is he okay?" Grace twisted around to look at the little dog.

Tiffany nuzzled him to her face and they snuffled and snuggled. "He's been through worse," Tiffany cooed.

In a few minutes, Connie turned into the town park and across the gravel lot. She wound past the honey wagons and utility trucks.

"Where is everybody?" Tiffany looked around at the deserted compound.

"At the theatre in town working on the fundraiser." Grace opened her door and stepped down, tilting her seat so Tiffany could climb out. She offered a hand for support, but Tiffany leaned her bandaged arm against the frame and climbed down by herself.

Grace launched into her prepared speech. "Tiffany, with all the crew in town, you're going to be all alone out here." She shut the door closed behind her. "Everyone knows you're out of the hospital. Why don't you grab some of your things and come and stay with Dr. Mark and me? I can make you some home-cooked—"

"I can take care of myself." Tiffany set Leo on the couch, allowing the trailer door to slam shut.

Grace shrugged at Connie.

"That was rude."

"I'm not giving up on her, come on." Grace reached up, opened the door and climbed up the stairs. Connie followed.

The customized trailer, with its plush carpet and rich fabrics, almost felt homey. They watched Tiffany glance at envelopes and magazines, sorted through a stack of papers. Except for the accumulated mail, the temporary living quarters appeared clean and tidy.

"Mail?" Grace stepped toward her.

Tiffany studied a sheet of paper. "My call sheet. I have lines to work on for a scene. But thanks for the ride." She didn't look up.

"I'm pretty sure all the filming on *The Scrapbook* is postponed," Grace told her. "The fundraiser's tonight and everyone's over there."

"You want to come watch?" Connie brightened. "Grace is the opening act. She's—"

"Connie's our backstage manager...." Grace changed the subject. "She can put you in a VIP seat where you won't be bothered."

Connie wouldn't be deterred. "I'll bet you can't guess what her talent is."

Tiffany sighed. "I'll change and give you your clothes back." She unzipped the jacket and handed it to Connie. "Anyway, I need my cell charger." She disappeared into a room down the hall.

When the door closed, Grace leaned into Connie. "She's forgotten more about performing than we'll ever know. She's not interested in our little talent show."

"You're probably right." Connie reached for the doorknob. "I'll get my clothes later. No hurry," she called. "The telethon's on Channel 56 if you're interested in watching it." She eyeballed Grace. "She'd be surprised at some of the talent we grow in our small town."

Grace flicked her hand dismissively at Connie then added, "I'm leaving you my cell number in case you change your mind or need anything." She scribbled on an envelope and propped it next to the microwave.

Tiffany whistled from the bedroom door and Leo jumped off the sofa and trotted down the short hallway. The door opened, they heard "Bye," and just as quickly, she pulled the door shut.

"If you go out, call a bodyguard or something!" Grace attempted, then turned back to Connie with a shrug. "She's probably tired." Opening the door, she checked to make sure it would lock behind them. "Don't worry. Tiffany surely won't go anywhere tonight."

Connie checked both directions before turning onto the tarmac from the dirt lot. "I hope she's okay. If the press finds out she's in that trailer they won't leave her alone."

Grace dug in her purse, left another message for the Sheriff, then dialed the hospital. "I'll tell Mark, we've been made."

Connie shot a quizzical glance. "Huh?"

Grace held the phone away from her ear and lifted a shoulder. "I watch spy movies, too you know."

Mark filled her in on what happened after their getaway. "The driver was more embarrassed than hurt. His insurance will buy us a nice new dumpster." Mark laughed. "I was getting tired of that old one anyway. When I heard the commotion in the parking lot, I went across the street and told them Tiffany developed complications we couldn't handle and I'd transferred her for consultation."

"You didn't!"

"Then I put a couple of orderlies in EMT uniforms and told them to drive slowly." She could hear the amusement in his voice. "Not so slow they'd catch on, though."

Grace thought a beat. "You sent them on a wild diva chase!" As suddenly as that realization occurred, her glee faded. "She didn't want to stay with us, though. She's all alone in that trailer."

Grace could hear Mark's insistent beeper. "I'm sure she'll be all right. Oops! got to run." Mark's end went dead.

Connie looked over. "What did he say?"

"He told the reporters that they were transferring Tiffany, then sent a decoy ambulance to Franklin City Regional on Cypress."

"That's the hospital where I was born." Realization spread across Connie's face. "Wait, they moved it a couple years ago, didn't they?"

"They did."

"What's there now?"

"Now it's a Red Cross blood bank. I read in the paper they're having a donation fair today."

"There's an irony, they're out for blood and...that's funny, Miz Grace!" Connie slowed to take the rotary toward town. "Do you need to go home first, or should we go straight to the theater?"

"Dropped my costume off yesterday at the theater, but I need my bike from Maggie's. We should stop and get it, check and see if she's there."

"I'll run out and check water bowls!" Connie trotted toward the barns when they'd pulled in.

Grace climbed the stoop and pulled the door closed. Still no sign of Maggie, everything looked the same as it had earlier; including the muffins. She searched the cabinets for something to put them in, and finally settled on a plastic grocery bag. It would have to do until she could get them to the theater. Maybe the props people would lend her something nicer to display them on.

A few minutes later, they lifted the bike into the jeep. "I didn't expect to find her here, but I had hoped she'd come home and confessed to running off just to scare us." Grace admitted to Connie as she brushed tire-dirt off of her hands.

"Is that something Maggie might do?" Connie clicked the ignition. "Up and leave her responsibilities, her animals, and worry her friends like that?"

"I wouldn't put anything past Maggie to tell you the truth." Grace thought of how cruel that sounded under the circumstances. What if Maggie really was hurt? Or worse? "Speaking of animals, I'll call Rose to ask her to take the evening feeding in case I can't make it back before dark." Grace called as they drove into town.

"I'd be happy to," Rose agreed. "And break a leg tonight. I'll be watching you on television."

Grace's stomach lurched. "I'd almost forgotten. My mind's been on Maggie."

"Don't worry, I'm sure Maggie is fine, just cooling off somewhere. And you're going to knock it out of the ballpark. Or theater as it were. You never cease to amaze me, Grace Harkins."

On the way back to town, the low battery warning on Grace's cell phone flashed. "I'm calling the sheriff's office to see if there's any word on Maggie before my cell dies."

The dispatcher told her there were no new developments. "Please make sure someone patrols the trailers." Grace thanked her then hung up. "They're stretched thin but she's going to alert them that the Eagle is in her nest."

"If it weren't for Maggie missing, this would be too much fun." Connie turned onto the rotary toward the theater. "It's almost like being in a movie or something." She cut a glance over. "Speaking of acting, you ready for tonight?"

Grace's tummy squirmed. "It's only two minutes, I can get through it."

"It's only the two counties," Connie teased. "Just a couple thousand people will watch."

Grace felt the blood drain from her face.

Connie reached over and patted her shoulder. "Don't worry, Sheriff Don has his people looking for Maggie, and you're doing a good thing helping raise money for the animals." Connie braked to a stop in the bumper-to-bumper traffic. "Mind if we pull into Loaves and Dishes for a bite? It's going to be a long night for me."

"Sounds good." Grace regarded Connie. "Why don't you perform as well? You have a pretty singing voice."

The traffic snarled down Main. "I prefer stage managing, in the back in the black. I'll leave the glamour and hard work to you talented people."

"Don't sell yourself short. I know what goes on backstage."

Connie waited while a car pulled out then zipped into a space in front of the Loaves and Dishes.

Grace and Connie stood on the sidewalk outside the deli. "They're packed, it may take a few minutes to get something." Grace checked traffic. "Help me get the bike down, I'll lock it up then get us a table while you wait in line."

After helping, Connie braved the crush inside while Grace wheeled her ride behind the theater. She thought about dashing in with the box of muffins she'd brought for the greenroom, but a line of autograph seekers blocked the backstage door, so she left them in her basket. If someone took them, God bless the soul who needed to take her muffins, anyway. She lifted the front tire into the rack and scooted back across the street to search for a table where they could eat their meal.

"Traffic's heavy and the parking's already a mess." Grace took the tray from Connie as she ducked to avoid hanging ferns.

Surges of people moved past on the sidewalk, and stood in line at the theater across the street to buy tickets. After Grace offered a quick blessing over their meal, for Maggie's safe return and for the production, Connie indicated the turnout with a nod. "I bet we sell out."

Grace set down her fork and willed her tummy to settle down. "Your dad coming to watch?"

Connie split a scone in half. "Said he'd stop by for a bit after his rounds. Hope he can find a place to park, I don't want him to miss our opening act."

"I'm a bit rusty, so no fair pointing and laughing." Her insides twinged a revolt. "But it's a good cause. The animals and all."

"You've known Maggie a long time, haven't you?"

"Since junior high." Grace welcomed a distraction, but talking about Maggie only brought up other concerns.

"Has she always been…?" Connie bit into a tomato and the juice trickled down her jaw.

"Has she always been gruff?" Grace wiped the girl's chin with a corner of her napkin.

Connie swallowed. "She wanted to stop the movie and stuff. You seem cool with it, though."

"She's outspoken, always has been. Sometimes friends…sometimes people…" Grace stumbled to get the words from her brain to her tongue.

"Sometimes people…" Connie prompted, watching Grace's face.

"Never mind. Let's just say there has been some… awkwardness."

"Dish. What happened?"

Grace buttered the scone, nibbled then returned it to the plate. "Do you have plans for the summer besides working part-time?"

"Oh no you don't, girlfriend. You've got a story to tell, and we've only got a few minutes until call time. Go."

"Look at us. Just last year I was your English teacher. Now we're BFF's, sneaking Hollywood movie stars past the paparazzi."

"Wait, you're changing the subject again." Connie narrowed her eyes peering over the rim of her tea glass. "Back to the story."

"Reader's Digest or long version?"

"Long."

"Many years ago, back in the dark ages …" Grace expected an eye roll that didn't happen. She continued, "…when I was about twelve or thirteen…My daddy took me on a business trip to Chicago. Except for the flight, which is another story, it was exciting. I'd never been further than Franklin City. Anyway, after his meetings, we went to a film festival. They were showing *Gone with the Wind*. I fell in love with the plantation, the scenery, the costumes. I wanted to be Scarlett O'Hara. So brave and in charge."

"I think they run that on TNT once in awhile."

"A classic. Fast-forward a few years to our junior-senior prom. I wanted to be on the decorating committee. Correction, I wanted to *be* the decorating committee. I had the whole thing planned."

"Lemme guess." Connie nibbled her scone. "*Gone with the Wind*."

Grace reconsidered a bite of oily lettuce dripping with dressing and set the fork down. Why did she open up to Connie? She'd never even told her own daughter about the incident that caused the rift between herself and Maggie. Connie's wide-eyed gaze plunged her further into the backstory.

"I managed to get myself appointed as the chairman of the committee. I started months early, picked the orchestra—" Loud banging on the plate glass window made her jump and she dropped the fork, splattering Caesar salad across the room.

"Hey! Whatcha doing?" Holly's muffled voice hollered at them from the other side of the large pane of glass. "It's call time, let's go!" She zigzagged across the street through bumper to bumper traffic.

"Jiminy Christmas." Connie shoveled a last bite of salad and wiped her face. "Look at the time!"

Grace tossed their trash in a receptacle and trotted outside. She held her hand up to stop the flow and followed Connie between the line of cars winding down Main. "You have to tell me the rest later, Miz Grace." Connie pulled the backstage door open. "And break a leg!"

CHAPTER NINETEEN

Tiffany pushed the power button and watched the screen pixilate and dark spots bloom and recede. She punched off and dropped the remote on the sofa. Still in Connie's clothes, she inspected herself in the mirror. *So, this is what a teenager looks like. Weird.*

Leo yapped at his empty dish, and she dutifully filled it with his organic kibble, pulled a frozen meal for herself from the fridgette. When the microwave timer beeped, she lifted a corner of the paper and sniffed. Disgusted, she dumped the smelly mess into the sink. "Worse than hospital food. At least you liked your dinner." She scooped up and carried her pocket-dog down the steps, and waited for him to salute the trailer railing.

With his business finished, they meandered through the quiet compound, passing more trailers, honey wagons, the portable dressing rooms, and equipment trucks. At the far side, an opening in the four-foot, three-rail fence led away from the park through a copse of cedars at least as tall as a soundstage. Leo followed Tiffany. He lifted paws and stepped gingerly into the taller grass, his tiny nose sniffing the piney air.

"You're digging this, aren't you, bud?"

He answered with a dainty sneeze and hopped behind her, pausing to explore the flora and sniff messages left by other fauna. The path they took wound behind the park, and past farmhouses and outbuildings.

"Hey, buddy, you don't miss riding in your bag?" Leo trotted past her. "I'm crushed. I paid a lot for that."

Leo broke into a bouncy trot, his nose lifted high, and he, moving ahead of her along the pathway apparently followed some intriguing odor. "Hey, don't go too far!"

Before she could close the distance between them, growling and snarling invaded the afternoon quiet, and from beyond a grove of trees, coming toward them at lightning speed through the undergrowth, a pair of snarling dogs exploded through the weeds, hurling themselves at the trembling Yorkie.

They strained and pulled against metal chains that flipped and bounced behind them. They ran full speed until one of the chains wrapped itself around a tree trunk. One dog slammed at the end and flipped over rivaling an Olympic floor exercise. He landed on the fern-covered forest floor with a thud.

The other dragged a chain bunched up with weeds and dirt. As he ran, the clods broke apart and with the weight gone, he gained momentum.

Tiffany broke into a run, but the pink borrowed sneaker was too-big and flopped on her foot. She tripped, and toppled over several yards from Leo.

"Leonardo, come here!"

He stood in the middle of the path, cocking his head in confusion. "Come here, baby!" She was terrified the dogs would make fast food of him.

She slipped the shoe back on and shuffled toward him, screaming at the monsters. The chains bought her some time while they strained and lunged, then something cracked, and one of their anchors broke loose and he launched airborne. Snapping teeth bared, he flew toward Leo. The other one managed to free himself as well, and together they closed in on their prey.

Tiffany panicked and looked around for a stick or a rock, anything she could throw to hurt or distract them when a gold and brown streak shot past her. Petrified Leo would be the victim of a three-way tug-of-war, she sobbed and screamed. "Go away! You horrible mutts! Stop it!" Tiffany kicked off the ill fitting sneakers and ran.

Rushing Leo, the horrible twin hounds, fangs bared and drool motors in high gear, made it to their afternoon snack. Bounding onto the trail within snout's reach of the little dog, they ran between fence posts and straight for him. Rounding the obstacles, they angled, misjudged, and head butted with a full speed thud.

In the time it took for them to turn on each other, the flash of fur from the west sped into them at full growl, another canine voice added to the confusion.

She snatched Leo up into her arms just as the canine hero dove at the culprit dogs. The chomp-fest commenced in growls and snapping jaws. *Superdog* sunk fangs into an exposed flank releasing a high-pitched yelp. Now he commanded the undivided attention of the snarling dervishes and urged them with bared choppers to reverse their position and retreat.

In a doggy-ballet of tangled flailing legs and ears pinned flat in submission, the two interlopers spun around, pirouetted, and tore away in the direction from which they'd come. Tiffany could hear their skedaddle through the undergrowth punctuated by flying sapling bits, clods of dirt flying, and broken chains snapping in their wake. The rescue dog disappeared after them, nipping and snarling at their skinny heels.

The popping and crashing, barking and snarls faded into the distance, and Tiffany examined Leo. The successful fang ripped open a two-inch long flap in his neck, and blood seeped, dripping down her arm.

She wrapped her hand over the wound and blood oozed between her fingers. Not makeup blood, but the real thing. She swallowed back the queasy taste that bubbled into her throat and patted her pockets. She remembered now she'd left her cell charging.

Tiffany searched up and down the path. Cradling Leo, she lowered herself to sit, reassuring the trembling little dog and pressed her palm to his wound.

"We'll get this bleeding to stop and go back for help, babe," she cooed.

"Hey!" All of a sudden, a nasty cigarette odor gagged her as someone grabbed her from behind. "What are you doing snooping around?" He yanked her to her feet.

"Ow! Let me go!" Leo bobbled in her grasp, yelped in pain. She squeezed him tighter. What kind of creep are you?" Tiffany surged forward but he had a firm grip.

"Get back here. You're not going anywhere." The smelly man threw a grimy cloth over her eyes. He shoved her forward, blinded and still clutching the limp dog to her chest. She gagged at the foul odor reeking from man and material.

"I'm not snooping." She struggled and stumbled. "Stop touching me. I need to get Leo to a vet."

"I ain't lettin' nobody go nowhere. You seen too much."

"I didn't see anything except your out of control dogs. Who are you, anyway?" Tiffany stiffened. "And if you think you're going to get funny with me, I have a black belt."

"I got a brown belt says you're not in any position ta argue. You're goin' with me." He gave a rough shove. Unwilling to let go of Leo, she knew she couldn't fight back.

"Ow!" The creep's gnarly grope forced her to stop in place.

A door squeaked open and he pushed her through what must have been a doorframe, her shoulder scraping splintery wood. "Stop it!"

"Git in there. And shut up."

She caught herself from tripping as he pushed her over a doorjamb, terrified of letting up pressure on Leo's gash. He whimpered and shivered as the thug jostled them and slammed the door behind them.

"Don't come out of there, girly, or I'll shoot you dead." He pounded on the door. Tiffany stood still, listening to his threat followed by a loud whistle as the goon called for the runaway dogs. His footsteps faded away.

After all the years of dodging stalkers and paparazzi, the worst had happened. Not only had she been kidnapped, but her precious Leo was hurt. She fought tears and tried to remember what her body guard had taught her about this kind of situation. "Don't panic, don't provoke and never give them any reason to think they won't get what they want as long as you're alive."

She tried to remember his cautions then realized the goon hadn't tied her hands. She balanced Leo on one arm, holding her hand over his wound, and lifted the foul cloth off. She waited for her eyes to adjust to the darkness. A late afternoon dusky haze filtered through window grime behind her. She could make out a concrete floor, a workbench and tools like set contractors used hung on the wall. Some sort of workshop.

"Hmmm!"

Something—or someone—lurked inside. "Hello?" Tiffany whispered. Who else was in town worth kidnapping?

"Hm-hm-hmm!"

She tiptoed a couple steps. "Who is that? Where are you?"

"HMMM!"

She squinted, unsure if the form in the darkness was people or animal. Her eyes cleared and on the floor against the opposite wall, something squirmed.

"Ohmigosh!" A woman with her hands and feet tied, her eyes and mouth taped over, lay hunched against the wall. "Are you okay?" Tiffany squatted next to her.

"MMM!" the tied-up blob insisted.

Tiffany shifted Leo so she could free her hand and tug duct tape off the captive's lips.

"Ow!"

Next, Tiffany pulled at the piece across her eyes, but her lids stuck to the tape. She looked up in a creepy, zombie glare.

Tiffany peered closer. "What are you doing here?"

"I'm having a bake sale, care for a brownie?"

Tiffany blinked. "He kidnap you, too?"

"Yes, brainchild." The woman turned sideways. "Now untie my hands."

"Why are you here? You rich or something?" Tiffany managed to loosen the rope with her one free hand.

"Not by a long shot. You're Tiffany Lane, aren't you?" The old lady rubbed her lips. "You think this is about you?"

"I've gotten kidnapping threats all my life, it was just a matter of time. I was always okay until I came to this stupid little town." She looked down at the injured dog in her arms. "We were taking a walk and his mutts attacked Leo. Probably to distract me so he could get his grimy hands on me. Then me and Leo got shoved in here." She looked up at her fellow captee with conviction. "Let's get out of here."

"I hate to break it to you, but there are more than one, so it may not be easy to get past them. They call each other Stupe and Idiot, and they live up to those names, let me tell you." She rubbed her wrists and sat up.

"What do they want if they're not my stalkers? It doesn't make sense." Tiffany cuddled Leo. "How long have you been here? You must be starving and stuff."

"Yeah. And stuff." She unwound gray tape from her ankles, creakingly freed her legs, and rubbed her backside.

Tiffany watched her. "You know who I am, what's your name?"

"Maggie, Maggie Neville. Nice to meet you. And your little dog, too."

"Welcome to the First Annual Talent Telethon for the benefit of Cherryvale's Animal Rescue and Petting Farm!" Jeff Field, tuxedoed up and polished down to the shoeshine, opened the evening as emcee.

"Where's my first act? Grace?" Connie spoke into her headset mic, her voice could be heard in the dressing rooms over backstage monitors. From her desk on stage right, she would make sure each act waited to go on as Jeff announced them. A bank of telephones manned with volunteer pledge-takers sat on stage left. The audience, packed to standing room only by the draw of celebrities and the news of Maggie's disappearance, surged into every available seat.

"Where is Grace? She's up!" Connie searched behind the curtain legs into the wings.

She gave the stretch hand signal and Jeff stalled through the opening introductions. Grace's cue followed a three-minute video of Maggie's place but they couldn't wait too long, the broadcast had already gone live and Sam had scheduled the evening down to the last second, running into the wee hours of the morning.

"Sorry. Here I am!" Grace clicked up to Connie. "My zipper stuck. Costume's been packed away a few years."

Connie spoke into her headset, and showed Grace to her mark as video playback rolled.

Grace posed on her mark and smoothed her costume. She drew her left heel to its beginning position, took a cleansing, calming breath, and tried to look at the audience to see if Mark had made it over from the hospital. The stage lights blinding her, she was only able to see up into the rafters of the theater. Above each side of the stage, screens showed the video of Cherryvale, a short interview with Maggie about the plans for the farm.

Grace tried to recall what Connie told her the final scene would be before the film ended and it would be time for her dance, but she decided to just watch and wait. It was an odd angle, and she had to crane her neck, but she could see most of the video screen if she leaned out a skosh and balanced on her leading foot. Besides, she hadn't seen the video Sam told her was designed to get the hearts softened and pocketbooks opening for Maggie's rescue operation.

Her own heart warmed when she recognized Carl waving at the camera from the cockpit she'd been in so recently. He'd flown the camera crew, called a second unit she'd learned, for aerial shots of the fire's devastation. The voiceover sounded as if the plea for donations was about to begin and she lifted her arms to await the first notes. But something unusual caught her eye and she jerked back to look up. The image flickered off and a picture of Maggie taken for the church directory last year appeared with the news about her recent disappearance. "Anyone with information as to her whereabouts, please call the pledge line," the announcer said. It took a second or two, but it dawned on her. *Could it really be that simple?*

In a flash, she knew where Maggie was, and as she'd suspected, was probably there against her will. Most definitely against her will. Grace searched the faces of the Valers in the audience. Again, the bright stage lights blinded her, but from the sound of their applause, it didn't seem anyone else caught what to her was so obvious.

Her heart thrumming, she forced herself to remain on her mark, her arms still poised, but she twisted toward the wings. "Psst! Connie!"

Hand on headset, Connie's lips moved, and Grace knew she was giving lighting the order to begin. Connie gave her a thumbs up and smile of encouragement as the video screen went dark.

"No, I'm not nervous!" Grace hissed. "I have to tell you something." Before she could make Connie understand, the lights flashed on, and the familiar first bars of "Yankee Doodle Dandy" poured from the speakers. *Well, maybe a little nervous.*

Grace lifted her baton, the audience clapped politely, and a little tittering came from the front row. Instead of discouraging her, a surge of adrenaline inspired by their doubt urged her into action. She started with a slow shuffle, and her rhythm increased as the tempo built, feeling the beat, the old movements coming to life in the routine she'd performed hundreds of times years ago in her competition days.

Her tap shoes kept time through a series of shuffle hops, cramp rolls, bombershays and fast wings. As the music crescendoed, Grace spun around, and with her back to the audience, flicked a tiny switch on her baton. She twirled, both ends of her baton popped and snapped, sparklers launching tiny pins of stinging heat onto her bare arms as she spun it around and around, overhead and behind her back.

Grace twirled, tapped, and ended the routine with a step ball change. She threw the flickering baton over her head, up and out of camera range, caught it on the downside, and landed on the stage floor in a full split, left hand on her hip, the still-sparkling baton above her head in a dramatic ta-dah flourish.

The audience paused in collectively stunned silence.

Someone started clapping slowly, a lone sound. Ripples of applause picked up, and soon the room erupted into whistles, "you go girls!" and cries of astounded congratulations.

Jeff Field entered from stage left, grinning into the camera. "Wow! What can I say? How about that?" He clapped in Grace's direction then turned back to the audience. "How about one more round for that amazing start to our show? Please dial the number on the bottom of the screen if you liked that spectacular performance by our own Grace Harkins, best friend to Maggie Neville, tonight's benefactress. I'm sure Maggie would be extra proud of you."

Again, the audience cheered, Grace waved, but the reminder about Maggie spurred her to make a hasty exit. She leaned toward Jeff's microphone, "Thanks..." she caught her breath, " "please call in your pledges," waved at the camera, then exited, tap-tapping her way off-stage as quickly as she could without actually breaking into a not-so-cool run.

Off stage, she whispered into Connie's available ear, "I think I know where Maggie is! We have to hurry. Have you seen the sheriff? Where's security?"

She lifted the headset off her ear. "Mic feedback. Great job. We'll chat later." She patted Grace on the shoulder and motioned to a dog act to take their mark.

Grace searched the desk lit by a dim blue light. She found a pencil nub and scrap of paper, scribbled her suspicions and handed it to Connie, but a poodle needed extra encouragement to go onstage and she scurried away without reading it. Grace tucked the paper into the cue notebook and pointed to it dramatically, but she couldn't tell if Connie saw her in the dark wing from the brightly lit stage.

Unwilling to wait any longer, Grace wiggled past performers, prop tables, and costume racks lining the hallway to stuff her street clothes into a gym bag in the ladies' dressing room, now empty as all the performers for the first hour were waiting in the wings. She didn't take the extra time to squirm out of her spandex bodysuit, but she kicked off her tap shoes and crammed grateful toes into more forgiving Keds.

Laces untied and trailing, Grace dashed through the backstage door onto The Path and circled around to the sidewalk next to the street. She searched for anyone in uniform, a security guard, or a deputy, shoot, she'd settle for the postal carrier at this point. Even with Main Street looking like Hollywood on Oscars night, there was no one she could recruit to help on her mission.

She grabbed her bike and ran-walked toward the street, but a wall of people surging toward the doors blocked the sidewalk. Opposite the line of humanity, a cordoned area fenced in the press and their cameras and microphones, utility trucks and scads of heavy equipment. Cars of curious tourists clogged the streets. What could have been a blessing to Maggie's financial problems might end up being the reason she would come to harm, that is, if Grace couldn't find some way to rescue her.

"Look, maybe that's somebody!" A reporter cried to a cameraman and all eyes focused on Grace. "She's nobody, never mind."

"I might have a lead on where Maggie is, do you want to come help me? You'd get the scoop?"

The reporter shook his head. "Nice try. I've got orders for pictures of Tiffany Lane. Try a cable unit, they're more gullible." He guffawed and as Grace turned away in a near panic, she heard them tease each other, something about never believing amateurs.

She ran into another people wall and ping-ponged for a couple of frantic seconds trying to get through. She caught a glimpse of a uniformed deputy directing traffic, but he either didn't see or just plain ignored the tiny bespangled woman jumping up and down trying to attract his attention amidst the sea of surging bodies. As one clump stepped aside to let her pass, another mob filled in, blocking her from moving across the sidewalk to reach him on the street.

Surrounded on all sides and feeling more than a little claustrophobic, she summoned her most authoritative teacher voice and hollered, "Make a hole, people!"

The crowd parted, she trotted to her bike, grabbed her handlebars, and pedaled onto The Path toward Maggie's farm.

"Oh, you're the one they're having the telethon for!" Tiffany sat cross-legged next to Maggie on the shed floor. "Shouldn't you be over at the theater? It starts pretty soon!"

Maggie cut a sideways glance at the young girl. "I thought I'd hang out awhile in my garage first and do some bleeding." She gingerly rubbed the back of her achy head, caked with blood from the goon's knockout blow.

"Oh, sorry. Speaking of bleeding, look at Leo."

"Here, let me see." Maggie took Leo from Tiffany and palpated his coat for tooth punctures. The skin around his neck flapped and still leaked a little blood.

Leo managed a half-growl, half-whine.

"Good job stopping his bleeding. I'll make a bandage." Maggie untucked her cotton button-down shirt and bit the edge to start a tear. She ripped enough to wrap around the tiny dog a few times. "We also need to make sure he doesn't go into shock."

"How do we do that?"

"Keep that pressure on it, like you're doing, until it stops bleeding. I don't think it's very deep." Maggie looked around for a blanket or anything to wrap him in. "Need to keep him quiet and warm. Hold him against your skin, that'll work, and it'll reassure him as well."

Tiffany opened her top button, laid the pet on her chest and then re-buttoned. Only his round head stuck out. His ears relaxed and he quit whining.

With Leo settled, Maggie used a section of fabric to dab at her own head wound then ripped several inches to wrap her thumb where the splinter had pierced the skin. Feeling woozy, she sank against the garage wall and eyed her cellmates. "You look like Kanga and Roo."

"Who?"

"Didn't you ever read *Winnie the Pooh*, or watch the movies?"

"I think I was in a commercial with him once."

Barking outside erupted and Leo quivered.

"They're back. He's scared of those devils, aren't you, honey?" Tiffany cuddled Leo closer and covered his ears.

"You two shut up in there!" a gruff voice warned.

"What do you want from us?" Maggie shouted, forgetting she was supposed to be gagged.

"Shut up, old lady!"

"Well. Of all the nerve."

"Clam up or I'll come in and gag you again!"

The barking quieted and it appeared the rude man had gone away. To be safe, though, Maggie kept her voice low. "If he opens the door, be ready to run. I'll distract him." She looked around for something heavy to hit him over his bad-mannered head and grabbed hers as pain shot through.

"Can we open that big door?" Tiffany indicated the large car-sized sliding door.

"The slider's got a combination padlock on the outside. Besides, it makes a ton of noise when you open it, even if we could get it unlocked. And the other door opens fine, but the dogs are tied up just outside. Either way, Idiot and Stupe are sure to hear and catch us before we can run away. If I can run. Maybe you can get away and run for help." Maggie held her head between her hands.

"How do you know so much about this place?" Tiffany nuzzled the top of Leo's head.

"It's my garage. We're at the back of my own property."

"The place that keeps catching on fire?" Tiffany's voice went up an octave. "Are we going to burn up in here?"

"I hope not. I guess it's a possibility."

"We have to think of something. In a Movie of the Week once, we got out of a trap like this through the roof. Props brought us a ladder."

They looked up, but darkness loomed over their heads. "My stunt double actually did the climb, though," Tiffany admitted.

"Does it look like we have a props crew here? Or stunt doubles?" Maggie shook her head and regretted the movement. "Ouch."

"At least I came up with an idea. If it wasn't for me, old lady, you'd still be bound and gagged."

"If it wasn't for me, your little dog would be going into shock."

As they retreated to imaginary corners to pout, devil-dog barking started again. Leo whimpered.

"I've got to answer a nature call." Maggie pushed herself to her feet and grabbed for a bit of wall to steady herself. When the room stopped spinning, she tiptoed around Baby. Next to the tool cabinet, she found a bucket to tinkle in. Much relieved, she stood up again and waited for her head to clear. Then she remembered the phone extension near the tools but remembered when she lifted it she'd turned it off to save money.

"This phone used to connect to the house, but I had it shut off after Joe died." Maggie gingerly hung the earpiece back in its cradle. I used it to call him in to supper." She returned to the wall and sat down next to Kanga and Roo.

"What are we going to do?" Tiffany's voice trembled. "No one knows we're here. Everyone thinks I'm safe in my trailer."

"I don't know." Maggie leaned against the wall to pray.

CHAPTER TWENTY

Rousing herself to some sort of action, Maggie looked over. "You don't have a mint or something, do you?" She doubted the starlet could carry an extra piece of lint in that too-tight outfit.

"I wasn't going to say anything, but now that you mention it, your breath—"

"Not for my breath. I meant to eat. Those creeps haven't given me anything." Maggie shook her matted red curls. Of all the luck to be stuck with genius here. She held her head in her hands. "Wish I had my bag, the least those chuckleheads could have done was kidnap my purse with me. There's no money in it, if that's what they were after." She realized Tiffany had gone silent. "What's on your mind?"

"Leo doesn't think you like us. He's usually right about people."

"Why does he—why do you say that?"

"I didn't get a 'thank you' for untying you. And your 'tude stinks. I'd have thought you'd be glad to see me, or anyone besides the kidnappers. What am I, too bridge-and-tunnel for you in your perfect town?"

Maggie couldn't believe the nerve of this girl. "Is it always about you? You realize you're a cliché, don't you? It's not like I'm having a tea party. I was knocked clean out and brought here unconscious." She regarded Tiffany's lower lip and wondered if it was an act or legitimate emotion.

"Don't worry, we'll get out of this. Anyway, what were you doing out alone? Don't you go everywhere with body guards or an entourage or something?"

"Budget cutbacks." Tiffany kissed Leo. "We went out for a walk after I got home from the—after I got home."

Maggie glanced at Tiffany's bandaged wrist and gestured at the dog. "Come here; let me see how he's doing. Let's start over. Sometimes—okay, usually—I'm too quick to judge." She lifted the cloth from Leo's wound. "At least he's not growling at me this time."

"He recognizes your scent. He has to rely on smell."

Maggie searched Tiffany's then Leo's face. "Why?"

"He's blind."

Realization dawned. "I'm sorry." Maggie suddenly felt an intangible connection to the pair.

"The vet says he sees blurry objects in motion, but that's about all. But he never forgets a person's scent. And if anyone's mean to me, look out, mister."

"I can tell you're inseparable."

Tiffany took a long pause then, "How long has your husband been dead?"

"Almost three years."

"You two married long?"

"We met in college. About 28 years."

"Wow. Kids?"

"No kids." Maggie leaned back and studied Tiffany's face. "I heard you tried to commit suicide. Wanna talk about it?"

Tiffany slid her bandaged wrist down to her side. "I did not try to—why does everyone think that? I slipped against the shower door."

Maggie tried a different angle. "I know what it's like to feel depressed. Lately I've been angry at my husband for leaving me. I know it's silly. He didn't want to have a heart attack and die. But I can't help feeling abandoned." Of all the people in the world, she bared her soul to Tiffany Lane? Something about the dark room, the uncertainty of their situation, opened Maggie's heart—and mouth—to this girl.

They sat silent for a few moments, the companionship melding. "I kinda know what that feels like. I never knew my father. Ruby doesn't want anything to do with me, except when she wants to be seen on the red carpet at my premieres."

"Ouch."

"I'm used to it, I guess." Tiffany spoke slowly, her voice soft and unlike any character Maggie had heard her perform. "It's funny, but when they told me about this movie, I never knew how it would make me feel to say the words. I mean, I read the script but it didn't affect me until...somehow living it out like that..."

"You can tell me." Maggie studied Tiffany's face shadowed in the darkness. Without the harsh makeup and severe lighting, she was a natural beauty. "Not like we're going anywhere soon."

An unmistakable touch of melancholy tinged Tiffany's explanation. "It's about a girl raised in the foster system because her mother's a druggie. She ages out and her social worker gives her a scrapbook with pictures of her bio family. She uses clues from them to look for her real dad."

"Does she find him?"

Tiffany nodded, a lock of golden hair swinging off her shoulder. "That's who Jeff plays." She shoved the strand of hair behind her ear, careful not to jostle the sleeping canine. "Those are the scenes we're doing here in Bananaville, but..." Tiffany buried her face in Leo's fur.

"Go on." She prodded the girl with a gentle elbow.

"When the television series I grew up on ended, it felt like I'd lost my family."

Maggie gave her a minute to regain control. "I never thought what working on a set would be like for a child."

"I know it's lame." Tiffany drew in a ratchety breath. "And you're going to think this is weird, but something about this town and the way the people are with each other..." she flicked her palm across a wet cheek, "made me miss having a home and family more than ever."

"I'm not surprised. There's something special about the Vale." Maggie dug in a pocket for a tissue but came up empty. "I'm sure you'll find if you let people in..." Maggie realized she was preaching to herself as much as the girl next to her, and prayed for the right words to offer as Tiffany sagged against her.

"Sometimes God sends us love in strange places." Maggie blinked back tears as she focused on the irony, "and through people we'd never seek out on our own. Kind of like right now."

Maggie wrapped an arm around Tiffany and Leo. "Seems like you and I have a lot in common. You mind if I add you to my prayers?" This famous face, fresh from the cover of gossip rags, hid real feelings, real hurts. Money and fame don't make up for loneliness. Neither did shutting out people who most wanted to love us.

"No. I don't mind...but..." Tiffany peeked at one-browed Maggie. The absurdity combined with raw emotion tipped her into a giggle, but she caught herself and hugged Leo. "You were the one trying to get us to stop filming weren't you?"

Maggie winced and stared through the grimy window. "A person has a right to voice their objections when their community is affected."

"You're like everyone else who thinks the worst of someone before they get to know them."

"So what I read in all the gossip rags about you has been rubbish?" Maggie challenged. "The partying, the arrests?"

"Well. I guess I could have been hanging with some of the wrong crowd, it wasn't my fault."

First a snort then under her breath, "Blame-thrower."

"What's that mean?"

"You have no idea how to live like most teenagers your age. Going to school and making good grades, working a part time job and preparing for college. Everything's been handed to you."

Tiffany bristled and sat up, Leo whined. "Nothing's ever been handed to me, I work hard. Besides..." She resettled him, shushing and cooing.

"Besides what?"

"I think I kind of would like to try living like a normal, as you call it, teenager, like Connie. Maybe see if I can hack it at regular school."

"So what's stopping you?"

"If you didn't notice, I live in a different world. Even if I went to school…it wouldn't work."

"Who said it wouldn't work?" Maggie twisted to look her in the eyes. "If that's something you really want to do, no one should stop you." She brushed a strand away from the piercing sea green eyes. "I'll help you, just tell me what I can do."

"Well, I guess it would help if I could start over somewhere away from Los Angeles."

"Like Cherryvale?"

Tiffany brightened. "Like Bana—" She corrected herself, "like Cherryvale. First I'll need someplace to live. I could rent an apartment or something."

"Nonsense. You can live with me. My house isn't glamorous. In fact it's downright shabby. But I'm all alone and I could use the company."

"I couldn't impose, I insist on paying."

"No way. I'm not taking any money from you, what do you take me for, one of your superficial homeys who only cares about you for celebrity and handouts?"

Tiffany flinched. "Don't dis my friends."

Maggie softened. "You'll be my guest…" Maggie shot her an uncertain look. "I've never had a daughter or anyone your age around. I may be difficult to live with."

"That's okay, I've been told I'm impossible to live with!"

Maggie and Tiffany looked at each other, and burst into the giggle fit they'd been holding back.

"I'm not going to let you slack, though," Maggie warned. "It's all about making over Tiffany, academically and socially. Whatever else you want to improve upon."

"Deal." Tiffany looked away, doubt seeping into her tone. "Why are you doing this?"

Maggie pondered that a sec. "Sometimes God places us in challenging situations to shape us into who He wants us to be." Maggie's gaze peered into the darkness. "Got to admit I never saw this coming, though."

Tiffany half-snorted. "I've never really been into the God thing."

"How's that working out for you?"

"Not so good I guess," she admitted. "One more question."

"What's that?"

"How's your God getting us out of this mess so we can get started on *His* new plan?"

Her rubber tires bumped and skidded as Grace steered over The Path's trampled patches neglected since last summer. She pedaled as fast as her fifty-something legs could go, the grassy patches slowing her down. The perimeter road would have been shorter in distance, but the traffic snarling into town meant CherryPath would have to do.

She glanced toward the horizon, checking for the sun. Twilight had set in with a wink of the first evening star beyond a full moon, gray and dim.

The mysterious caller's warning jostled loose in her mind as her bike thunk-thunked over the rutted thruway. *After the sun goes down* droned the voice on the answering machine. What will he do after the sun goes down? She pedaled faster and regretted never mastering no-handed steering. Her cell phone lay somewhere in the bottom of the gym bag now bumping against her bottom. She swung the bundle around with one hand and steadied her handlebar with the other. The bag lodged under her chin, she bumped her knees in rhythm.

She fumbled and scooped under the clump of street clothes, but came up empty handed. She skidded to a stop and kneeled to rummage through the bottom. A run in her dancer's tights zipped from her knee and skidded up her thigh.

She palmed the phone's smooth cover and pulled it out, flipped it open and punched numbers. The black screen mocked her. *Drat you, Grace, you have to plug the dern thing in.*

Back on the bike, she slung the bag across her shoulder, changed her mind and ducked free, throwing the whole shebang on the grass. Unencumbered, she leaned on the pedals with her full body weight, the bike's frame creaked then responded with a burst of speed and into the filming compound.

She serpentined past the honey wagons and equipment trucks. Her thighs burned, tall grass dragging the rubber tires. She knew running would be faster, provided her now over-stretched and under prepared legs would cooperate. She jumped off like a ten-year-old and fell down like a two-year-old. One shoe flew off, tripping her into a full on face plant. She'd only stepped into the toes of her shoes without pulling up the heels and they'd scattered like chickens in a windstorm.

Hand to nose, she checked the grass nearby for the airborne sneaker but gave up and kicked the other one off. Her earlier splits-action left its own brand of sore. *Dancer up, Grace!* Barefoot, tights in shreds, sweat and no telling what else streaking her stage makeup, she soldiered on, limping and trotting toward Maggie's place.

Grace slowed when she caught sight of the clearing where the ancient garage stood. Feeling like a spy in one of those action movies Mark loved, she slowed, and checked the area for sight or sound of anyone suspicious. Her breath sounded like a surfacing whale, she doubted she could sneak past a hibernating bear, much less those really big, really mean-looking guard dogs chained up next to the shed.

She tiptoed from behind one tree to the next, trying to hide her red, white and blue spangled bodysuit that insisted on twinkling in the rising moonlight.

Diversion, we need a diversion. Grace racked her brain for something to distract the dogs from eating her. *Aha!* She retraced her steps back to the bike. Several muffins meant for the green room lay near the handlebar basket having spilled out of their bag.

She snatched them up and sneaked back, maneuvering as close as she dared to the shed in the clearing. The dogs snoozed, muzzles resting on outstretched paws. She un-wrapped a muffin, tore off a small piece, and threw it about five feet from of the closest one. He didn't stir.

Encouraged her plan might work, she tossed several balls of muffin dough further and further until the last bit landed as far as she could fling it. Holding her breath and taking careful steps to make as little noise as possible, she circled wide, creeping behind the garage on the opposite side of the still dozing canines. Her stocking feet forced her to choose her steps carefully, testing each footfall before shifting her entire weight to move forward. Eventually she made it to the wall. She searched the ground, and in the fading haze of dusk, picked up a shiny pebble. Grace drew her arm back and hurled it at the Shepherd's flanks, perhaps a mite too hard. He scrambled to his feet, barking, startled and angry. The Rottweiler joined in.

A "shut up!" warning came from a van parked across the clearing.

Circling in confusion, the Rottie caught a whiff of something tasty. His sniffer on overdrive, he stuck his nose in the dirt and soon enough, found the first bite. His companion, alerted to the possibilities, lunged at him. They snarled and postured then each stuck a nose to the ground, searching for more tidbits.

Grace knew she would have only a few minutes to circle the shed. Over the dogs' smacks and warning growls to each other, a tinny AM radio played inside the van.

Though the smaller door beckoned, she didn't dare try it or risk being seen by the Rascal Flatts fan, so she tiptoed around to the other side of the building.

The good news, now she was out of sight of the strange vehicle. The bad news, a large, rusty padlock held firm.

Her blood thickened like cottage cheese to her knocking knees. She whisper-shouted, "Maggie!" keeping an ear alert for the imminent return of the dogs but her heartbeat thrummed a retreat signal and she wondered if she'd hear a train headed for her. She squeaked, "You in there?" and held her breath. A cricket tuned up in the darkening woods.

About to cut and run and look for someone to help, she turned to tiptoe away. Something niggled in her mind. "Sometimes God puts people in our lives for His reasons. Not ours." Shelby's wisdom replayed. "You gonna come through or think of yourself first?"

The combination lock appeared to be the same one she remembered from the days when she and Maggie used the garage as their playhouse. They had spent long summer afternoons re-imagining it as everything from a deserted island a la *Robinson Crusoe* to a hutch in Africa described so eloquently by Joy Adamson raising the lion cub in *Born Free.* Grace realized her love of literature spawned their journeys of imagination, and Maggie's thirst for adventure had inspired her wanderlust and desire to explore the four corners of God's creation. Their friendship had been more compatible than she'd realized, her desire to find Maggie unharmed stronger than ever. New found determination prompted her to study the lock. She dove into her memory dashing at cobwebs. *I remember*!

She tipped up the lock to catch light first resting at 12, backward to 29, then stopping at 52. Maggie's birthday. No luck. She tried again, clicking, pausing, still listening for dogs or thugs. She took a deep breath and let her eyes and fingers rest. She heard a noise from inside the shed and thought about calling out again but knew her time would be up soon, the dogs would surely return from their muffin hunt and find her standing there. She didn't want to hasten their return.

She spun again, more deliberately and a little panicky this time. She forced herself to make slower movements and turned the dial all the way around to clear it. Once again she started over. After two more tries, the lock finally loosened, the hook let go and Grace lifted it from the latch.

Holding her breath, she pulled the door with enough force to start it along the track. *Please Lord, keep the squeaks and scrapes silent.* She stuck one leg through a narrow opening she created, sucked in her belly to squeeze through and looked up to see the silhouette of farm tools poised high and ready to bash in her head.

"Wait! It's me!" She covered her head with her hands.

"Ohmigosh!" Maggie tossed the weapon aside and grabbed her. "We thought you were one of the kidnappers sneaking in to... "

Tiffany shoved the door closed behind Grace's spangled back.

Maggie released her and Grace breathed in relief then grabbed

Tiffany in concern. "What are you doing here? I thought you were in your trailer?" Leo's head bump prevented a full on hug and she realized he blinked up from Tiffany's shirt cradle. "What's wrong, is he hurt?"

Tiffany gave her a quick update on her walk, the dog attack, and her incarceration with Maggie.

"Do you know who they are, Maggie?" Grace's eyes adjusted and she looked around. "What do they want with you?" She didn't mention the obvious reasons why Tiffany might be here; stalkers, crazy fans...she'd never seen Cherryvale in such upheaval. Maybe Maggie was right about the movie crew ruining their town.

"I certainly have no idea. They haven't made any threats except, of course, rudely shoving me in here with nothing to eat or drink." Maggie lifted a remaining eyebrow in scorn. "How did you know where to find us?" She stepped back for a look at Grace's get-up. "And how did you get to be such a mess?"

It's a long story." Grace ineffectively smoothed down loose spangles. "But a patriotic mess, don't 'cha know? I'll explain later, but for now, how are we going to get out past the dogs and their goons?"

"Call someone on your cell phone gadget," Maggie commanded.

"Of all people, I thought you hated them new fangled things." Grace patted nonexistent pockets in her leotard. The phone, gone in her abandoned gym bag.

"I know you have one, so you might as well use it to call for help. But at least you're not on it all the time like some people who can't go a minute without that thing attached to their ear..."

"Fresh start, Maggie!" Grace shot a warning finger.

"...and it can be so rude when you're trying..." Maggie paused. "There I go again." She smoothed her ginger-colored bangs and lifted her chin. "What I meant to say was that they can be quite useful in some circumstances."

"Good girl." Grace held up her hands. "But for all that, I don't have it with me."

Tiffany watched the women in disbelief. "Here we are about to be eaten or worse and you two work on your relationship? Seriously?"

Maggie sighed. "She's right. Speaking of which, how did you get past the dogs?"

"Muffins. I threw itty-bitty pieces to lure them away. So I could get close enough to the building to get in."

"That's smart." Maggie nodded. "I admire your ingenuity. Now what's your plan?"

"Isn't there a phone in here?"

"Disconnected. Thought of that already."

Grace peeked out a grimy window. "Even if we could get past the dogs, what about whoever's in the van? How many do you think are in there?"

Tiffany stood in front of the window. "We think there are two by the voices, we never got a look at them." Grace pulled her away.

"We call them Stupe and Idiot," Maggie added and Tiffany snickered.

Maggie lowered herself to the floor. Grace shrugged, folded rubbery legs and set her bottom on the concrete next to her. Tiffany, holding Leo against her chest, sank down across from them. They grew quiet and considered their situation. Somewhere by the tool rack, vermin claws skittered.

"Remember the kingdoms and make believe worlds we set up in here?" Grace reflected.

"We'd sit in my dad's tractor and pretend we were Laura Ingalls in her covered wagon crossing the prairie. Right over there where Joe's car..."

Grace startled and looked at Maggie. As one, they sat up and whisper-screamed together, "Baby!"

"You two slip her cover off. I'll get the spare keys." Maggie tiptoed to the workbench.

Grace and Tiffany lifted the canvas cover off the 'Stang, and quietly laid it on the floor.

"Found them," Maggie announced, opening the car door.

"As soon as we start opening the slider, they'll hear it," Grace reasoned.

"And as soon as I start the engine, they'll hear that," Maggie added.

"Should we try to open the door and push her out in neutral then you can start it?" Tiffany suggested.

"I have it." Grace moved to the door. "You two get in the car. While you start her up, I'll open the door, Maggie, put her in first gear, and I'll jump in the back." Grace flicked a thumb. "Easy-peasy!"

"We should put the top down so you don't have to crawl in the door." Maggie fiddled with the ragtop locks.

"Why don't you let me open the door and jump in, I'm, uh…" Tiffany suggested, one hand on Leo, the other on the heavy door.

"No, you hold on to Leo in the front seat." Maggie said. "We don't want to take any chances with his condition."

Grace nodded. "On the count of three, I'll open the door and jump in as you drive by. If I miss, leave me and save yourselves!"

Grace stood ready at the rolling door. Maggie turned the ignition to the first click so she could operate the mechanism to lower the convertible top. She stopped the lowering process a couple of times, listening for signs Stupe and Idiot might have heard. In a few starts and stops, the canvas top settled into its cradle.

Maggie moved the gearshift from neutral to first several times. Satisfied the gearshift was greased and ready, she placed her left hand on the steering wheel, her bandaged thumb resting at the top like a tiny turbaned head peeking over the dashboard. Tiffany rode shotgun with Leo's nose peeking above her shirt.

On Maggie's nod, Grace slid the door. Loud scraping and metal popping stopped her. She felt a sick giggle work up her throat. If the goons would come take a look at this crew of bandaged, two-headed, spandexed escapees, they wouldn't have to break out. They'd merely have to wait for their captors to pass out laughing.

She sobered and composed herself, realizing how dangerous it could be if this didn't go as planned. This wasn't a make believe game like the ones she and Maggie played when they were girls. This was for keeps.

"Let's go for it, Girlfriend," Grace whispered from her post at the door. "When I say go, I'll pull the door back. You start Baby, and kick her into gear. I'll jump in as you go by." She felt herself stall while her emotions roller-coastered between numbing fright and reckless bravery. "We'll be halfway to town before they know what happened. Ready?" She leaned back, gripping the door with both hands. She paused for a deep breath and a quick prayer. "Set, go!"

Grace reared back, tugging on the heavy sliding door with all her strength.

On cue, Maggie turned the ignition, let out the clutch and eased into first, inching forward, the tires beginning to slip against the concrete. Grace's stocking feet slipped and slid as well, but she managed to drag the door back. When it looked like Baby would clear the door, Maggie pushed on the gas and nosed through the wood frame. Grace leaned over the car's window ledge to roll into the backseat and pull her legs clear. She misjudged. Baby slid past her. She grabbed for the canvas top, sprawling across the trunk's custom wax, bent her knee, searching with her toe to steady herself on the slippery narrow rim of the chrome bumper.

Maggie shifted into second, her eye on Grace in the rearview mirror. "Hang on!"

"I'm trying!" Grace's toes barely made purchase on the slight lip as Baby made a piercing screech. The engine surged with horsepower straining for release. Its spinning tires laid rubber tracks and filled the garage with a cloud of smoke.

Maggie let off the clutch."Oops!"

Baby lurched onto the gravel drive, Grace still clinging. Her toes lost their grip and she slid back and forth across the polished surface like a dog wagging its tail. The car churned through deep gravel and fishtailed. Grace's fingers lost their tenuous hold, she slid off and rolled into a ravine.

Maggie jammed on the brakes and backed up. Tiffany and Maggie looked down the slope.

Grace sat up. "I'm okay." She scrambled up the slick grass in bare feet. Over the rumble of Baby's motor she heard noises. "Let's go! They're coming!"

The outline of two running men appeared from around the side of the garage.

"There they are!" One shouted to the other. "Follow those brake lights!" Behind them, the dogs scrambled, still attached to the chains. All four headed straight for them, and men, dogs and chains tangled. The stooges shouted and ignored orders back and forth, while the dogs alternated yelping and snarling.

"Get in!" Maggie shouted as Grace swan dove into Baby's back seat.

"Step on it, they're coming!" Tiffany squeaked.

Maggie let her foot off the clutch, and from the man-dog jumble, they heard, "Get in the van! They're getting away!"

Grace twisted around to watch the van bump across the pocked and overgrown yard toward them, its one headlight wild, disappearing up into the trees one second, then down a ravine the next. "Once they hit the driveway, they'll gain on us. Hit it Maggie!"

Maggie geared into fourth, and Baby's rear wheels kicked up rocks and gravel. This increased the distance between them, the ancient VW climbed onto the smoother driveway but coughed and sputtered, unable to keep up with the finely tuned precision engine. Nearing the pavement, Maggie slowed Baby until the front tires cleared a deep trench. This narrowed their lead and Grace watched the van make the last turn down the driveway.

Instead of slowing at the lip, the van's wheel rim lurched and jolted against tarmac. The driver manhandled, over-corrected, and the momentum spun the vehicle. The gyrospin launched the other man out the van's slider door and into the dirt downwind from Baby. As Maggie straightened the 'stang onto the highway and shifted up, Grace watched the van topple, twirl in a complete circle, and slide into the mud.

"Are they all right?" Maggie tapped the brake and shouted over the squeal of the crash.

Two men in silhouette against the lone headlight, one short, one tall, rose up and sprinted across the asphalt glittering in the new moonlight. Grace yelled over her shoulder, "They're running after us! Pedal to the metal, sister!"

Maggie punched the gas and Baby fishtailed then straightened, speeding toward town.

"Where should we go?" Maggie floored the gas.

"I see lights on at the McCoy's." Grace pointed as Baby picked up speed. "Pull in there!"

Hours later, Connie cleared breakfast plates and poured coffee into mugs. A television in the adjacent living room played the early morning news. Maggie accepted a second helping of scrambled eggs and Sheriff continued his questioning.

"What were you hoping to find in those files, Maggie?" Don scribbled in a pad and waited for her to chew.

Grace hung up the phone near the doorway and returned to sit with them at the kitchen table. "Mark's going to check the E.R. for anybody who looks like they've been in a car wreck." She eyeballed Maggie. "He says for you to let him know if you feel dizzy or nauseated after that blow." Grace lifted a curly lock to get a better look at Maggie's gash.

"I need to find proof of ownership of my property." Maggie ducked and waved her fork to shoo her off. "The county seat has only kept records since the 1950's, but my great grand-dad purchased the farm in the 1890's." Maggie held her cup out for Connie to refill. "Even if there's not someone trying to get my land, I'll need to borrow money against it to rebuild since the insurance company says the fires were arson related." She took a bite of toast. "I've been thinking I should sell Baby to raise cash. She's running darn good."

"No!" Grace and Tiffany protested in unison.

"Baby saved our lives." Grace sank into the chair next to Maggie and her voice hit a melancholy note. "We all know how much that car means to you. And now to all of us."

"Grace, how did you figure out Maggie's location? And why didn't you call me?" Sheriff turned to her and scolded. "You could've been seriously hurt."

"I know, but my cell phone died." She nibbled a corner of toast. "I watched the video from my mark onstage. Plain view of the van parked next to Joe's old garage, dogs tied up outside. Maggie would never have dogs tied that way."

"The devil-dogs!" Maggie and Tiffany sang together.

Grace nodded. "Baby lives in that garage, and Maggie doesn't own a van. As soon as I finished my number, I tried to tell Connie, but backstage was chaos. I left a note."

"You mean this one?" Connie reached into her pocket, handed a paper scrap to her. "I couldn't make out what it said."

Grace examined it. "Yeah, what a mess. It was dark and I was pepped up on adrenaline."

"Never mind, Don, thanks to her, we're out of there." Maggie shuddered. "No telling what they had planned for us." Grace laid a hand on her shoulder.

"Look, our super hero's on the morning news." Connie picked up the remote and raised the volume on the television.

"Your old baton routine from dance recital!" Maggie pointed and laughed at a clip of Grace's fiery act. She punched her arm. "You swore you'd never perform that again after you set the curtains on fire!"

"Miz Grace!" Connie shrieked. "More ancient history?"

Grace rubbed her arm. "Lost my grip and it went flying. Besides, it's the only talent I have. Not much call for someone doing stand-up crosswords. It was "Star Spangled Girl" or nothing." She peeked under the cotton robe Connie had loaned her. "Still fit in the leotard after all these years, too. Did anybody notice that?"

"She did set the place on fire. Metaphorically this time." Connie beamed. "The phones started ringing before she hit the splits."

Don cleared his throat. "If we could get back to the matters at hand." He turned to Tiffany. "Have you been threatened since you came to town, could this be someone after you?"

"I always have kooks out there trying to get close to me, but nobody's made any threats lately." Tiffany shook her head. "And why would they take her first, anyway?"

"Doesn't make sense, does it, Don?" Grace agreed.

Headlights shone through the kitchen window. "Maybe that's Mark." She jumped up and padded over to open the door. Instead of her husband, a burly dog burst in and licked her face, paws on shoulders. "Buckwheat! What are you doing here?"

Rose clomped up the steps after him. "Sorry, Grace. Bucky, down!" She grabbed Buckwheat's collar. "He ran across the street and I followed him. What's Baby doing here? Isn't that Maggie's car?" His tail whipped in excitement and Bucky strained against her grip.

"You're not going to believe what happened." Grace wiped her moist cheek. "Look who I found."

Rose looked past her into the kitchen. "Maggie you're all right!" She let the dog go and ran over for a long neck hug. "We were worried like crazy. Morning, Sheriff, Connie."

Sheriff touched the pencil to his forehead and Connie jumped up. "Coffee? Have a seat."

Grace introduced Rose to Tiffany, who sat up straight. "That's the one that chased the devil dogs. He came out of nowhere. When they saw him, they dropped Leo and took off."

"What a good boy." Grace rubbed Buckwheat's ears. "What happened last night? Can you tell us, fella?"

"What do you know, Rose?" Sheriff asked. "Did you see or hear anything unusual last night?"

"Now that you mention it, I had a hunch something was up. When I got home from the telethon Bucky had gotten out of the tack room where I leave him." She nodded thanks to Connie as she set a cup of coffee in front of her. "Otherwise he rounds up the horses out in the pasture even if I don't need them up. Gotta work on that." Rose shook her head at the dog. "Anyway, I guess he'd climbed up on some boxes and pushed the screen out through a window I left open for fresh air. When I got home it was pretty late, but he was barking and running back and forth up The Path toward your place, Maggie." She stirred sugar into her coffee and caught her breath. Don flipped a page over on his pad. "I went over and knocked, but you weren't home, so I gave up and went to bed. I guess he was trying to tell me something."

"Did you walk over on The Path, or take the road?"

Rose thought as she sipped. "I walked over on the road, it was pretty dark and I was still wearing sandals. Not good for that deep grass along The Path."

"That's why she didn't see any lights or the devil-dogs." Grace suggested.

Don looked up from his pad. "Go on."

"He must have heard me scream. I thought he was just another wild dog after me and Leo." Tiffany added.

"Where is Leo?" Rose looked around. "Is he all right?"

As if on cue, Doc McCoy entered the living area wiping his hands on a towel. "Rose, what brings you by at this hour?"

Grace filled Greg in on Buckwheat's heroics, and he knelt down to inspect for any wounds. "He's fine, just a scratch." Then he met Tiffany's anxious gaze. "You can go through and see your boy now. He'll be fine soon enough. I want to keep him for a day or so on IV fluids, but he's resting comfortably. Someone gave him excellent emergency care." He winked at Maggie, then to his daughter, "Connie, can you take Tiffany in for a quick visit?"

"Sure. C'mon, Tiffany, let's go see Leo." Connie beckoned to Rose. "Wanna see him? After all, Bucky saved his life. And do I have a story to tell you." She glanced at Tiffany, "unless you want to tell her. It's so cool."

Bucky followed them into the clinic. Greg watched the swinging door close, then poured himself a cup of coffee and sank into a chair. "What do you think of all this, Don?"

Sheriff Melton flipped his notebook closed. "I'm putting out an APB for the kidnappers and a description of the van." To Maggie. "You describe it as an older model hippie van, I assume that's one of those VWs. Call me if you remember anything else." He settled his Stetson on his head.

"Only has one headlight, I just remembered," Grace offered.

Maggie held up a hand. "Hang on." Her eyes narrowed. "The head blow did kinda knock me silly, now you mention it..." she focused at a point in the middle distance, "I've seen that van before." Maggie recounted the visit from the man in the bad suit several days ago. "Tried to hide a ponytail in the neck of his shirt. Gave me the creeps."

"I'll send over a sketch artist, anyway." Sheriff nodded. "Couldn't hurt."

Maggie rubbed her temples. "It was dark and they made sure we didn't get a glimpse. I can describe their dogs."

"Isn't it enough that the van was parked on her place?" Grace rubbed Maggie's neck. "Is she even safe to go home?"

"They were trespassing, not as serious as kidnapping. We still also need to know their motives, that might help us know who they were." His radio squawked. "I've gotta run. I'll send squad cars by to patrol your place." He paused at the kitchen door, his tone changed from professional to concern for a friend. "Maybe Grace is right, maybe you should move to town until we get this sorted out."

Greg walked Sheriff onto the porch then returned to the kitchen. "If you ladies don't mind, I'm going to shower and get ready for my day. Make yourselves at home." He closed his bedroom door, and they could hear the shower running.

"Do you want more toast or some juice?" Grace sank down next to her and studied Maggie's face with concern. "Mark says for you to wait here until he can examine you. We can give Tiffany a ride to her trailer, then go home with you. You'd better pack a bag and stay in our guest room." She studied Maggie's face.

"Nope. I'll load up the .22 and defend myself, they're not chasing me off my own property." She stretched. "I could use some fresh air after all night in that garage."

Grace gestured toward the path-side door. "Let's go sit. I recall a lovely cushioned settee out there. I'll pour us another cup." She held out an elbow but Maggie refused the help.

Outside, they settled themselves into soft cushions facing The Path. "Thanks again for using the old noggin to get me out." Maggie lifted her cup to salute Grace. The she told her more about getting clocked while she was searching Sam's files, and the long night held captive in one of her own buildings.

"She's not such a bad kid." Maggie remarked when she got to the part about her conversation with Tiffany. She thought a minute and watched a jogger go past. "Sometimes it's like she's speaking a foreign language though. Any idea what 'bridge and tunnel' means?"

Grace shook her head. Morning sunrays crawled up the steps and warmed the porch. She yawned then sat up straight so fast coffee sloshed over the rim of her mug. "I totally forgot. We didn't find out how much money we raised at the telethon."

CHAPTER TWENTY-TWO

Later that week, Grace stepped out her back door and breathed deeply, the morning jasmine sweet and spicy. She stepped onto the flagstones, leaned over and slowly stretched calf muscles and still slightly tight thighs before opening the gate onto The Path. She'd passed on that morning's Walk and Rollers but after Mark left for his shift at the hospital, she decided to walk on her own. Her new leather Keds needed their white toned down, so she set out to see how far she could get around The Path before dark and finish planning the clean-up list for Founder's Day.

Grace picked up speed to increase her heart rate, ignoring complaints from her thighs. *Next time, let's end the dance number with a lady-like bow instead of splits,* she huffed and swung her arms and paused, noticing Jeff's rented suburban parked on the street.

"I thought you'd be on the road with that act of yours by now." Jeff called. He wore overalls and work boots, looking like quite the Cherryvaler. He waved her up the walkway. "You were quite a hit."

"Not me! I only appear for command performances!" She soft-shoed a shuffle ball kick for him in the grass. "And likewise, I thought you'd be on a plane back to LA. What's going on here?"

"I'll have to go back for post-filming work, but I did it." He barely repressed excitement. "I made an offer on this place." He beamed up at the structure, then over at her.

Grace beamed right back. "That's terrific. How did your daughter take the news?"

His look went dim. "Looking forward to it like a cat looks forward to a bath. But I know it's the right thing to do."

"The Lord will bless you and your daughter greatly." She laid an encouraging hand on his shoulder. "And if there's anything we can do, we're just a holler away. I'm pretty good with a paintbrush, and I've got a list of contractors I can recommend from my kitchen makeover." She watched him surveying the place. "You really love this place, don't you?"

Jeff nodded and reached in his pocket. "I borrowed the keys. Can I show you my plans?" Without waiting for her reply, he disappeared through the brush. "Watch your step," he hollered.

She followed him up the steps. Rainwater had leaked through a hole in the roof and warped the hardwood floorboards at the transom, but further inside, although dusty and scarred, they lay straight and true. The kitchen sported a layer of grime, but the walnut cabinets and tile countertops looked solid. Brittle paper curled down the wall, and broken glass from wall sconces crunched underfoot.

"We'll have to come up with a new name for this place. I'm guessing it won't be 'The Pit' much longer."

He gestured toward the living room. "You're right, I love it. Broken chimneys, pink and green tiles and all.' He pulled his phone out of his pocket and aimed at a rubbish heap almost as high as the mantle. "I'm going to take some pictures for the before and after."

Grace wondered at his pensive tone. This place could be a metaphor for his life. She prayed for a word to give him, speaking up when it felt right. "Just when we're at our worst, He comes in to love us out of our rubble." Grace spoke while he snapped photos. "What was old is now new again."

"I would appreciate your help. It'll be nuts while I'm flying back and forth." He leveled the phone at the kitchen and snapped shots from several angles. "Am I crazy for taking this on and trying my hand at being a dad at the same time?" They moved toward the door. The inside was growing darker as the setting sun gradually removed any daylight that filtered through the dirty windowpanes.

"Helps to be a little crazy when you're raising kids." Grace waited while he checked the lock. "I'm looking forward to meeting Julie."

Jeff slid the phone into his pocket. "Oh, I almost forgot. I'm pretty sure they're planning on showing a preview of *The Scrapbook* in Cherryvale. Good PR with the telethon tie-in and all."

"For which we Valers will be eternally grateful." Grace checked the time by the shadows on The Path and hurried to finish her walk. "The check presentation is in a few hours. I'll see you there."

Cherryvalers mingled with a few Vaders who remained behind. All waited for the ceremony to begin. No one but the accountant knew the amount pledged for Maggie's animal sanctuary, so the excitement ran high. The movie crew and their new friends had catching-up and good-byes to say before heading back to LA.

Grace stood chatting with Maggie, the Sims family, and the Mayor. Mark strode in and joined them. "Did I miss anything?"

"No, you're just in time." She turned to accept his quick peck on the lips. Tiffany wandered in from the lobby, a bandaged Leo cradled on her arm.

"Excuse me. I'm sorry to interrupt, but can I say something?" Tiffany fiddled with Leo's ear as she approached the group.

They opened up the circle. "What is it, dear?" Carolyn Sims smiled at her.

"I…uh, I wanted to a-apologize. To Cassie. And all of you. I was a real bi –uh- butt before, uh, on set, and well, you know." She knelt in front of the little brown-eyed girl. "I'm sorry, Little Bit." Tiffany's new nickname for the young girl suggested her repentance was truly genuine. "It wasn't your fault when I couldn't get my line right. I shouldn't have yelled at you. And I'm sorry you got hurt in the fire and all."

"Cassie?" Carolyn nudged her wide-eyed daughter. "What do you say?"

Cassie looked directly into Tiffany's face. "It'th okay. You didn't mean it. You had a lot of words to say. I sorry I thnored."

Tiffany bit her lip. "I don't blame you a bit. Sometimes I bore myself, honey."

They all laughed.

Tiffany hugged the tot, and Leo took the proximity as an invitation for a quick ear sniff. "He'th sorry for hurting me too." Cassie giggled, wiping her wet cheek with the back of her hand. "Can I hold him?"

"You sure can, but he might lick you to death."

"No, he won't, thilly." She looked down. "Will you sign my cast?"

"Of course!" Carolyn handed her a marker and she left-hand-scrawled a sweet message to Cassie.

Grace sucked in a breath as Tiffany finished her cast-signing with a flourish of her left hand. Cassie set off to show the autograph to anyone who would look. Grace put an arm around the teen's slender shoulder.

"Walk with me, talk with me." Grace led Tiffany a few steps away. When they were out of Cassie's earshot, Grace beamed at Tiffany. "You really didn't try to commit suicide, did you, honey?"

"That's what I've been trying to tell everyone. Finally you believe me?"

"I've always wanted to. I watched you signing the cast. You're a south paw."

"South what? Oh, you mean a leftie. Yeah. So?"

"It's your left wrist. No one cuts first with their awkward hand." Grace assumed a smug look. "You learn how to watch for things like that when you're a school teacher. And for clues by watching a few hundred episodes of *Murder, She Wrote*."

Maggie caught her eye with a questioning look. "What's up, ladies?"

From the corner of her eye, she saw Sam Madison walk to center stage, mic in hand. "I'll tell you later," she mouthed.

"Can I have everyone's attention, please? Find a seat, and let's get started with our presentations so we can get to the fine table of refreshments in the lobby." Tittering and scuffling while they found seats, soon they were quiet. "Pastor, will you do the honors?"

Pastor thanked the Lord for the talent, both on stage and off, and for the generous contributions toward the animals' needs. He added praise for Maggie, Tiffany and Leo's safe return. "And all God's people said..."

"Amen!" The room answered.

Sam took the mic back. "And now if you'll direct your attention to this short video montage our *Scrapbook* friends have put together for us."

They watched highlights of the telethon, including short segments of several acts, a few hilarious outtakes followed by still photographs of volunteers who made the evening a success. The ending scene featured Grace's sparkly baton act followed by a long list of everyone's names in credits. The appreciative audience clapped for themselves, thumping shoulders and teasing each other's mishaps and foibles.

The lights came on and Sam walked onstage again. "Let's hear it one more time for all our talent, the crew, and especially all of you who pledged to make Cherryvale's first annual Talent-Show-Telethon a success!"

More applause and whistles, then as he opened his mouth to speak again, Emmett John stood up. "Before you go on, Sam, we want to say something." He excused himself as he edged into the aisle. Hank followed him up the steps.

"We passed the hat for Maggie. The crew of *The Scrapbook* would like to present her with this check for five thousand dollars."

Maggie straightened by Grace's elbow.

"This is terrific." Sam beamed and waited for the applause to die down. "Before you go, Emmett, Hank, I want to remind everyone what part you two played." He wrapped an arm around Emmett. "Ladies and gentlemen, from the moment they heard us in the Bucket talking about Maggie's troubles, Emmett and Hank and most of their crew jumped in to help without our even asking. With their technical expertise, we were able to broadcast to three counties. And all in a matter of a few days. Let's hear it for Emmett, Hank and the crew!"

Cherryvalers jumped up and cheered. Unaccustomed to the bright side of the spotlight, Emmett and Hank ducked their heads and shuffled their Doc Martens. They scooted down the steps with shy waves.

Sam waited for the room to quiet. "And also, a big thanks to everyone who performed, and to Jeff Field for being our most gracious emcee." More appreciative applause.

"Now, before we present the check to Maggie, we have a special presentation. The Main Street Merchant committee has decided to honor one act with a special award. This year our recipient not only impressed us with her onstage talent, but also with her sleuthing abilities to help rescue Maggie and Tiffany—and Leo—from alleged kidnappers. Gotta say it that way so we don't get into trouble with the law, right?" Everyone laughed and looked at Lew sitting in the back row. He gave a thumbs up.

"Anyway, ladies and gentlemen," Sam continued, "Help me honor the first recipient of the Main Street Top of the Telethon Talent award. The award goes to Grace Harkins for 'Star Spangled Girl...uh, er-Lady."

The roomful of heads swiveled, hands clapped and many stood to their feet. Mark affectionately elbowed Grace and kissed her cheek warming with the unexpected attention.

"Grace, don't be so humble, c'mon up here, and accept your award." Sam beckoned. Mark stood to let her in the aisle.

"Oh, I almost forgot." Sam waved an envelope. "Cherryvale Travel and Party Planners has donated two round-trip airplane tickets to anywhere Explorer Airlines flies."

Grace flourished a good-natured red-carpet wave as she crossed the stage, inspiring louder applause.

"Thank you, my fans, thank you." She accepted the trophy, an acrylic shooting star on a marble pedestal. "And thank you all for everything you've done to help Maggie's place."

When she returned to her seat, Mark pressed a kiss to her cheek, whispered. "I'm proud of you."

On stage, the lights lowered and a taped drum roll played over the speakers. "And now!" A spotlight found Sam center stage. "With all the pledges in and counted, we are ready to make our final presentation to this year's benefactor of the first annual Cherryvale Talent Show Telethon. Maggie, will you please join me for the announcement of the grand total?"

The spotlight followed Maggie up the steps. From stage right, four members of the telethon committee carried an oversized cardboard check covered with a black cloth to conceal the total from the audience. Maggie joined Sam in his circle of light.

"First, it's my turn to say a few words." Maggie took the mic from Sam, who threw his hands up with a grin and stepped back.

"I don't know how, but I want to somehow thank all of you. Both my old Cherryvale friends and my new ones. I guess you know that before you even got here, I nicknamed you Cherryvaders." A ripple of laughter followed her confession. "I didn't keep it a secret that I didn't want 'your kind' coming to our town. I assumed I knew about you. That was wrong. You've all been a tremendous blessing to us. To me, especially. We are going to miss you.

"Not because you helped with the telethon, but because you've become our friends. You dropped everything to help us search for Cassie, and you generously offered your time and equipment to help bail my farm out of trouble..." Maggie stopped, her face wrenched, eyes filling. Unable to continue speaking, she kissed the tips of her fingers and signed her thanks.

While they clapped in response, she regained her composure. "And to all my beloved Valers, what can I say? I thought the fires might be the end, but you've tried to help by raising money for me, and I'll be forever grateful..." Her voice caught and she shook her head, handed the mic back to Sam and leaned into his shoulder, his arm around her waist. "I know Joe'd be mighty proud."

He motioned with the mic, and the committee carried the check downstage. When they hit their mark, he nodded, and Mayor removed the cloth that covered the amount.

Sam lowered to a deep radio announcer voice and read, "Pay to the order of Maggie Neville - $12,000!"

Maggie gasped and covered her face with her hands. A burst of applause erupted, but when she gulped a mournful cry and disappeared off stage, the room silenced, stunned to mute.

"Uh, I guess she's too overwhelmed to speak." Sam glanced at her and back at the audience.

While everyone still sat, stunned, the back door swung open. As one, they turned in their seats. Sheriff Melton shoved two scruffy thugs ahead of him. Their handcuffed hands tight behind them, their heads bent forward as if they were bowing.

"Where's Maggie?" Sheriff demanded as they scuffled up the aisle. "I need her to identify if these are the suspects who abducted her. Found 'em holed up, chased down by their own dogs."

Laughter and some applause flicked awkwardly through the audience.

He caught Greg's eye. "Their mongrels are pretty starved. Doc, I've got them over at the station. VIP cell. You should come over and check on 'em when you get a chance. Think one of 'em has a broken rib or something."

Greg stood and glanced at Jeff on stage. "'Course, Sheriff, I'll be over right after the ceremony."

"Where is Maggie, shouldn't she be here for her big night?"

Sam peered into the stage wing. "Maggie?"

"Ma-ggie!" someone in the crowd chanted.

"Ma-ggie! Ma-ggie!" everyone joined in.

CHAPTER TWENTY-THREE

Red curls appeared from behind the curtain leg. "Can't a person have a good cry around here?"

"There you are." Sheriff shoved his suspects toward the stage. "Are these the scoundrels who kidnapped you?"

Maggie moved onstage and shaded her eyes. "I really can't tell."

"Come down here out of those lights." Sheriff commanded and roughly escorted them closer to Maggie.

"That's not what I mean, Don." She obeyed and stepped down. "I never got a look at them."

When they passed Tiffany, Leo squirmed from her grasp and jumped into the aisle, sniffing and snorting, yipping and twirling.

"Shut up, mutt, get away!" The taller one kicked at Leo.

"Stop that, you!" Sheriff jerked him back so the blow didn't connect. "What about you, Tiffany?"

"They covered my eyes. I didn't see faces, but Leo recognizes them!" She lifted the angry dog out of the creep's boot-kicking range.

"He never forgets a person's stink!" Maggie announced. Everyone, except the thugs, laughed.

"Sheriff, you know that won't hold up in court." Lew warned, stepping into the aisle.

"Soon as I get a chance to fingerprint and do a search on 'em I bet I'll have me a coupla long sheets of outstanding warrants. Besides, I've got enough to hold 'em on suspicion and search their van. At least charge them for trespassing on Maggie's property. We found their tent and beer bottles." He looked over the short round one to Maggie. "You'll press charges against them, right?"

"Of course I will."

"Come on you two."

Maggie followed as he turned them toward the exit. "Wait just a minute, Don. I've got a bone to pick with them."

Someone from the back yelled, "Get 'em, Maggie!"

She marched up and peered down into the short one's stubbly face. "Shame on you. What would your mother think of you? Does she know what you're up to?" She turned to the taller guy. "And you! You could do so much better with yourself than... Wait a minute. You came to my farm last week, didn't you? I know you, don't I?"

He suddenly developed a keen interest in a stain on the carpet and dug at it with a boot toe.

"What's your name?" She moved closer to him.

"Henry, ma'am."

Grace handed her trophy to Mark and got up for a closer look. "Wait a minute. I recognize them. They were at the movie shoot. Holly?"

"Yes, ma'am?" Holly stepped into the aisle to join them.

"What happens with the pictures you take of all the extras?"

"We use them for consistency," Holly explained. "To make sure we keep costumes the same and—why?"

"Sheriff, I think if you go through the pictures from the other day, you'll see these men were in Cherryvale. I gave each one of them a muffin in the holding tent." She took her turn at the men. "Henry took the last blueberry and Max liked my cranberry. You see? I never forget a muffin!"

"Holly, I'd appreciate seeing those pictures." Sheriff turned the two toward the door. "Names, busted alibis. And two, make that three, reliable witnesses. You two are toast. Thanks, Maggie, Grace. And Leo."

"Wait, Sheriff." Maggie commanded. "I'd like to know why these men kidnapped me."

Lew held up a hand. "Sheriff, for the record, have you Miranda-ized these two?"

"Sure did, when I slapped the cuffs on. Anything you two say now, well, you've got a lot of witnesses."

Max clammed up, but Henry shot Maggie a guilty glance then mumbled. "We were looking for something. We didn't mean to hurt you. Honest. We were trying to find the file, and I wanted to scare you so you'd give it to me, but I got skeered you'd recognize me, so I panicked." The words rushed out as if they'd been percolating, ready to boil to the surface for ages. "Sorry you got hit so hard."

"Recognize you! From the day you came in that ridiculous suit to my farm?" Maggie studied the lined, ruddy face, and reached up to pull off the grimy knit cap. A stringy grey braid fell down his back.

Max elbowed Henry. "Keep your trap shut."

Recognition lit Maggie's face. "Sister Sara's sauces! You're Henry Weston! We used to play in the hayloft together. And you kidnapped me?" She thumped him on the shoulder. "What were you thinking?"

"I told you, we needed them files so my family would be better. Max, he beaned you in the office so's you wouldn't get them. Max said we better not leave you there because you might tell the poh-lice what we look like." Henry took a hiccup-y wheeze. "I never wanted to hurt you, Peggy."

Max rolled bloodshot eyes.

"Peggy!" Grace searched Maggie's face for a reaction. "Your mom's pet name for you."

"Ask him about the will, Maggie," Lew urged.

Maggie gaped. "So that's what this is about?"

"Uh-huh."

Maggie leaned in, her one remaining eyebrow raised high. "Spill it!"

"Stan was all, 'Maggie's place' this and 'Maggie's place' that. Somethin' bout ninety-nine years endin' and the money bein' gone. I thought he loved me like a brother when he took me in from the group home, but

Stan's always mad. I was tryin' to make him proud a' me." Henry dragged a dirty sleeve across his eyes. "Now I just wanna go back..."

"Shut up, Idiot," Max hissed, but the Sheriff yanked him quiet.

"Any of that make sense to you, Lew?" Maggie put her hand on Henry's shoulder, but glared at Max.

"I think this is going to take some research." Lew scratched his head.

Maggie returned her gaze to Henry. "Did you set the fires, too?"

"Fires? Nu-uh, not fires, only one. Me and Max, we come to the petting farm and we seen where you keep the files. He said we should get rid of them and we had some matches for smokes and gas in my van cuz the gauge ain't workin'. Stan promised he'd get me a new car, only I don't drive good and he wrecked his car and got another one for hisself."

Maggie pointed. "Do you know you almost killed poor little Cassie?"

The little girl looked up at the mention of her name.

"That were a accident. I heerd about that on the radio. Honest! I went out walkin' and had a smoke, and Max, he yelled at me and told me not to get too close to your house so nobody would see me. I never wanted to hurt nobody, I swear Peggy. I'm so sorry."

Grace whispered to Mark. "Well that accounts for two of them, anyway."

Maggie continued her interrogation. "Did you make those phone calls, too?"

Henry's shoulders sagged lower with each confession. "Max thought if we skeered you, we could get you to move."

Maggie turned her inquisition on Max. "What did you expect to get out of all this?"

Forgetting his own better interest, Max snickered. "You ever seen the way he lives? There's money and lots of it."

Lew cleared his throat.

"I'd advise you to shut up," Sheriff warned. "Want me to add making threats to the charges?"

Max's face drained pale. "Naw."

Her attention back to Henry, Maggie went on. "And what did you do with the file from Sam's store?" She rubbed the back of her still sore head.

Sheriff interrupted. "Is it an old, thick file held together with a large clip, says something like 'Ebenezer Elmsley' on it?"

"That's it. He was my great grandfather." Maggie cast a stern look at Henry. "You came by my place to make sure I was the right person then followed me, didn't you?"

Henry nodded again.

"And you placed it on top of the file cabinet," Grace chimed in, caught up in the reconstruction.

"Yes, and got a splinter in my thumb." Maggie held up her bandaged digit. "That's when I got beaned."

"I knew there was something fishy about your disappearance." Grace furrowed her own eyebrows at the sheriff.

He ignored her. "That file was in their gear I confiscated."

"We'll want to see that," Lew chimed in.

"You know the procedure, counsel." Don seized the scoundrels firmly by the handcuffs and pushed them toward the exit. "I've got all I need. I'm taking them for processing. You all go back to the celebration. How much did we raise, by the way?"

"It's a very generous amount of money." Maggie gestured to the check held by the committee members. "Maybe enough to help me move."

"Move?" Grace felt her voice tremble. "Why would you move when we've raised money to keep you in business?"

"It's still not enough to rebuild."

"Maggie, don't jump to conclusions." Lew laid a hand on her shoulder. "I have a gut feeling that in their bungling way, those two will lead us to a solution to your dilemma. Let me see what I can find out about these mysterious files they were so anxious to get their hands on."

Grace and Maggie waited outside Lew's office and Maggie knuckle-rapped insistently. "I know he's in there. I can hear him."

The door opened from inside, and Lew, phone to his ear, gestured at two wingback chairs. He returned to his own worn leather seat behind his desk.

Hand over the mouthpiece, he whispered, "Good stuff, Maggie, be right with you. Hi, Grace." He put the receiver back to his mouth. "Great, Steve, thanks for the info. Say hi to the family…I appreciate your help." He punched the phone off and looked across the desk at them, a grin spreading.

"All right, Maggie, I think you're going to like this. I called in a couple of favors and dug up some pretty interesting info. Nothing's for certain, yet. This is what I've found out so far. Would you like some coffee, first?"

"No, tell me. Please." Maggie leaned toward the attorney.

"Do you remember anything about a ninety-nine year lease?"

"Ninety-nine year…" She twiddled her purse straps around her bandaged thumb.

"I remember ninety-nine yearlings, Mags," Grace reminded.

"Remember? You made it up? We used to chant it when we skipped rope."

Maggie explained to Lew. "My grandfather talked about 'ninety-nine yearlings.' I figured it was some kind of Wild West reference to back in the day when mustangs ran on our place. But he was saying a 'ninety-nine year lease'?"

Lew nodded. "Apparently your great-grandfather gave Henry's great-grandfather a lease in the amount of one dollar. Right after the flu epidemic."

Grace knew that part of the town's history by heart. "Mark's great-grandfather was the town doc during that epidemic. Lots of folks died."

"Yes." Lew nodded. "Henry's great-grandfather lost his first wife and child to the illness. To help him start over, Maggie, your great-granddaddy, known for his charity, let him use thirty acres carved out of your property. They built a wagon repair business, the next generation converted to tractor repairs, and now we know it as the lawnmower parts factory."

"Wait." Maggie pondered that. "You said my property?"

"Let me finish." Lew's countenance lit up as he rose to address his audience. Grace imagined how his energy and presence helped drive points home for juries. "In his will, Henry's father entered a clause reminding his heirs and the Board that the land would revert at the expiration of the ninety-nine years."

Grace did some mental math. "The flu epidemic was in 1911." She turned to Maggie whose look of astonishment mirrored hers. "That means the ninety-nine years is up."

"That's right." A grin spreading, Lew licked a finger and shuffled through a file. "That's why they panicked, especially Stan Weston, Henry's brother.

"Little Stan?" Maggie uttered under her breath. "He was always teasing us and getting in trouble. They sent him off to military school or something."

"Maybe. He's in financial trouble. Almost bankrupt from what I can gather. Can't afford to buy new parts to meet contracts. The Board is taking over control from him and investing venture capital to keep the factory going. He's about to lose his cash cow."

"Been robbing Peter to pay the proverbial Paul." Lew sat again and looked directly at Maggie. "The factory's actually been doing well financially, but Stan's been dipping in and giving himself perks."

Maggie sat stunned and speechless.

"What will happen to Henry?" Grace asked.

"He's provided for by a trust." Lew thought a beat. "My hunch is somehow that Stan's been dipping into that as well, that's why he moved Henry back here to live with him." He picked up a gold pen. "Henry had been doing very well, living in a group home. I'll make some calls to prevent Stan from stealing any more from Henry."

Lew scribbled and looked up at Maggie. "Here's what affects you. Since you own the land, they're obligated to pay you fair market rate when the lease expires. Based on current land value, here's what I recommend we ask for, under the new contract." He scribbled again and slid the amount toward Maggie.

Maggie stared without touching it. Grace laid her hand on Maggie's clenched fists, careful not to bump the injured thumb. Maggie looked at her, then at the paper. Grace followed her gaze to read the astonishing number for herself. She felt a giggle burbling up when she realized what the figure suggested. "That's enough to feed the animals, fix the place up, and maybe even expand!"

Maggie nodded, her gaze still locked on the paper. She brushed at her cheeks, wiping moisture from under each eye.

Grace couldn't remember seeing Maggie this speechless for this long. "How did Henry get involved in all this?"

"Henry misunderstood and thought they would be evicted. He was only trying to help, although he picked the wrong partner and means."

"Where did he find Max anyway?"

"Stumbled on each other somehow. Max just got out on parole. He's a piece of work. Already back where he belongs."

Maggie finally found her tongue. "Lew, how much trouble is Henry in?"

"He's facing time as well, although he doesn't have any priors, not too much."

"Is it possible that he could make restitution instead? Couldn't you speak to the D.A.? "

Maggie's offer of mercy startled Grace.

Lew twiddled with his pen. "Under the circumstances, I guess he might listen. What do you have in mind?"

"I don't think prison is the right place for him. I've known him all my life…well, I knew him when we were little together. He was never harmful, just misguided. He could help me rebuild."

"We'll still have to go through the court." Lew's expression softened. "I'll make some calls."

Grace and Maggie took the stairs down to street level. "Maggs, this means you'll never want for money for the farm," Grace considered. "As long as the parts factory does good business."

"That silly ditty about ninety-nine yearlings was really a prophecy in a way, wasn't it?" Maggie's expression belied her relief.

They stepped onto the sidewalk and paused next to Maggie's truck. "Thanks for going with me to Lew's. I thought he was going to tell me I was out of business."

"I'm so happy for you."

Light drops began to fall and Maggie looked up and pressed the button to remotely unlock the door. "Better get, looks like rain."

Grace moved forward for a hug, but Maggie hopped in. Grace leaned in before she could roll up the window. "We'll have you over for dinner soon."

"I'll check my social calendar." Maggie drove off without another word. Grace sprinted to her bike. The drops turned to sheets as she steered toward home, wondering if Maggie had been distracted by the weather, Lew's news, or something else entirely.

The next day, Grace set two salad bowls, a basket of strawberry-rhubarb muffins, and a plate with butter on the patio table. Mark put down his Blackberry cell phone and picked up a fork.

"Now you can get back to your list." Mark reminded Grace after they'd exhausted the news about Maggie. "You must be thrilled."

"Indeed." Grace nibbled her salad then set her fork down.

"You know, Gracie, there's nothing wrong with having an organized to-do list." He cleared his throat. "As long as it doesn't get in the way of what's really important."

"Has my need to clean finally made you crazy?"

"No. You know that's not what I'm driving at." Mark drained his tea glass. "Good lunch, honey. I need to get a haircut before my shift." He pecked her lips when she tipped her head back. He pointed heavenward. "He's listening. I love you, Grace."

"Love you more."

Mark drove away a few minutes later. The patio stippled with sunlight through the canopy of mature trees they'd planted for shade many years ago. The rain had lasted for hours and freshened the air. After a hot shower, Grace spent several hours dragging boxes and greenery out of the Christmas closet. The seasonal decorations now lay strewn across the family room ready to sort through and reshelve.

She clicked on the dishwasher and padded down the hallway, bolts of shelf liner tucked under her arm. At the door to their bedroom, she froze. Against all her urges to organize before doing anything else, she spun left and dropped the spools on the bed. She went in her closet, slipped on her shoes and walked out the back door. Under normal conditions, she would never leave the house like that. Today would be different. Household chores and selfish to-do lists would have to wait.

"Knock-knock! Anyone home?" Grace called over voices inside. "Maggie?

Tiffany appeared at Maggie's screen door with Leo in her arms. "Hey, Miz Grace."

"Hey back. It's good to see you." She noted the little dog's bandage. "How is Leo?"

Tiffany bounced the dog in her arms. "He's a lot better. Doc's taking really good care of him." Tiffany found her manners and shoved the screen door open for Grace to step in.

Grace picked up a cone the size of a kitchen funnel embellished in rhinestones and a fur trim. "Where'd you find a designer cone?"

"Maggie bought the googahs on one of her trips to Franklin City and I glued them on. Doc says he only has to wear it if he bites at the stitches. Have a seat."

Tiffany's bling free outfit—more appropriate than her previous too-small tops and thong-revealing—flattered her. "He looks great. You look good too." Grace admired Tiffany's teal blouse. "That top is beautiful with your eyes."

"Thanks." Grace detected a slight blush in the girl's unmade up face. Tiffany buried her nose in Leo's head. "She's meeting with architects. Should be back soon."

Grace sat on the overstuffed chair by the small fireplace. A television played a blurry episode of *The Waltons.*

The family, clad in skirts and overalls passed food across the dining room table. "One of my favorite shows." Grace rested her elbow on a chenille blanket.

"Huh?"

"*The Waltons.* Erin's my favorite. Such a sweetheart."

Tiffany sat, and held Leo in her lap. "I never knew real families could be like that. Until I came here."

"Even on *Forever Family*?" Grace tipped her head. "Your own show?"

"They were just scripts." Tiffany's eyebrows knit together as she watched the onscreen family laughing and talking. "I always wished it could be real."

Grace fiddled with the remote, wondering if this was as good a time as any. "I'm glad you've seen what people who care about each other can accomplish." She eyed Tiffany to see if she was listening. "We may not be perfect in the Vale, but with the Lord's help we try to be there for each other." She looked around. "I don't miss her animal-cage-with-odor-de-poo."

"We carried the last of the cages out yesterday into the temporary sheds." Tiffany watched a commercial for miracle fabric. "Can I ask you a question?"

"Sure."

"You used to be a school teacher, right?" Tiffany fiddled with Leo's collar.

"For twenty-three years."

"Do you think you could…help me?" A hint of color tinted her cheeks. "I mean, I never finished high school. Maggie invited me to stay here for a while. I thought I might go to college." She shrugged and Grace caught a hint of unmasked pain. "But I need to get my diploma first."

"Well, of course I will!" Grace tried to control her excitement lest she overwhelm the girl. "I'd be honored. But does this mean you're giving up your acting career?"

"I can always fall back on that if my education fails me." Tiffany grinned.

"There's an ironic twist. How many kids are told to get their education first and then try acting? Seriously, you'll do great." Grace patted Tiffany's knee. "And I know you'll be a success at whatever you try."

Tiffany hugged Leo sheepishly, but when she lowered the dog to the floor, Grace noticed a smile light the young woman's face.

The screen door squeaked open and Maggie stumbled in, her arms full of papers. "The big business world'll drain ya. Give me my work boots and a tractor any old day." She caught Grace's eye. "What's up?"

"Thought I'd come by and see if I can help with chores, then I thought we could go to the Garden of Eatin' for supper. I want to try their California sushi roll she's put on the menu in honor of our new connection to the coast."

"Garden of Eatin'?" Tiffany rolled her eyes. "This is some town."

"So you've decided to stay?" Grace grinned.

Maggie dropped the papers onto a side table already sagging with magazines and mail.

"Yeah, I guess I'll give small town life a whirl. You people need someone to bring you into this century." Tiffany arched an eyebrow. "You're kind of old school you know."

Maggie added a hillbilly accent to her words. "She's even gonna show us how those newfangled iPods work." She plunged into the soft cushion next to Grace. "I brought you something." She kicked off her shoes before handing Tiffany a bag from the Read and Reel bookstore.

Tiffany opened the shopping bag and slid a book out far enough to read the title. "*The Many Adventures of Winnie the Pooh*." She looked up at Maggie, a look of realization flashing. "Aw, you rock! Thank you!"

"A classic. Maybe some things from the past are cool, after all." Grace admired the artwork on the cover. "But why Winnie the Pooh?"

Before anyone could explain, they heard Connie's Jeep outside. Tiffany jumped up and beckoned through the screen. "Wait'll I get my stuff."

Connie stepped inside, greeted the women and scratched Leo's ears.

"Where are you two going?" Maggie asked.

Tiffany reappeared in the doorway. "I'm going to help Connie clean kennels." She slung an overnight bag over her shoulder. "Then its movie night! You mind keeping Leo, or want me to take him?"

"She's going to tell me what everyone in the 'wood's really like." Connie grinned. "I got the lingo."

"Now girls, even if they are celebrities, is that nice?" Grace looked sideways at Tiffany. "You should know better, haven't you been the subject of gossip and paparazzi often enough?"

"All right, all right. No harm in telling her who's nice and which guys are good kissers." Tiffany picked up Leo. "But if I'm supposed to clean up my act, I think it's time you two did the same."

Grace plumped a throw pillow. "Us?"

Maggie examined her bandaged finger. "He can stay here with me."

Tiffany laid the dog in Maggie's arms. "See? You two put your game face on in public, but we know better. C'mon. Tell us when your friendship jumped the shark."

Grace watched Leo lick up at Maggie's stony face.

"She means, what happened that changed everything for the worst?" Connie sat down. "Grace started to tell me about it."

Grace studied frayed edges of the embroidered pillow. Maggie stroked Leo's head.

Connie softly prompted, "Something about a dance?"

Tiffany sat on an ottoman at Grace's feet. "Whoa. I love ancient history. What kind of dance?"

"They probably wore leopard-skin gowns and rode t-rex to the Jurassic-torium." Tiffany and Connie laughed at their jokes.

"Haha. You girls better run along." Maggie glanced at Grace. "Some things are best left alone."

"Nuh-uh! You promised." Connie tugged Grace's shoelace.

With a glance at Maggie, Grace began. "Tiff, I already told Connie that it had always been my dream to design our prom around the movie *Gone with the Wind*."

"Oh. Tara and 'Frankly, Scarlett, I don't give a d—'"

"That's right," Grace interrupted. "My dad took me to a film festival and I fell in love with the dresses and the music and the romance."

"But when she started planning it as the prom theme, there were people in town who, shall we say, had previous bad feelings about it." Maggie joined in, her tone ratcheting up a notch. "You should have gotten the hint and changed it."

"You mean to 'Under the Sea' or another cliché?" Grace flicked a thumb to her chest. "I was the decorations chairman, I'd kept notes for weeks, made all the calls. Besides, it was my choice, and the school board approved it. Changing it wasn't fair."

"It wasn't fair that you were determined to make it an issue when it stirred everyone up."

"What?" Tiffany urged when the women grew quiet. "What could *Gone With the Wind* possibly stir up?"

Grace paused, then, "It was…racial." Her cheeks warmed. It had been years since anyone discussed the town's infighting during their senior year of high school.

"Racial?" Connie's face grew serious. "How?

Grace's teacher gears whirred to life. "The movie was made in 1938, before Martin Luther King and civil rights." She watched Connie for the spark of understanding. "Back in the day, when the book was being made into a movie, Cherryvale split over it."

"It was a book first?" Tiffany stopped inspecting her manicure. "Who knew?"

"Anyway, I didn't realize I was stirring anything up with the…" Grace paused, embarrassed to say the words.

Connie's eyes grew wide. "You don't mean the—"

Tiffany breathed out, "The what?"

"The KKK?" Connie whispered.

"Ohmig…" Tiffany's eyes grew.

"Yes," Grace confirmed. "When they were writing the screenplay based on the book, the director, Selszman or something—"

"Selznick," Tiffany corrected.

"Yes, him. He wouldn't allow them to use any references to the Klan."

"I should hope not." Connie shuddered.

Tiffany nodded. "Why was that so bad?"

Maggie stared out the window. Grace continued. "In the book, Margaret Mitchell refers to them helping Scarlett after Tara's attacked. It was a different time. Doesn't make it right."

"I don't get how that caused a problem so many years later in Cherryvale," Connie wondered.

"It did." Grace chewed her lower lip and shot Maggie a look. "What was wrong is that—"

"I'll tell it." Maggie spoke, her voice flat. "My great grandfather was in the Klan."

Tiffany and Connie drew breaths together.

"He was a grand poobah or whatever you call it." Grace stopped when Maggie glared holes through her. "Sorry. You finish."

"No way!" Connie's eyes saucered.

"Way."

"But I thought he was a good guy, giving people land to use and all."

Maggie nodded slowly. "Not proud of it, but there you have it. Besides, that was the other side of my family."

Grace watched Tiffany. The young girl had only seen her own father once from a distance. Familiarity with past generations' deep dark secrets must be foreign to her.

"What did that have to do with your prom?" Connie brought Grace's attention back to the moment, but Maggie answered.

"When Grace started talking about her dream theme," —Maggie emphasized dream with a dramatic flourish— "some old timers started teasing my mom."

"How sad." Connie whispered.

"My parents were wonderful, loving people. So were my grandparents. Each generation removed from that era coped with the shame a little differently. Looking back, I wonder why they didn't just admit it happened and let everyone move forward. But they'd worked so hard to keep it a secret, it seemed impossible to do otherwise. Turns out they never let my mom see *Gone With the Wind*, or any other movies, really." She glanced at Tiffany. "They called all movies evil."

Tiffany's face morphed into understanding. "That's why you were so dead set against having a movie made here?"

Maggie nodded. "Proving I didn't learn from my parent's mistakes this many years later."

"What happened to the prom?" Connie's attention riveted to their back-story.

Maggie looked down at a braided rug worn from generations of use.

"Somehow I got to be the chairman. Since my mother made the fuss and Grace wouldn't change the theme, I did."

"Wait." Connie furrowed her brow. "Weren't you best friends or something?"

"She did a splendid job." Grace watched Maggie's face. "She went with a 'Summer in Paris' theme."

"You hated it," Maggie began then paused. "Hang on. I thought you didn't even go. Cindy Ferguson told me you never bought a ticket."

"Nobody asked me. But my parents convinced me I'd have only one prom, and I should go anyway."

"Did you even dance with anyone?" Connie asked.

"No warning, you just up and went?" Tiffany wrinkled her nose. "What did you wear?"

"What I really wanted was a gown that looked like Scarlett's." Grace focused dreamily on a distant point, hands clasped over her chest. "You know the one trimmed with green ribbons? I ended up wearing a long skirt my mom had in her closet."

"You didn't yank down the curtains and wear them?" Connie and Tiffany giggled.

Grace dropped her hands in her lap, the dream vanished. "My dad dropped me off and waited in the parking lot. I walked around the punch table, looked at everyone having a good time and left." She caught Maggie's eye. "But your decorations turned out beautifully."

"Why didn't you look for me?" Maggie sounded hurt even though her lips turned up in a slight grin.

"I asked Principal Sanders to tell you I'd stopped by. Didn't he tell you?"

"Mr. Sanders spent most of the evening policing the bathrooms. Someone smuggled in wacky tobacky."

Tiffany hid a smirk behind Leo's head. Connie pulled out her cell phone. "Look at the time. We better get back. My dad's making us his homemade pizza."

The girls started out the door, but Tiffany stopped. "I remember there was something else about that movie."

Always glad to instruct and inform, Grace nodded. "When the movie premiered, the actress who played Scarlett's maid didn't want to go to the opening because it was being held in a segregated theater in Atlanta. In solidarity, Clark Gable threatened not to go. But she made him."

"She didn't go at all?" Connie sounded shocked.

Tiffany raised an index finger. "No, but she was the first African American to win an Oscar."

"That's so wrong, I mean about the segregated premiere," Connie went on. "But you know what?"

"What?" Grace and Tiffany chorused.

"That Clark guy was a good friend for standing up for her." Connie tipped up her chin.

"The best." Grace cut a glance at Maggie.

Tiffany paused, her hand on the door. "I'd like to read *Gone with the Wind.*"

"That's a brilliant idea," Grace agreed. "I collect copies. Some have illustrations..." She realized the girls were anxious to leave and stood waiting for her to finish. "We can talk about that later. You two have fun tonight."

The screen slammed and the girls clattered down the steps, chatting about what plantation life must have been like. "Think we can download it from Netflix?" Connie suggested as they drew out of earshot.

Grace hurried to the door and called through the mesh. "The movie's never as good as the book!" Then she remembered something. "Wait!" She leaned out.

"What?" Connie stopped, her hand on the Jeep's door handle.

"Bridge-and-tunnel?"

Tiffany threw her bag on the backseat. "New York snobs call New Jersey-ites 'bridge and tunnelers.' Like they aren't good enough to be in the same crowd. In other words, stay on your side of the river, we don't want your kind here."

"City-ism," Connie named it. "Is that a thing?" She opened her car door and tossed her purse inside.

"People always find ways to distance themselves from each other for petty reasons." Grace shook her head. "Let's just pray we don't make the same mistake. 'Night!"

The doors slammed in unison and the girls sped off. Grace settled into the deep cushions next to Maggie, whose expression remained unreadable.

Grace knew it was time to face their own -isms. "Can we talk?"

CHAPTER TWENTY-FIVE

Maggie broke the silence. “I guess every generation has their own form of prejudice. I was pretty bridge-and-tunnel toward the movie crew.”

“You’ve had a rough year since you moved back.” Grace tried to make her voice soft without denying the truth of her statement.

Maggie thought a minute. “You’re still angry with me for taking over the prom committee.”

“We were young. We should have talked about it.” Grace fidgeted. “What hurt was that you took over without including me.”

“I knew you loved to be in control, it’s how you’re wired.”

Grace sucked in air.

Maggie tipped her forehead and peered at Grace from under her one and a half eyebrows. “Okay, be uber-organized, if you will.” Maggie’s eyes swept over a bookshelf in disarray with magazines, old mail and dusty knickknacks piled high. “Back then I thought you had to be in charge of everything in a show-off kind of way.” She picked at a loose end to her bandage. “Now I realize it’s a gift.”

Grace felt a little of the heavy weight lifting. “You’re good at lots of things, the way you’re wired with compassion for the forgotten animals...”

"Hold on. Let me have my say." Maggie's voice resumed its healthy timbre. "I'm no good at planning things or even keeping this place organized, Joe always—" Her gaze traveled to a photo hanging next to the door. A younger Maggie and Joe posed in front of the pyramids in Egypt.

Grace couldn't help herself. "You have lots of strengths. You know all about living in foreign countries, how to exchange dollars for euros, how to find your way around the Paris metro..."

"None of that's of any use here." Maggie picked up Leo.

Grace watched her stroke the dog's head and leaned forward. "You have a soft spot for animals. And for people when you'll admit it. Or you wouldn't have invited Tiffany to stay here with you. But when you left town, I never heard from you except a postcard or Christmas letter. What was that about?"

"I thought you were mad. That you didn't want anything to do with me. And I was so jealous of you..."

"You were always so intent on moving away, going somewhere else. I missed you. I kind of..."

"Kind of what?" Maggie insisted.

"It's stupid. I took it personally how much you wanted to leave the Vale. But now I realize you always wanted to see the world." Grace thought of the occasional Christmas cards that didn't replace the real intimacy they'd shared growing up then something occurred. "Wait. You were jealous of me?"

"Still am. I move back to my hometown and it's not the same anymore. Most of the people are new. I may have wanted to leave Cherryvale, but I loved it here as well. My granddad's tales of Europe during the war probably spurred my wanderlust. In the back of my mind all those years Joe and I traveled, I missed Cherryvale something fierce." A thought passed behind her eyes and her voice grew soft. "Whenever I got homesick, I made Joe listen to tales of our adventures in the hay mow or swimming in town pond. Remember that time I dared you to go skinny dipping?"

Grace felt herself blush. "Shh! Good Lord when those headlights shone across the pond I thought I'd die."

Maggie guffawed. "I never saw anyone hold their breath as long as you did." She sighed. "I wanted to return to that place, not a town full of strangers and sightseers, I wanted to get away from that. Not to mention Vaders! Uh, sorry. When the movie crew and photographers hit town, everyone's distracted and I'm left alone getting this place going..." Maggie heaved a quiet sob.

Grace squeezed her shoulder, sensing the need to remain quiet and just listen.

"Of course I'm jealous of you." Maggie continued. "You've got the perfect life, successful grown kids, a great husband to come home to. On top of that, you almost single-handedly transformed this entire town, much as I hated it at first, you saved it from going under. There's not a life or a business that hasn't benefited from the touch of Grace."

She fought a tickle of pride and shut her eyes, then opened them. "Maggie, two things."

"What?"

"First of all. The perfect life as you call it was made even better when my best friend moved back."

Maggie's voice caught in her throat a little. "And the second?"

"I owe you an apology."

The bandaged hand waved. "No you don't. Besides, this is about me apologizing."

"The stupid prom thing? Forget it. I've always been self-centered, pushing for what I wanted. Can you forgive me?"

"You? Self centered?"

"Please let me off the pedestal, it's lonely up here!"

Maggie chortled. "All right. I forgive you. But that doesn't mean I don't appreciate your gift from time to time. I don't mind admitting I could use a little help." Maggie leaned back, her arms resting on the chair. She regarded Grace. "Now your turn. At least admit you still miss never having the Tara-themed prom."

"No question." Grace wove her fingers together, laughing at her lingering teenage dream. "I've always wished I could have danced at least once. But I meant what I said, you did a beautiful job."

"Did you know I forgot to hire the band ahead of time?"

Grace shook her head and fought against a smug grin. "Oh?"

"So I used the budget to hire another more expensive band at the last minute. My mom and grandmother made the food because I ran out of money for the caterer." Maggie rolled her eyes. "Told you some of us have it, some don't. You make it look easy."

Grace smiled and answered simply, "Thanks."

"Some people call it meddling, I call it genius."

"Whatever you call it, I thank God for the opportunity to use it for His glory." Grace watched Maggie massage her sore thumb. "Turns out you have the gift of hospitality, asking Tiffany to stay and all, you've already made her feel welcome. That reminds me, what's this about Winnie the Pooh?"

"I'll tell you about that while we do the evening feed, and then I'll take you up on that meal. I haven't had good sushi since Joe and I attended the coronation in…oh never mind." She rubbed her belly. "Since my days in lockup, I've had an enormous appetite." She chuckled down the hallway. "Can you imagine our Hollywood starlet cleaning dog pens?"

Grace called after her. "I know today she seems like any other teenager heading off for a sleep-over, but you know she's not cut from the same fabric as our small town kids around here. Issues are likely to come up."

Maggie leaned around the doorpost. "Tiffany wants to learn about taking care of animals, change her lifestyle and clean up her act. I don't think any of this was an accident, do you? About the time I could use an extra hand around here to fix the place up, she's dropped into my world and wants to—no—*needs* to live with me."

Grace realized the irony of world traveler and street wise Tiffany settling down to live with Maggie. They might come from different backgrounds but in a way they were more alike than disparate. Maybe it would work out without problems.

A few minutes later, Maggie emerged, morphed from her business-meeting suit and city pumps into a seersucker shirt, khaki slacks, and loafers. Grace helped her fill bowls with dog chow from cans on the porch, and they carried them outside for the German shepherd and Rottweiler that Henry and Max conscripted as stakeout sentries. Their bones still gave them an angular look, and Greg's stitches showed along the shepherd's hip, but their eyes were eager and their tongues lolled, drooling and eager for dinner. Their tails circled while they dove into their dinner bowls.

Are you keeping these two?" Grace watched, pleased they were turning out to be friendly. Maggie could use their type of devotion and companionship.

"For now. Apparently they'd been abandoned near the bypass. People should be shot…I've put an ad in the paper and sent word to nearby rescues, but no responses."

"Didja name them?"

Maggie considered the hounds. "What about Scarlett and Rhett?"

"Love it!" Grace laughed.

The women strolled to the farmyard to continue feeding.

"I know it was the Lord, Maggs, why Tiffany's here I mean. Don't you find it ironic that the very people you were so against coming here—"

"You don't have to say it. I get it." Maggie waved her hand, pointing heavenward. "It doesn't take a big hammer to teach me a lesson."

Grace glanced at her.

"Okay, maybe it does." Maggie smirked. "I thought they were causing my trouble, and they ended up being the reason I was found."

"And you got a sort of new daughter out of it." Grace finished filling the bucket and turned off the spigot.

"I'm going to need lots of help from an expert." Maggie eyed Grace.

"You'll do fine, with a lot of prayer, and patience. Feeling responsible for someone else can wear you down."

Maggie took the buckets from Grace and stacked them in the feed room. They sat on the steps to wait for the donkey's water trough to fill. "What's this I hear in your voice? You admitting to being worn out?" Maggie dangled the hose over the rising water.

"Not exactly, not physically."

Maggie gently bumped her. "What could possibly wear down Super Grace?"

Grace huffed and inspected her thumbnail. "I'm worn out running from the Lord."

"You? You're the most righteous person I know, why would you—"

"I'm serious." Grace felt her face warm.

"You mad because I didn't say thank you for finding me? I know if you hadn't been watching the video when you did, and ridden your bike to the rescue, I—"

Grace's voice grew small. "I wasn't fishing for thanks."

"Always finding something that needs fixing or re-purposing. Now I'm your project, right? I thought we worked all this out inside, what now?"

"I admit I have goals for myself and my family." Grace fumbled for the right words. "I don't expect…I mean I never meant to set the bar for anyone else to jump."

"I see how you have to bite your tongue around me." Maggie adjusted her grip on the hose as it bobbed. "Still don't get why you of all people, think you have been running from the Lord."

Grace had a tough time admitting even to herself she had flaws, but she owed her oldest friend honest transparency. "You've had a rough time since you moved back to the Vale. I could have been a much better friend and support to you." She rubbed Maggie's back. "I'm sorry about Joe dying, you know that, Maggie."

Water dribbled down the hose and Maggie scooted her feet aside. "Huh. Losing him has made me even harder to get along with, that's where you're going with this."

Grace handed her a tissue she'd remembered to stuff in her pocket that morning. "No matter how hard you are to get along with…" Grace laughed through her tears as Maggie shot her a mock look of shock. "You're entitled to some off days, let me put it that way. But I'm sorry to say it almost took losing you to…" Grace choked before she could speak the possibilities of what might have happened to Maggie and Tiffany. "It took almost losing you to make me realize you're more important than any old to-do list. That's why I'd been running from the Lord until I realized what He was trying to tell me."

Maggie swiped at wet lashes. "Remember what you said on Greg's porch? When you called me your best friend again after all these years? That meant a lot to me." Grace opened her mouth but Maggie shushed her. "Let me finish. You organized a telethon and then danced in it for me. And I never thanked you. I'm a terrible friend all wrapped up in my own pity. It was not your fault whatever happened to my place." She looked up. "The truth is, the first fire was shabby wiring we should have replaced years ago, and the others set by Max and Henry were not something you had any control over. She bumped Grace's shoulder. "You can not control everything in the Vale, sister, so just give up trying. Admit it feels good to give up all that responsibility and leave it to God." Maggie twisted the faucet to stop the hose.

Grace heaved a sigh. "You're absolutely right."

Heads together, they listened to the sounds of animals crunching until Maggie spoke again. "Shall we call today our Fresh Start?"

"Yes, please." Grace thought over the past few days. "Speaking of fresh starts, get this. Tiffany's not the only Vader to become a Valer. Jeff Field's fixing up The Pit."

"Oy. We're going to have two movie stars living in our midst? I guess I'll have to learn to take these things with a more Grace-full attitude, I was looking forward to the drama subsiding." She shoved herself off the step and curled the hose. "Let's get going. I'm ready to put on my own feedbag."

Maggie held a hand out and pulled Grace to her feet. They strolled to the house and gathered purses and shut off lights.

"Wait a sec, one more thing." Grace pulled an envelope from her back pocket. "Here. I hope you can take one more change."

"What's this?" Maggie worked open the seal.

"The other night when I stayed here to feed your animals, I kind of snooped around looking for clues to your disappearance. I stumbled across your list again. Well, stumbled is wrong. I up and looked for it."

Maggie slid out papers and read aloud. "E-ticket confirmation."

She scanned the sheet and up at Grace. "Jumping johnny's jungle gym! These are the airplane tickets you won. That's a hoot. You and Mark going in an airplane?"

"Not me and Mark." Grace beamed and gestured toward the itinerary. "You and me. We're going to England. Number fourteen."

Maggie stared at her and then back at the papers.

"I Googled and found us the perfect pony trekking holiday. We're going for a week in September."

Maggie fell onto a chair. "What about your fear of flying?"

"Already started working on that." Grace held her head high as the clouds. "Remember, I went up with Carl? That's how I realized that van parked near the shed was all wrong."

Maggie gaped and pointed at the ceiling. "Of course. What an eye for detail you have."

"I might not have realized what was out of place if Carl hadn't shown me the town from up there. It's all so beautiful from up there, you just don't realize..." Maggie cast her a smug grin. "Of course, you know about air travel. That's why you're the perfect person to take me on my first big trip."

"No, honey. Go somewhere with your husband." Maggie fingered the tickets and held them out. "I doubt if I'll be able to get away by September. I've got to rebuild, and..."

Grace closed her hand over Maggie's and shoved the tickets back. "It was Mark's idea. And I've already spoken to Connie about taking care of the place while we're gone." Grace's words gathered speed, along with her confidence. "Think about it, now Tiffany's here to help too. Greg will lend a hand, and I asked Rose to look in on them. Everything will be grand."

Maggie read over the description of the holiday, letting it soak in. She beamed at Grace, her cheeks moist from happy tears. "I may never get over losing Joe. But, when I thought I'd alienated any friends at all, including you, the entire town...and then some...came to my rescue. Led by my spandexed, baton-twirling, toe-tapping, super-friend!"

Grace shrugged to hide her blush. "Aw shucks, what are super-friends for, anyway?"

Virtually the entire town turned out for Founder's Day assignments. All morning, Grace rode her bike the length of The Path, supervising as one group filled potholes with dirt and another planted new bushes to replace those that died over the winter. New fence railings went up and painted, fresh directional signs nailed in place. By noon, volunteers completed the work on Grace's punch list to her satisfaction.

Later, she and Mark scurried around their kitchen, preparing meat for patties and buns for the burgers. Grace flicked a floral gingham cloth over the patio table and placed a glass bowl filled with colorful peonies in the center.

"I'm going to shower, then I'll fire up the grill." Mark covered a platter of ribs with plastic wrap and slid them into the fridge. "Give these babies a chance to marinate."

Grace lifted the lid on the cooler to make sure ice still covered the soda cans. She took one last inventory of the kitchen island covered with plates, utensils, and napkins for their buffet lunch. At one end, she placed a deep basket lined with red gingham holding a double batch of cranberry and blueberry muffins.

The Sims family arrived with smiles and waves. Cassie and Carson played with a bottle of bubbles Grace set out for them as the adults discussed the improvements to The Path, plates piled high with ribs, burgers and dogs fresh off the grill.

Jeff arrived and exchanged pleasantries then chose a lawn chair near the table.

When everyone was settled, Grace carried a tray with two bowls over, offered up to Jeff. "Did you make any calls to those contractors I gave you?"

"I did, and I have two meetings tomorrow." He helped himself to guacamole and a handful of chips.

Rose came out of the kitchen, her own plate full.

"Have you seen the changes he's making, Rose?" Grace stood from her perch on the bench.

She slid her long legs in between the seat and table. "Changes?"

"Jeff bought that fixer-upper a few doors down from me. He's planning a complete renovation."

Rose stopped fiddling with her braid, gave it a toss behind her back. "When I lived in England, I rode with a fellow who approved historic renovations for the National Registry. He showed me some of his projects." She bit into her hamburger.

Jeff sat up, his chair creaking under the shift. "Care to take a walk and see it before we go to the park?"

"I'd love to." Rose set down the burger and wiped her hands.

"I'll keep your plate warm." Grace took it from her. "You two hurry or it'll be too dark to see anything in there." She avoided Mark's glance, clearing the table of the other dirty dishes.

"Anyone else want to come along?" Jeff offered.

"I'd love to see it." Mark rose, but before he could follow, Grace interrupted.

"Oh, honey." She caught his eye, crooked her finger. "Will you help me put a basket of food together for Maggie and Tiffany?"

Mark glanced at Jeff. "I guess I'll need a rain check." He followed Grace into the kitchen where she poked her head inside the refrigerator.

"Oh, I get it." Mark goosed her bottom. "You wanted to get them alone, didn't you?"

She backed out and handed him a bowl of potato salad with a sheepish grin. "See if anyone wants more of this. I made way too much."

"Someday you're going to pay for meddling in other people's lives." He took the bowl but gave her a stern look.

"Is it my fault I want everyone to be as happy as we are?" She batted her eyelashes at him.

"You're incorrigible." He caved in, and kissed her square on the mouth.

Jeff unlocked the front door and stepped back so Rose could walk inside.

"Oh, I really like the oak beams and wood trim." Rose tiptoed past piles of rubble.

"It's got good bones. I've done some checking into its history." Jeff laid a hand on the wobbly banister as if it were a rare gem. "The original owner built it in 1920. He met a woman in California, fell in love, and had her childhood home copied and built here. Right down to the last post and beam. After it was complete, he asked her to marry him."

"And she couldn't refuse him?" Their eyes met. Somewhere in the house, a branch scraped against glass and broke the silence. Rose cleared her throat. "Kind of like what you're doing for your daughter? Grace told me you'd like to move her here." She stepped away, her sandals slapping against the floorboards. "What happened to them?"

"Who?"

"The man and the girl he proposed to?" She examined a loose stone in the generous fireplace.

"She accepted and they had five kids. Married for 43 years." Jeff delivered the last line in his best voice over style. "Romantic, isn't it?"

"It could be the premise of a movie itself. Who let it get in such bad shape?"

"Maybe we've stumbled onto a new reality show." Jeff had a faraway look in his eyes. "Apparently it was most recently owned by a couple who couldn't make a go of it in the recession. Sad." Jeff indicated doors leaning against the hearth. "These belong on the bottom cabinets of the built-in bookshelves. No telling how long they've been off."

"You've got quite a project. I thought you were just going to need new carpet and paint."

"Sometimes, change needs to happen far below the surface." Jeff paused then turned to her with light in his eyes. "The more I research these homes, the more excited I get about the historical renovation. I want it accurate down to the last mortice and beam." They stepped back outside onto the porch and Jeff locked the door. "I've gone on about myself. What about you? Have you lived in Cherryvale—er, the Vale, I guess locals call it—for long?" He held her hand to steady her as they maneuvered down the uneven walkway, then kept hold of it as they walked along The Path.

"Not long."

"How did you end up here, in this town?"

"I was looking for a small farm, large enough to board a few horses for income, teach lessons. It's in a central location. I can show on the circuit when I have a horse to sell." Rose stumbled, grabbed Jeff's arm for balance and lifted her foot. "I have a pebble." He indicated a stone bench by the walkway and helped her hop over to it.

A rotten log rested across a murky pond, and a couple of squirrels scampered back and forth over its length, busily doing whatever squirrels do on a summer afternoon.

"I like it here, but I was looking for a quiet place to settle." Rose slipped off her flip-flop, brushed a hand over her bare foot. "Are you sure you're ready to make such a big lifestyle change. I mean, aren't you afraid you'll go into shock living in such a small town after Los Angeles?"

"One can feel lonely even when surrounded by people." Jeff's shoulder touched hers, the bench barely long enough for both of them. "As soon as we arrived, I felt connected somehow." He slid a glance over to her. "I thought places like this only existed in hokey women's network movies. The way Cherryvale pulled together hit me right here." He smacked his broad chest. "I think I'm going to really like it."

"What about your career?" She brushed the bottom of her foot absently.

"I'm ready for something different. I've got some money put away, if that's what you mean."

Rose fumbled to slip on her shoe. "I know enough about the biz to know you risk being forgotten if you're away too long."

Jeff chuckled. "Don't worry about me. Really. But I appreciate the concern."

She stood up, a tinge of embarrassment coloring her cheeks. "We'd better get back. It's about time to head over to the park." She stepped onto the crumbling walkway.

"Rose, wait." He grabbed her hand and she teetered, her sandal fighting for a level spot.

"What is it?"

"Are you seeing anyone?"

"Well." She grew quiet then set her chin. "Not really. No."

His movie star perfect teeth flashed white at her. "Good to know. Allow me." He helped her safely through the growth and uneven flagstones. "I need to hire a bushhog first thing." He grunted, pushing the gate open through tall weeds.

Back on the lane they strolled, admiring the improvements completed that morning and discussing the contractors Jeff had lined up to begin making bids on the makeover. They rounded The Path as the others stepped out the Harkins's gate. Rose dropped Jeff's hand as they approached the others.

"Isn't that a fascinating project he's taking on?" They stood so close to each other Grace fought back the urge to grin. "I think he's going to need all the help he can get."

Family and friends set up chairs and spread out blankets to lie on for the best view of the Founder's Day fireworks later that night. Grace, Mark, Rose, Jeff, and the Simses found a spot among them.

The Cherrypickers' rollicking banjo and harmonica melodies filled the evening air from a temporary stage near the water's edge. Carolyn sat down on the blanket while Carl scampered after the twins in an impromptu game of freeze tag. Rose and Jeff meandered away as well, hand in hand again. Grace and Mark relaxed in lawn chairs and settled in to enjoy the music.

"I see your matchmaking worked." Mark tapped a toe in rhythm with "Orange Blossom Special."

"They do look cute together, don't they? I think he's interested in finding a mom for his daughter and Rose is kind of young for that but she seems so mature—"

"Look Miz Grace!" Carson and Cassie burst through the crowd, their cheeks glistening from a combination of what appeared to be cotton candy and wet paint. She tipped Cassie's chin up. "Love the beautiful butterfly that's landed on your cheek."

"It's just paint, thilly." Cassie giggled. "Carthon got Spiderman." Cassie pointed at her brother, who proffered his cheek for a closer look.

"Love those super heros!" Grace cooed over his choice. "Now, who wants to go over to Maggie's petting corral?"

"I do!"

"I do!"

"I'll walk over there with you." Carolyn tucked her sandaled feet under her and stood. "I ate too much at your barbecue. I need to walk it off. You coming, Carl?"

"I think I'll sit this one out if you don't mind, babe." Carl lay back on the blanket and shut his eyes. "Think I pulled a muscle in that potato sack race."

"It's okay you didn't win, Daddy." Cassie patted Carl's forehead. "Old people can't hop as fast as us little kids."

Carl swiped playfully at the giggling twins as they raced off.

Grace lifted a wicker basket, heavy with food and a thermos of lemonade. "Be sure and listen for a special announcement if your hearing's not gone, old man."

Carolyn and Grace followed the twins over to Maggie's petting corral. A Shetland pony nibbled at hay while a sheep huddled in the corner with her lamb.

Tiffany, Leo nestled in the crook of an elbow, wobbled on high heels trying to keep a toddler from pulling the lamb's ears.

"Happy Founders Day!" Grace greeted Maggie across the fence. A pot-bellied pig nuzzled Grace through the wire. "How's your day been?"

"Busy." Maggie leaned against a hay bale, watching Cassie show Carson how to properly pet the sheep's wooly, white back.

"This is the one that jumped over me in the fire," Cassie explained. She lifted the hem of her shorts. "Thee?"

Grace bit her lower lip. "My brave little one."

Maggie kept a keen eye on a young girl poking at her pig. "How was the barbecue?"

"We ate too much and enjoyed every bite." Carolyn patted her belly.

"Mith Maggie," Cassie called, "what did you name the lambs?"

"I haven't named them, yet."

"Hey, why don't you have a contest?" Grace's wheels turned. "It would be good publicity for the grand re-opening."

"We'll have a drawing. I'll give the winner a yearly pass." Maggie gently pulled back the little girl before she succeeded in pulling the pig's tail. "Scratch his back like this, honey." She glanced up at the sky. "Time to get them put away before it gets dark." She eyed Grace's basket. "I'd love some of that barbecue, if that's what you're hiding."

Grace jumped. "I almost forgot. The least I can do is feed you."

"Sorry, folks, the animals need to get ready for bed." Maggie stood aside as the visitors left, and then walked around to the truck.

Grace waited for Maggie to back the trailer up to the enclosure so they could load them up. She watched Tiffany perched on a bale of hay flicking mud off her heels with a piece of straw. *A lot of good those ridiculous shoes were on a day like this. It's a good thing she's here at all, though, or her surprise would be ruined.*

A young woman interrupted her thoughts. "Excuse me." The pot-bellied pig poker peeked out at her from behind her mom's candy-striped capris. "My daughter told me you're the tap dancer from the telethon."

"I am." Grace grinned at the little blondie who looked to be about seven or eight years old. "You're absolutely correct."

"Allie wants to know if she can have your autograph. She's learning how to dance. We taped your performance and watch it over and over."

Grace felt herself blush. "That's terrific, Allie. I'll bet you're really good at dancing."

Allie's mom handed Grace a torn bit of paper from her purse and

Grace wrote her name and thought a second, then added, "Always Dance for the Lord," and handed it to the little girl. "I never thought I would be signing autographs. You've made me feel very special, Allie. Thank you." She wiggled her fingers in a goodbye wave and scooted over to help Maggie shoo the animals up the ramp into the stock trailer.

The doors locked and the animals safely settled, Grace folded back a cloth covering the picnic basket and lifted out a couple of plastic wrapped plates. She handed a plate to Maggie then held one up to Tiffany, who supervised Cassie holding Leo. "At least try a rib. Mark's rub is to die for."

Carolyn took the plate and handed it to Tiffany. "I'll say. I'll supervise Leo and the twins. You eat."

Grace watched Tiffany inspect a rib, nibble at it, then glance at the stage where the 'Pickers were noisily taking down their equipment.

Connie ran up. "Hey, everybody, enjoying the day? I took care of that special item you needed. Isn't it time, Miz Grace?"

"I didn't realize how late it was getting." Grace shoved the basket in Maggie's direction then pulled it back. "Connie have you eaten? There's a plate for Henry but I haven't seen him."

"I left him working on one of the burn sites." Maggie munched on a corn muffin and tugged the basket back. "I can take it to him for later. What's got you wound up?"

"It's time for our special event." She emphasized special with a jerk of her head toward the stage. "You remember. Carolyn? Don't you want to get Carson and Cassie…uh, ready?"

Realization spread across Carolyn's face and she sprang up. "Oh, yes, come on kids. Let's go get ready for that…thing I told you about." She handed Leo back to an astonished Tiffany and held her hands out.

Carson grabbed his mother's hand. "Is this the—"

"Shhhh!" Grace, Carolyn and Connie cautioned him at once, and they ran toward the grassy field.

"You go on. I'll take care of the basket." Maggie swallowed and sat down next to Tiffany. "You eating that rib or memorizing it?"

On stage, the Mayor stepped up, did a rat-a-tat on the mic. "Ladies and gentlemen." Mayor stepped up to the podium, his baritone attracted the crowd's attention. "This year we are starting a new Founder's Day tradition. This event is in honor of one of Cherryvale's newest friends. Grace, since this was your idea, as most of the ideas in town seem to be," he waited while laughter and clapping died after that comment, "Why don't you come up here and make the announcement?"

Grace climbed the steps and stood too close to the mic. While the feedback receded, she saw Carl jump up to follow his family. "Hello, everyone." She tried again. "First I want to thank you for your hard work today. The Path looks terrific. Give yourselves a round of applause." The townsfolk cheered themselves heartily.

"Like the Mayor said, we thought Founder's Day needed a new event, something all ages could participate in, but first, let me invite the honoree to the stage." Grace held her hand over the microphone, more painful feedback shot from the loudspeakers. "Can someone get Tiffany up here?

Connie ran over to the petting enclosure, said something, and without hesitation, Tiffany set the rib on her plate, wiped her mouth, and made her way across the field.

"You come up here too, Maggie." Grace returned focus to the waiting audience. "Ladies and gentlemen, the owner of the to-be-rebuilt petting farm brought several animals over at no charge today." Maggie moved toward them. "She wanted to let you know how much she appreciated the fundraiser to get the animal rescue operation back on its... hooves and paws, as it were."

Everyone laughed. Maggie shook a couple of extended hands as she walked through the crowd. A sheepish grin spread over the usually stoic woman's face.

Climbing the steps in total ease, Tiffany turned to wave at the crowd. Leo sniffed the air for familiar scents, and Grace leaned toward her as the applause died down.

"You don't know what this is about, do you?"

"I've done lots of appearances at these little events." Tiffany's brows knit. "Key to the city?"

"Good, just checking." Grace held a note card out for Tiffany and stepped back to give her room. "Here, read this."

Tiffany scanned the card.

Grace leaned into mic range again. "Out loud, honey."

When the crowd's laughter ceased again, Tiffany began. "Ladies and gentlemen, boys and girls, it is my honor to present the First Annual..." She stopped, staring at the card.

"Go on." Grace motioned.

Tiffany cleared her throat, her voice softer now, and she began again. "It is my honor to present The First Annual Tiffany Lane Kites and Kids Just-for-Fun Event."

Connie climbed the steps with a large kite and handed it to the Mayor, who presented it with a flourish of his hand.

"This...I don't know what to say." Tiffany turned the kite to look at it, awkwardly hitting Grace over the head with it. "Sorry! And thank you."

Grace rubbed her noggin and held up two palms. "No, it's yours. Cherryvale's gift to you."

Tiffany looked back at the crowd. "This is better than all those stupid keys I usually get."

Again, the crowd erupted. Her arm around Tiffany, Grace leaned over and announced, "Kids, go fly your kites!"

From across the field toward Main Street, dozens of boys and girls appeared over the slope and into the field still sprinkled with tomato red poppies. They ran downhill toward the lake, clutching strings, pulling and tugging to keep their paper ships aloft in the warm breeze. Moms and dads, grandmothers and grandfathers followed, trotting behind them lifting kites that were homemade or store-bought, long tailed or short, all ready to catch the wind.

Tiffany stood motionless as they topped the small hill and flung the kites into the afternoon breeze blowing off Cherryvale pond. The happy shapes lifted, the strings grew taut. In moments, the sky filled with kites shaped like diamonds, dragons, boxes, and animals, every color in the rainbow dancing in the wind.

"Let's go, honey!" Grace tugged at her elbow, moving toward the steps to the grass. "Don't you want to try yours?"

Tiffany hesitated for just a moment before flying down the steps where Connie and Maggie waited.

"Lemme have Leo." Connie took the dog from her and Maggie grabbed the kite, leaving Tiffany holding the string. Tiffany clutched the kite and wouldn't let go.

"I've got it." Maggie tugged.

"Honey, you need to let it go so Maggie can launch it for you." Grace pointed up the hill. "Run."

"I've never actually flown a kite before," Tiffany admitted.

"Well, today there's no stunt double, so you're doing your own tricks, girl." Connie sprinted after Maggie, who lumbered up the hill at a brisk pace.

Tiffany hobbled and wobbled, balancing on her toes. Every time she rocked back, her heels sunk into the deep grass and Maggie had to stop and wait.

Finally, she looked down, and one by one, flicked the eight hundred dollar shoes into the deep grass. She handed Leo to Grace, motioned to Maggie and took off running barefoot, shouting, "Let her go, Maggie!"

Maggie sprinted but couldn't hold on any longer as the breeze lifted the midnight blue kite, sprinkled with stars and glittering tail high, dancing and soaring over Cherryvale Park.

Grace trotted up to Maggie who leaned over, hands to knees, catching her breath. "I've never heard her laugh like that."

"How'd you..." Maggie panted, "...organize this so fast?"

"I went viral with it."

Maggie twisted sideways and lifted an eyebrow.

"I sent out an emergency email yesterday. Pastor let me use the Sunday school enrollment. I told everyone to bring a kite. Some already owned them, others made theirs at home." Grace waved at the Simses running by with theirs.

"Love the homemade ones." Maggie straightened, and they watched Carl and his kids working two expertly crafted diamond shaped kites.

Beyond them another family's newspaper covered creation dipped and spun.

"Mark found a pattern that uses stuff around the house, and we included that as an attachment to the email. When this town gets into re-purposing, we don't stop at buildings."

"Mith Grace! Look at mine!" Cassie jumped up and down, pointing to her kite, string slipping, then she clutched it again in the excitement. "My daddy helped me make it."

"It's beautiful, and it flies like a bird," Grace called. "Yours is great, too, Carson."

"Why kites?" Maggie had caught her breath, yet her face was still red making her freckles more pronounced than usual.

Connie ran up. "Great idea to use her tattoo to connect with her Miz Grace."

"Tattoo?" Maggie's eyebrow rose.

"You caught on to that?" Grace laughed.

"What tattoo?" Maggie insisted.

Connie looked at Grace who nodded permission, so she explained. "We found out she has a tattoo, hidden from the world." Connie motioned toward her backside. "They often mean something special."

Maggie leaned over to pick up Tiffany's discarded shoes.

Grace continued the story. "The only time she saw her father was from a distance. Flying kites with another little girl."

"Probably his other daughter, right Miz Grace?" Connie suggested.

"Whoever the girl was, it must have hurt to see that." Maggie clomped Tiffany's shoes together. Muck freed from the heels, plopped into the deep grass.

"We didn't tell anyone else the reason for the kites to keep Tiff's privacy. But doesn't it make for a great addition to the Founder's Day celebration?" Grace's gaze swept the sky dotted with the colorful flyers. "Reminiscent of how our ancestors would have spent a beautiful afternoon. We thought it would give Tiffany another reason to connect with the Vale. Maybe touch her in a place no one's reached before."

"I'll get it!" Connie ran to help Tiffany regain altitude when the breeze faltered, causing her tail to drag.

Maggie and Grace headed gratefully for their blanket and chairs where they could see Jeff signing an autograph for a fan.

Maggie elbowed Grace. "You better take notes. Seems I recall you saying 'no one's going to want our autographs.' I saw what happened at the corral."

"That was a fluke."

"Next thing I know you'll be signing with an agent and wearing ankle-turning shoes like these." She poked at her with one of Tiffany's stilettos.

"Right. Hollywood…or possibly even Broadway…will be knocking on my door," Grace mused as she settled into the chair next to Mark. "Hear from Shelby? I hope she can find us before dark." Leo snoozed in Mark's lap. "You two look cozy."

"Call me the pocket dog whisperer."

A giggle caught their attention. The fans gone, Rose and Jeff lay with their heads together in deep conversation.

Cassie and Carson scampered up, Carolyn and Carl close behind. Carson climbed into his mom's lap and Cassie collapsed next to the cooler, ran her hand through the ice and drew out a juice box.

"Toss me one, would ya, Sissie?" Carl lay back on the blanket, Carson and Cassie climbed on, and he rolled over, tickling them 'til they giggled and squirmed away, then came back for more. Grace remembered Mark doing the same with their own children and was glad to know there were still dads like them in the world.

In a few minutes, Tiffany and Connie joined them on the blanket. Tiffany's long blonde hair lay tousled and uncombed down her back and her cheeks glowed. Grace glanced around, relieved to see no photographers lurking. Maybe Tiffany could settle in Cherryvale and have a normal life with people who really loved her. Perhaps one of these men could be a surrogate father to her. Her sweep of the happy scene landed on Greg.

She'd almost missed his arrival in the gathering dark. Sitting next to Connie on the opposite side from Rose and Jeff, the look on his face reminded her of a kid who'd been left out of a kickball game. He watched the others, particularly the lovebirds, with a longing in his eyes. *Need to find someone for him*, she made a mental note to herself. She glanced at Mark who was watching her. "What?"

"You've been quiet for too long. What are you thinking about?"

"I want to make sure Greg's had dinner is all," she said with a slightly defensive edge. "Greg would you like to sit over here by us?" She patted an empty spot on the blanket. "There's a plate of food in the basket with your name on it." *A little white lie. Henry hadn't shown up, Connie turned it down. It was going to waste sitting there.*

"No, thanks." He drew his long legs under him and stood up. "I just remembered there's a sick, uh…cow I need to check on. The vet's eyes focused on the top of Rose's head. She was still deep in conversation with Jeff.

"Dad, you'll miss the fireworks." Connie's head rested on Tiffany's stomach.

"Doesn't matter. 'Bye, everyone. Happy Founders Day." His boots clumped heavily as he left.

The rest of the evening, Jeff and Rose snuggled, Tiffany and Connie giggled, and Shelby, who arrived in time for the fireworks, chatted with Maggie and Grace about the hungry crowd at the Bucket that day. Carolyn and Carl hugged their twins, who were still a touch afraid of the noise, and Grace and Mark held hands like teenagers.

As they were gathering up their chairs and blankets to go home, her only regret was that pesky twinge of guilt over Greg's hasty departure.

How can I help that man?

CHAPTER TWENTY-SIX

Grace rolled over and studied the fuzzy face on the alarm, trying to make sense of the day and time. Mark should have been showered and shaving by now, but his still form lay motionless next to her.

"Hey, sleepyhead, the alarm didn't go off. You're going to be late." She leaned over to peer at his face half-hidden under the comforter.

"Mmmhfph."

"You sick?" She reached over to feel his forehead.

"Changed my weekend. A little birdie told me there might be something special about the day."

"You didn't have to do anything for me. Last year's surprise will last several birthdays." Her sparkling almost brand new kitchen would warm her heart for years to come.

"Can I at least take the day off to spend it with you?" Mark rolled over and pulled her close. "What would you like to do? The day's yours."

The birthday girl laid her head on his chest. "Let's just stay home. Maybe see a movie later."

"It's a beautiful day. Why don't we take a drive in the country—" the phone on the bedside table rang, interrupting his invitation.

Grace reached over, but Mark grabbed it, glanced at the caller ID and rolled away from her. "Um, it's the hospital. I'll take it in my study. You stay there, and I'll make you some breakfast in bed. Hello?"

Mark disappeared, shutting the door behind him. Grace lay still for a millisecond then jumped out of bed and shoved her toes into her house slippers.

Might as well get the coffee going. A few minutes later, she stood at the open kitchen window filling the carafe with water. Joggers, people walking dogs, and other strollers were already out enjoying the morning.

"Good morning!" she called to Carolyn and Cassie as they passed by on The Path.

"Happy Birthday!" Cassie called to her, and Carolyn gave a quick wave and pulled her along.

"Thank you, sweetie." She shut off the faucet.

Mark joined her, set a bowl down, and took a bowl of Shelby's fresh brown eggs out of the fridge. He set a skillet to heat on the range, and soon the sound of his fork clinked in the bowl of dark yolks for their scramble.

She listened as it spit when he poured the goo into the hot skillet. "Everything okay at the hospital?"

"Hmm?" Mark picked a wooden spoon out of a carafe behind the stove. "Don't you want breakfast in bed?"

"I'd rather eat outside. It's a gorgeous day."

"Lovely idea, birthday girl." Mark pecked her on the lips as he set plates on a tray.

They spent the morning reading the paper on the patio, and Mark took a few phone calls, always in his study.

"You don't have to go in. I'm used to hearing you give orders on the phone." Grace looked up from her crossword after he returned from a lengthy call.

"I just don't want to bother you on your special day, hon." Mark kissed the top of her head and stacked the dirty plates. "I'm going to shower. Just let the machine get the phone while I'm in there. You ready for that ride in the country?"

"Why don't we just dust off your bicycle and we'll ride around town, maybe go to the Bucket."

"Actually I've been looking forward to getting out of town." He shot a guilty smile. "You know whenever I run into patients, they always want to talk about their ingrown toenails or blood pressure."

"I get the point." The door shut behind him and she concentrated on an unfamiliar clue. She made her best guess and filled in the last box for the solve, stuck the newspaper under her arm, and picked up their coffee cups. The phone rang and she absently picked it up, forgetting about Mark's request to let the machine answer. "Hello?"

"Oh, Grace." Maggie's voice sounded strained. "It's Maggie."

"Good morning." She laughed at the sudden formality. "I recognize your—"

"Is Mark there?"

"He's in the shower. Why?"

"No reason. I'll see ya. Oh, um. Happy Birthday." Click.

She replaced the receiver as Mark entered the kitchen buttoning a fresh polo shirt, his hair still wet from the shower. "Who was that?"

"Maggie. She wanted to know if you were here." Grace searched his face. "What is going on? Either you're seeing someone behind my back or you're cooking up something."

"Yes, I've been meaning to tell you that I'm running off with Maggie."

Grace snapped a kitchen towel, barely missing his hiney. He grabbed her in a bear hug. "Not really. You're the only gal for me."

"I know you get all sorts of invitations, but Maggie?" Grace leaned into his soap-scented chest.

"Honestly, I tried to arrange a party or get-together, but we've all been so busy with the telethon and the movie people." He pecked her on the lips. "We just couldn't pull anything off. Guess we're not as organized as you. I'm sorry, honey. I'll make it up to you next year, I promise."

"I don't want anything special. A quiet day with you will be just what the doctor ordered."

"Now, go get your purse and things. I made lunch reservations at that new little restaurant on the road to Franklin City."

Mark whistled as he cleaned the kitchen. On the other end of the house, Grace took birthday calls from the kids then puttered in her bedroom, pulling out several outfits. She finally settled on a cotton sundress, sandals and her pearl earrings. She thought of Maggie and made a mental note to remember her birthday in some special way this year.

In a few minutes, they'd loaded up in Mark's car and turned toward the highway down Main Street. Grace expected Mark to pick up speed as they passed the town park, but instead, he slowed in front of the stables.

"Why are we stopping here?" Grace watched a smirk spread over Mark's face. "You did cook something up. What? A trail ride? You're getting on a horse? Wait, I'm not dressed to ride."

"We're not riding. Not exactly." Mark pulled to the side of the lane and turned the car engine off. "Just trust me, you'll like it."

Mark didn't move to open his door right away. But they didn't wait long. From down the lane, Rose drove a carriage pulled by Jake. She had draped garlands of summer wildflowers along the sides and braided colorful ribbons in his mane.

"What's this?" Grace watched them approach as Mark walked around and opened her door. She stepped out, her eyes never leaving the beautiful rig as it pulled to a stop next to the car. "It's gorgeous!"

Mark helped her step up onto the carriage and climbed up to join her on the white leather cushion.

"Happy Birthday, Grace!" Rose lifted the reins and Jake pulled the buggy across the lane as they clip-clopped back toward the stables.

"This is terrific. I never would have dreamed…is this the picnic you planned?" Grace smiled up at Mark.

"You'll see."

As they rounded the end of the fencerow, Grace noted several cars in the visitor's lot, then she heard band music.

"An orchestra? Whatever did you…?"

Rose drew the reins up and Jake slowed to a stop just as the carriage neared the barn. In the meadow beyond the riding arena, a dozen or so picnic tables covered in white linens, laden with bowls and platters of food, waited. What caught her attention were the people. All the women were dressed in hoopskirts and carried parasols, and the men wore riding breeches, long-tailed coats, and top hats.

Grace stepped out of the carriage, and Jeff, dressed in his own plantation fashions, held out a gloved hand to help her down. Maggie, Shelby and Carolyn, each in an elegant gown, surrounded Grace. Jeff hopped up into the carriage and Rose clicked her tongue at Jake, who pulled away.

"Thanks for the ride!" Grace called, but the two were deep in conversation and didn't respond. She looked around at her friends, who'd gathered in a half circle in front of her. "Maggie, I haven't seen you in a dress since, well, since your wedding!" Grace stifled a giggle.

"Get a load of it." Maggie swished the hoop skirt. "It'll be at least another century before you see it again."

"And so you don't miss the fun, we brought one just for you." Shelby led Grace into the women's locker room, covering her eyes. "Okay, you can look now."

Grace squinted and blinked her eyes until they focused on a pale green gown trimmed in dark green ribbons.

"Don't forget your hoopth!" Cassie tugged at Grace's hand. "Thee, I have them too." Cassie beamed and tipped her skirt, exposing pantaloons and hoops dainty enough to be a doll's costume.

"She's a mini-me." Carolyn crooned.

"So that's how you knew today's my birthday." Grace hugged the little girl.

"Your party's waitin.' Change, girl." Shelby pushed her toward the costume.

"I'll stay and help her wrestle into her get-up." Maggie waved at the others and they bustled out. "Let's get you dressed." Maggie lifted the gown from its hanger and held up the hem so Grace could slip it over her head. Grace tied the matching hat under her chin while Maggie worked the long row of buttons down her back.

"Now I know why you were calling my husband this morning. You sneak. This was your idea, wasn't it?"

"A few of us put our heads together. We wanted to do something for our hometown hero. Really, Gracie, you thought you were going to retire and take it easy, but you haven't had a moment's rest all summer."

"Oh, fiddle-dee-dee. What are friends for, anyway?"

"Hey in there," Mark called from outside the locker room door. "Is my belle ready?"

Maggie slipped the last button through. "She'll be right out, Rhett."

Grace adjusted the feather-plumed hat at an angle on her head, and twirled in front of the mirror. "This dress..."

Maggie slipped her arm through Grace's and they swished toward the door. "It's an exact replica of the one Scarlett wore to the barbecue, just like you described. Holly found it at a costume shop and sent it out as a favor."

Grace smoothed the frock, tugging at the boning, and tried to twist around to check the sash tied around her waist. Maggie's red curls bobbed as she bent over to straighten her skirt over the hoops. They'd been through so much together, and their friendship had grown deeper as a result. Instead of the resentment she'd felt only a few weeks ago, Grace's heart swelled with joy at the hurdles they'd overcome. Maggie stood up.

Grace clutched Maggie's hands in her own. "How can I thank you?"

"By dancing with your hubby, that's how." Maggie stood back and considered her handiwork. "You're gorgeous. Now, go!" She pushed her toward the door.

Grace had a new appreciation for the phrase "burst her buttons," and she almost did so with happiness as Maggie escorted her outside and the crowd's chorus rose up in "For She's a Jolly Good Fellow."

Mark bowed low, held out a gloved hand to his lady, and drew her arm up, covering her hand with his own. He kissed her forehead and they strolled toward the field where a meadow full of Cherryvalers, both new and old, waited to celebrate Grace's life and God's blessings of true friendship.

For Immediate Release:
Cherryvale to Host Movie Preview
By Cynthia Walker

Producers of the recently completed film *The Scrapbook*, starring Tiffany Lane and Jeff Field, announced today that the movie, due to be released in time for the Christmas holiday, will have a pre-release preview in Cherryvale. Most of the final scenes were filmed in the village known for its recent restoration to resemble its original 1890's appearance.

The cast and crew will return to the town where they worked side-by-side with the townspeople to help raise money in a telethon. During the final weeks of filming, a local petting farm suffered extensive fire damage, and the telethon raised money for its repair.

"I've been able to begin rebuilding my farm, thanks to my friends, both in town and from the movie," farm owner Maggie Elmsley told this reporter. "And thanks to my best friend, Grace Harkins, I can take a much needed break after all the summer's excitement. We're traveling to England for a two week pony trekking holiday this fall."

Maggie plans to reopen the farm when she returns from her European vacation in time for the Autumn Harvest festival.

Beverly writes from Southern California where she lives with her husband, Gary. They have two grown children; son, Evan, and daughter, Lindsay.

Beverly also writes nonfiction. She co-authored *Lessons from the Mountain, What I Learned from Erin Walton* (Kensington, March 2011). The book describes Mary McDonough's memories playing Erin on the award winning television drama, "The Waltons."

Beverly Nault is a graduate of Texas A&M University and the Christian Writer's Guild "What's Your Story" apprentice program. A technical and business writer for many years, she also worked in entertainment onstage, as well as "in the back in the black." A props coordinator and set decorator, she also won a regional award for costuming. She is a certified judge for Miss America local competitions, has taught classes in stagecraft and improvisation, and has judged national improv competitions. Beverly also draws on her experience showing hunters and jumpers in the United States and England.

Find Beverly online at:
www.beverlynault.com & Twitter @bevnault

CPSIA information can be obtained at www.ICGtesting.com
224205LV00002B/57/P

9 781600 391828